The Teutonic Cross

James Muench

DEDICATION

This novel is dedicated to the wonderful storytellers whose work has inspired and entertained readers, listeners and viewers through the ages.

.

ACKNOWLEDGMENTS

I wish to thank my wife, Fran, whose wise counsel and patient encouragement has helped me bring this novel to life, and my children, Nolan and April, who have stoically endured the torment of living with a student of history and literature.

I wish to thank my editors, Rebecca Graf and Lisa Binion, whose effort made the novel much better, even though my journalistic side chafed at the sight of all those new Oxford commas.

I also wish to thank those teachers who instilled my love of literature and history. Along with many others who freely gave their help and encouragement along the way, I wish to particularly thank Dave Collins, Wayne Zade, Everett Rees and Jenni Teel.

Finally, I wish to thank my parents, Laurence and Esther Muench, and my grandparents, Albert and Virginia Muench and Roscoe and Esther Moulthrop, who also shaped my love of history and storytelling.

CHAPTER 1

CHAPTER 1

The last swig of cool beer slowly rolled off the back of Heinrich Kueter's tongue and slid down his throat. He eyed the multiple images of the menacing drunk behind him in the small circles that ringed the bottom of the glass mug. He had simply wanted to enjoy a cold beer straight from the tap in peace. Apparently, the drunk had other plans.

Heinrich put down the mug and stared at the wall behind the bar. The tear-off calendar nailed to the rough-wood paneling showed July 12, 1913, punctuated by a ruddy smudge that looked like blood. Perhaps the tavern owner's dirty paw had made the print, or perhaps it was one of the meat packers who frequented this Chicago watering hole.

"This ain't no Kraut house," repeated the sandy-haired ignoramus with bloated biceps. His thick accent sounded either Ukrainian or Lithuanian. For emphasis, he poked Heinrich in the shoulder with a thick index finger.

Sent to the local tavern to fill up the tin growler pail, so named for the sound it made when filled from a bar tap, Heinrich hadn't expected a fight. Usually filling the growler was a job for grade-schoolers, but, feeling nostalgic, he had decided earlier that evening to buy the beer and fill the growler for the neighborhood. Perhaps it was a need to reconnect with his earlier self, he thought, a self he liked better. His safe return from the Filipino war had generated a strong desire to carry out activities from his youth and filling the growler was one of them. He had performed the task so many times as a child; the neighbors would share the cool beer and celebrate their friendship before sleeping on their porches in the blistering summer heat.

Heinrich sighed, knowing his dying father would not approve of what he was about to do.

"Mister, I'm no Kraut, and I have no problem with you," Heinrich said through clenched teeth. "I'm a veteran, just served in the Philippines, and I've seen enough fighting."

"Served with the goddam Hessians, I'll bet," the drunk announced loudly to the entire room. "Did you wear one of those goddam spikes on top of your head?" The drunk's buddies, still wearing bloody smocks from one of the nearby packing plants, laughed nervously.

Heinrich pretended to laugh too, and, looking up at the ceiling for a second to apologize to his father, slammed the beer mug on the oak bar. Pieces of his shattered mug flew across the room. Rapidly pushing his right fist with the palm of his left hand, and quickly twisting his waist like the release of a coiled spring, he rammed his right elbow hard into the drunkard's gut. As the man bent over to clutch his belly, Heinrich interwove his fingers behind the drunkard's neck and drove his knee into the man's face.

The drunk collapsed on the sawdust floor. Heinrich quickly grabbed the most menacing jagged shard from the beer mug with his left hand and passed it to his right. He broadened his stance, bent his knees, and lowered his center of gravity. Ready for the next attacker, he shifted his weight to the balls of his feet and held the shard in front of his body.

The drunk's buddies looked at each other in surprise, unsure what to do.

"Gentlemen, I have no quarrel with you," Heinrich said. "I simply want to take my growler back to my house in peace. It's up to you."

The biggest one, a stocky fellow with dark brown hair, shrugged his shoulders. The menacing veteran who faced him obviously meant business, and any chance to take the young German easily had passed. SPACE "Hokay," he said in a gravelly voice, dehydrated from too much alcohol. "No hard feelings, Kraut."

Heinrich took the slur without a comment. The tavern keeper handed him the growler pail filled with lager, and Heinrich backed his way out.

"Sorry about the mess, Joe," he said from the doorway. "I'll make it up to you later."

Joe Boston nodded. "Kueter, do me a favor; go wreck somebody else's bar next time."

As the screen door swung shut behind him, Heinrich heard Joe announce to the other patrons, "I swear, every time that damn preacher's kid comes in here, he brings a fight."

With a pang of guilt, Heinrich knew that word soon would get back to his father, who would scold him again, as he had so many times before, even from his sickbed. At 28 and not yet completely out of his father's house, he was still never too old for a good sermon from the Reverend Papa Kueter.

The doctors had said his father would die any day now, but Heinrich did not want his bad behavior to put the last nail in the old man's coffin. He said a silent prayer for his father and gingerly carried the growler bucket home. Childhood practice had honed his mastery of the skill. He stepped carefully to make sure the golden summer nectar did not slosh out onto the sidewalk, and he avoided the alleys with their foot-tall summer weeds.

A month later, Heinrich leaned forward in the saddle on the road to Franklinton, Missouri, on this hot and sticky August day. The bay mare underneath him moved with a determined gait. Heinrich thought about his father and realized it would be a long time before he didn't think about Papa Kueter's death daily. At least his father had seen him finish his master's degree at the University of Chicago in May 1910 and return safely from his three-year tour with the Army in the Philippines.

Technically, the 6-foot-tall, blond-haired, blue-eyed Heinrich wasn't really "out" of the Army, since he had to report to a local recruiting office periodically and to serve as a reservist for four years, but he doubted anything would happen that would cause him to be called up. Congress had passed a seven-year enlistment law the previous year. It allowed soldiers the option to be transferred to the reserves after three years instead of the usual four, as long as the soldier did not plan to reenlist later. Heinrich had taken that option; he hoped he was done with the Army, and done with killing.

The dirt and gravel road from St. Charles offered periodic shade when it moved from open farmland into patches of woods. Otherwise, the heat could be unbearable. The road was the main thoroughfare across the north-central section of Missouri, but you wouldn't know it from counting the scanty traffic. Young Heinrich tipped his hat to the occasional horseman or wagon, but people appeared few and far between. He wondered if traffic might pick up as he neared the outskirts of Franklinton.

The day before his father died, the old man had grasped Heinrich's hand and made him promise to follow the way of the cross. "Son, you anger too quickly and are prone to violence," he said. "Do your best to avoid the violent reaction. God appreciates patience. Let your Teutonic cross remind you of your duty." A slow smile spread across the old man's wizened face as his head dropped back on his pillow.

Despite their frequent, heated disagreements, Heinrich had loved the stubborn old grouch, who had been a medal-winning distance swimmer on Lake Michigan before losing the use of his legs to adult polio in his 50s. As the last in a long line of Lutheran pastors that stretched back to medieval Germany, the Rev. Georg Kueter had wanted Heinrich to follow in his footsteps. Heinrich had considered the ministry, but he preferred history. Although his choice of careers had disappointed his father, the old man had appeared to get over it after grumbling and praying for an evening or two.

Heinrich reached into the left breast pocket of his brown, pin-striped suit, now covered in road dust, and touched his lucky cross to make sure he hadn't lost it. Although his father had admonished him sternly one day about his superstition, saying that belief in luck could lead to idol worship, Heinrich couldn't help himself. Hard combat experience had led him to believe in luck and fate. A bullet either has your name on it, or it doesn't.

The cross had been a gift from his father on Heinrich's twenty-first birthday. The silver Teutonic emblem hung from a tri-colored silk ribbon of black, red and gold — the colors of German nationalism. Papa Kueter had scowled when Heinrich asked why a man of peace would carry an "Iron Cross," which in recent decades had become the symbol of German imperial militarism.

"It's not an 'Iron Cross'; it's a Teutonic cross," Heinrich's father said, "It is not a symbol of militarism but of the spirit of the crusaders. It was given to your grandfather at the University of Giessen by Senator Carl Schurz. It carried him safely through his flight to Zurich, Paris and London after the failed revolutions of 1848, and it will carry you safely as long as you remember to fight for what is right." Indeed, the cross had seen Heinrich through many a tough spot. It had given him good luck in his college and graduate studies, and it had even deflected a stray bullet during his recent military service in the Philippines.

The horse continued on toward Franklinton with a rhythmic clip-clop gait that encouraged Heinrich's mind to drowsily wander in his own past and wonder what new adventures might await him in his first job as a history instructor. Folded in his other breast pocket was a letter from his mother who spurred him to greatness. In the letter,

4

Virginia – no one dared call her "Jinnie" on pain of death – again pushed the ministry as an option. "Never say never," she wrote. "Life's trials have a way of leading young men in directions that they may not expect." He had acknowledged the comment with a roll of his eyes, then felt guilty about his response.

Suddenly his horse's ears perked up, and Heinrich felt the animal's muscles grow tense under his legs. Hearing a loud bang behind him, he quickly whipped his torso around to the left to see what it might be. It sounded like the crack of a rifle, similar to the carbines with which he had grown accustomed in the Philippines. He stopped the horse at the side of the road, and he and his mount turned to watch in unison. A tiny black speck on the northeast horizon hurtled toward them. It grew larger by the second.

At first Heinrich thought it might be another horse, but it moved like a locomotive —only there weren't any tracks, so it had to be an automobile. Heinrich had seen a few of them, most recently when he had stopped for dinner in St. Louis. A Cadillac dealership next door to the cafe had displayed several shiny new motorcars in various gleaming colors from royal blue to metallic red. He especially remembered viewing a coupe, a roadster, and a touring car, although he couldn't remember the exact differences between them. The touring car, which held six people, stuck out in his mind because it was maroon with pink velvet seats. A car for a wealthy dandy, he imagined. It certainly did not fit his taste. This one was a darker color and coming fast.

His horse began to snort and fidget nervously under him, so he steered her over to the grassy shoulder next to a tree at the side of the road and patted her flank to calm her nerves as the vehicle sped by.

It was a new 1913 Model T convertible touring car, with a glossy, dark blue paint job. Heinrich had seen Fords before too, painted in multiple colors, on a Chicago showroom lot near his father's home. The driver, an attractive woman with blond hair, large white straw hat with a white fuzzy plume, and long, tan driving gloves, shouted out an apology as she shot by Heinrich at breakneck speed. Heinrich soothed his horse with quiet words and gave its dark brown mane another soft pat as he watched the driver and mechanical beast fade into the distance. The wispy white angel in her blue shell disappeared in a cloud of dust that he could taste on his teeth.

About an hour later, still a few miles from town, Heinrich and his horse crested a steep hill and headed down into a wooded hollow.

Entering the trees, Heinrich felt the influence of civilization disappearing. The wildness of the woods was both intimidating and alluring. It drew him in willingly.

Heinrich spied a dark object on the other side of the hollow that looked like a giant cockroach. He realized it was actually an automobile parked by the side of the road. Looking left and right, he could see no nearby farmhouses; if the driver had left his motorcar, he was in for a long walk to find help. He thought it odd to see two automobiles on the highway in a day.

He spurred his horse to a trot and rode to the parked car. As he came up the hill, he realized it was the same blue Model T driven by the blonde woman who had shot past him earlier.

She had already lifted the rear driver's side wheel properly by pumping the jack under the axle. Leaning over the still-attached wheel in her white dress, now grayed some by road dust, she attempted in vain to pry its flat tire off of the wooden wheel. Her fists strained against her tan driving gloves as she pried at the tire with a crowbar. Hearing him approach, she straightened up and wiped perspiration off her brow with her gloved right hand. She grimaced at her dirty gloves.

"May I help you, Miss?" Kueter asked.

"Giddings," she said. "Sally Ann Giddings. And, other than my knight in shining armor, you are...?"

He laughed. "Teutonic Knight Heinrich Kueter, at your service."

"Kee-ter," she repeated. "The new history professor."

He nodded and bowed. "New to town and in person."

She curtsied in response, then quickly checked to make sure her now dirty gloves had not completely spoiled her white dress. "The dirt is divine punishment for wearing white while driving," she said with a laugh. "I've almost got the tire off," she said, "but I could use some help."

She handed Heinrich her iron crowbar, and he gingerly pried the tire off the wheel. He had seen a friend conduct the procedure once, although he had never actually performed it himself. After pitching the damaged black rubber tire into the back seat at her direction, he removed the punctured inner tube from the wheel and replaced it and the tire with new ones that Miss Giddings handed him.

"Ford supplied these as part of the repair kit that came with the vehicle," she said.

"Good thing, too," he replied. "Otherwise, it's a long walk to town."

Seeing that he would need a screwdriver to maneuver the tire into place on the wheel, Sally opened a red, wooden toolbox and handed him one.

"Smart drivers should carry along tools on outings of any length," she said. "I read it in the newspaper, so it must be true."

Sally laughed as she then handed Heinrich the hand pump from the repair kit. "Do you mind?" she asked.

"Papa always told me to make myself useful," he answered, attaching the pump to the tire and pushing the pump's piston-like plunger downward. It was quite a workout, pushing and pulling for several minutes as the tire slowly plumped with air. By the end of the effort, the exertion had soaked Heinrich's starched cotton shirt in sweat.

When the job was done, and the tools were stowed in the toolbox, Miss Giddings asked Heinrich if he would like a ride into town. He answered that, while he would love the experience, he needed to take care of the horse.

He cranked the engine to get her started again. Before she drove away, she thanked him for his help and welcomed him to Franklinton. "Maybe we'll see each other in town," she said.

"I would like that," he replied.

He watched her drive over the hill and then got back on his mare and continued the journey. She was a fine looking woman, and he earnestly hoped he would see her again.

The dirt road became Main Street as Heinrich reached the Franklinton city limits, and the road surface changed to a rich, red brick when he reached the edge of downtown. The brick pavement reminded Heinrich of the summer-kitchen fireplaces he had seen in antebellum homes, an idea that fit the heat of this dusty and sticky day. He could see a tall church steeple in the distance; it was probably the Worcester College chapel. Its bells were busy marking the five o'clock hour. He stopped and secured his horse in front of the Tapped Keg pub.

As he reached for the polished brass doorknob to open it, he noted that it was embossed with a carving of a phoenix, the symbol of the Irish Fenian movement. Heinrich thought about the incident at the neighborhood tavern in Chicago. Anti-immigrant sentiment, especially against the Germans and the Irish, was very strong these days. Franklinton was an insular, southern-leaning town of the sort that wouldn't have looked kindly on the nearly universal support among German-Americans for the Union during the Civil War fifty years ago.

A German had to be careful when imbibing for fear of acting to stereotype. While in basic training for the Army, his grizzled drill sergeant took sadistic pleasure in labeling him "Dutchie." One day the sergeant had accosted Heinrich nose-to-nose. "Dutchie, I think you Germans are a lop-eared, good-for-nothing, race of pure cowards," the sergeant shouted in Heinrich's face. His lips were practically frothing as he spat the words. "I think you couldn't fight a real man without some Dutch courage. You'd need to get all liquored up. Isn't that so?"

"No, sir!" Heinrich responded, red-faced, at the top of his lungs. Looking pleased, the sergeant responded, "Good answer, maggot!" and stepped over to harass the next soldier.

Heinrich's fists had tightened; he ached to pop the sergeant in the mouth. Seeing that he had gotten under the young German's skin, the sergeant goaded him to throw a punch, but Heinrich didn't dare do it.

The drill sergeant smiled, pleased with the recruit's discipline. "That's a smart trooper, Private Kueter," he said, and moved on to the next victim.

It was a change to which Kueter knew he needed to adjust. In the Army on a foreign post, a certain amount of drinking was expected, even encouraged. But back in the States, America's predominant Anglo-Saxon/Scots-Irish culture frowned upon the German and Irish practice of enjoying wine or beer along with a good meal or on Sunday afternoons with music and friends. Ostensibly under the belief that drinking with friends was a sin and imbibing on a Sunday was a mortal one — but mainly to combat the influx of foreigners and their strange ways — many Midwestern communities had passed blue laws and called for various forms of temperance legislation. Far better, Heinrich mused with a mischievous grin, for the proper American WASP gentleman to drain that hidden whiskey bottle in private and beat his wife on Saturday night. That way the Sabbath was left secure for sober confession and communion with the Lord.

Heinrich laughed to himself. Of course, to be fair, he knew it wasn't quite that simple. Many in the temperance movement enjoyed wine and beer while frowning at the use of distilled spirits. Likewise, many in the temperance crowd discerned the difference between the good neighborhood tavern and the evil saloon, which tended to breed all manner of licentiousness and vice in its back rooms.

The Tapped Keg looked like a standard neighborhood Irish pub, assuming he interpreted the Fenian phoenix on the doorknob properly, and it might be more inviting to a "foreigner" like him. It had been a long ride from St. Louis, and Heinrich was ravenous. He needed directions to Yaeger's boarding house, a bite to eat, and a cold draft, not necessarily in that order.

As he turned the knob and prepared to step inside, a short, plump man in a crisp gray business suit came striding down the boardwalk. A gleaming gold pocket watch fob swung to and fro across his stomach. He had the look of a captain of industry about him, in a starched white shirt with French cuffs, diamond cufflinks and spats on his expensive black shoes. A black derby hat covered his balding dome, and gray, bushy hair stuck out on the sides from underneath. Perhaps most interesting, the man carried a cane with a silver handle on top. It looked like the type of instrument wielded in antebellum cartoons by Southern legislators beating down Northern abolitionists in Congress. He might have been a banker, but a swagger in his step, a 3-inch scar that adorned his left cheek, and a sneer in his eyes provided a sinister hint of menace.

Deciding to introduce himself, Heinrich raised his hand, "Sir? I am new to town; might I inquire about a good local bank..."

The man ignored the question and shouldered past Heinrich without a word. Heinrich couldn't hear exactly what the man mumbled, but he muttered something about "damn lop-eared Dutch" as he marched away.

Welcome to the small-town South, Heinrich thought. The old expression the man had used derived from the view that lop-eared animals like rabbits were stupid, so the epithet amounted to calling somebody a "dumb bunny." In the Civil War, the term also had signified cowardice, as when soldiers ran like rabbits. Heinrich was taken aback; he hadn't expected such a response.

He shook his head, turned toward the door, opened it, and entered the bar. The gnarled screen door spanked the frame behind him. Above the bar mirror hung two flags, one dark green with a golden harp, and one a tricolor of green, orange, and white. Heinrich guessed them to be Irish; he was fairly certain he had read the phoenix accurately.

The burly bartender with a handlebar mustache saw him eyeing the flags and said, "Welcome. The flag with the harp is the traditional flag of the Irish. The tricolor is a symbol of what Ireland might become. The white stands for peace between the green Irish and the orange Protestants."

Heinrich nodded, perched himself on a brown leather barstool and wiped the road dust off his face with a red bandana from his pants pocket. The proprietor handed him a glass of water and gave him a smile.

"Needless to say, I'm Irish. The name's Mike Murphy. I own the place."

Heinrich eyed the glass for a second.

"Don't worry. It's clean."

Heinrich's face turned red. "No offense meant, Mr. Murphy."

"None taken," Murphy laughed. "You can't be too careful when you're traveling."

Heinrich held out his right hand, and Murphy shook it. "Mr. Murphy, I'm Heinrich Kueter."

"Glad to make your acquaintance, Professor Kueter. So it rhymes with 'Peter.' I wondered about that."

"How do you know my name?"

Murphy laughed. "Don't worry. I ain't no fortune teller. The college has been looking for you to arrive. You're the new history professor, right?"

Kueter nodded. "I will need directions to Yaeger's Boarding House. That's where I'm staying."

"No problem." Murphy pointed to a high-backed walnut booth at the back of the room that Kueter hadn't noticed at first. "Tommy Lee lives there too. Hey, Tommy, could you lead our new professor over to Yaeger's later?"

A young Asian man stepped from a shadowy walnut booth. "Sure," he said. His black hair and black-marble eyes shone in the late afternoon sunlight streaming in through a window. He began to bow at the waist slightly in the Asian manner, as if it were a natural reflex, then caught himself.

"That is, after he's had a bite to eat, right Professor?" Murphy asked.

Kueter nodded and held out his hand to Tommy, who shook it. "Tommy Lee, Heinrich Kueter," Murphy quickly introduced. "He's the new history professor."

"Pleased to meet you," Lee said, with a slight bob of his head. Heinrich nodded the same.

"What will you be havin' then?" Murphy said to Heinrich.

"What have you got cooking in the pan there?"

"Oh, that's some morel mushrooms for Herr Dahlen. He finds them in the woods from time to time, and I cook them up for him. It's about the only time I can get him to buy a beer or two from me, the cheap bastard. No offense meant."

"None taken. How about a steak?"

"You bet."

Heinrich was famished. The medium-rare sirloin and potatoes Murphy fed him were delicious, and not too expensive. He figured he'd become a regular at Murphy's. The bar felt comfortable, warm and inviting, especially compared to the hundreds of other bars he had visited throughout the world. This one did not push his background, but seemed to absorb it like a beloved and worn chair.

"By the way, do you know a rather pudgy, well-dressed gentleman who..." Heinrich began.

"I saw him, and what he did to you," Murphy said. "No matter how he's dressed, he ain't no gentleman. That's Truman Fairchild. Be wary of him. He's the local political boss here, our presiding county commissioner. He runs the Democratic machine as well as most of the vice in town. He learned his craft at the feet of Boss Tom Pendergast in Kansas City. Rumor has it he had to leave town after killing somebody in a fight, but he stuck around after he realized there was business out here in the sticks."

"Sounds like a real operator," Heinrich said.

"Yeah, he acts like a big shot. He rents the top floor of the Franklinton Bank building, where he has an office and some rooms for party business that are accessible only by a back stairway. There's usually a thug or two standing around guarding it. You'll see the sign up top of the bank: 'Franklin Democratic Club.' He's also the head of our local Know-Nothing contingent, or whatever they call the "nativists" these days, and there's a reason. He really doesn't know nothing!"

Heinrich laughed. "You think he smelled my 'Germanity?'"

Murphy laughed. "That and the fact that you were heading for my tavern probably didn't help. He and I don't get along too well. I'm too Irish for his taste."

"Glad to hear it; it means more beer for me," Heinrich said, draining his mug and passing it back to Murphy. "I'm too German; I need another lager."

Murphy refilled his mug, and Heinrich took a swig. It tasted wonderfully wet and cool. He looked around the room, which held the obligatory dart board and pool table. "You've got a nice place here," he said to Murphy.

Murphy nodded. "I run a friendly tavern, professor. None of the sleaze you see over at the Lucky Strike; that's Fairchild's saloon," he said. "It's a nightmare of gambling, whoring and thievery, the kind of place that'll stick us with Prohibition someday, you mark my words."

Heinrich cocked an eyebrow and gave Murphy a dubious look.

"Let me tell you, professor, I've heard stories about that place that frighten me, and I don't frighten easily. They beat and roll drunks for their wallets on a regular basis over there, and there's toothless whores in the back room who'll rob men blind. I heard tell of one drunk troublemaker who won too big at the crap table. They killed him, dumped him in an alley across town and ran him over in a staged buggy accident."

That widened Heinrich's eyes; he whistled. "Where were the police?"

"The sheriff couldn't prove anything. Hell, Fairchild owns the mayor and county commission anyway."

Heinrich took another gulp, glad he'd chosen the right tavern.

He finished his supper, paid his bill, thanked Mike Murphy, and left with Tommy Lee. They walked the two blocks down Main Street to Dahlen's stable as Tommy led Heinrich's mare. The young man explained in a thick accent that Presbyterian missionaries in Korea had sent him to the States for his education.

At the stable, Heinrich could get the horse fed, watered, cleaned up, and bedded down for the night. When they arrived, they saw an older man with short gray hair standing in the doorway. His back was turned to them, and he was listening to someone yelling inside.

"You goddam Chink! How many times must I tell you? The roan in number four needs oats! Do you hear, Chop Suey? I said O-A-T-S, oats! It's over in the bin, dammit!"

The man at the door responded in a thick German accent, "That's enough, Billy! Show more patience. You won't teach him anything by berating him. Mr. Chang, please try to pay closer attention to the feed for the horses."

Heinrich's horse nickered, and the man turned apologetically to face them. In the dimming light of an oil lamp, Heinrich could see that the man had light brown hair, a broad nose with freckles, and a stocky build, which all hinted at German heritage. He reminded Heinrich of a shorter version of his father.

"Please excuse the unpleasantness, gentlemen. It's hard to keep well-trained hands these days, so I have to rely right now on Chinamen such as Mr. Chang, who can only speak a few words of English."

Digging a match out of his pocket, he struck it on a rough brick on the outside of the building, lit a Meerschaum pipe, drew in a puff, and exhaled a smoke ball. Manfred Dahlen was usually a cheerful man, always ready with a smile or a joke, and he looked as if he were made to wear lederhosen in some Alpine village.

"Herr Dahlen," Tommy said, "This is Heinrich Kueter, our new history professor."

"Ah, we've been waiting for you, Professor Kueter. So glad you made the trip in one piece," Dahlen said as he showed Heinrich a potential stall for his mare. Kueter nodded that it would suffice and paid Dahlen for a week's keep.

"*Sprechen Sie Deutsch?*" Dahlen asked, counting the money.

"*Ja,*" Heinrich said.

"It's good to have another German-speaker in town," Dahlen said. Kueter smiled, nodded, and shook the older man's hand. He hoped his German would be up to the task; his family rarely used the mother tongue anymore.

"You'd probably best get on to the boarding house," Dahlen said. "Knowing Mrs. Yaeger, she will be nervously awaiting your arrival."

Heinrich nodded, shook hands with Dahlen, and left with Tommy. They walked northward to Yaeger's boarding house. Tommy told Heinrich that Manfred Dahlen was Austrian.

"Ask him to show you his white Lippizan horse sometime," Tommy said. "The gleaming white coat is beautiful. It looks like an angel's horse."

Yaeger's boarding house, a large Victorian home with light blue paint and white trim around the windows, was handily positioned three blocks away. It sat one block up the street from the college chapel, a magnificent stone Gothic Revival building built in 1880, thirty years after the college's founding by a Presbyterian minister.

Heinrich gestured at the pointed tower on its southwest corner. "My home in Chicago had a witch's tower like that," he said. "It was great fun to play in as a boy." Tommy looked puzzled, and Heinrich explained that traditional witches wore pointy hats. Tommy nodded, unconvinced. He wondered why any self-respecting witch would want to dress that way.

Heinrich rang the bell, and Mrs. Yaeger met them at the door. A short, plump matron with tired brown eyes, she wore her gray-streaked brunette hair pulled back and tied in a bun. Herr Dahlen had sized her up pretty well. She looked like she'd be a handwringer when events did not go strictly according to schedule.

"Professor Kueter, so glad you found us," she said, pulling his arm inside and toward the stairs to the second floor. "I was beginning to worry that some mishap might have occurred on the way to Franklinton. Unfortunately, you missed dinner."

Heinrich hadn't known he was expected. Tommy looked the other way, stifling a grin.

"I apologize," Heinrich said. "The journey from St. Louis took longer than expected."

"I could pull some leftovers from the icebox," she offered.

"Thank you for the kind offer, but there is no need. I managed to grab a bite on the way."

"No matter," she answered and pointed up the stairs. "Your room is the second one on the left."

Tommy obligingly carried the professor's worn leather suitcase up the oak steps, which creaked quietly as their feet climbed the risers. Looking down, Heinrich could see worn spots in the staircase veneer from right-footed people; unconsciously, he made an effort to step on the other sides of the stairs, just to keep the wear even.

Tommy turned the key in the carved brass doorknob and opened the door. Heinrich followed him into the room. The oak flooring in the bedroom displayed a lighter shade than that in the hallway, and Heinrich guessed it had been sanded and revarnished more recently. Heinrich could see a mahogany chest of drawers and a matching wardrobe on the inside wall, and a dark walnut four-poster bed with decorative turned posts in the center of the room.

The bed's sheets were decorated in a violet pattern and folded over a star-patterned quilt. Above the bed hung a ceiling fan whose brass finish was tarnished and whose crown held an electric lightbulb. Though no longer rare in larger cities, Heinrich could tell that electric lights were only beginning to replace gas in Franklinton as the technology of choice.

Heinrich noticed a small, walnut cabinet door in the wall next to the wardrobe and opened it with a snap of a spring latch. Inside was a hole, framed by a square duct that headed straight down. He guessed it was the laundry chute. Laundry would cost extra, so he would need to pinch his pennies.

Tommy put the suitcase down on a walnut desk next to a dormer window. Looking out, he saw that the sun was beginning to set in an intricate mosaic of orange hues.

Heinrich unpacked his suitcase, while Tommy sat on the bed.

"So, Master Lee, if you are Chinese, how did you wind up in Korea?"

Tommy smiled, apparently used to the question. "Exile," he said. "I was born and raised near the city you call Peking, but my parents died in the Boxer Rebellion 13 years ago. My aunt and uncle adopted me, but we were exiled to Korea after the rebellion. Our good friends, Reverend and Mrs. Scott, were Presbyterian missionaries in our village near Pyongyang. Much of my tuition is paid for by a Boxer Indemnity Scholarship, arranged by Reverend Scott. He was an alumnus of the college, and they lent me the rest of the money needed to come and live in America."

Heinrich, wondering what to say, nodded solemnly as Lee recounted the history. "Don't worry," Tommy Lee said. "Life is good now. I miss my parents, but I don't mind talking about it anymore. I hope to return to China once I get my degree, and perhaps work to build our new republic, maybe even help Sun Yat-Sen create a democracy as great as America's."

"Yes, I suppose China would be more promising now, while Korea is much less so, after the Japanese takeover?"

Tommy nodded. "I fear for the Reverend and his wife, even though the invasion is over. The Japanese are ruthless killers and treat the Koreans with contempt."

"Hopefully, they will treat Americans with more respect."

Tommy looked unconvinced. Wanting to change the subject quickly, Heinrich tried another tack. "So, Master Lee, where does one look to find female companionship in this town?" As soon as he said it, Heinrich realized his words were probably a bit too familiar for the situation. He had to remember he was no longer in the army.

Tommy turned red and began to stammer a little as he fought for the right words. "I wouldn't know, professor. It depends what you mean. There are quite a few co-eds and some fine girls who live in town. For instance, I danced with a local girl the other night, and I enjoyed her company very much. She's a bit young for you, though, I should think."

"Ouch! That's a punch to the gut." Heinrich laughed. He took on the voice of an aged man. "Don't worry, sonny. This old man won't steal your girl."

Tommy looked worried. "I didn't mean to make offense, sir."

"No offense taken, and I apologize if my tone was too informal," Heinrich said with a grin. "May I call you Tommy?"

Lee nodded. "Tommy, you're a good man, and I hope to see you in class soon. But I need to get my things unpacked, and I'm really tired. I plan to turn in early. Thank you so much for the help and conversation this evening."

Tommy bowed his head. "You're welcome." He turned and left, closing the door behind him. The heavy door stuck a little, and Heinrich gave it an extra push to shut it. He finished putting his underwear into a drawer in the armoire. Sitting down on the springy bed, he pulled off his black leather riding boots and laid his head back on the pillow.

He fell asleep in less than a minute, looking up at the tarnished ceiling fan and thinking it needed polish.

Heinrich stood in the scorching sun at the Army's camp on the volcanic Mount Bagsak in the Latiward district of Jolo island in the Philippines. Bathed in sweat like most of his comrades, he stood at attention in the wet-hot steambath that was pretty much every day in the Philippines, where either the humidity beat you down, or it rained, which was a relief only if you could stay out of the mud. Today, the afternoon sun bore down upon them as the soldiers waited for General Pershing.

The general arrived on horseback with a contingent of staff in tow. Pershing's bay mount snorted in the heavy air and made a sound like a fire-breathing dragon on the prowl. Meanwhile, the fire-breathing general dismounted stiffly and sauntered briskly down the line of men. He inspected their uniforms with professional disdain and pointed his swagger stick at the occasional dull boot or tarnished button.

A capable tyrant, Black Jack Pershing held the aura of authority. Command seemed to be his true nature. His men did not love him; they respected him, and that was enough.

Pershing was a national hero back home for leading the fight for Christian decency against the Moros, Black Jack had even won the respect of the Filipinos. They even bestowed upon him the noble title of Datu during his previous stint in the Philippines in the early 1900s. Then he had cleaned up the district around Lake Lanao on the island of Mindanao. This time, the American forces had endured attacks from the Moros for four days as they slowly surrounded the enemy fortress on Bud Bagsak, or Mount Bagsak. Tomorrow, if all went as planned, he intended to crush the Moro rebellion for good on at the summit of the volcano.

Now Black Jack was upon him. The Datu looked piercingly into Heinrich's eyes, and Heinrich tried hard not to look back. "Don't eyeball me, soldier!" the general said with a scowl. He stepped back and marched to the front of the column.

"At ease," he commanded after a moment, and the regiment stepped to the side, their feet about shoulder-width apart and their hands behind their backs. "As you know, men, we have surrounded the enemy's forces in his fortress at the top of the mountain," he said. "Tomorrow, at dawn, we storm it, their last stronghold in the Philippines. I don't need to tell you how brutal it will be, but we must crush this rebellion and punish our enemies so that they never revolt and threaten us again."

Pershing paused for dramatic effect. "Tomorrow, when you finish off the Muslim Moros, your job will be complete. Many of you will soon be home, and someday, you'll tell your grandchildren about your grand adventure in the Pacific."

Black Jack paused again, and appeared to look each soldier in the eye. "Tomorrow, you achieve glory..."

...Suddenly, the following morning arrived, and Heinrich charged with the rest of the army uphill as fast as he could. The entire American line surged toward the enemy's wooden battlements on the summit as the U.S. siege guns roared and spat flame. A countercharge of screaming Moro warriors armed with barongs, kris and spears climbed out of the trenches to meet the invaders.

Heinrich dodged a slashing barong — a Moro sword that looked like a long, curved kitchen knife — and fired his carbine to fell the warrior who wielded it. He then quickly turned to meet a running, shirtless warrior swinging a curvy kris sword in Heinrich's direction. On impact, the wavy sword would do double-cutting damage to its target, and Heinrich had no intention of letting that happen. Using his carbine like a spear to keep the warrior at a distance, he plunged his bayonet in just below the man's ribcage. The warrior's tortured brown eyes stared up at him as he put his boot on the man's chest to extract his bayonet...

...Then Heinrich felt the bodies squirm underneath him as he ran across a swirling sea of wounded Moros while the Americans surged across the enemy trenches. He didn't pause to look at the pool of waving arms extended toward heaven. Crossing the moat, he reached the timber parapets, made from apitong or other dipterocarp trees, he figured. The wooden wall had been shattered by the bombardment, so that it looked a bit like brown Swiss cheese. He climbed through a large hole in the wall behind another soldier yelling a rebel "Eee-yah," like the Confederates of fifty years ago. He continued to charge the now routed Moros to the lip of the volcanic crater at the summit of the mountain. Surrounded, the Moros trapped inside the crater tried to charge their way out, but the soldiers ringed the crater several ranks deep and poured continuous fire into the hole. They gunned down the proud Muslim warriors – literally like fish in a barrel.

Heinrich emptied his carbine into the crater, then traded his rifle for another handed to him by a soldier in the rear. Like an unthinking machine, he continued to fire. He pumped round after round into the seething mass of Muslims in the pit. The bodies in the crater piled one on top of the other as desperate Moros tried to claw their way out, only to place themselves in the rain of gunfire. Heinrich continued to shoot until he had emptied a dozen rifles, and his finger hurt from the constant motion. He stared down into the pit; a Dantean pile of body parts and dead eyes stared back at him. The eyes of the dead...

Heinrich felt the urge to vomit and backed away from the crater.

Staggering back through the ranks, he fell on his knees and retched in the volcanic black sand. He sat up, unblinking, and wanted desperately to go home.

The eyes of the dead...

Heinrich awoke with a start, but he could tell it was still the middle of the night. The ceiling fan spun with fervor. He turned over and tried to go back to sleep. He knew that, during the five-day battle, as many as two thousand Moros died – many of them in the volcano's maw on that final day. Pershing would report only six troopers killed and seven wounded.

A few evenings later, Heinrich cut into the pork steak with apricot sauce at the Emperor Hotel grill, Franklinton's finest restaurant. He savored the first bite and thought how much better it was than the rubbery chops he had eaten at the college dining hall a few nights before. The Emperor Hotel grill offered both an excellent meal and a wine cellar, and it ought to at $4.95 a meal, he thought. The best thing on the menu at Murphy's cost fifty-five cents.

As he took a second delectable bite, out of the corner of his eye he saw Sally, the blonde woman whose car he had rescued on his journey into town. Smartly attired in a flattering blue floral dress, she moved gracefully about the dining room. He found her figure very pleasing to the eye and had to work to avoid staring at her. He inviting look of confidence and her air of maturity strongly contrasted with a group of white-gloved girls from the local finishing school dining at a nearby table. Their loud giggles caused Sally to glance at them disapprovingly.

She saw him looking her way and smiled. Getting up demurely, she walked to him with a silken gait. Forgetting that his mouth was still mostly full, he awkwardly stood up to greet her.

"Hello, Miss Giddings," he half choked.

"May I sit with you?" she asked, with a laugh. "Please finish your food. And you may call me Sally."

Heinrich looked around quickly, then nodded, chewing and swallowing the piece of pork in his mouth as quickly as possible. She held out her gloved hand, and he gripped it, suddenly nervous and unsure of himself. He bowed, kissed her hand valiantly, and wondered if he was being too old-fashioned and whether her skin was as soft as the satin glove. Her eyes were soft too, radiant and deep blue. He could swim in those eyes, he thought.

"Likewise, please call me Heinrich," he said, motioning for her to sit down and desperately trying to think of something to say.

"And how is your motorcar?" Dangerous, he thought, but playful.

"I haven't run anyone off the road recently, if that's what you mean," she said with a laugh.

He grinned. "You could stand a little more practice, I should think," he said.

"What do you mean? I have practiced," she said. "I made you run for cover, didn't I? That maneuver wasn't easy to master."

A sense of humor too, he thought. "So what do you do when you aren't motoring?" he asked.

"I'm the editor of the local newspaper," she said. "The Franklinton *Democrat*. Perhaps you've read it?"

Heinrich nodded again, although he often found the newspaper too parochial for his taste. Perhaps he ought to give it another chance, especially since she was its editor. He usually read two-day-old copies of the *St. Louis Post-Dispatch* at the college library, and its relative, the German-language *Westliche Post,* also printed in St. Louis.

"I understand you're a descendant of Friedrich Muench," she said.

His jaw dropped. "Yes. How on earth did you know that?"

"Word travels fast around here," she said. "I'd like to interview you sometime."

"Do you want to be run out of town on a rail?" he asked, only half in jest. "Coverage of Union-loving Dutchmen might lose you a few readers. I could lie and say I'm related to Robert E. Lee, but nobody would believe it. Or maybe I should conjure up some other famous, but slightly more obscure, Confederate relation — Nathan Bedford Forrest or P.G.T. Beauregard, perhaps?"

"Professor Kueter, I am a journalist and would never stoop to printing an outright inaccuracy such as that," she said with a mock sniff. "The fact that you are a distant cousin of Alexander H. Stephens will do nicely."

"Who?"

"Vice president of the Confederacy, from Georgia," she said. "And you call yourself a history professor. Tsk. Tsk."

"Impressive," he said. "Apparently I will have to learn more about him if he is to be my relative. Hannibal Hamlin and I bow to your superior knowledge, Miss Giddings." He bowed obsequiously with a theatrical wave of his hand.

"Thank you, fine sir," she replied. "And Hamlin was Lincoln's vice president; don't think for a minute that I wouldn't remember that one."

Heinrich laughed. "All right, you win the historic trivia challenge. I won't dare to underestimate your prowess ever again."

She nodded. "Too bad our locals don't share your wisdom. Most of them gave up on me long ago. After all, I am a crazy woman doing man's work, don't you know. They let me get away with it, though, because I'm a good reporter."

"I'm not sure you get away with as much as you think you do," he said, wishing he hadn't said it as soon as the words came out of his mouth.

"Oh, really? Do tell."

"I apologize. I've said too much."

"You can't say something like that and leave it hanging in the air," she said. "You launched the boat, so you may as well sail it."

"Oh, all right. My landlady warned me about you. She said you are a loose woman who should be avoided at all costs if I want to keep my reputation intact."

She laughed. "Mrs. Yaeger has led a hard life and has every right to her opinion, even if I disagree. You need to understand, Heinrich. For us local celebrities, it is far more important that we be spoken about than to be spoken well about. If people read my paper only because there is a hint of scandal wrapped about me, so be it. When they stop reading it, then I'll worry."

Heinrich decided to go deeper. "But what have you done to merit such gossip?"

She grinned. "A few times, just to shake up the ladies' garden club, I mentioned that I believe women should be treated as equal to men and deserve the suffrage. I told them, "No woman is without honor in her own country – just without the vote – and that is an injustice in the land of the free and the home of the brave."

"Ah, so I'm speaking to a real live suffragette!"

She fluttered her eyelashes. Her blue eyes weren't so soft now, more serious. "Darn right, sir," she said. "I marched in Washington back in March, and I even picketed for a few days in front of the White House. If President Wilson won't back us, maybe we'll try vandalism or arson like our British sisters are doing right now."

"That would certainly ruffle a few feathers at the ladies' garden club," Heinrich said with a laugh.

"It most certainly would," she said. "Then, when their conversation begins to languish in such banalities as the best quilting stitch or the priority of placing fish-shaped soap 'just so' in the bathroom, I bring up the merits of free love and free thinking. Such radical ideas really set their hearts aflutter."

Heinrich laughed again. "Sally Giddings, I daresay you display the temperament of a Lolly bomber! I would love to be a fly on the wall the next time you splash a well-tossed stone!"

As soon as he'd said it, he regretted his descent to toilet humor. This was an awkward moment for a reference to the boyish prank of dropping a rock into the privy pit to create a splash when the target sat down to do business on the other side of a two-seat outhouse. "I apologize, Miss Giddings. My attempt at humor was inappropriate."

"Indeed, Professor Kueter, and I'm shocked. You should be ashamed of yourself for resorting to such potty-mouthed humor," she said with mock sternness. "I should wash your mouth out with soap."

"Fish-shaped soap?" he said with a snicker.

She laughed and stood up. "I'd better let you finish your meal, and I have work to do," she said. "May I call on you someday soon for that interview?"

He nodded.

"Great. It was nice seeing you again." She walked away with a swaying gait, while he took another bite.

The next day, the chairman of the History Department saw Heinrich in Academic Hall. Chairman Goforth waved him into his moldy office and then motioned for him to take a seat across from his carved, claw-footed desk. A friend of Heinrich's father who had helped Heinrich gain his instructor's post at the college, the slow-moving Professor Erwin Goforth was a white-haired, wrinkled southern gentleman in a fraying black frock coat that seemed to be awash in chalk. He leaned on his desk and eyed the junior faculty member with a look of fatherly concern.

"I'm not quite sure how to broach this subject, my son," Dr. Goforth said. He nervously rubbed his hands together as if wiping the sweat from his palms. Goforth called everybody "My son," even women occasionally, by mistake. It was his way; it simply would not do to be offended. Everybody knew Goforth meant no harm, so one tried to ignore his eccentricities or laugh them away.

Goforth put a hand on Heinrich's shoulder. "So here it is, my son. I do hope you understand that members of the faculty must tread lightly and do their best not to embarrass the faculty – or to injure its reputation in public."

What on earth was the old man babbling about? "To what are you referring, sir? I don't believe I've done anything that would ..."

"I know, Heinrich. You would never do anything on purpose that would jeopardize your position, but you met with a woman yesterday evening over supper."

"Sally Ann Giddings? Yes, she came to my table and introduced herself. She said she wanted to write a story about me sometime."

"Yes, quite. Well, I thought it my duty to inform you that you should avoid her company. She is a fallen woman, not of high repute."

Kueter frowned. "The conversation was quite professional, I assure you. I learned she is a suffragette, and that is about all."

"I'm sure," said Dr. Goforth. "But I was instructed to give you a quiet warning."

"Instructed? Somebody ordered you to tell me with whom I can associate?"

"It's not me, Heinrich."

Probably the president of the college, Heinrich thought, or his obnoxious first lady, Wilhelmina "Minnie" Tichenor, a notorious battle-axe. The mousy Goforth was so desperate to keep his own position until retirement that he might have given some offhand remark by President Joseph Tichenor too much credence, Heinrich thought. Or the president could be a meddler; Heinrich made a mental note to get to know the president better in the future.

"Frankly, I do not care with whom you frolic," Goforth said. "But there are eyes and ears all over this town. If your reputation gets sullied in any way, it could put your position in jeopardy."

"Being introduced to someone in public hardly constitutes a frolic, sir," Heinrich stood up, his ears beginning to burn.

"It's for your own good, Heinrich. Consider it a friendly warning."

Heinrich pointed his finger at Goforth. "I thank you for your help in the past, Dr. Goforth. You are a good friend and colleague, but don't ever tell me to whom I can and cannot speak. I am a free man and will do as I please. Good day, sir." He turned on his heel and curtly walked out of the office, worrying that he had just jeopardized his job.

A week later, Heinrich nursed an orangeade drink made with orange syrup and water. He would have preferred some spirits in it, but unfortunately he worked for a Presbyterian college. He grinned at the thought, and quickly shook it off, instead smiling sociably and pretending to listen to Dr. Goforth's monotone drone. It was the Fall Mixer, a tedious college tradition but politically necessary, and he was currently grouped in conversation with the old man and another middle-aged professor of biology whose name he had already forgotten. Heinrich would have to look at last year's yearbook to make sure he got the name right before running into him again.

Faculty had to at least be seen at the mixer. It was one of the few annual events at which town met gown. Goforth blathered on about some legendary professor from his early days at Worcester College. Heinrich felt his eyes glaze over, and he excused himself to get more ice.

He tended to feel ill at ease at these types of purely social events. He had never been a master of small talk and much preferred to discuss items of greater significance. But this event would have been unwise to skip. It was his chance to meet President Joseph Tichenor socially. The first impression would be important for his future.

For the occasion, Heinrich wore his second-best suit, a summer seersucker with blue pinstripes, and a royal blue bowtie. He had purchased the outfit at Schattinger's Men's Store in town and hoped it would help him blend in better with the southerners here in Little Dixie, although it felt as out of place on his shoulders as a suit of armor.

He glanced at his pocket watch. Only an hour into the party, and it felt like a week. Heinrich had spoken with several professors and department heads and was working his way slowly toward President Tichenor, who was holding court near the rear of the pea-gravel parade ground. The president stood six-foot-two and was extremely thin, with bony features and a long, hooked nose. Behind his back, the students called him Ichabod Crane, in reference to Washington Irving's character from The Legend of Sleepy Hollow. When the academic dean broke away from the president to get another cup of punch, Heinrich saw his chance and introduced himself.

"Ah, yes, our new German history professor," Tichenor said with a laugh. "Sprechen Sie Deutsch?" It was amazing how many used that line as their opening gambit with Heinrich. Being a fourth-generation American, he thought people would have gotten over his ancestry by now.

"Only a little Bitte, I'm afraid, spoken at home from time to time," Heinrich answered with a tinny laugh. "I studied French instead. My ancestors are probably rolling over in their graves."

Tichenor laughed politely to acknowledge that a joke had been made, but Heinrich could tell the president really didn't get it. "You'd think they would have forgotten Napoleon, who conquered them, but these blood feuds last forever in Europe," Heinrich said.

Tichenor nodded, but Heinrich could tell the president was not pleased. Clearly, President Tichenor was one of those people who always had to be the most knowledgeable person in the room, or else.

Heinrich attempted a rescue. "I'm impressed, sir. There aren't too many on the faculty who would have understood the Napoleon connection," he said.

Tichenor smiled. "Quite," the president said. "Luckily, I studied French history way back when. The French are so much more civilized than the Germans. It's no wonder the Russians have copied their ways."

Heinrich decided to ignore the slight. Perhaps later, once the president got to know him better, there would be more chances to display the better points of his ancestors' German culture.

"You aren't planning to open up a beer garden on my campus in the near future, are you?" Tichenor said with a loud laugh. "I simply won't have it. And there will be no swordplay amongst the fraternities."

Apparently, Tichenor had heard about the Burschenschaften, the German political fraternities of a century ago in which the young male students of the Romantic Era, their blood boiling with virility, dueled over their political beliefs. Those Romantic students, such as Carl Schurz and Franz Sigel, later would become the leading agitators in the failed democratic revolutions of 1848 in Europe, and many would immigrate to America. Heinrich decided it was time to leave before the president began making jokes about the "scrubby Dutch" women he had seen in St. Louis or some other bigotry.

"I promise, sir, to leave no scars," Heinrich said, performing an imaginary fencing move as a graceful exit. Tichenor laughed as if dismissing Heinrich and turned to somebody who looked more important than a mere history instructor.

It was a relief to walk away. Heinrich looked at his pocket watch, which registered only a little over an hour to go. Profs were expected to stay a couple of hours before quietly disappearing to let the students have their fun. At some point later, the punch would inevitably get spiked, but much boredom would have to be endured first.

Heinrich swished away a fly. It was a pleasant evening after a warm September day. The summer-dormant bluegrass had long since changed to the full green turf of autumn. He remembered hearing the shouts of the football team at practice from his office window earlier that afternoon.

"When you hit that dummy, I want to hear your war cry," Coach McPherson yelled. "Rahhh…" each young man yelled in response while hitting the stuffed bag with his shoulder. "Come on, show me your guts!" The shouts got louder as the coach pushed his charges to train harder.

It was funny, though. As the sun headed toward setting on the party, now the boy's shouts seemed even louder, but less menacing. Boisterousness and beer, that's what tonight would soon be about, he thought.

Then there she was, chatting with an older gentleman — a vision in a stunning sky blue dress trimmed with lace. Heinrich knew little of women's fashion, but he knew enough to know that Sally looked good in just about anything, especially shades of blue. "Well, Professor Kueter, it's good to see you out enjoying the weather for a change, rather than skulking around the town tavern," she said.

"It's how I avoid protesting suffragettes," he answered. "Besides, is there anything wrong with a good skulk now and then?"

"None at all." Her eyes flashed, radiant with life. "In fact, I…"

Her voice trailed off, and his eyes diverted to a scene unfolding nearby.

On the far side of the parade ground, near fraternity row, Tommy Lee stood calmly, ringed by four other young men. Tommy Lee suddenly bowed to one of them and then shifted into a fighting stance, his weight on his back foot and his hands open, one covering the side of his head and the other in front as if mesmerizing his forward opponent like an Indian snake charmer.

From a distance, Heinrich could see a short wooden baseball bat in the hands of the attacker behind Tommy's back. Before Heinrich could yell, "Look out, Tommy!" young Mr. Lee leapt forward and landed a front kick with the ball of his foot on the first young man's chest, sending him sprawling across the parking lot. Having lurched forward only to miss Tommy on a downward stroke, the boy with the bat took another step toward Tommy and brought the bat upward in an angled blow toward Tommy's ribcage.

Tommy blocked the bat with his forearms, and, grabbing it with his left hand, pulled it toward him while sliding his right elbow along the bat and into the other boy's chin. Bat boy fell on the ground. Grabbing the club with both hands, Tommy then jammed the butt end into the gut of his attacker on the right, who let out a grunt and also fell backward onto the pea gravel.

Twirling the club expertly in his right hand, Tommy advanced on the lone remaining assailant to his left. Tommy jumped and twisted in the air 360 degrees. He twirled the bat above his head and shouted a fierce "Kee-yap" as he landed. He waved the bat in a figure-eight pattern as if daring number four to come get his beating. Recognizing defeat, his final assailant instead turned tail and ran off down the street.

Tommy grinned, brought his feet together, bowed to the retreating cloud of dust, and then turned to give a bow to his audience, which by now pretty much included everybody at the party other than his attackers, who were still moaning on the ground. The crowd of onlookers, Heinrich included, gave Tommy an ovation, although Heinrich could see that President Tichenor was not amused by the display of martial artistry. It clearly did not match his image of the proper behavior of a college gentleman.

Another woman grabbed Sally's arm during the commotion and led her away. Sally gave Heinrich a resigned look, and he waved while mouthing the words, "See you later." Thinking that he would recruit Tommy to be president of his Burschenschaft fraternity were he to start one anytime soon, Heinrich decided to make his exit.

CHAPTER 2

Suddenly time stood still, as if Heinrich and the Moro warrior running toward him at breakneck speed were the only people in the plaza.

The crowd at the Jolo marketplace parted. They ducked and ran for cover behind baskets of exotic tropical fruit and fresh fish, to watch the charge of the barefoot warrior, his skin painted vivid red, the Moro war color. He wore blue trousers with a shiny gold sash and a red turban and had clearly gone juramentado, the Moro version of a personal jihad. A warrior gone juramentado usually worked himself into a trance, and then executed an unnerving charge at high speed while screaming as if berserk and slashing with a weapon, often a barong, a short, wide-bladed sword that was the preferred weapon of the Moros. However, this time the weapon of choice was the kris, an exotic Moro sword with a long, wavy blade that tended to hypnotize its target as it danced through the air toward its intended victim.

Surprisingly calm, perhaps because this was his third juramentado attack, Heinrich purposefully set his feet at about shoulder width and gripped his Colt .45 sidearm in his right hand. Sergeant Brady had trained him for just such an occasion by ordering the men to keep their sidearms loaded at all times with holsters unbuckled. The policy led to a few stolen guns, but it saved precious seconds during an attack. Heinrich slipped it from the holster in a fluid movement that seemed like slow motion, but which only took a few seconds. When the bellowing warrior got to within ten feet, he squeezed off three shots, aiming low as he had been taught. Aim low, and you have more chance at hitting something.

Struck in the stomach and chest, the dazed warrior, tangled hair blowing in the breeze, sank to his knees and dropped the kris, which fell on the cobblestone pavement with a clank and a clatter. The warrior toppled face forward, and Heinrich matter-of-factly walked over, carefully placed his booted foot between the warrior's sweaty shoulder blades, and pumped two more shots into the back of his head to finish him off. The soldiers had learned through deadly experience not to let a Moro get up again, especially once he was down, during a one-on-one fight. Heinrich turned the body over. The Moro's glassy eyes and contorted mouth gave his face the look of a landed fish caught in a net...

Shivering and sweating profusely, Heinrich awoke with a start. He wondered why this particular Moro had taken over his dreams lately after the dozens of others he had killed in combat. Why did this one matter more than the other two Moros on juramentado he had shot? Perhaps it was because it was his final juramentado killing, perhaps it was the warrior's use of the kris instead of the barong, but he suspected it was mainly because this particular killing had been so cold-hearted and clinical. By that time, killing for him had become so nonchalant that blowing another man's head off was no more momentous than taking out the garbage. Had he really become the mechanical killer he saw in the dream? Heinrich hoped not.

And it was the image of the glassy, brown eyes staring up at him; the eyes of his dead men had begun to haunt him.

There was no way he could go back to sleep now, and he would have to get up in an hour anyway. So he got out of bed, put on yesterday's clothes, and headed for the kitchen. If Mrs. Yaeger hadn't started brewing the coffee, he'd put it on for her.

On his way out the door, he remembered Tommy's own combat the night before. He stopped at Tommy's door and knocked. When he got no answer, he continued on his way.

Heinrich yawned, caught himself and said "Excuse me" to the young men of Kappa Psi, with whom he was lunching that day. Faculty members were expected to dine with the students when invited. His yawn hardly mattered. The hungry youths were deep in conversation with each other and hadn't noticed.

Heinrich wished he had gotten more sleep the night before, but he hadn't been sleeping well for some time now. He hated having to lie to Mrs. Yaeger when in the morning she asked him how well he had slept. He could tell she was worried about him, but he didn't dare tell her about his evil dreams. He had learned the wariness of the military man toward showing weakness. Better to suffer in stoic silence than to let it be known he might not be mentally fit.

Still itching to speak with Tommy about what had precipitated the boy's battle at the mixer, Heinrich knocked on the young man's door before leaving to teach his Western Civilization class, but still there was no answer.

Heinrich took another bite of rubbery fried chicken.

"So, your family is German?" a clean-cut, hawk-nosed senior across the table asked, trying to spark a conversation. He was John Fairchild, president of the fraternity and the son of the powerful political boss who had given Heinrich the cold shoulder on his first day in town.

Heinrich looked down at the red gingham tablecloth. "Yes, we immigrated in 1834."

Fairchild wrinkled his nose; Heinrich frowned and waited for what young Fairchild would say next.

"Sorry, Dr. Kueter. No offense, but you Dutchmen were never very popular around my house. You're the reason Missouri stayed in the Union."

Heinrich grimaced and took a sip of sweet tea, which only heightened his sour face. Never much of a tea-drinker, Heinrich preferred it straight when coffee wasn't available. But here in Little Dixie, it was a matter of Southern pride to load it down with sugar. A small glass of fruity Riesling might have made the chicken more palatable, but imbibing even a tiny amount of alcohol during the workday would be frowned upon at a Presbyterian college run by staunch teetotalers. Like most employees, Heinrich thought it best to follow the "When in Rome" adage; when the imperious president proudly displays a photo of Carrie Nation on his office wall, one does as the Romans do.

As it was, sweet tea symbolized the North-South divide that made discussion of the Civil War difficult. Many Missourians still fought the Civil War in their hearts, no matter that it had ended 50 years ago. In addition, for Missourians, the war had taken on a decidedly "insider-versus-outsider" aspect not always seen in other parts of the country. That insular resentment had never dissipated amongst the older settlers toward the German and Irish immigrants who had streamed through St. Louis since the early 1800s and either built new communities or swelled the populations of established ones.

Heinrich's maternal great grandfather, Friedrich "Papa" Muench, had led a group of idealistic German dissidents to this supposed "Land of the Free" only to see blacks whipped and sold in chains at the courthouse square in St. Louis. Outside Franklinton, on a hillside meadow filled with daffodils, blacks had been auctioned like cattle on a table-shaped granite boulder known forever as "nigger rock" to folk throughout the Little Dixie region. But the Union-leaning, highly educated German "Latin farmers" detested such practices and saw slavery as feudalism warmed over. After escaping police harassment back home, leaving much of their wealth behind, and enduring disease and death on their journey, most Germans would not support a similar system of medieval serfdom in the New World.

When Civil War came, and the governor and legislature threatened to secede, the Union formed the Federal Home Guards, a mostly German force under Captain Nathaniel Lyon, which steamboated up the Missouri River and took the state capital by force. They chased former Governor and militia General Sterling Price, secessionist Governor Claiborne Jackson, and legislators out of Jefferson City. The action made a lasting impression on the insiders, whose bushwhackers later were reported to kill men on the road merely for looking "too German."

Heinrich could see that Young Fairchild awaited his reply. Although he often tried to avoid the touchy subject, Heinrich decided to challenge the young man's assumptions. "Is it so bad that Missouri stayed in the Union?" he asked.

"It is in my family. My grandfather fought with Old Pap Price."

Former Governor Price became the Civil War hero of choice in Little Dixie after defeating Lyon at Wilson's Creek in 1861. Three years later, his last-ditch raid through Missouri had been meant to rekindle the secessionist flame, but a decade of deadly guerrilla warfare and Union Order Number 11, which had emptied the farms along the Kansas border, had destroyed any desire to flock to the lost cause. Heinrich eyed the Confederate battle flag over the mantle above the Kappa Psi crest and remembered that Missouri had a star on that flag even though the state had technically remained in the Union.

"A fine gentleman and a historic figure," Heinrich said diplomatically. Fairchild nodded.

An awkward moment of silence ensued as the group searched for a less contentious topic.

"Professor Kueter, what do you think about the Kaiser throwing his military weight around and sending his battleships to face down the French in Africa?" interjected another young Kappa Psi from farther down the table.

Ah, yes. Every American of German origin must answer for the imperial homeland, Heinrich thought. No matter that his Germans were democrats who had left before the country had even become a unified nation precisely because they were unhappy with its authoritarian political system. Most American Germans had hoped for a unified, democratic Germany, not one centered on Prussian militarism.

"The Kaiser is a child and a bully, prancing around in military uniforms and showing off his toy battleships," Heinrich said.

"You have to admit, though, that the Kaiser sure seems to have acted as a peacemaker in the Balkan wars this year and last," Fairchild responded.

Heinrich nodded. "We'll see. I suspect the Balkan peoples are not through fighting each other yet," he said. "While I hope the German government will change for the better, we may have to wait until the world powers stop carving up the earth and squabbling over the pieces."

Fairchild grinned. "White man's burden," he said.

Racist attitudes like that were the burden, Heinrich thought, but said nothing. He looked at the Confederate flag again, and then at the wizened ebony face of Benjamin "Old Ben" Jones, the aged Kappa Psi "houseboy" standing stoically in the corner. He was waiting to bus the dishes of these young southern gentlemen.

"Old Ben" was a peaceful man with gray stubble on his head and prune-like fingers who was universally beloved by the students. Sometimes, in the evening after a hard day's work, Ben would sit on the front stoop and tell stories about the old days. Old Ben was reputedly a cousin of Morris Slater, the infamous "Railroad Bill," a southern Robin Hood who stole goods from L&N line trains in Alabama and gave them to fellow poor blacks. When asked, Ben would act out Railroad Bill's saga. When lawmen tried to disarm him in 1895, Railroad Bill killed a sheriff and his deputy. After that, a white posse hoping to hold a "necktie party" for the desperado. To flush out the outlaw, they murdered numerous blacks in the area. The law finally caught Railroad Bill a year later; he died in an ambush at a general store in Atmore, Alabama. He became a martyr of black lore.

On a recent evening, Heinrich had listened to Old Ben recite the town's Civil War legend. Ben clearly didn't share the pride Franklinton's white folks took in the story, but young Fairchild certainly would.

As the story went, after Missouri decided not to secede from the Union, Franklinton County seceded from the state. A committee of its most prominent secessionist citizens declared it the sovereign "Grand Duchy of Dixie," complete with its own elected Duke, an older gentleman who would later receive a 21-gun salute at his funeral in the 1890s. When the Union Army showed up, because all the eligible young men had left to join the secessionist militia, the remaining locals made the town appear fortified by painting logs to look like cannons and sending boys on stilts to man wooden ramparts. From a distance, it looked convincing. The Union commander signed a peace treaty with the Duchy, and the townspeople never forgot their brief, shining moment of sovereignty.

It was a quaint, romantic tale, certainly more fun than delving into the domestic face of Rudyard Kipling's "White Man's Burden," which Heinrich knew by hard experience to be a simple euphemism for "suppression by brutal violence." The European empires and their Japanese and American copycats merely used the argument to excuse their gobbling of territories and raw materials from less sophisticated peoples under the guise of educating and bringing religion to the "savages." Young Americans learned their racism at home and exported it overseas. Heinrich, by gunning down Moros with his carbine and Colt .45, had served the new empire's machine firsthand.

Another young man down the table piped in eagerly, "I hear you served with Pershing in the Philippines. What was it like fighting the Moros? Are they as fierce as people say they are?"

He inrich nodded, afraid of where that road of conversation might lead. The intense dreams broke his sleep nearly every night. It had only only three months since the Battle of Bud Bagsak, but it seemed like forever. It had been the most awful, ter, he had caught the boat for home.

He wanted to forget the Moros, the slaughter of innocents, the butchering of bloody place of slaughter he had ever seen, and it had come in the last week of his tour of duty. Three days la kris-wielding tribesmen and the gunpoint robbery of their freedom, but the faces of painted Moro warriors haunted his dreams. Worse still was the vision of a young Moro boy on the opening day on the slopes of Mount Bagsak.

Having just flattened a charging Moro warrior with the butt of his rifle, Heinrich had seen a sword flash behind him in the corner of his eye. Instantly, fired by pure adrenaline, he whirled around and shoved his bayonet into the attacker's belly. His assailant screamed in pain and dropped his *barong*. The boy looked to be about 11 or 12 years old, merely one of the 500 women and children who fell to U.S. arms during the three-day battle. Realizing he had just killed a boy, Heinrich sank to his knees and cried. A few weeks later, he was back in Chicago, a civilian again, comfortable but numb.

As Heinrich searched his mind for something witty that might turn the conversation to some other less painful subject, another student with a ruddy complexion and carrot-red hair staggered up to the table and draped his arm around Fairchild's shoulders. Spitting as he spoke, the newcomer was clearly tipsy.

"It's time we taught the Chink a lesson," he said loudly, as if he thought nobody but Fairchild would hear. Heinrich realized he probably meant Tommy Lee.

Fairchild gave his fraternity brother a steely-eyed look of disgust. "Martin, you know the fine for public drunkenness."

Martin Mason seemed to suddenly realize where he was. Upon noticing Heinrich, his face turned ash white. "Sorry, Professor Kueter. I guess I had a few too many."

"I apologize for Martin's behavior," Fairchild said. "I'd better help him to his room."

"Apology accepted," Kueter said. "But perhaps I can help. Tommy and I room in the same boardinghouse. If Tommy has done something to provoke you, I could talk to him." Fairchild shook his head. "No, Professor Kueter, Martin and Tommy just had a little disagreement yesterday; that's all. We'll work it out." Fairchild got up, put Martin's arm over his shoulder and walked him up the hall.

Heinrich watched them leave the room. He stood up, but, before he could pick up his dirty dishes, Old Ben took them. Heinrich said, "Thank you," and Ben nodded.

Heinrich followed the young men down the hall. As he turned from the foyer into the main hallway, he saw Fairchild push Mason up against the wall and shake his finger under the other boy's nose. When he saw Heinrich, Fairchild quickly pulled Mason into a nearby room and shut the door behind him. The sight made Heinrich uneasy; under the surface of the situation lurked something more than public drunkenness.

Just after breakfast the next day, Heinrich found Tommy on the grassy field behind the freshman dormitory. He watched in wonder as the young man performed a series of what looked to be calisthenics and martial arts maneuvers in a slow, fluid dance under the shade of an elm tree.

"Hello, Professor," Tommy said, aiming a slow punch at the midsection of an invisible opponent. He continued the routine.

"Hello, Tommy. That's an interesting dance," Heinrich observed.

"It is called Tai Chi Chuan, an ancient Chinese martial art. My father taught it to me. It gets my energy flowing. I often mix it with the Tae Kwon Do I learned in Korea."

Tommy slowly circled his arms around his body like a large windmill and came to a stop. Holding position for a moment with his eyes closed, the young man then opened them and bowed.

"It may look like a dance, but the form represents a fight with an imaginary opponent," Tommy said. "The moves can be used for offense and defense, yin and yang, hard and soft, at the same time."

"Somewhat like a boxer might use an offensive punch to prevent getting hit first?" Heinrich asked. He had learned some boxing moves at a German athletic club back home.

Tommy nodded. "Boxing is a western martial art. Tae Kwon Do is similar in that it uses closed hands, while Tai Chi uses open hands. Closed hands can sometimes mean fewer injuries, but open hands can allow for fast reaction. Often, that is most important in a fight."

Tommy showed Heinrich how to make a tight fist and a knife hand. "Now, you did not really come here to learn the knife hand. What can I do for you, professor?" Tommy asked.

"Well, I don't mean to pry into your personal affairs, but I thought I ought to warn you that Mr. Mason appears to be upset with you." Heinrich related what had happened the day before at the Kappa Psi house.

Tommy frowned. "We had strong words a couple days ago, but I think the matter has been resolved. Somebody showed me an advance copy of the yearbook, and under my name was a caption that contained a slur against me."

"The Chink."

Tommy nodded. "As you know, Marty Mason was the editor of that page, and I told him I did not appreciate it."

"That is understandable, but remember your sticks and stones."

"What do you mean?" Tommy asked.

"Sticks and stones may break my bones, but names will never hurt me."

Tommy nodded again. "A silly saying; words hurt too. Marty and I fought with words. He told me not to dance with white women, and I told him I would freely dance with whomever I choose."

Heinrich tried another tack. "What do you do when someone pushes you?" He pushed Tommy's left shoulder, and the young man stepped back with his left foot and turned his body to back his shoulder away from the push. The move effectively neutralized the force of the blow.

"Precisely," Heinrich said. "Do the same when someone calls you a name."

Tommy laughed. "If someone keeps pushing you, then you must follow with an attack."

"All right, so I suppose the method isn't perfect," Heinrich said.

"As in this situation. They attacked me the other evening for the same reason, as you may have heard."

"I saw it. Be careful, Tommy," Heinrich said. "Don't go looking for trouble. You can't win every fight, although I must say you conducted yourself rather well against those four assailants."

"Thank you, professor. I do not look for trouble, but it often seems to find me."

Heinrich nodded, thinking as he left the young man with a half wave, that the same could be said about himself.

With silent concentration, Heinrich worked through the possible ramifications of moving his rook. Manfred Dahlen had purchased the exquisite chess set, with its ancient Chinese warriors in hand-carved ivory, at an outdoor marketplace in Shanghai. Tommy had told Heinrich that Dahlen was a "serious" chess player, and Heinrich did not want to embarrass himself by making a stupid mistake in front of the Austrian gentleman. Dahlen had invited him over this evening to play chess and drink tea, which turned out to be hot green tea from China, a nice respite from the Southern sugared variety. Heinrich made his move, and then got up to stretch his legs while Manfred surveyed the board.

To the left of the brick fireplace stood a common rack of fireplace tools: poker, spade, broom and bellows. They were hidden behind a green, leafy plant until the winter chill arrived. To the right, housed in the bottom of an antique butter churn was another eclectic collection of tools. Heinrich recognized a branding iron and fireplace toaster among other interesting implements. They appeared to be artillery tools.

Dahlen had told Heinrich of his boyhood as the son of a blacksmith in an Austrian village near Salzburg. A widower, he had married his childhood sweetheart, the daughter of a merchant. Dahlen had volunteered for the Austro-Hungarian Army, had been assigned to an Imperial *Landwehr* Field Artillery Battalion and rose from the rank of *kanonier*, equivalent to a private in English, to *feuerwerker*, equivalent to a sergeant.

In January 1900, Dahlen was assigned to the Austro-Hungarian legation in Peking and was granted permission to bring his wife, who was a month pregnant. Six months later, the Chinese Boxers besieged the Legation Quarter, and Dahlen helped organize the small Allied defense that maintained the siege until an Allied expedition, marching from Tianjin, relieved it by taking Peking in August. The legations only had one old, muzzle-loaded cannon, which became known as the "international gun," because its barrel was British, the carriage was Italian, the shells were Russian and the crew was American, with some token assistance from Dahlen. Unfortunately, Liesl Dahlen was killed by a sniper's bullet while helping Christian missionaries and children under their care move into the compound.

Heinrich studied the mantle above the fireplace. Two ornate beer steins depicting a Germanic male and female flanked the walnut mantle. "Are those *Siegfried* and *Brunhilde* from Wagner's opera?" he asked Manfred.

The Austrian nodded and grunted affirmatively, still contemplating his next move. "I find it interesting that even we Westerners have our yin and yang characters."

In the middle of the mantle, below an ornate mirror, sat a blue porcelain saucer and an octagonal teacup adorned with the painted figure of a winsome girl. "What's this one?" Heinrich asked.

"A teacup from China. It was a gift to my wife, Liesl; I keep it to remember her. As you know, she was killed by the Boxers… and I still miss her terribly."

"I'm sorry to bring it up, Manfred."

"It's all right. It seems a long time ago now," Manfred said as he moved his bishop to pressure Heinrich's rook. "She was the love of my life, the yin to my yang."

"Hmm," Heinrich said, surveying the board and trying to think of something else to say. One good thing about chess, he thought, is that silence is not impolite. Sometimes not having to think of something to say could be quite handy. Manfred sensed Heinrich's unease.

"Don't be uncomfortable, Heinrich. We all must learn to cope with the death of those we love. However, I doubt I will ever forgive the Boxers."

Heinrich continued to stare silently at the board. He could think of no good response.

Manfred pointed to the gaudily framed mirror above the fireplace. "As for the mirror, it comes from a brothel in San Francisco," Manfred offered, laughing. "She came cheap, but I wouldn't want to lose her either."

Heinrich joined the Austrian in laughing at the rescue, delighted to extricate himself from the difficult subject of Manfred's lost love. It was then far easier to focus on the masculine art of chessboard warfare, as good a yang activity as there ever was.

The following week, Manfred invited Heinrich to join him on an early morning hike to see Eagle Cliff, a local landmark and home to several eagles. Manfred said local birders had sighted at least one prominent pair of bald eagles recently and suspected there were more in residence.

Heinrich met Manfred at the stable at four in the morning. Manfred had baked muffins to eat along the way. He had used a recipe left behind by his deceased wife, he explained. They brought along canteens of water and a Coleman gasoline lantern to light their way until dawn. It was a chilly fall night, pitch black.

The rugged path began on the far side of Stephens Creek, west of Worcester College. After about a half-hour hike, they stopped on a large flat rock to rest. Manfred turned down the lantern and put it into a hole in the underside of the rock to hide the light. He explained that he only had about a dozen matches with him, so it was best to keep the lamp burning. It was still very dark, with only a hint of the coming dawn apparent in the sky. The light of town lay far away, and the full cascade of stars was visible in the heavens.

"I love to look at the stars," Manfred said. He showed Heinrich how to find the Milky Way and how it intersected a triangle formed by three bright stars.

"That formation is called the Summer Triangle, formed by Altair, Vega and Deneb, and it attaches the classical constellations of Aquila, Lyra and Cygnus," Manfred said. He pointed to Altair and Vega. "Do you see how Altair and Vega lie on opposite sides of the Milky Way? To the Chinese, the star we know as Altair is Niulang, the cowherd, and Vega is Zhinu, the weaver girl."

Heinrich nodded, trying to keep up.

"The young cowherd spied the beautiful fairy while she was bathing and stole her clothing as a joke. Because he saw her naked, she had to marry him secretly, but it was truly a match made in heaven. She was a wonderful wife, with a great talent for weaving. He was a fine husband, and they fell madly in love. Unfortunately, the girl's meddling mother, the Goddess of Heaven, became enraged. She wanted a better match for her daughter."

Heinrich nodded. "There's usually an evil mother-in-law lurking somewhere."

Manfred laughed and continued. "With her hairpin, she angrily scratched out a wide river, the Milky Way, to separate the lovers forever. Zhinu now spends eternity weaving colorful clouds on her loom, while Niulang is forced to watch her from a distance across the sky."

Heinrich nodded in admiration. "So cowherds in China can't swim?"

Manfred laughed again. "I suppose not." He looked at his watch and picked up the lantern. They continued their hike. "And they certainly can't govern themselves either."

"Come now, Manfred, Germany was once as fractured as China is now."

Manfred nodded. "Fractured and feudal, perhaps. But lawless? Not like the Chinese. They're damn devils."

Heinrich needled him once more. "Come now, Manfred, China's empire and its law flourished long before Europeans knew any organized government beyond the tribe."

"You're a good man, Heinrich; you see the best in people," replied Manfred, shaking his head. "I once thought the Chinese could be civilized too, but I saw their barbarity firsthand."

Clearly, Heinrich had touched a nerve, so he decided not to push the subject.

A half-hour later, at the crest of a hill that looked down into a swampy valley, they stopped again to rest and watch the dawn, a beautiful light display of orange and yellow hues waking up the natural realm.

As they started heading down into the valley, Heinrich saw a stand of large, round, off-white mushrooms under a tree beside the path. "I wonder if those are edible," he said.

Manfred shrugged. "They appear to be puffballs, which are usually edible, although you would need to cut them open to make sure they weren't brown inside, which would mean they would taste bad," he said."You also would need to make sure they aren't poisonous Amanita mushrooms, which sometimes look similar. Personally, I prefer morel mushrooms. Mike Murphy sometimes cooks them for me with a steak; they taste wonderful cooked with a beef-juice gravy."

Eagle Cliff rose above the valley that held the dirt path they were following. The cliff overlooked Franklinton Lake farther west. The thin, winding path wound westward through the marshes leading to the lake, and Heinrich could tell that parts of the path had been shored up by wooden railroad ties.

Along the trail, the two men talked about religion, although in careful terms. Heinrich,the son of a Lutheran pastor, and Manfred, who had served as a Catholic missionary in China, talked about various points of theology. It was good to live in a country where people did not kill each other over religious matters, Heinrich mused to himself. No need for a European-style Thirty Years War here in the land of the free.

"I suppose it's good that we keep improving our government here in the United States," Heinrich said.

Manfred nodded. "Yeah, except I wouldn't count the income tax as an improvement."

The momentous and long-debated income tax had arrived with the passage of the 16th Amendment the previous February and was only now going into effect. Heinrich had few resources and believed that government could do great good with more resources, so he welcomed the move, but those more affluent than himself had more to lose and did not often appreciate the new tax burden imposed by the federal government. When combined with the recently created financial institution, the Federal Reserve, some viewed the two moves as a government conspiracy to take over the economy and push the nation toward socialism. Heinrich guessed that Manfred might take that view, so he decided to avoid the subject and asked instead about another recently passed amendment.

"What do you think about the direct election of senators? It should eliminate some corruption, don't you think?"

Manfred snorted. "On the day politicians eliminate corruption, hell's residents will hold a snowball fight."

They walked in silence for a minute. Then, Manfred asked about Heinrich's family and how his relatives came to America, which led Heinrich to talk about how Germany had at first spurned its democratic-leaning citizens. This move eventually led the country to become a unified nation under Prussia's influence only about 40 years ago. He told how his father had hoped that Germany might include Austria as well in a "Greater Germany," but those hopes had been dashed by European dynastic politics. Manfred agreed with Heinrich that Germany's coalescence under Prussia had not been a healthy development because it had resulted in the triumph of Germany's militaristic elements.

"With the balance of power as it is now in Europe, all it would take is some spark to engulf them in a war," Heinrich said, but Manfred shook his head.

"The Europeans are too civilized for that. Cooler heads will prevail," Manfred said. "They have too much at stake. At worst, there might be another war between France and Germany, but the other countries will quickly pressure them to come to terms."

Heinrich nodded. His friend's point made sense. If only the Kaiser didn't enjoy throwing his troops around the chessboard so nonchalantly, he thought.

Soon they reached a good spot from which to view the eagles. Manfred pointed toward a hole in the cliff above them, where a stand of old-growth forest stood. Heinrich pulled out a pair of binoculars he had recently purchased on a trip to Jefferson City and soon found a couple of nests in the treetops. The birds' stark white heads with black bodies and golden beaks were fascinating to behold as they soared high above on the wind currents of the valley.

Heinrich shared his field glasses with Manfred and thanked the Austrian for bringing him to this special place. "The view is certainly worth the walk," he said.

The following weekend, Manfred accompanied Heinrich to the black-tie "Titanic Ball" benefit hosted by the Tichenors at the Emperor Hotel Ballroom. The H.M.S. Titanic had sunk the previous year. Stenciled paper portholes had been placed around the dance floor, and a ship's wheel had been strategically located on stage with the orchestra.

The event began with a banquet with large round tables and seating organized by the Tichenors. While married couples had been placed together, Heinrich and Manfred were ushered to a round table with place cards that intermingled bachelors with bachelor-girls and their chaperones. Heinrich sat between a blushing brunette co-ed with a pronounced overbite named Jill Worth and her aunt, a sour matron named Mary Hazeltine. Sally had been placed at a different table, and Heinrich suspected their separation was deliberate.

The eight-course meal began with a chilled Franklinton cocktail, basically a spiced tomato juice. Heinrich tasted pepper in it and an Italian flavoring he recognized from spaghetti sauce, perhaps oregano. The soup course that followed was composed of consommé a la royale, a hearty beef broth with egg custard pieces shaped like boats. Next came baked stuffed black bass a la meniere – breaded fish with a butter sauce – served on a lettuce leaf, followed by tomatoes frappe – a tomato jelly – en mayonnaise. The chilled dish had a consistency similar to a milkshake, except that the interesting mixture was more tart than sweet.

After the fish course, President Tichenor stood to remind everyone that the party's purpose was to benefit the children of maritime disaster victims, and he recognized the donors. Guests who paid the highest donations got to play the role of the passenger or crewman of their choice. As host, and for $100, President Tichenor chose to be the captain and received a Titanic ship's hat from his wife. Powerbroker Truman Fairchild paid twice that and chose to be John Jacob Astor. As the top female to make a donation, Sally Ann Giddings chose to be the Unsinkable Molly Brown. She received a cigar to augment her costume, which consisted of a stunning pink taffeta and chiffon dress with a shiny satin bodice and dollar bills safety-pinned in strategic locations. Of course, she chose to light the cigar and smoke it – just a few puffs for comic effect – with great bravado, much to the horror of many a society matron in attendance.

As the males laughed at her performance, waiters rolled out the fifth course of broiled Philadelphia squab – a small game pigeon – on toast, served with grilled sweet potatoes and French peas. As an interlude, the guests received a small glass bowl of crushed pineapple ice to cleanse their palates. When the diners stood up to stretch for 10 minutes, the men smoked cigarettes in an adjoining room.

Although many of his military compatriots had picked up the smoking habit to kill time overseas, Heinrich had not. Instead, he had habitually spent time roaming the Philippine street markets and small shops looking for good imported wines. Of course, the wine customer needed to shop with care because too often the unschooled natives would leave wine in the sun and ruin it. As Heinrich's wine palate evolved, he found his taste gravitating toward rich, red wines.

So today he obtained a glass of French burgundy from the bar and joined the men for a few minutes of conversation. Across the room, he could hear his department chairman, Erwin Goforth, expounding on the merits of a ban on boxing, so he walked over to listen.

A few months ago, a boxer named John "Bull" Young had died of a broken neck in a fight with Jess Willard, and California reformer William E. Brown was leading a coalition of clergyman and women to ban boxing matches. Promoters had skirted California's law against "prize fights" by calling them "boxing affairs."

"You mark my words, gentlemen," Goforth said. "The women might just kill off boxing, and maybe it should be killed off. And we all know that the next thing they'll go after is liquor, and maybe that's a good thing too."

The men grumbled. Women had received the vote in California two years before and were pushing for the vote across the country. Among the usual print advertising and colorful posters, their California campaign had employed the innovative marketing tactic of giving male voters up-close looks at luxury and racing automobiles in exchange for speeches on the benefits of giving women the vote. And when police tried to arrest suffragettes for not having public speaking permits, the women sang about their message instead. There was no law in California against singing in public.

Heinrich smiled at the thought. It sounded like something Sally would have done. Hopefully, her dance card would not be full tonight after the interminable dinner.

Goforth pointed a bony finger at him, snapping him out of his thoughts. "You're something of a brawler, Heinrich," Goforth said. "What say you about boxing?"

The men grinned and turned to hear his response. Heinrich looked from man to man. He raised his glass.

"Gentlemen, a good boxer knows when and when not to fight," Heinrich said. "I support the well-regulated sweet science of pugilism, but I defer to my department chairman's judgment as he is far older and wiser than I."

Goforth laughed, and the others raised their glasses. "Here, here!"

When the guests returned to the dining room, waiters served roast spring chicken with chestnut dressing, accompanied by lobster salad, new potatoes in cream and asparagus tips in butter. Soon after, the meal ended with a dessert of vanilla ice cream and cake nuggets, served with black coffee. Once again, the men finished by adjourning to a nearby room to smoke cigars, while the women went to a dressing room to prepare themselves for dancing.

Sally allowed Heinrich to fill in his name on more than half of the 24 dances on her dance card, an action that would have been seen as improper for younger unmarried women, who were expected to spread their attentions evenly amongst all the bachelors in attendance. In addition to the standard two-steps, waltzes and foxtrots, the ball featured popular ragtime tunes by Scott Joplin, such as the "Weeping Willow Rag," "The Maple Leaf Rag," "The Entertainer," and some songs by other ragtime artists such as Louis Chauvin and Thomas Turpin. Old Ben Jones, his wrinkled fingers skipping across the keys and lights glinting off his thick Prince Hall Masonic ring, played the piano with the orchestra on the rags.

When the old gentleman stepped outside for a break, Heinrich shook his hand at the doorway and complimented his playing. Ben thanked Heinrich.

"Will you be joining the dance later after your set?" Heinrich asked, and instantly realized it was a stupid question. Ben was the only colored person in the room other than a few women serving drinks and hors-d'oeuvres.

"No, no, Professor," Ben said with a laugh. "We ain't invited, but don't you worry, my folks will be getting together for a Shine party later this evening."

Heinrich looked puzzled. At that point, Sally Giddings came up and grabbed his arm. "Ask Sally. She knows what I mean," Ben said with a wink as he walked out the door to grab a smoke.

"Heinrich Kueter, apparently I have to use physical force to get you to ask me to dance," Sally said, mockingly perturbed.

"Hmm.Physical force.Sounds interesting."

She swatted him. "Stop it. Let's dance."

Sally pulled him out on the floor for a foxtrot. He did his best. His steps were rusty, but he found his rhythm.

"Old Ben told me he is going to a Shine party this evening and that you would know what that was."

Sally laughed. "Legend has it that Jack Johnson, the famous boxer, was denied a ticket on the Titanic, and a stoker named Shine was reputedly the only black man allowed on board. The blacks sing songs about him. Shine was not allowed on the upper decks. He was only there to shovel coal and otherwise stay out of sight. When the ship sinks, he out-swims whales and sharks all the way to New York in the frigid waters even though the captain and passengers offer him money and sexual favors to stay aboard. Some versions of the tale are quite ribald, I'm told. By the time the news of the sinking arrives, Shine is already half-drunk in Harlem and laughing at the white people."

Heinrich nodded. "So tonight the black folks will be putting one over on us fancy-pants white people with a party that's more fun."

"That's about the size of it. Now dance."

Ben Jones came back inside, then sat down at the piano. He rubbed his ring for good luck and began playing "The Magnetic Rag."

"Have you ever tried the Turkey Trot?" Sally asked. "Let's do it."

Heinrich had seen it done once, but he found the new dance a little silly. He looked around the room. He might wind up paying for it later in sore muscles and strange looks, but what the heck. Life is short, he thought. If Sally wanted it, he would do his best.

Considered somewhat scandalous, the Turkey Trot was a version of the foxtrot in which the partners held their arms out like turkey wings and hopped in four-beat time. He and Sally stepped in time on the first beat, hopped three times, and then gave four run-walk steps to complete the pattern: step-hop-hop-hop and run-run-run-run. Other younger dancers followed suit, while several of the older ones left the floor in disgust at the vulgarization of the genteel foxtrot.

When the song was done, Sally and Heinrich left the floor. It had been an exhausting dance, and they wanted some punch. At the punch bowl, they met Mrs. Tichenor, whose face held a visage even more disapproving than usual.

"Professor Kueter, my husband and I would like to visit with you after the dance to get to know you better. Do you think you could spare us a few minutes?"

Mrs. Tichenor stood before them imperiously, her plump frame enclosed in a red and white dress with severe corseting underneath and practically every inch of skin covered. Her bony nose let out small sniffs as she spoke, punctuating her demands as if she were whipping her serfs with air.

The tone of Mrs. Tichenor's voice made it clear that Sally was not invited. Sally touched his arm. "I need to step away for a minute."

He nodded. "Of course, Mrs. Tichenor, I would be delighted."

"Good, then please meet us in the sitting room off the foyer at the end of this soiree."

Only Mrs. Tichenor would call such an event a "soiree," he thought, dreading having to pretend to enjoy her company. When the dance ended at 10 p.m., Heinrich told Sally and Manfred to go on without him. He trudged to the sitting room and opened the door.

The cheery crone's voice greeted him with a hearty "Come in!"

President Tichenor shook his hand and motioned for him to take a seat. He was ready to start the interrogation. He and his wife peppered Heinrich with questions about his family, religious beliefs, hobbies – you name it, they asked it, all under the guise of "getting to know him."

Heinrich gritted his teeth and bore their tedious questions, hoping desperately for a chance to leave, but it was clear that they wanted to make it impossible for him to spend any more of his evening with Sally.

When they could think of no more questions to ask him, they began to regale him with inane small talk. Desperately trying to keep his eyes open, he prayed to be released into the company of Sally, Manfred, Murphy, or even Old Ben. That Shine party sounded better with each interminable tick of the grandfather clock across the room.

The President told Heinrich a sonorous story about how he'd negotiated a favorable deal on his last horse. Tichenor was extremely cheap and loved a good bargain. Heinrich only half-listened, wondering how the man found it in his heart to part with $100 for maritime relief. It must have been his wife's idea.

And boy did she have ideas, most of them based on the premise that Missouri was a far-lesser state than her beloved Virginia. As the clock continued to tick, Heinrich began to wish Thomas Jefferson had never purchased the land west of the Mississippi. He began to think he would willingly swear allegiance to Spain or France just to get out of the room.

Then Mrs. Tichenor launched into a truly insipid tale about how she had saved money by purchasing a barber's kit when they were first married. She cut the future President's hair herself. No wonder it looked so thin now — ha, ha, ha, she tittered at the tiny joke — for which Heinrich could only force himself to generate a smile.

When President Tichenor finally stood up to say politely that he needed to use the restroom, Heinrich saw his chance. Making his apologies that Mrs. Yeager really didn't like him to come in too late, he ran away as fast as his legs could carry him, thanking God for Tichenor's bladder problem. It was a well-known malady that had generated jokes told in hushed tones among the faculty. The president had become notorious for constantly needing to urinate whenever he traveled.

If a full bladder was to be his rescue, he'd take it. Maybe he could still catch up with Sally at Murphy's.

The next Friday found him pausing before his Western Civilization class. Today, the subject was the colonization of the Americas. A student had asked an intelligent question that deserved some thought before Heinrich could give his answer.

"The question, if I may paraphrase you, Mr. Jordan, is, 'Do we in the "civilized" Christian world have a responsibility to impose better government and religion upon the poorer, uncivilized peoples of the world?' Is that a fair characterization of your inquiry, Mr. Jordan?"

Paul Jordan, one of Heinrich's brighter pupils, nodded. "Those people need our help, don't they?" the student added.

"It is a fair question and one very much in the public mind these days, what with developments in Africa and Asia, and with our war against the Filipino people, which I have had the opportunity, unfortunately, to see firsthand," Heinrich answered. "It may be that, while they may need our help, they may not want our help in the way that we tend to impose it.

"As Rudyard Kipling said some years ago:
'Take up the White Man's Burden,
Ye dare not stoop to less—
Nor call too loud on Freedom
To cloak your weariness.
By all ye will or whisper,
By all ye leave or do,
The silent sullen peoples
Shall weigh your God and you.'"

The young men in his class gave him that bleary-eyed Friday stare; he hoped he hadn't looked so obviously bored in front of the Tichenors the other night. "Let me put it another way. For instance, I felt my motives were pure once too. I thought we soldiers went to the Philippines on a mission to bring democracy and Christianity to a heathen populace. But the reality was quite different. Rather than teaching and helping people down on their luck, I found myself forced to kill them instead. When a fierce Moro warrior gone *juramentado* charges you waving a razor-sharp sword under your nose, you learn the only way to survive is to shoot first and ask questions later.

"Standing in formation, we were ordered to fire on the natives, and we mowed them down in great numbers most furiously. I regret that. And later, when I had time to think about it, the fear and contempt I learned to feel for these brown-skinned people was perhaps most frightening for the state of my soul. Therefore, I find it disconcerting when we are told that it is our duty to subjugate native peoples. I have seen the results of such policies in action. We men possess a marvelous, yet dastardly, capacity to tell ourselves that it is perfectly correct to do wrong as long as we do it for all the right reasons."

He paused for dramatic effect, but he could tell the students no longer cared to hear about his experiences. Heinrich could tell he was losing the class. "So, I guess I cannot answer the question for you; you must decide for yourselves. How's that for an evasive answer, eh?"

The class laughed.

Heinrich thought for a minute. "I will leave you with another thought. My great grandfather, Friedrich Muench, one of the early Missouri Germans, wrote in an 1862 article that: '...Slavery and true freedom can not, in fact, exist next to each other.' In reality, he said, the freedom of speech for Missouri's citizens had been diminished because they could not speak or write what they truly believed for fear of retribution from slaveowners. Therefore, systematic enslavement of blacks meant that other Americans lost some of their freedom as well."

The blank stares told Heinrich the students didn't grasp the concept. "OK, what about here in the United States?" he asked. "Back in April, when the postmaster general segregated the Postal Service, did any of you take notice?"

A youthful head or two gave a weak nod in response. It was a losing battle on a Friday afternoon, but he pressed on. "Maybe you didn't notice, but didn't that action, which took away a right for colored people, also take away the white workers' right to associate with them? I ask you, why was that necessary or desirable?"

"Why would we want to associate with Darkies?" asked young Doug Hanratty, who enjoyed making provocative statements to gain a laugh.

Heinrich gave Hanratty a mock swat with his hand in the air, which Hanratty ducked, to student laughter. "Because they might have something to teach us, perhaps."

The lily-white class murmured in disgust. Heinrich was losing this argument in the court of popular opinion, even though he knew he was in the right. "Okay, Okay, I can tell you don't agree, but I, for instance, would love to learn to box as well as Jack Johnson."

That comment brought a mix of laughs and jeers. "Settle down, settle down," he said. "What I'm suggesting is this: I believe that when we take away freedom from other peoples, whether overseas or right here at home, even when we believe it to be for all the right reasons, we give away some of our own freedom because social pressure takes away our ability to question the morality of our actions. Perhaps, rather than subjugating other peoples, our duty as Americans lies in doing the opposite. What do you think about that?"

Heinrich looked around the room. Not one student raised a hand. The omnipresent glassy-eyed stare in the eyes of the young men — predominately clean-cut, wealthy WASPS — told him he had lost his audience. It was time to carry on with the real lesson for the day. "All right, then. Who can tell me something about Hernando de Soto?"he said, turning toward the blackboard.

"Hello, Professor Kueter," said President Tichenor, taking Kueter's hand in his slippery grip of a handshake. Tichenor had just cornered Heinrich on his way from teaching class as he was walking from his office toward the library. They stopped under a large oak tree that shaded the brick walkway. It had been a long day, and it was about to get longer, Heinrich guessed.

"Hello, President Tichenor."

"Professor Kueter, would you please walk with me for a moment?" the president said in a stiff, cold manner.

"Certainly," Heinrich answered. "What can I do for you?"

"Well, I heard that you expressed some controversial political opinions in your class yesterday, and it caused some consternation among some of your students."

"I'm sorry to hear that, sir. They asked my opinion on an issue, and I gave it."

Tichenor took on a pedantic and curt tone, as if he were instructing a schoolboy. "I understand," Tichenor said. "However, I have found the wisest course of action in these instances is to give fewer opinions and instead to impart the information that you have been hired to deliver. In the future, please stick to the history in question, Professor Kueter."

"Sir, how can the students begin to understand their role at this moment in history if they are not allowed to assess the mistakes of the past?"

"That is not your concern. Simply teach them the material they need to know. No more opinions, if you please."

"That is an impossible request. You can't hold me to it..."

"Then resign. I'll find someone else, preferably someone without your Dutch stubbornness. That is all."

Tichenor strolled on with an imperial gait, dismissing Kueter as if he were a mere plebeian, of little concern.

Kueter held back, unsettled and frustrated, and watched the lanky president march on to his next meeting. Gritting his teeth, Kueter kicked a nearby pebble on the path and sent it scurrying into the grass. He then marched onward to the library to prepare for tomorrow's class, the Saturday morning pretense in which neither teacher nor all save the most dedicated students enjoyed participating.

That evening, still smarting from his encounter with President Tichenor, Heinrich joined Manfred at Murphy's tavern. After they had tossed back a few lagers, Murphy announced that it was time to pursue some manly entertainment outside. Heinrich and Manfred looked at each other, wondering what that might mean, but Heinrich suspected the activity was not illicit. Knowing Murphy to be a sucker for tales of the earliest pioneers and mountain men who had blazed the trail into the American West, he figured it might have something to do with that area of interest.

Indeed, after telling his nephew, Brian O'Toole, to man the bar, Murphy led them out the back door and handed them each a hatchet. Heinrich asked if he had engaged them in a Tom Sawyer-like stunt to get them to clear brush.

Murphy laughed. He pointed toward the brick wall that marked the back of his property, about 20 feet away. "No, we're going to play a real man's game tonight, a mountain man's game."

Attached to the brick wall, about five feet from the ground, was a wooden target about a foot square with a red bullseye on a white background and a blue outer ring. Murphy explained that the bullseye was worth five points, the middle ring worth three points, and the outer ring worth one point. He drew a line in the gravel and dirt that lay on the ground.

"Here's where you throw from," he said.

Heinrich and Manfred looked at each other. Heinrich laughed first. "I suppose I'm not much of a mountain man," he said. Manfred laughed and nodded in agreement.

"Just try it," Murphy growled. "You'll find it relieves anger," he said, then pointed to Heinrich. "Just think of the target as Tichenor's face."

Heinrich laughed again, weakly. Not wanting to anger his friend, he stepped up to the line. Dutifully raising his hatchet in front of his body, he sited with his eye down the head of the hatchet toward the target.

"If I may...," suggested Murphy, interjecting. "Don't look down the head of the hatchet. Just look at the target and raise your hand naturally above your shoulder, like this." He adjusted Heinrich's stance to shoulder width, with Heinrich's left foot slightly in advance of the other. When he got out of the way, Heinrich threw the hatchet toward the target. It missed, low by a foot. He had to admit that it did feel strangely therapeutic to mentally strike at Tichenor's face.

"Good, good," Murphy said, handing him another axe. "Now this time, don't twist or flick your wrist. Let the weight of the head in the air make it turn over naturally and hit the target."

Heinrich did as he was told and tried again. He gripped the smoothed pine of the handle, but loosened his grip as his hand came forward. He let the axe head flow forward, the base of the handle lightly scraping his palm as it left his hand. This time, he was only off to the right by about six inches.

"You get three throws; then let Manfred try," Murphy said.

On his third attempt, Heinrich hit the high side of the target's outer ring and pretended it had been Tichenor's forehead.

Manfred stepped forward to try his luck. "I know who I want on that target," he said. "One of those Boxer devils."

While the Austrian made his throws, Murphy whispered to Heinrich, "He means the Chinese, not the bare-knucklers. They killed his wife, you know."

Heinrich nodded. Manfred's hatchet hit the outer ring on his second throw to tie Heinrich's score. On the Austrian's third throw, he shouted, "Die, you devil!" He scored a hit in the middle ring and promptly bet Heinrich a dollar he could beat him two out of three. Heinrich accepted the challenge.

Manfred won the first game 4 to 1, and Heinrich won the second, 3 to 2. On his final ax in game three, down 3 to 1, Heinrich stared at the target intently, and, because his second throw had fallen short, stepped back a foot. He raised his hand and let the axe fly. It traveled the distance in two attractive arcs and stuck in the bullseye for a win. Manfred laughed and paid Heinrich the dollar.

"I'll get you next time," he said. "At least I can still drink you under the table."

They all laughed. Murphy had been right. The game had been therapeutic, and they would play it from time to time over the next few months.

Martin Mason closed his eyes and shook his head to clear it, but it didn't work. His fraternity brothers — pillowcases with cutout eyeholes covering their heads — wouldn't let him get his balance. He could taste the blood dripping into his mouth, but they just kept hitting him.

"You just couldn't keep your mouth shut, could you, Martin?" He recognized John Fairchild's voice under the sheet.

"I didn't tell. I didn't tell."

His nose bleeding badly, he put up his arms to block their blows. He couldn't see anymore.

A squirt of scarlet stained the white pillowcase. "Bullshit, Martin. That time at dinner, when you almost finked us out to that Kraut professor…that was bad. Now somebody else heard you drinking and nearly spilling the beans tonight over at the Gamma Sigma house. That's really bad."

"I'm sorry, John, I didn't mean to… please, give me another chance," Mason sobbed.

Two hooded men grabbed Mason's arms. Fairchild punched him in the gut, and Mason fell to his knees. "You know how we deal with snitches, Martin."

"John, I swear to God..."

"I don't want to hear it." Fairchild raised his fist and sent a right hook into the side of Mason's head, hitting the young man in the temple. Mason crumpled to the ground.

One of the young men knelt down to look at him. "Shit, John. I think he's dead."

Fairchild looked up at the bright stars. "Damn," he snarled. He hadn't meant to shut the kid up permanently. What to do now? What to do now?

"All right," he said. "Get that team of horses out of the barn, and hitch them up. Mason's going to have an accident."

Sally Ann passed the *Franklinton Democrat* across the table. The story was on the front page. She and Heinrich were having dinner at Murphy's pub.

"What a shame," Heinrich said as he read. "A man run over by a team of horses at so young an age. To think I was eating dinner with him just the other evening."

"They really should have been more careful," Sally Ann said.

Heinrich nodded. "Some fraternity business, probably with too much alcohol, I suppose. Young men tend to think they are indestructible."

Mike Murphy came over to their table. "Couldn't help overhearing. The boy was a regular here," he said. "Marty Mason was never much of a horseman. To me, it sounds fishy, like what the Fairchilds did one time to that unruly drunk. I don't know what they'd be doing with a team of horses in the middle of the night, but I guess boys will be boys."

"Certainly frat boys will be frat boys," Sally Ann said.

"Yes," Heinrich said. "But, when handled correctly, fraternities can channel young men toward doing good. My forefathers were members of the *Burschenschaft* in Germany. They did a lot of dueling in those days, but it was over politics, in the name of democracy."

"Our frat boys do the same, only in the name of beer and spirits," Sally Ann said, shaking her fork in Heinrich's direction.

"Glad to know there are still things worth dying for," Heinrich replied, and put another piece of medium-rare steak in his mouth.

Sally Ann clucked. "You really shouldn't joke about such things. Marty Mason was a good kid. And every boy has a mother."

Heinrich shrugged. "Sorry."

"That's okay, Heinrich. You know, I just love your name. It's just so … foreign."

"I'm glad you approve, Sally Ann. And I just love your name too. It's just so… Mark Twain."

She gave his arm a swat with the back of her hand. They laughed and turned to other matters.

With his right hand, young mister Fairchild smacked the top of the ax handle into his left palm. It made a loud "pop" in his gloved hand. He stared in the mirror, framed in a scratched and dented walnut to match the wizened wooden cabinets built by some long-forgotten class of Kappa Psi alumni. His pillowcase cut with eyeholes made a suitably fearful visage for a good baldknobber. It would do for this evening's purposes.

His fraternity brothers were gathering in the foyer, chattering in hushed tones and thinking about the midnight prank they planned to play on that upstart Chink. Mr. Tommy Lee wouldn't be so uppity after tonight, Fairchild reckoned with a laugh.

A knock sounded on his door. Joe Entwhistle poked his head inside Fairchild's room.

"You about ready?"

Fairchild nodded. "Do we have the horse and the buckboard?"

"Smitty got them."

"Then it's time." He took one last look at himself in the mirror and followed Entwhistle out the door.

CHAPTER 3

Peering through the open second-floor window and through the ragged eyeholes of his makeshift pillowcase hood at the sleeping Tommy Lee, Fairchild grinned and stifled a laugh. He never thought it would be so easy to hoodwink "The Chink." Tommy was sleeping soundly except for an occasional low moan.

Fairchild quietly descended the ladder and grabbed Mike Foster by the arm. "Get the buckboard," he whispered to Foster. Mike nodded and ran toward the Kappa Psi house.

The window was already open about six inches; Fairchild quietly pushed it open wide, climbed through and motioned silently for more of his hooded Kappa Psi brothers to climb the ladder.

Quietly pulling a blue pillowcase off a spare pillow, with Lee still sound asleep a few feet away, Fairchild stood with a finger to his lips. One by one, five of his fraternity brothers quietly climbed the ladder and crossed through the open window. They gingerly worked their booted feet over the threshold into the room, making hardly a sound. The operation went well until Mike Foster kicked his leather boot heel a little too hard against the window frame.

They froze. Tommy Lee mumbled something unintelligible in his sleep and clutched his stomach, but did not wake. Glaring, Fairchild handed Mike a bandana from his back pocket. He motioned for his brothers to circle the bed.

It was a simple procedure, sometimes performed on wayward pledges. Each man grabbed an arm or leg and held it, and Foster stuffed the hanky in Tommy Lee's mouth. For a moment, Tommy's eyes bulged with fear, but then his face fell limp. Fairchild then dropped the pillowcase over the Asian student's head, and Tommy reacted, rolling his head from side to side under the pillowcase in panic and snarling through the rag in his mouth. Then they rolled Tommy up in his bedclothes. Holding him fast, they carried him quickly out the door, along a short corridor and down the grand staircase to the solid mahogany front door, which was unlocked, like most doors in Franklinton.

The blonde caressing him in his dream quickly faded as Heinrich awoke with a start to the sound of footsteps outside his door. Quickly putting on his slippers, he hurried down the stairs toward the front door, which was gaping open. In the moonlight outside, he could see a mummy-shaped pile of bedclothes being tossed in the back of a buckboard along with a half dozen young men riding along.

A sleepy Mrs. Yaeger appeared at the top of the stairs. "What's goin' on? We bein' robbed?"

"I don't know," Heinrich answered. "Let me look."

He stepped outside and didn't see the blow coming in time to block it. Out of the corner of his eye, Heinrich watched a fist fly toward him. It crunched into the right side of Heinrich's face as he exited the door.

The hooded owner of the fist then grabbed the back of Heinrich's head with his left hand and smashed his right elbow into the left side of Heinrich's face. Staggered by the two blows, Heinrich fell to his knees. The hooded man then hit Heinrich in the head with a short piece of two-by-four, and he crumpled onto the dewy lawn, his face in a patch of dirt. Leaving him there, the hooded man ran after the escaping wagon.

Fairchild laughed under his hood as he and his fraternity brothers headed for the large silver maple tree in the front lawn of the Kappa Psi house. He never dreamed it would be so easy to grab the Chink straight from his bed! What unfathomable good luck! He and his brothers had expected the so-called master of the Oriental martial arts to put up a fight.

Their prey had been downright disappointing so far. "You're not so tough, are you, Chink?" he yelled at the struggling mass of bedclothes. He punched the writhing pile of sheets as Foster passed him a bottle of Jack Daniels. A big swig warmed him. Now it was time to really put a scare into the Chinaman.

At the Kappa Psi house, somebody threw a noose over a bough on the silver maple tree that shaded the yard and porch, upon which sat an old Napoleon cannon, captured by Joe Shelby's troops at Ford Davidson during Pap Price's 1864 Missouri raid. The fraternity men fired it once a year during their annual antebellum party, a costume ball during which the young men dressed in Confederate uniforms, while their dates wore the hooped gowns of Southern belles.

The young men quickly donned their hoods. A little baldknobbing would teach Tommy Lee not to dance with white women again.

They pulled off Tommy's shirt and tied his hands. He struggled a bit, but mainly moaned and clutched his stomach as if he were in pain. Fairchild knew he hadn't hit him that hard. Fairchild grabbed Jimmy Smith's shoulder and pushed him. "I told you not to rough him up," he said.

Smith bristled. "We didn't. He must be sick; maybe he ate something that didn't agree with him."

Mike's brother, Danny, grinning only as a successful thief can, came running with Dahlen's Lippizan stallion from the stable. The horse's white coat glowed eerily in the moonlight. "I thought it would add to the effect," he said.

Fairchild nodded approvingly as the boys placed Tommy on the horse. He struggled to maintain his balance atop the mount. He seemed more aware now, as if coming out of the comatose sleep in which he had arrived. That was good, Fairchild thought. They wanted to scare the Chink out of his wits.

"No, no! Don't!" Tommy moaned as the fifty fraternity men gathered round.

"He squeals like my girlfriend," Jimmy sneered.

"Since when did you get a girlfriend?" Mike retorted, then laughed as Jimmy fired a fake punch his way. Fairchild frowned at them.

"Tommy Lee, you are hereby sentenced to death by the Kappa Psi fraternity," he said. "We don't take kindly to foreigners, and we are going to make you sorry you ever came to pollute this great country of ours. String him up, boys."

Jimmy placed the noose around Tommy's neck, tightened it with a jerk, and then reached up to secure it to the tree limb with a hastily tied knot. No longer hooded, Tommy clawed at the rope around his neck with his fingers, desperately trying to loosen its grip. He continued to snarl unintelligible mumblings through the hanky stuffed in his mouth. Tommy seemed to be somewhere else, as if he were delirious with fever.

"This horse is a symbol of our pure, white virgin women you want to ride," Fairchild said. "But tonight, you will be purified!"

Out of the corner of his eye, Fairchild could see sparks from a burning fuse coming from the back of the Napoleon cannon on the porch. Although he couldn't see who had primed the cannon, an operation that included inserting gunpowder into the barrel and threading a short length of fuse into the touch hole at the back, apparently a fraternity brother had decided to fire the aged beast.

Suddenly, smoke began to pour out of the front of the cannon's bronze barrel. Something wasn't right. Fairchild opened his mouth to say something, but it was too late. A fraternity brother yelled, "Run!" and they all leapt for cover as the old cannon exploded in a fireball.

Hearing the deafening roar, the startled horse reared up and galloped off, its frightened ruddy albino eyes tearing as it ran frantically from the scene, leaving Tommy Lee swinging by his neck, like a pendulum, gurgling and choking as he fought for breath.

"Heinrich, wake up!"

Heinrich stirred as Mrs. Yaeger shook him by the shoulders. He rolled over and sat up, his vision blurry. His face hurt all over. He gingerly rubbed the back of his head, which had taken the brunt of the board.

"Ow."

Mrs. Yaeger shook his left shoulder. "Heinrich, they've grabbed Tommy."

"What?"

"Men in hoods. They took him in a buckboard."

She pointed down the street toward fraternity row. Hazily, from two blocks away, he could see a large group gathered in front of the Kappa Psi house.

Heinrich quickly regained his wits. He grabbed the short piece of two-by-four the hooded man had used on him and took off running. "Go get the sheriff. I'll go try to help Tommy."

"Be careful!" she yelled as he sped away.

The board might be moderately useful in a fight, but Heinrich wished he still had his Colt .45. The army had made him turn it in upon his discharge. His revolver had saved him many a time before and would have given him a comfortable edge.

After four blocks, Heinrich reached the Kappa Psi house and sized up the scene. A large crowd had gathered around the house. There were no hoods to be seen. Apparently, all hoods had been stashed quickly after matters got out of hand.

He found Fairchild kneeling beside Tommy Lee, trying to revive the young Chinaman. Although Lee no longer had a rope around his neck, the skin on his neck was clearly inflamed and bruised. It sure looked like a rope burn, Heinrich thought.

He said nothing. Though seething inside, there was no time to waste on anger. On his knees, bending over Tommy, Heinrich leaned over, placing his ear above his friend's mouth to listen. Tommy was still breathing, but only faintly.

Heinrich pointed to a nearby fraternity brother. "You. Go get Doctor Harris." When the boy hesitated, Heinrich said simply, "Now." The boy nodded and hurried away.

Heinrich turned to Fairchild. "What happened?"

"We don't know. We were about to hold a ritual to assign pledge fathers to our pledges, and we were preparing to fire the cannon when it exploded somehow. Then a buckboard sped by and dumped this man in our front yard."

With one eyebrow raised, Heinrich studied Fairchild's face. They both knew it was a lie. Heinrich only hoped they had cut Tommy down quickly.

"Did you see the men who did it?" Heinrich asked.

"No, they wore hoods."

Heinrich nodded. "Naturally."

"What is that supposed to mean?" Fairchild snarled.

"You're a smart boy, young Fairchild. You figure it out," Heinrich answered.

Doctor Harris came running up with his black leather medical bag and took over, checking the young man's wounds and pulse. "Let's get him back to the boardinghouse," he said.

A group of Gamma Sigma brothers from the fraternity house next door built a makeshift stretcher out of two poles and a worn, brown blanket. The young men put Tommy Lee on the stretcher, and the Gamma Sigs carried him home to Yaeger's Boarding House.

Heinrich watched as Doctor Harris hurriedly checked Tommy's pulse at the wrist. His friend was limp and pale. Tommy Lee's handsome Asiatic face appeared frozen in a faraway grimace, as if he had just learned some incredible truth.

As he watched Doc Harris minister to Tommy, Heinrich thought about the summer afternoon just a couple of months ago when he'd met Tommy. He had grown to really like the boy. Tommy was an outsider, a condition Heinrich understood.

The young man's arm was clammy with sweat from the fever he had endured for several days because of brain trauma, the doctor had said. He'd been clinging to life by a thread, but the strand was now cut. Heinrich could see in the doctor's face that the young man was finished.   Tommy Lee would never get his chance to chase the American dream.

"Damn," Harris swore under his breath.

"Is it over, Doc?"

The doctor nodded.   He listened to the young man's chest one last time and sighed, "Yes, it's over."

The doctor pulled the light blue bedsheet up and over Tommy's face.   From a leather-bound notebook he had carried in with him, he took out a "Preliminary Death Report" form and began to fill it out. Under "Cause of Death," he wrote "fever of unknown origin, probably due to infection from external trauma," and signed the form.

In response to Heinrich's quizzical look, Harris said, "It's for the coroner."

"Sometimes these fevers are brought on by external trauma," he continued.   "The bruising around his neck is consistent with a rope, which appears to have severely strained his neck, even though it isn't broken, which might mean he didn't hang for long.   There are also internal injuries, which caused the patient to cough up blood."

"So he was lynched, but they chickened out?"

"That would be my guess," the doctor said.

Putting his palm on the student's forehead, Heinrich said a last silent good-bye to his young friend.   As he left the room, he wiped a tear from his eye.

Feeling especially low, he decided to lose himself in the willows on the bank of Stephens Creek for a while, thinking of the times he had spoken to Tommy both in and out of class.   Tommy Lee had died too soon.   Heinrich decided he would do whatever he could to locate the boy's killers.

Word spread quickly through town regarding the vile nature of Tommy Lee's death.   One rumor suggested the attack was committed by anarchist vigilantes, another that it was launched by descendants of Jesse James, and still another that it was organized by a revived Ku Klux Klan, which officially had died out in the late 1800s.   While there had been occasional lynchings of blacks by mobs from time to time in central Missouri since before the turn of the century, there had been no organized bushwhacking or bald-knobbing — the name for such activities in the vernacular of the nearby Ozarks and popularized in the 1907 Harold Bell Wright novel *The Shepherd of the Hills*.

Heinrich knew in his heart that Fairchild and the members of Kappa Psi were responsible for Tommy's death.   They were the instigators, but he couldn't prove it... yet.

Depressed about the loss of his young friend, Heinrich had tried at first to lose himself in his work. But today, the hurt had come back with a vengeance. Tommy Lee's funeral was to be held at Franklinton's First Presbyterian Church, and Heinrich had been asked to speak on the boy's behalf. He had to think of something good to say.

He sat down at a table in the back of the college library, hidden behind the stacks, trying to compose something worthwhile. A solitary person by nature, he often lost himself in books. He had always felt the musty library smell of old ink on paper to be strangely comforting.

There were so many questions swirling through his mind. Why would people commit such a vicious crime against a good kid like Tommy? Although he suspected involvement by Kappa Psi men, which ones exactly were involved, and why would they perpetrate an attack on Tommy? What had he done to merit such an attack? And why were there no witnesses to the crime? Surely somebody saw the lynching. Of course, the answer was probably fear; witnesses were afraid to come forward.

His mind was befuddled. What should he say? What reading should he use? He opened an American Standard Version of the Bible from the stacks to find some appropriate passage.

"Psst." A whisper from behind the book shelves startled Heinrich. He jerked his head up from a passage he was reading and looked around to find the source.

"Psst... Professor Kueter," the whisper came again.

"Yes?" he asked hesitantly.

"The Kappa Psis killed Tommy Lee." The voice, still very quiet, now rose slightly above a whisper. It was a young man's voice, a relatively high-pitched tenor. He could see a shadow of a not-too-large man in the stacks behind him.

"How do you know? And who are you?"

"I'm a friend, a Gamma Sig. A group of Kappa Psis killed him. We saw them carry him to their house in a wagon. It was an accident. Fairchild only wanted to scare him by putting him on horseback with a noose around his neck, but the cannon blew up and spooked the horse."

"Why are you telling me this? Why not tell the sheriff?"

"I have to be careful. I can't be seen going to the law. But I couldn't keep silent. I figured you'd know what to do."

Heinrich heard feet walking quickly away. He got up and looked around the stacks, but the whisperer was gone. All that remained were scuffmarks in disturbed dust on the floor where the informant had stood. Heinrich sat down at his table again and stared at the piece of paper in front of him.

After slamming a quick hamburger for lunch at Murphy's and mulling over the message from his secret informant, Heinrich decided to visit the sheriff. Heinrich had shaken Sheriff William Thackeray's hand at the fall mixer, but he doubted the man known locally as "Old Stumpy" would remember him. Somebody had pegged the nickname on Thackeray because he was short and wrinkled like an old tree stump. Sally Ann had warned Heinrich that the old man might be getting a bit senile.

Heinrich found the sheriff in a rocking chair on the front porch of his office, whittling intently on a stick.

"Hello, Sheriff," Heinrich began.

Stumpy squinted at Heinrich. "Hello. Professor Kueter, isn't it? What can I do for you?"

"Surprised you remember me," Heinrich said. "I'd like to talk to you about the murder of Tommy Lee."

"Kinda figured you might, seein' as how you were a witness to the events in question. What's your plan? Are you confessing?" The sheriff grinned.

The old man had a sense of humor. "To missing a sucker punch, yes," Heinrich answered. "Somebody gave me quite a wallop that night. But the reason I'm here today is I received some new information." Heinrich explained what had happened to him in the library. Stumpy continued whittling as he listened.

When Heinrich finished, Stumpy said, "Well, it confirms my suspicions. Thanks for the information. I'll take it under advisement."

Heinrich was taken aback. He had expected some action.

"Don't worry about it too much, Sonny," Stumpy said. "This is a small town. There's rumors flying all over the place. Just let me handle it. It'll all take care of itself before long if we just let it." He continued his whittling.

Heinrich could tell the conversation was over. He walked away, deciding to write a letter to the Federal Marshal's office in St. Louis. That way, at least something might be done if the sheriff were lax in his duty.

At Dahlen's stable, Heinrich found Manfred bent over, attempting to reshoe a roan horse. Manfred's dungareed buttocks welcomed Heinrich as the professor strolled in. The acrid smell of stale horse manure made him wrinkle his nose for a moment.

The Austrian twisted his head around to look at Heinrich as he finished levering a rusty iron shoe off with a small pry bar. "It's a healthy fragrance, Heinrich," he said with a laugh. "Farmers love it."

Heinrich grinned. "I don't doubt it."

Manfred looked through a rack of tools on peg board to find the correct hammer. Choosing a heavy ballpeen from the rack, he turned to Heinrich.

"What's on your mind?" he asked.

Heinrich pursed his lips. "What can you tell me about the sheriff?"

"He's a good man. Why?"

Heinrich thought for a moment. "Because I believe he is doing absolutely nothing to solve Tommy's murder," he spat out.

Manfred said nothing, but took the shoe to an anvil and began to pound on it with the hammer.

"Well?" Heinrich asked.

"Well what?"

"What do you think, Manfred?"

Manfred looked at Heinrich with a fatherly gaze over his pince-nez glasses. "I think you are agitated and somewhat irrational over this matter. Tommy was a good kid, and we all miss him, but let justice take its course."

Heinrich gritted his teeth. "Do you think Stumpy's in Fairchild's pocket?"

"Heinrich, he has been sheriff for some time, since before Fairchild's machine grew strong," Manfred said. "He wouldn't have been sheriff for so long if he hadn't had the ability to deal with it. I don't believe he is in Fairchild's pocket, but he certainly does what he must to navigate the political obstacles as best he can."

Heinrich snorted, unconvinced. He told Manfred about the stranger's words in the library. "Stumpy told me he would take the information under advisement, and then just kept whittling."

Manfred laughed. "That's just his way. He's thinking. The sheriff is a shrewd customer, smarter than he looks. Give him a chance."

Heinrich nodded. His emotions were indeed raw; he recognized that. But he felt the need to do something, anything.

"Look, on the surface, what appears to have happened is that a fraternity prank got out of hand and led to a tragedy, right?" Dahlen said. "You want justice for your friend. So do we all. Stumpy just needs to figure out how best to proceed."

"So he whittles?"

"Among other things, yes."

Heinrich frowned, still unconvinced.

"Would you like some tea?" Manfred asked.

"No."

"Heinrich, take my advice. Quit rushing around like a whirling dervish. Go to the funeral. Then do something fun for a day or two. Go get your thoughts together. For today, honor Tommy Lee's memory. Then take your mind off of it. We have plenty of time to go after his killers another day."

Heinrich nodded and walked out. He needed to get dressed for the funeral.

"For all the Saints, who from their labors rest..."

Heinrich sung out with gusto on the hymn, a relatively new setting by English composer Ralph Vaughan Williams for an older set of words by Anglican Bishop William Walsham How. Heinrich liked the tune.

Many attending the funeral at Franklinton's First Presbyterian Church, which was about half full, mumbled through the prayers, choking through tears, but Heinrich always sang hard. Partly, it was his nature. Singing made him feel better, fully connected to God for a moment or two. And his father had taught him to sing that way. You should sing with feeling, allowing the music to surge through your muscles, making the sound flow sweetly through the mouth, reverberating in your sinuses as if you were playing an instrument, the old man had said.

After the hymn and readings from the Testaments, Heinrich walked slowly to the lectern. He placed his notes on the podium and quickly wiped his eyes with a handkerchief.

Gazing across the assembly, he began to speak. "Friends of Tommy Lee, we come here today to remember a friendly and kind spirit."

He told how Tommy had been a fine student who cared about his classmates, how he'd helped them in math and they'd helped him in English. He told the crowd how Tommy's class had made a Christmas donation for the poor, and how Tommy's gift had been a pair of Kara-shishi lions he'd carved himself, explaining that they were Chinese talismans placed at a door to ward off evil spirits.

While going through the litany of Tommy's good traits, he noticed John Fairchild in the audience, and it made him pause. Hypocrisy or guilt, it didn't matter; the younger Fairchild's presence at the proceeding did not feel right. Anger surged inside him, and Heinrich decided to change tack. The subject was eating at him, and he decided to get it out in the open. He put aside his written text.

Heinrich looked around the room. "If there was one fault Tommy had, it was that he placed too much trust in others. He never wanted to believe the worst about anyone, but I have reason to believe somebody did want the worst for him. It's possible he fell prey to a vicious person or group who didn't like him and wanted to harm him. Nobody knows the truth yet, but if such is the case, let me warn you. You will be found out. Sooner or later, you will be found out."

Heinrich looked sternly at the assembled crowd, many of whom were fidgeting uncomfortably. He could see some faces in the audience become angry and turn quickly to neighbors, and he could hear hostile murmurs break out around the room.

"And the Lord said to Cain, 'What have you done? Listen, your brother's blood is crying out to me from the ground.' Well, Tommy's blood is crying out to me, to all of us. We need to be our brother's keeper, and in this case, that means making sure our brother receives justice."

Heinrich picked up his papers and left the lectern as the strains of the next hymn, "Abide With Me," floated upward to the apex of the pointed wooden roof.

Watching Tommy's casket being lowered into the ground at the burial, a grief-stricken Heinrich couldn't help but think about the tragic waste of a good young life. Tommy had so much to give, yet he had been taken away, and the world was the worse for it.

After the burial, Heinrich walked home in the rain in his black suit. The dreary weather seemed appropriate for the solemnity of the occasion and for his mood. He noticed that the leaves were falling regularly now. Soon the trees too would be bare.

After following the boardwalk out of downtown as far as it went, he plied the puddles on the cracked sidewalk that led to his boarding house near the college. In his mind, he reviewed the faces of the many Filipinos he had killed, and how their faces had looked eerily similar to Tommy's. He had gunned down those Asiatics with nary a thought, much like Manfred had killed Boxers, but Tommy had grown into a true friend. In a small way, getting to know Tommy had helped Heinrich atone for the Filipinos whose lives he had taken. He wondered whether the human cycle of racist violence would ever end. Finally, Heinrich realized that he also felt intense personal shame; he had failed to save his friend from death in his time of need.

Passing two male students, he tipped his black hat to them. They responded in kind.

However, stopping for a minute to tie his shoelace, he heard them laughing. "Why would Professor Heinie care so much about a Chink student anyway?" said one of them.

Heinrich stiffened. Enough was enough. He whirled, grabbed the young man by the shirt and shook him.

"A boy is dead, you stupid fool!" he yelled and pushed the young man away. The youth slipped and fell onto his knees.

"Nobody does that to me and gets away with it, you kraut asshole!"

The youth got up and charged Heinrich, who, without thinking, deftly sidestepped and launched a right cross into the young man's jaw. It knocked the youth down, and he lay senseless on the ground. Heinrich leaned over him like a boxing referee giving an eight-count.

"Count yourself lucky, friend; I've killed many a better man than you," he said, instantly hating himself for saying it. He then turned rightward to the youth's friend and shot him a ferocious look through angry slits. Suddenly fearful, the young man took off running, high-tailing it around the corner, no doubt to get the sheriff.

"Heinrich!" someone said sternly to his left. It was Murphy, standing there with Dahlen.

It might as well have been his father admonishing him. Heinrich stood up straight. He knew he had done it again.

CHAPTER 4

Mike Murphy cleaned up the glass from his shattered front window. "That broken window'll probably swallow my profits for the day. Some baldknobber thinks he's real funny."

"Do you know who threw the brick?" Sally asked.

"Most likely one of Truman Fairchild's roughnecks," Murphy said. "It had a note on it that called me 'Paddy' Murphy — as if I hadn't heard that one a million times before. If they were going to make a mess, the least they could have done is tell a good paddy joke, but these goofballs just ain't funny."

Heinrich could tell one was on the way, and sure enough, Murphy had a joke to tell.

"...Like this one I heard the other day," Murphy continued. "Paddy Murphy walks into a Belfast bar and says, 'That Miles O'Donnell is a bastard. He beat me something fierce.' The barkeep looks at his cut face and says, 'He must've hit you with more than his fist. Was he holdin' somethin'?' Paddy says, 'Sure he was, he was holdin' a shovel, and he whacked me with it hard.' So the barkeep says, 'Wow, O'Donnell usually fights with his fists. It's not like him to take advantage. Were you holdin' somethin' in your hand too?' And Paddy says, 'You bet! Mrs. O'Donnell's breast, which was mighty fine, but it didn't make for much of a weapon!'"

Heinrich and Murphy rolled their eyes and laughed. Sally smiled, taking the off-color joke with lady-like grace. Murphy winked at her, "Beggin' your pardon ma'am, but once I started, I had to finish."

The brick most likely came from the hand of one of Fairchild's partisans. Heinrich suspected that Murphy's support for him after his recent confrontation with the student on the day of Tommy's funeral didn't help the Irishman's relations with either of the Fairchild factions. In return for their not pressing charges against Heinrich, Murphy had agreed to serve the student, Irving Winger, and his friends free beer for a month. Of course, Heinrich had to apologize to the young man and to accept a formal reprimand from the college, delivered by Professor Goforth and President Tichenor. It was only fair, Heinrich knew. He had stupidly lost his temper and throttled a student, hardly proper behavior for a professor.

Murphy had a pretty good idea what Heinrich was thinking. "Look, Heinrich, your fist-fight with the student is just the tip of the iceberg. This all started way before you came to town."

Heinrich nodded. "I'm still sorry for turning up the heat on you, and I appreciate all you did to help resolve it."

"What are friends for?" Murphy said, a twinkle in his eye. "Just remember, you may throw a solid punch, but you were lucky you were up against a stupid kid. Somebody like me would have taken you easily."

"I'll keep that in mind," Heinrich said. "Next time I tangle with you, I'll remember my brass knuckles."

"So you suspect the elder Fairchild?" Sally asked.

Murphy suddenly turned suspicious. "You'd better not be cooking up a story, Sally. If so, I'm not going on the record."

"It's news. I'll be discreet," she said, batting her lashes.

Murphy laughed. "You know I can't resist those beautiful eyes of yours," he said. "But this is off the record. Fairchild's been behind this push to institute blue laws in town for a long time, and he has unleashed his muscle to try to intimidate me. No liquor on Sundays is his plan."

Dealing with saloons, whether good and evil, was one of the thorniest social issues of the day, Heinrich knew. During the last decade or so, the Temperance Movement had become a political force to be reckoned with. There were many good people who had come to the conclusion that the power of the saloons and the liquor industry needed to be broken because of the damage they caused to society. Too many hardworking men put their families in jeopardy by getting drunk and allowing unscrupulous saloon keepers and prostitutes to roll them for their pay. It was a common practice — fill the man with booze to take away his judgment and then take his money in the back room through gambling, prostitution, drugs or old-fashioned thievery. The unfortunate mark would end up lying in the gutter, penniless in a puddle of his own puke, and later staggering home with nothing to pay the rent. That is, if he wasn't dead.

Trouble was, any legislation aimed at attacking the evils of bad saloons would also harm the good neighborhood taverns like Murphy's. And for every crazed fanatic teetotaler wielding a hatchet like the recently deceased Carrie Nation, there were moderates of various stripes who saw the necessity for reform. For instance, some believed that only distilled spirits, a product of modern industry, should be outlawed, while the wholesome fermented spirits of beer and wine, lovingly crafted for thousands of years, should remain legal. Although Heinrich preferred beer and wine over whiskey, he would occasionally imbibe hard liquor, so he generally stood against any Temperance legislation at all even though, objectively, he understood the need to clean up the saloons and supported more law enforcement to do so.

"You don't believe the Lord's Day should be free of alcohol?" Sally asked Murphy.

"The Lord made alcohol for man's enjoyment," Murphy said. "He knows Irish folk like to frequent the pub on a Sunday. It's their one day off, and He wouldn't want to take our enjoyment away. These authoritarian ignoramuses are sticking it to the Germans too, attacking their wine and beer gardens. The temperance fanatics want to make it a crime to enjoy a drink and a bit of good music on the Sabbath. After all, if they can suck the joy out of life for us, maybe we'll leave."

"Can I quote you on that?" she asked.

He shook his head.

"How 'bout if I paraphrase it?"

"Only if you say, 'a local source who wishes to remain anonymous,'" he said and sighed. "They'll probably guess it's me anyway. Maybe sooner or later they'll get tired of throwing bricks, but I doubt it."

At that moment, Murphy got called away to help a customer. Heinrich wondered if such talk would bother Sally. After all, the temperance and women's suffrage movements had been marching hand-in-hand for some time, mainly because women, as guardians of the home, bore the brunt of the problem when their husbands fell prey to the evils of the saloons.

"It would help if the liquor industry didn't throw its weight behind the opposition to votes for women," Sally mused. "It forces the temperance and suffrage parties into alliance and breeds fanaticism."

Heinrich looked ill at ease. Sally grinned and put her hand on top of his. "Don't worry. It's just business and politics. I don't take it personally. Murphy's a good friend."

Heinrich breathed a sigh of relief. "The world would be a better place if crazies like Carrie Nation weren't in charge," he said.

Sally shook her head. "Then give women the vote. The crazies wouldn't be in charge if men would simply allow women to participate in the political process. If women didn't have to fight so hard to exercise their God-given rights, which men have stolen from them, there wouldn't be so many radical women."

Heinrich hadn't considered the issue from that angle before. He decided it prudent not to argue the point.

Sally continued, "Don't you find it odd, dear, that even our neighbors in Kansas gave women the vote last year, but Missouri men won't show women the same courtesy?"

Murphy returned at that moment, rescuing Heinrich from answering and having to point out the difference between bushwhackers and jayhawkers. Sally went back to business.

"Do you really have any proof that Fairchild's behind this broken window?" she asked Murphy.

"No. But I know he's leading a recently revived group of Know-Nothings in town."

"You're kidding, right?" Heinrich interjected.

"I wish I were. No, they think it's great fun to try to secretly thwart immigrants whenever they can. They call themselves the Millard Fillmore Admiration Society. After all, if it's presidential, it must be patriotic. Put that in your story. I dare you," Murphy said with a smile.

"No problem, it's a great angle if I can get confirmation," Sally answered.

"Good luck. That's why they call them Know-Nothings," Murphy shot back.

"So now vigilante justice and secret posses will rule the night once again," Heinrich said. "Apparently, the spirit of Jesse James is alive and well in these parts. Just dress the outlaw up for a new cause, and the criminal becomes a hero."

"Make no mistake, the bushwhacker spirit is here to stay," Sally said. "In case you didn't know it, Truman Fairchild is not only kin to Sterling Price; he also claims relation to Bloody Bill Anderson."

"Quite a pantheon; the two sides of the coin," said Heinrich with another swig of beer.

"That's not the half of it. Judge Jameson is related to both William Quantrill and Will Doniphan," Murphy said.

"Forget just the Civil War;" she said. "They're still fighting over who was the real Missouri hero of the Mexican War, Doniphan or

Price."

Heinrich nodded. Doniphan had led the First Missouri Volunteers into Mexican territory on a 6,000-mile trek that created the framework for the state of New Mexico. Price followed with the Second Missouri Volunteers, cleaning up messes in Doniphan's wake, including the bloody Taos rebellion.

"Any chance these Know-Nothings are behind the killing of Tommy Lee?" Heinrich asked.

Murphy shrugged. "I wouldn't put murder past Fairchild. He'd have to be mighty worked up to go that far, but I've heard tales about his bad temper and the evil goings on at his saloon."

"I'm going to snoop around a bit," Sally said. "Don't worry, Heinrich, I'll be careful," she quickly added when she saw the look of concern on his face.

Seated in the green leather armchair across from Truman Fairchild, Sally eyed the ragged Confederate battle flag hung on the wall behind his desk. Even though Union forces had held Missouri throughout most of the Civil War, the state had been granted a star on the flag by virtue of its exiled secessionist legislators voting to leave the Union. Fairchild had told her once that his grandfather had taken the flag as a souvenir from Pea Ridge, the Confederate battlefield disaster in northwestern Arkansas that effectively lost Missouri to the Union.

On the adjacent wall to her right, an autographed publicity photo of Tom Pendergast's face stared cheerily at visitors. The notoriously corrupt political boss of Kansas City's Democratic "goat" faction seemed a much more appropriate symbol of where Fairchild's true nature lay, Sally thought. For years, Jim Pendergast's goats sparred with Joe Shannon's "rabbits," who were also Democrats, for control of the city. Although the true reason for the adoption of the animal mascots by the factions is obscure, common wisdom was that the rabbits lived down by the river, while the goats lived on the hillsides surrounding it. Of course, the wealthiest Kansas Citians lived in splendid mansions on Quality Hill, which overlooked the boisterous West Bottoms.

Fairchild had been a protégé of Tom Pendergast when the future Kansas City political boss's brother Big Jim had controlled the wide-open town. Although Tom would later assume command of the Pendergast empire, Big Jim had been the long-time alderman of the "Bloody Sixth" ward, which included the city's infamous, vice-ridden West Bottoms. Filled with bawdy houses, saloons and gambling dens, the West Bottoms offered many earthly delights, such as a five-minute "hell dance" in a dance hall with a half-nude woman for about 25 cents or with a totally nude woman for 50 cents.

Its railroad connections made the West Bottoms the natural location of the city's "tenderloin district," which offered prostitutes spread out amongst various "cribs." These were individual homes or rooms offering ladies who were either in business for themselves or who were sometimes employed or connected to saloons. A session involving sex would cost at least a buck or two in a crib, depending on the length of time spent and negotiations with the client. But that was better pay than an older, street-walking crone, who might only receive 25 cents for her services.

Likewise, the nearby red-light district, between second and sixth streets on the north and south, and Main and May streets on the east and west, offered similar fare, but in a more concentrated area. Those streets encompassed a region of about 130 brothels including the three largest, run by Madame Lovejoy, Eva Prince, and Annie Chambers. Chambers' "resort" was the most famous and served the wealthiest clientele. Annie's ladies reportedly earned as much as $200 a week. Progressive forces in Kansas City had been able to force the closure of her bordello in October, but she had reopened a month later and countersued the state.

In that milieu, Tom Pendergast, known now as "Boss Tom," had worked his way up from bouncer to ward captain, and later replaced Jim Pendergast, whose health was failing, as alderman in 1910. He then built a political machine that quickly exerted its grip on the entire city. Truman Fairchild had worked for Boss Tom 10 years ago. His job as a bouncer in Big Jim's American House on St. Louis Avenue came to an end when he had been forced to leave Kansas City quickly. A streetcar driver on break found one of Fairchild's rivals, a fellow bouncer who was rumored to have "turned rabbit," dead in a back alley. The murder remained officially unsolved, perhaps partly because of the Pendergast brothers' influence over the police force.

A man trained to revel in such dark matters should not be trifled with, and he scared Sally, even though Truman Fairchild could be charming. She continued to quickly scan the room. A mysterious Asian lady smiled demurely from a portrait in vivid yellow hues on the opposite wall. On a bookshelf next to a walnut cabinet, Sally could see a copper toy cannon and a boxing glove. She knew Fairchild had been a fair boxer in his youth. She did not know if the pretty Asian woman held any significance beyond decoration.

"Thank you for meeting with me, Mr. Fairchild," she said sweetly.

"Why, Miss Sally, you know the press is always welcome

here," Truman Fairchild replied. "I'm just a phone call away."

Fairchild loved pointing out his expensive, nickel-plated, tapered-shaft Stromberg Carlson "Oilcan" desk phone, ordered specially from Chicago and engraved with his initials.

Regardless of his words, Sally knew Fairchild was wary of her visit. Her relationship with him had always been courteous and professional, but not genuinely friendly. She suspected that he probably criticized her behind her back in the Southern way, that tradition that assumed attacking a person's character was fine as long as it was followed by, "Bless her/his heart."

After asking about his family and making other small talk, she decided to get down to business. "I understand there's a new group of Know-Nothings in town," she said, watching to see his reaction, which amounted to an icy stare. "I've heard they call it the Millard Fillmore Admiration Society. Have you heard anything about it?"

"I wouldn't know anything about that," he said, as if almost, but not quite, genuinely shocked at the question.

"Certainly," she said. She nodded and wrote in her notebook, allowing time for her message to sink in. "That's interesting. I was told you were the leader of the group; would you care to comment?"

"Why, that's simply untrue," he said, indignantly arching his neck and tightening his lips.

"You're sure?."

"Positive. People spread the most vicious rumors nowadays."

"You're sure you don't know anything about it?"

"I'm sure."

"Of course, if you did, you couldn't say because you know nothing."

Fairchild grinned, but didn't say a word.

"Also, I was wondering if you knew anything about the deaths of two students. Tommy Lee, of course, was killed in a lynching incident."

Although Fairchild's body and face remained relatively placid, his eyes widened slightly. Sally thought maybe her question had rattled him a little. "Oh, yes, an awful atrocity committed by criminals and hoodlums," Fairchild said. "A fine young man, I understand, even though a Chinaman, bless his heart. Our law enforcement officials need to catch the perpetrators. Quite a shame, a terrible tragedy."

She nodded. "And Martin Mason, who died in a buggy accident?

"I remember somebody mentioning the accident, probably my son. Another terrible tragedy, but I don't know much about it."

"Can I quote you on these matters?" she asked.

"Sure," he said. "But why would you ask me about them?"

"I'm asking the question of quite a few people. Somebody in town must know something about what happened, and a man of your stature in the community often knows 'most everything that goes on around here."

He grinned, unconvinced. "Thank you for the compliment, but I assure you that I know very little about the incidents and played no part in them."

"Anything else you'd like to not tell me?" she asked, only half in jest.

He shook his head and laughed weakly. "No, I'd say that'll do."

She thanked him, stood up, curtsied, and left. He stared after her for a moment, then picked up the phone's earpiece in his left hand and held the candlestick base in his right. Tapping the switch hook a couple of times, he put the earpiece to his ear. "Give me President Tichenor, please," he told the operator.

President Tichenor shook Truman Fairchild's hand firmly with a grip he had been taught many years before. He made a mental note to remind the fraternity boys of this important business skill in the near future: Winners don't give limp-fish handshakes.

"James, it's always nice to come visit the college," Fairchild said.

"And it's always wonderful to see you too," Tichenor responded. "You've done so much for this college."

Truman Fairchild's control over local government and his regular, healthy contributions made him a particularly important alumnus.

"To what do I owe the honor of your visit?" Tichenor asked. "Checking up on young John?"

"No, not this time. Has he been involved in something nefarious that I should know about?"

"Not that I know of. There is an apparently unsubstantiated rumor that he and his fraternity brothers were involved somehow in the recent death of an exchange student."

"That's part of what I wanted to speak to you about, actually."

"Oh, I wasn't aware that you knew Mr. Lee."

"I didn't, really," Fairchild said. "Saw him on the street once or twice, perhaps, and there was that excitement at the mixer last month that I saw from a distance. But I want to speak to you about a young professor of yours, Heinrich Kueter. I understand he's been snooping around with that newspaper woman and spreading misinformation about my son. They apparently believe John was involved in the murder, which is simply ridiculous."

Tichenor nodded.

"I don't need to tell you that if a vicious rumor like that were to become public scandal that I would have to rescind my offer of $50,000 for the new college library," Fairchild said. "Frankly, such a scandal would be disastrous for the college right now. And, last time I checked, people were innocent until proven guilty."

Tichenor frowned. "That's quite true. So what do you want me to do?"

"Tell young Professor Kueter to quit snooping and spreading lies about my son. John is innocent, and I would much prefer this library project to go forward, as would you, I suspect."

"Of course," Tichenor said. "I will speak to young Kueter, and please be assured that we do not make it a practice of spreading idle gossip."

Fairchild stood up and stuck out his right hand. "Thank you, Jim," he said, shaking Tichenor's hand. "That's all I needed to hear."

Heinrich straightened his black silk necktie one last time before knocking on Sally's door. It was their first official "date," and he wanted it to go well.

Sally lived by herself in a small but fashionable white bungalow with dark green shutters and a native stone façade on Conley Street, a few blocks from the newspaper.

He squared his shoulders and rang the doorbell. When Sally appeared, it was clear that she had put great thought into her appearance as well. She wore a purple dress with a lace collar that framed her face wonderfully.

"How do I look?" she asked.

"Stunning," he said. "I don't deserve to be seen with someone so lovely."

"Oh, you are too kind," she said, clearly pleased.

They walked the three blocks to the Emperor Hotel, whose dining room was decorated in a Napoleonic manner, complete with Empire chairs topped by eagles and golden bee figures embroidered on the scarlet upholstery. A fellow historian had told him once that the bee was an ancient symbol of the earliest kings of France, the

Merovingians, and before that, the Egyptian pharaohs. A master of propaganda, Napoleon had placed the symbol on his coat of arms and ceremonial mantle to cement his imaginary connection with the ancient line of French kings.

After they were seated and had ordered, Sally said, "I think this should be 'our restaurant.' Too bad I can't afford it very often."

He laughed. He couldn't either, but he didn't want to say so.

As they dined on roast duck, they talked about politics, international relations and history. It seemed Sally could discuss just about anything. Heinrich found her to be terrifically well read, and her journalism career had brought her knowledge about a broad variety of subjects.

It turned into a magical evening. They found they had much in common. They both liked ragtime music, and they even discovered a common affinity for science fiction, especially Jules Verne and H.G. Wells, whose *The Sleeper Awakes* she had finished recently. He promised to read it as soon as he could.

She told him she really enjoyed a poem, "Renascence," by a new poet, Edna St. Vincent Millay, which Sally had read in *The Lyric Year* anthology recently. "Many believe the poem is about death, but I believe it is clearly about spiritual renewal," she said. "It was quite a scandal in the literary community last year, taking only fourth place in the contest for the anthology. Many readers were incensed that it had not come in first or second."

Heinrich merely nodded self-consciously, as poetry had been the least item on his mind the previous year, having spent most of it in combat overseas, desperately praying for God to make sure he came home alive.

"But enough about me," she said. "What were you up to before coming to our small town?"

He really wanted to yell, "I was up to my neck in Filipino gooks, hoping I killed them before they killed me!" But he repressed the urge. Realizing that he was clenching the tablecloth with his hands, he quickly released his grip and smoothed out the wrinkles he'd made.

He took a deep breath. "I was in the Philippines with General Pershing," he said.

"Oh," she said with a gulp. "I'm sorry. It must have been tough."

"It was, but it's over now – and I survived," he replied.

She looked down at the tabletop. "I didn't mean to pry."

He looked down too. "No, it's OK," he said, clasping his hands together on the table in front of him. "It's just that I had to do things, bad things, and it's not a matter to discuss on a night such as this. I don't want to spoil the mood."

She wrapped her hands put her hands around his clasped ones. "Maybe, after we get to know each other better, the proper time will come, someday."

He nodded. She quickly changed the subject, asking him about his family.

They talked about family matters, friends and the news. After dinner, they walked back to her home, hand-in-hand, enjoying each other's company in the pleasant coolness of a fall evening. He hesitated, not quite knowing whether to end the enchantment and leave with a kiss.

She stood on the bottom step of her front porch. He put his hand on the stair railing's newel post, which was shaped like a pine cone, painted white like the rest of the porch. "It has been a wonderful evening..." he said, not knowing quite how to proceed.

She solved his dilemma by leaning over and kissing him passionately on the lips. At first a bit taken aback, he joined her lips in a second, long kiss and pulled her to him in an enthusiastic embrace.

They came up for air a few moments later. "Ordinarily, Heinrich, I would not be quite so forward," she said. "However, this evening has been glorious, I am getting older, and I fear that I ought not to pass on a chance for bliss."

He laughed. "Thank you, Sally. It was most pleasant and gracious of you." He kissed her again softly for good measure.

"We had better keep it at that, sir. People will talk."

"In Franklinton? No!" he answered with feigned shock.

She laughed. "Good night, Heinrich."

"Good night, Sally. May I call upon you again soon?"

"Most definitely. How about Friday?"

It was 3:30 Friday afternoon, the time when class seems to drag on   forever and the acquisition of knowledge falls prey to daydreams of weekend plans. Heinrich could see the young men in his class continually glance at the clock.

"All right. If I've learned anything from Black Jack Pershing, it's to never fight a losing battle," Heinrich said, to delighted laughter from the class. "That's enough for today. Class dismissed."

The young men hurried out, chattering like schoolgirls, only at a lower pitch, mainly about Saturday's football game against Missouri

Methodist College. Heinrich turned his own thoughts to the evening's date with Sally. He needed to finish some grading first, but that should mark the last item on his to-do list of academic "janitorial work" and fully prepare him for next Monday's class.

He gathered up his papers and wiped off the chalk board with a rag, laughing to himself that he was acting in the finest German tradition of the "scrubby Dutch." He didn't have to clean the chalk dust off the board, but polite professorial etiquette called for it. He headed for the front door of Liberal Arts Hall, a stoic stone building with ivy covering its back. To Heinrich, the building did not look man-made, but organic, as if it had grown out of the bedrock of the hill on which it was perched. Then he noticed an unwelcome apparition. Oh how wonderful, he thought. At the bottom of the building's granite front steps, a large, matronly woman with red hair stood impatiently tapping her buttoned-up foot.

It was Minnie Tichenor, the president's wife. Heinrich tipped his bowler hat. "Good afternoon, Madame Tichenor," he acknowledged as he passed by.

She blinked her eyes and curtly said, "My husband would like a word with you, sir."

"Oh?" Heinrich asked. "Is Monday soon enough?"

"Now, Mr. Kueter, in his office," she said, and stomped away down the lane toward town, her elephant legs pounding in the packed dirt of the pathway.

"Goddamn battle-axe," Heinrich thought as he watched her disappear. The Tichenors were from Virginia, and Mrs. Tichenor rarely let an hour go by without telling everyone how much more refined things were back home in Charlottesville, Virginia. At parties, she made a point out of calling Missouri "Indian Territory," then laughing haughtily as if everyone knowingly shared the same opinion.

Heinrich found it hard to understand what Joseph Tichenor saw in his wife, but one never knew with marriages. "Perhaps she wasn't always a swine," Heinrich thought with a grin. He marched up the hill toward Worcester Hall and the president's office.

Once again, Heinrich got that oily undertaker feeling he always did when he came in contact with "President Ichabod." Tall and toothpick thin, Tichenor reminded Heinrich of an oily undertaker he knew back home whose hands were notoriously icy. His close resemblance to Ichabod Crane, the Washington Irving character who had battled the Headless Horseman, led to his student nickname, "President Ichabod."

"Ah, Professor Kueter," Tichenor said, flapping his gangly

wings and grabbing his arm. "So happy to see you. Why don't you come into my office?"

It was a rhetorical question. It wasn't as if Heinrich could say no. Tichenor opened the door to his office with a false flourish.

"Have a seat, Professor Kueter; can I get you something to drink?" the president almost whispered, in a voice drooling with mock graciousness and oily Eastern snobbery. Heinrich shook his head and steeled himself for the worst.

"I've been hearing some good things about you, Professor Kueter. May I call you Heinrich?" Tichenor said.

Heinrich nodded.

"Have your classes been going well?"

"Fine, sir."

"Good, good." Tichenor paused. "Although I have heard good things about your classroom work… well, there are also some actions you've taken recently that disturb me," the president continued.

Heinrich remained silent and waited for the coming punch.

"The first is your unwarranted speech last week implying that young Tommy Lee may have been murdered. Such rash statements are completely uncalled for. We must not taint innocent people until they have been proven guilty."

Heinrich began to simmer, but tried not to allow it to show on his face. Tichenor continued.

"I know you had a great friendship for this boy, that you were a mentor to him, and that is admirable. But this is an institution of higher learning, where we teach that rational decisions are made based on reasoning, logic and evidence. We believe in self-restraint, Professor Kueter. Wild speculations and unsupported charges will simply not do."

Heinrich continued to say nothing.

"When you add the business of your physical attack on a student, I have to admit that I am growing concerned about your future here at Worcester College. A solid academic career is not built on rash actions."

Heinrich stood up. "Sir, if I have erred in judgment, I apologize, as I have already done in relation to my fight with the student, which I remind you was precipitated by an untoward comment on his part. Yes, my reaction was incorrect, and I assure you for a second time that it won't happen again."

"It had better not," Tichenor said. "An assault on a student is simply unacceptable."

"Yes sir, most definitely. But you must also understand that I no longer believe that Tommy's death was an accident. While my knowledge of what happened the night Tommy was kidnapped and I was attacked is not yet complete, I intend to find out more. My theory -- once fully formed -- will be entirely based on reasoning, logic and evidence. Tommy's murderer is not going to go free if I can do anything about it."

"Professor Kueter, if you have decided to play detective rather than attend to your work, I simply will not have it."

"I have excelled in my teaching duties, and what I do during my free time is my business," Kueter replied.

President Tichenor poked the desk with his index finger. "Which brings up another matter. I understand you've been flagrantly meeting this newspaper woman. Gallivanting around with a woman whose honor is most questionable will simply not do."

"Excuse me, sir, but if I am seeing her, flagrantly or otherwise, that information is none of your business."

Tichenor took a deep breath. "While I cannot tell you with whom you may associate, the honor of the College, Professor Kueter, is always my business. These matters are intimately related to its reputation, and I will not tolerate any activities that may embarrass the College."

"I don't see how forging a relationship with a fine woman from town who happens to have a mind of her own could possibly be an embarrassment to an institution that is supposed to promote the free discussion of ideas. I happen to love Sally, and, when the moment is right, I intend to ask for her hand in marriage."

Tichenor looked skyward. "Wonderful. Good god, man. That will provide fodder for the town's ladies for years to come!"

"Sir, I don't give a wit for the town's ladies. I refuse to live my life according to feminine gossip. If I can ignore it, why can't you?"

"It's quite simple," Tichenor said quietly. "I have a wife, not to mention that fostering the town-and-gown relationship remains an important part of my job."

"Then choose to look upon my budding relationship with Miss Giddings as an opportunity to forge stronger relations with the local press," Heinrich said.

Tichenor stood up, pushing his rolling, leather chair back behind him and tapping the desktop hard with his index finger to accentuate each point. "Don't get 'smart' with me, young man," he snarled. "If you insist on seeing this woman, you must keep any private liaisons under wraps and your public relationship completely upright, unsullied and above board. Is that clear?"

Tichenor looked Heinrich in the eye, his teeth clenched.

Heinrich looked straight back at him, seething inside. But he could tell this was not a battle he would win. Heinrich exhaled slowly.

"Certainly, sir. As always, I will do my utmost to maintain the honor of the college," Heinrich said.

"Good. And if you continue to insist on a relationship with this woman, I would also appreciate it if you would ask her not to harass our college's most important alumni."

So that's what this was really about, Heinrich thought. "Fairchild?"

"H ow perceptive of you," Tichenor said. "He contacted me yesterday about Miss Giddings and yourself. Your actions discredit you both."

Heinrich gritted his teeth. "I believe the college dishonors itself most when it sweeps the murder of one of its students under the rug. We're talking about a young man's life."

"Oh, come now. Surely you don't really believe that nonsense."

"I'm beginning to wonder."

"Now, see here, Professor Kueter. The College did not hire you to be a Pinkerton detective. We hired you to teach history, and you're a damn fine teacher. But I must warn you that if you persist in this inquiry, your employment here at Worcester College may be in jeopardy. Good day, Sir."

President Tichenor turned away from Heinrich. Apparently, Heinrich was dismissed. Fuming, Heinrich marched out of the president's office and headed toward his boarding house.

Sally moved in closer to Heinrich. They were eating a light supper at Murphy's. Actually, they were sharing. She said she wasn't hungry, as she often did. He therefore ordered an extra-large sandwich with extra coleslaw and potatoes, having learned that she would eat nearly half of the food even though she "wasn't hungry."

"So he doesn't want you checking out the Fairchild boy," Sally said. "That's interesting. Old Man Fairchild must have gotten to him. That may mean one of two things: Daddy Fairchild may be involved in this, or he may simply be protecting his son."

"Shouldn't we go to the police?" Heinrich asked.

Sally shook her head. "What do we have? The sheriff would never believe it yet. We don't have any proof."

"I suppose it's also possible that Tichenor was just throwing his weight around." Heinrich said.

"He is a gaseous old windbag, isn't he?"

Heinrich laughed. "Yes, but we've got to be careful. I need this job. We may need to lay low for a while, perhaps meeting mostly in secret."

She nodded. "Ooh, secret. How fun!" she exclaimed, and they laughed.

"You can count on me to be discreet," she said. "I still plan to pursue this story, but I'll find another reason for my inquiries."

Heinrich's face got serious. "Then you be careful."

"Professor Kueter," she said with mock sincerity. "Is that an order?"

"Would you take one?" Heinrich laughed. "I know better. No, it's simply a request. There are already two people dead."

"Heinrich Kueter, I'll have you know I am descended from Frank James, Jesse's smarter brother. I'm a survivor."

Heinrich threw up his hands. "All right, you win. Just keep it safe, O.K.?"

"I promise," she said, and kissed his forehead. "I've got to go. Meet me at the glade near the creek tomorrow at six." She got up to leave.

"That's good. I must do some research in the library tomorrow."

Hidden in the back stacks of the college library the next day, Heinrich tried to search diligently for information regarding the Frankish kings. But he couldn't help thinking about other matters — namely Sally Giddings, President Tichenor and Tommy Lee.

"Psst, Professor Kueter." It was a familiar whisper.

Heinrich looked up from a well-worn biography of Charlemagne. He couldn't see anyone.

"Psst, over here."

It was coming from the stacks. He got up and followed the noise. Someone was hiding in the shadows between two dusty racks of books. Apparently, it was the same secret whisperer who had passed him information before.

"Who are you?" Kueter said.

"You don't need to know," the voice said. "I'm a Gamma Sig. I was a friend of Marty Mason's."

"I'm sorry. He was a fine boy; it's a shame he was run over. Run over on purpose."

Heinrich lifted an eyebrow. "You mean he was murdered? By whom?"

"His fraternity brothers, the Kappa Psis," the man in the shadows insisted.

"Them again. Why?"

Heinrich could see the shadow fidget and look around. "He got too loose with his tongue about what they did to Tommy," the man said urgently.

"Do you have proof?" Heinrich pushed.

"Only what somebody told me. Also, I hear you are suspicious of John Fairchild. Fairchild told a friend of mine that something was wrong with Tommy when the Kappa Psis grabbed him. He said it was too easy, as if Tommy were drugged. I don't know if that means anything."

"It might mean somebody else was involved."

"Maybe. Look, I've got to go, but I'll keep trying to find out more for you."

"Wait...," Heinrich said, pushing his chair back and chasing after the voice through row after row of books until he reached the center foyer of the library. No luck; he had lost his quarry again. Heinrich retraced his steps to make sure he hadn't overlooked the secretive person, but the mystery man was already gone.

Heinrich returned to his "hideout" in the back stacks, abruptly sat down, rubbed his eyes with his fingertips and then his palms. Were the Kappa Psis simply fraternity boys on a prank gone wrong, or were they killers? And if someone had drugged Tommy before the hangmen had shown up, his real killer might still be on the loose. Who would do such a thing?

On a hunch, Heinrich walked to the back of the stacks and found the previous year's yearbook, bound in process-blue imitation leather. Flipping back in the book to Tommy's photo in the Juniors section, Heinrich found his photo and was appalled at the caption underneath, which said, simply, "The Chink," as Tommy had told him earlier.

Clearly, somebody thought it a funny joke; how cruel young men can be. He thumbed forward to the table of contents and looked to see who had produced the yearbook.

Lo and behold, the editor-in-chief was John Fairchild, pre-med major. All roads seem to lead to him. Heinrich closed the yearbook and stared at the shelving.

Heinrich surveyed the interesting playing board, which was in the shape of a six-pointed Hebrew star.

"That's really different," he said to Manfred Dahlen. "I've played regular Halma, with its square board, but I've never seen this before."

"It's called 'Star Halma,'" Manfred said. "I picked it up on a trip to Germany and Austria about ten years ago. Everybody was playing it."

Heinrich thumbed through the rules booklet. It was in German, and his was rusty. "I remember that Halma was a bit like checkers; the board was square, only it had twice the number of squares, and you played from corner to corner."

Manfred put his right hand out flat, palm-down, and rolled it from side to side. "Yes, there is jumping as in checkers — the name comes from the Greek word for "jump" — but you don't take the man when you jump it. You simply use the jumps to move your men to fill up the opposite player's camp. Star Halma is the same, only there are fewer men."

"The game board looks a little like the star on the Chinese flag too — no, never mind, the Chinese star has more points on it," Heinrich said.

Manfred nodded and moved his first marble, a blue one. "To me, it looks more like a Hebrew star, and I much prefer it. As far as I know, there are no Boxers in Palestine, which is a good thing," he said. "Our one little hybrid cannon had little chance against them."

"That's right, you were an artillery man." Heinrich moved one of his green marbles.

"Yes, it was a desperate siege. But it was a reactionary assault against us foreigners, far different from the successful Wuchang Revolution a couple of years ago. Apparently, they needed a modern army to overthrow the monarchy, and they have one now. I understand they have learned to use artillery with some competence, which is a big step toward modernity for the rabid devils."

"Maybe they should train our students," Heinrich joked.

Manfred laughed. "That old Napoleon was a disaster waiting to happen. They should have rendered it inoperable years ago," he said. "It was a downright tragedy that it aided in Tommy's death, but we're lucky there weren't any more people killed."

Manfred's voice trailed off, and his eyes were focused on something far away. Heinrich nodded sadly. He missed Tommy too. He moved another marble in an effort to build a convoy of jumps toward Manfred's home base.

Heinrich watched a blue jay hop from limb to limb and listened to the bird call out from the trees. The bright fall reds, yellows, and oranges of late October splashed radiant color over the campus.

He watched the wind rustle through the leaves and the translucent water fall over a rock, generating a white foam. Waiting for Sally was strangely fun. Having been told not to meet with her made their secret liaisons that much more exciting. Perhaps Romeo felt the same with his Juliet, Tristan with his Isolde, or Lancelot with his Guinevere. Of course, Isolde and Guinevere had been already married; at least he didn't have to worry about a jealous husband coming after him with a sword...

He heard the snap of a twig. It was Sally, wearing brown, leather English riding clothes and a starched, white blouse.

They embraced. "I didn't know you rode," Heinrich said.

She nodded. "There are a lot of things you don't know about me, Professor Kueter. I keep a horse over at Henry Clay College. It was a good excuse to use in meeting you."

Clay College was the women's finishing school on the other side of town. Its social life was closely connected to Worcester's, and it had a riding program.

Sally looked in his eyes. "What's wrong, Heinrich?"

Heinrich looked down. "President Tichenor is after me again."

"Ichabod? I wouldn't worry, Heinrich. You know how he likes to pick a scapegoat of the week. It's probably just your turn."

"No, I don't think so. This time it's serious. He has told me not to see you anymore."

She stepped back. "You've got to be kidding. I knew my reputation was bad, just not that bad."

"It's just a small step, you know, from suffragette to free-love fanatic, and then socialist to communist," Heinrich said.

"And what if I did believe in breaking the legal bondage of marriage?" she asked.

"It's not that I care that much,' he said. "It's just that this is my first professorship. I'd hate to lose my job."

Sally first looked as if she would cry, then just looked angrier. "So I guess this means..."

Heinrich pointed his index finger at her to interject. "No! I will not give you up."

Sally was startled by his forceful, Teutonic side expressing itself.

"Sally, I have never been so happy as when I am with you," he said. "I will not give you up."

She embraced him. "Thank you. I had hoped..."

"I love you, Sally."

"I love you too."

They gazed into each other's eyes for a moment, then laughed in unison.

"Heinrich, we'll have to be very careful from now on. We cannot be seen together too often."

Heinrich nodded. "Perhaps time will bring acceptance. Perhaps we will need to get married first."

"Is that a proposal?" Sally laughed.

"Of course it is," he said.

She smiled. "Heinrich, you aren't ready for that type of commitment, and, frankly, I'm not ready either. We hardly know each other. When you are ready, you can propose properly. I can wait."

"But why won't you marry me? Don't you want to be married?" he asked.

"Don't be hurt, my love," she said and hugged him. By the look in his eyes, she could see he wanted more explanation. "You must understand, Heinrich. On the one hand, I would love to marry you, but I fear that marriage would mean giving up my vocation."

"It wouldn't have to mean that."

"Maybe not in New York, but we don't live in the big city," she said. "I enjoy my work. I'm not yet ready to quit and have babies."

Heinrich nodded, a glum look on his face. "You may be right. I don't want you to sacrifice your work. I wouldn't ask you to not be you."

"Thank you, my love. I promise you that I will give your proposal due consideration," she said, and kissed him.

"Unfortunately," he said, "I need to be me too. President Tichenor ordered me to quit sleuthing into the death of Tommy Lee, but if I don't do it, who will? I'm not sure what to do."

"Do what you always do, Heinrich," Sally said. "Do the right thing. And let your friends, like me, help."

It hadn't been easy for Sally to get her ticket to the "Old South" dance at the Kappa Psi house. Her friend, a housemother at Henry Clay College, owed Sally a favor and let her take her ticket. It meant pretending to chaperone, but it got her in the door.

Though elegant, Sally's peach dress was a bit snug, requiring the strings of her corset to be pulled so tightly that she could barely breathe. She hoped she hadn't put on a few pounds since she last wore the dress. Probably too many big meals with Heinrich, she mused. When had she last worn it? Somebody's wedding, she thought.

Nobody challenged her. The young fraternity gentleman at the door tipped his hat and said, "Good evening." She would busily fill her role as chaperone until she could find a chance to slip away.

Near the punch bowl, two young ladies were speaking intently to each other, gossiping about something interesting from the looks on their faces. Like a good chaperone checking the punch, Sally ladled herself a cup of the reddish concoction and listened in. The punch tasted of strawberries, nothing more. Too bad, she thought, grinning. For a moment, she wondered if she should feel guilty about eavesdropping, but being a reporter had taught her to bend the rules of decorum from time to time. She had told herself some time ago that she would never cross the line into unethical behavior, but, as her career progressed, she often pushed the line further out to provide wiggle room.

"Isn't it just awful about Tommy Lee?" one young woman asked the other between sips of punch.

"Oh, yes. For a Chinaman, he sure was smart."

"And athletic too. Quite the warrior."

Knowing nods from both. "Can you believe this? I heard John Fairchild was involved somehow, maybe even led the attack that kidnapped Tommy. He was angry that Tommy had danced with his girlfriend. What is her name again?"

"Rebecca. There's also a rumor going around that they staged the accident that killed Martin Mason too. Martin said a little too much about their plans after he got tipsy."

The other girl looked at her punch. "Speaking of tipsy, the punch is good. I hope they didn't spike it."

"I wouldn't mind it if they did, but I can't taste anything illicit." She laughed.

A male voice from behind startled Sally.

"Miss Giddings, isn't it?" It was John Fairchild.

She turned, nodded and curtsied. "Sally Ann Giddings, chaperone for the day, at your service."

He bowed, "President John Fairchild," he said, somewhat warily.

"Thank you for inviting the girls," she said.

"Our pleasure. Is Mrs. Semple all right?"

"She needed to take a trip to Jefferson City and asked me to cover for her."

He nodded. "Women of good breeding are always welcome at Kappa Psi."

She smiled, wondering what she-wolf had suckled him. He bowed and continued to circulate around the room.

Seeing her chance, she excused herself to find the designated ladies' room. She quietly melted into the foyer and nonchalantly climbed up the stairs to the members' living quarters. She paused outside the door of the first room to her right. Hearing laughter and mixed company inside the first room, she realized she had probably already failed in her role as a chaperone, but she was on a mission. She aimed to find evidence of a connection between the Kappa Psis and the murders of Tommy or Martin.

The next room had an oak sign with white letters tacked to the door: "President." She tried the doorknob, which turned. She drew her breath and pushed. It opened with a creak, and she stepped inside quickly, keeping her petticoats from brushing too noisily on the doorjamb.

She knew she didn't have much time. The room was dimly lit; as her eyes adjusted, she looked around. There was a Confederate battle flag, the stars and bars, displayed proudly above the window, and a painted Kappa Psi crest in wood on the far wall.

Clearly, the room's occupant was male. She snickered at a pile of clothing in the corner alongside a pair of shoes with some smelly socks hanging out. No woman would put up with that, she thought.

And the bed was sloppily made up, with the covers simply yanked up to the pillow without any smoothing of the bedclothes. But Fairchild had good taste in sheets, she had to admit. She recognized them as an expensive cotton weave she had seen in a Montgomery Ward catalog.

She headed for the built-in dresser attached to the far wall and quickly rifled through the five drawers without causing a mess. Then she turned and opened the door to the closet. Another pile of smelly laundry had been stuffed in the bottom below the jacket, pants and shirt hanging on the bar above.

A small gray pillowcase crammed in the back of the closet caught her eye. It was clearly a much cheaper fabric of the kind she had seen for a nickel a yard at a dime store in Jefferson City. She took it out and saw that it had eye holes cut into it, giving it an intimidating visage. It clearly was a hat meant for some fraternity hijinks, or, as she suspected, it was the kind of mask Heinrich had told her the baldknobbers had used when they kidnapped Tommy Lee.

She folded the mask and put it into her patent leather handbag, closed the closet door and quietly left the room with her heart beating so loudly she thought it might give her away. As she stood in the hallway for a second, deciding her next move, Fairchild came up the stairs and saw her.

Thinking quickly, she pointed at the room with the male and female laughter still going on inside. "Mr. Fairchild," she said. "As president, would you do me the honor of discreetly breaking up the party inside this room? While I have no intention of getting any ladies in trouble with their parents, as their chaperone, I must be vigilant about their reputations."

"Certainly," Fairchild said.

"Thank you," she said. "And would you be so kind as to point the way to the ladies' room?"

"Of course, it's down at the end of the hall, to the left."

Nodding her thanks, she headed in that direction.

John Fairchild knocked on the door of his father's leather-and-cherry paneled office.

"Hello, son!" the wizened Truman Fairchild called from inside. "Come on in."

John walked in and sat down. "You wanted to see me, father?"

"Yes. I don't know how best to broach the subject, so I will be frank. You didn't have anything to do with this business about the death of the young Chink lad, did you?"

"No, sir," the young man said with a straight face and in a sharp tenor voice. "Why would you ask?"

His father clasped his hands and dropped his forehead slightly, still looking his son in the eye. "The word is around town, and I wanted to make sure before I pull some strings," the elder Fairchild said in a coarser baritone, made rough by years of smoking too many Cuban cigars. "You didn't have anything to do with the death of young Martin Mason either?"

"No sir."

Something in his son's voice made him wonder if he didn't know more than he was letting on. The elder Fairchild looked his son in the eye with an intense gaze.

"You're sure you don't know anything? It's important that I know the truth so that I may help you should the need arise."

John Fairchild nodded slowly. "No. Nothing."

"Good, good. As you know, I have big plans for your future;

we cannot afford a scandal that might scuttle them."

John rolled his eyes. "I know, Father, I know."

"And another thing," the elder Fairchild said. "That newspaper lady apparently suspects something. I heard she invited herself to your latest dance as a chaperone so that she could snoop around. Any reason why she should feel the need to do that?"

John Fairchild shook his head. "I had my eye on her. Let her snoop. There's nothing for her to find."

"Nevertheless, she's a bit of a crusading muckraker who wouldn't hesitate to take us down if she could. And look out for that Kraut professor too. Apparently, he is investigating you too, although I've spoken to his superiors and hope to have solved that problem by threatening to revoke my gift."

John Fairchild nodded, but stayed silent. Truman Fairchild studied his son's face intently. When his son bit his lower lip and licked his lips, the elder Fairchild knew.

"Boy, you never could lie to me," Truman Fairchild said. "You were involved, weren't you?"

His son put his head in his hands, and Truman Fairchild knew for sure. "Good God, John. What were you thinking?"

John Fairchild looked down. "It was just a prank, Dad. We just wanted to scare him."

A prank that had morphed into murder. His son's future might now lay in ruins.

"I wanted you to keep your nose clean," Truman Fairchild said. "I wanted you to take a different path. I didn't want this sort of life for you."

John said nothing, his eyes closed. Truman sighed and closed his eyes for a second or two too. He shook off a vision of his home burning and reopened them.

He grabbed his candlestick desk phone and dialed. "I'm getting you a lawyer, Son. We've got to be prepared."

Sheriff Thackeray was sitting at his usual post outside his Main Street office, asleep in his oak rocking chair on the shaded boardwalk, a pocketknife and a partially whittled stick in his lap. The tip of his felt cowboy hat had fallen almost to his nose.

It had been a busy day for Heinrich so far. In addition to teaching three classes that day, Heinrich had paid a quick visit in the morning to biology Professor Miles McGovern, who currently served as county coroner. Cause of death was rarely at issue, and Franklin

County could not afford a full-time coroner.

Now it was time to wake up the sheriff. "Sheriff Thackeray?" Heinrich asked.

No response, other than a light snore.

"Sheriff?" Heinrich nudged his chair and said it louder.

Thackeray woke with a start. "Sorry, professor, I must have dozed off."

Heinrich nodded. "Sorry to disturb your nap, but I was wondering if you have had any luck in investigating the Tommy Lee murder."

"No, I checked around town some, talked to some people, but I haven't made much headway."

"To whom did you talk?"

"The Kappa Psis, Mrs. Yaeger, Dr. Harris, Mr. Murphy and Truman Fairchild. There just isn't any evidence that would indicate any connection to the murder."

"If I had evidence that would prove a connection, would you use it?"

The Sheriff squinted his eyes. "What are you getting at?"

"If I had something that could prove a connection between the attack on Tommy Lee and the Kappa Psis, would you do something about it?"

"I always do my duty, sir. And I'm not sure I like your tone."

"No offense meant, Sheriff."

Heinrich pulled the pillowcase hood from his pocket. "This item was found in John Fairchild's closet at the Kappa Psi house. It's what the attackers were wearing when they took Tommy and killed him."

The sheriff looked at the hood. "Come now, Professor Kueter. That's just a silly hood that fraternity boys might use in one of their harmless rituals. That scanty evidence won't stand up in court."

"Even if it has drops of human blood on it?" Kueter asked almost innocently.

Thackeray's jaw dropped. "Let me see that."

Heinrich handed it over.

"It's definitely human blood?" the sheriff asked.

Heinrich nodded. "I showed it to Professor McGovern, and he confirmed it. I suspect if you search the Kappa Psi fraternity house, you may find more evidence. If you question the boys, you might even get confessions."

"You may be right. I'll need to get a warrant from the judge," said the sheriff.

Three days later, Sheriff William "Stumpy" Thackeray and two deputies served the search warrant on the Kappa Psi house with an almost military precision that Heinrich would have thought was beyond the old codger's ability. As he watched from across the street, the sheriff and his two deputies entered the stately Tara-style mansion that served as the fraternity house.

Their search of the fraternity yielded more of the pillowcase bald-knobbing masks and other evidence such as the worn length of rope that had been used to string up Tommy Lee. Behind the house, they found the buckboard that had been used to convey the boy to his doom, and they impounded what was left of the old Napoleon cannon from the front lawn as evidence.

To the great private amusement of the townspeople, although most usually expressed great shock and anguish about the matter in public church-gatherings and such, the deputies found an illegal still in the basement of the fraternity house and an equally illegal full bar in one of the rooms. Although state law in Missouri generally had been interpreted to allow no drinking until the age of 21, when a young man officially had assumed adulthood, there was much leeway given to counties and towns in regulating local drinking. However, such stills and bars in college housing were definitely against college regulations.

Equally problematic in this case, the hidden, private tavern was adorned with a Tiffany glass barroom chandelier and a mirror behind the marble-topped bar that had reportedly come from a New Orleans house of ill repute. Its polished brass frame, which featured bare-breasted nymphs, brought many a snicker from the men and much horrified consternation among the town's female population. It was as if the bawdy mirror trumped murder amongst the town's women for a short time.

For several days, the sheriff questioned each young man individually about the events involved in the kidnapping and murder of Tommy Lee. As the Kappa Psi members began to crack under questioning and turn on each other, the story slowly emerged regarding the facts of the Lee murder case and the related murder of Martin Mason, which it became clear had been disguised as an accident.

The 18 members of the Kappa Psi house who had participated in the events related to the two murders were arrested and held for trial. Several fraternity members turned state's evidence in return for plea agreements that gave them short prison terms and probation. John Fairchild and his three top officers were arraigned for trial.

The Worcester College Interfraternity Council expelled the Kappa Psi house from campus for a year, and President Tichenor made a great show of tendering his resignation to the Worcester College Board of Trustees, who registered their most sincere indignation at the criminal behavior of the young men. In the end, however, the trustees decided to retain him in the presidency. Tichenor had, after all, doubled the endowment.

Over the ensuing weeks, fall turned to winter. The trial moved forward slowly, while Heinrich and Sally's romance grew quickly. They were very much in love. After a few dates, she invited him into her home for coffee, and they talked late into the evening.

Then one night in late November, after a fine dinner of roast pork at the Emperor, she invited him in as usual. But, after only a few sips each, the coffee was left, forlorn in its china cups, until the next morning.

Passion took over, and they abandoned themselves to it. She was saying something about an ongoing strike against an Andrew Carnegie-owned coal mine in Colorado as they sat next to each other on her antique couch with walnut carvings.

"It's only a matter of time before Mother Jones becomes..."

Heinrich kissed her on her ripe lips before she could finish her sentence. "I don't really care about Mother Jones, do you?" he said.

She shook her head and kissed him back. He continued, kissing her face, neck, and ears as she caressed the back of his neck.

After embracing most passionately for half an hour, Sally led him to her bedroom. Quickly, they peeled each others' clothes off and made love in Sally's walnut four-poster bed, their shadows intertwined in the soft, flickering light of a gas lamp turned down low. As they caressed in the lamplight, he enjoyed the silky texture of her glowing skin, an intoxicating luxury he hadn't known before.

Tonight, Heinrich found himself happy that he had waited to pursue the delicacies of sexual enjoyment. He knew that many of his comrades in arms had sampled the delights of local girls or prostitutes in the Philippines, but Heinrich had not sought out such companionship. He knew the public would be shocked, for instance, if it were ever to hear of the rumored overseas sexual exploits of such storied officers as Black Jack Pershing that ran rampant in the army. A drunken aide to Pershing had told him once that the general made a mysterious $50 payment each month to a lawyer in Manila on behalf of a child who was the result of an affair with a native woman.

Heinrich had been tempted and certainly was no prude. For some soldiers, he knew, liaisons helped relieve the strain of combat. He simply had not wanted to risk disease or an unwanted child with a native woman demanding child support or a ticket to the states.

As he and Sally lay in the afterglow of their pleasure-filled pursuit, he felt a little guilty for taking advantage of her.

"Sally, my love," he asked slowly and deliberately, "will you marry me?"

Her answer surprised him. "Oh, Honey, I am touched and honored by the proposition," she said, "but let us wait. Let's make sure we are ready and truly love each other."

Before he could object, she continued. "Dear, I was married once, when I lived back East, but it was a disaster. We got an annulment. It's the main reason I left Philadelphia. I needed to start over."

Heinrich nodded, "But you said you would at least consider my offer. I love you."

"Of course, dear," she responded. "And I'm still considering it, daily. But give me time." She caressed his chest hair with her index finger. "Let's not make a hasty decision based on one night's lovemaking."

Sally sat up in bed. "A poem," she said, and gave a quick oration:

"And you, my lover, kneeling here before me
With tender eyes that burn, warm lips that plead,
Protesting that you worship me, adore me;
Begging my love as life's supremest mead,
Vowing to make me happy. Ah, how dare you!
Freedom and happiness have both one key!
Lover and husband, by the love I bear you,
Give justice! I can love you better, free!"

Heinrich rolled his eyes. "Always the suffragette. Okay, I give. Where is the verse from?"

"Charlotte Perkins Gilman," she said. "From the *Women's Journal.*"

"Sally, you amaze me. I think you really do believe in free love."

She laughed, and they kissed again. "Mainly the vote, dear; mainly the vote."

The next morning, Heinrich left by the back door and snuck back to his boarding house. He had overslept and slinked in late to breakfast. Although Mrs. Yaeger simply sniffed and raised an eyebrow, he could tell his story that he had stayed overnight with Murphy didn't fool the old woman one bit.

CHAPTER 5

A legend in local legal circles, Prosecutor Robert Blunt rarely lost a case. Murphy had once overheard him professing the worry that several of his accused might have been found not guilty if they had received competent representation. The prosecutor was rather tipsy at the time, and Murphy thought it might have been an empty boast. When sober, Blunt spoke about his faith in the jury system to find justice even when the system was stacked against a defendant.

Today, Heinrich watched Blunt circle young John Fairchild on the stand like a tiger who had cornered his prey, looking for the best moment to pounce.

"Young man, you've told the court that you abducted Tommy Lee for fun."

"Yes, sir. It was just a prank."

"You wanted to play a joke on Mr. Lee."

"Yes, sir. We planned to give him a fright by peeking in his window and making noise."

"So what made you decide to go further?"

"He was sleeping so soundly, we decided to grab him instead."

"And this was all a big joke?"

"Yes, sir."

"So, just to reestablish the facts, the six of you climbed through the window?"

"Yes,   sir."

"And then you gagged and tied him in his sleep, and took him from the room?"

"Yes, sir."

"And this was all in fun?"

"It was just a bit of bald-knobbing. We just wanted to scare him."

Blunt paused before delivering the next blow. "And when did it turn into a lynching?"

"Objection!" shouted Larry Lyon, counsel for the defense. He had been brought in from Kansas City and was rumored to be a good friend of the Pendergasts. "Counsel's assertion assumes guilt of the witness and would cause the witness to incriminate himself."

Judge Harvey Jamison nodded. "Sustained. Gentlemen of the jury, please strike that last question from consideration."

"Fair enough," Blunt said. "Mr. Fairchild, did you, or your fraternity brothers, put Mr. Lee on a horse?"

"Yes."

"Did you tie a noose and toss the rope over a tree limb?"

"Yes."

"Did you put the rope around his neck?"

"Yes, but…"

"You killed Tommy, didn't you?"

Fairchild began to sob.

"Objection!" shouted the desperate Mr. Lyon, a high-priced attorney from Kansas City. "That is a conclusion for the jury. The prosecutor is leading the witness."

"Objection sustained," said the judge quietly. "Strike that last question from the transcript. Again, members of the jury, please pretend you did not hear that last exchange."

Heinrich looked at the jury box. Several members of the jury nodded but looked unconvinced. He leaned over to Sally, "His goose is cooked," he whispered. She nodded.

"Your witness," Blunt said to his counterpart.

Lyon walked to John Fairchild on the stand. "Mr. Fairchild, you never intended to kill Mr. Lee, isn't that so?"

"Objection," Blunt said. "Counsel is leading the witness."

"Overruled," the judge responded. "Leading questions are allowed in cross examination. The witness may answer the question."

Lyon pointed into the air with his right index finger. "In the spirit of fairness, I will gladly rephrase the question. Did you mean to kill Mr. Lee?"

"No, sir. We never meant for that to happen."

Lyon nodded. "Sheriff Thackeray testified that the old Napoleon cannon did not fire by itself; a fuse had to be placed properly and lit manually. Did you or one of your fraternity brothers fire the cannon?"

"I did not fire the cannon, and I didn't see any of my fraternity brothers fire it either."

"But somebody must have placed and lit the fuse, and then fired the cannon?"

"Yes, somebody must have installed and lit the fuse to make it blow up and spook the horse."

"And you have no idea who that might have been?"

"No, sir."

"Then who do you think fired the cannon, Mr. Fairchild?"

"Objection," Blunt said. "Counsel is asking the witness to guess about an important point. This is complete conjecture and has no evidence to back it up."

The judge nodded. "Overruled. Although the question requires the witness to speculate, the witness was a direct observer of events. As such, his opinion may carry some evidentiary value."

Blunt shook his head and began to shake a finger. "Your Honor, I…"

Judge Jamison cut him off. "Counsel, I want to hear his answer."

Blunt nodded and sat down.

Lyon repeated, "Who do you think fired the cannon, Mr. Fairchild?"

"I don't know. None of us can figure it out. The cannon hadn't been fired since last school year. We always keep it disabled until we needed it for our annual Old South celebration in the spring. We only buy a short length of fuse at that time, and there wasn't any left over from last year."

"So you have no idea who fired the cannon?"

"No sir."

"And you have no idea whether the cannon blast that spooked the horse was intentional or accidental?"

"No sir."

"You have no idea who caused the action that caused the horse to bolt?"

"No sir."

"And you are aware of no intentions on the part of you, your fraternity brothers, or anyone else, to injure Mr. Lee?"

"No sir, just to frighten him."

"Are you aware of the previous testimony from Doc Harris, which indicates that Mr. Lee's neck was not broken, only severely strained?"

"Yes sir."

"Objection!" Blunt interjected loudly. "Defense counsel is leading the witness again."

"Sustained," said the judge.

"All right then," Lyon said. "Mr. Fairchild, once again, do you know who fired the cannon, which caused the horse to bolt, which caused the rope to jerk, which in turn injured Mr. Lee's neck?"

"And this is the house that Jack built!" cried a young male voice from the crowd. The courtroom laughed.

Judge Jamison, furious, shot up and slammed his gavel onto the dais. "Silence! I will have no such outbursts in my court!"

Lyon repeated the question.

"No sir," Fairchild responded. "I have no idea who caused the horse to bolt. The horse bolted upon hearing the cannon explode, but I have no idea who fired that cannon."

Lyon paused for a few seconds. "Was Mr. Lee easy to capture?"

"Yes, sir."

"Did you find it odd that he was so easy to capture?"

"Yes, sir. We expected more of a fight. He was supposed to be some kind of martial arts expert."

"What information led you to believe that?"

"Students had seen him fight several times, most recently at the fall mixer."

"But he didn't put up much resistance on the night in question?"

"No, sir. He was sleeping really soundly, and he was groggy when we grabbed him. It was almost as if he never totally woke up, like he was ill. At one point, he clutched his stomach and mumbled something about it hurting."

Now it was Blunt's turn to object. "Your honor, there has been no evidence presented of any illness, drugs, or bad food; the defense is grasping at straws."

"Objection sustained. Gentlemen of the jury, as I have told you, the legal issue comes down to whether the defendant intentionally took it upon himself to impose, without due process, violent punishment or execution upon the victim for real or alleged crimes."

John Fairchild put his head in his hands.

A bald man in his mid-forties, Judge Harvey Jamison was very proud of his connections to Black Jack Pershing. Missouri's celebrity general held command in the Philippines, where he led the U.S. Army's drive to suppress the Moros, much as the army had tamed the native "Indians" of the American West.

A native of Grand Island, Nebraska, Jamison had studied law at the University of Nebraska, where he had met the driven young 2nd Lieutenant Pershing, who was the university's professor of military science. At the same time, Pershing had been earning a law degree, so the two men often studied together.

Jamison's family had money and helped Pershing finance his military drill team, at the time named "Company A" and which, after the future general had left the university, later became known as the "Pershing Rifles." Heinrich had heard Jamison proudly boast about his 1892 Company A team, whose only loss in national competition had come at the hands of the crack cadets of West Point. It was a moment of great pride for the judge.

But that was 21 long years ago. Now Jamison sat in judgment over a murder trial. He wondered what Pershing would think of him now.

Larry Lyon approached the bench, crafted from nearly black, hand-carved mahogany, which was part of a similar motif around the entire room. Next to the white plaster walls, the wood created a black-and-white effect. No shades of gray in this courtroom, Heinrich thought.

He was startled to hear Lyon say, "Your Honor, I call Professor Heinrich Kueter to the stand."

Nervous, Heinrich looked left and right, then stood and walked to the witness stand, where the bailiff directed him to raise his right hand. "Do you swear to tell the truth, the whole truth and nothing but the truth?" asked the bailiff.

"I do," Heinrich answered. He sat down on the mahogany witness chair, and Lyon strutted forward.

"Professor Kueter... it is Professor Heinrich Kueter, isn't it?"

Heinrich nodded.

"Heinrich... that's German for Henry, isn't it?"

"Yes."

"Hei-i-i-n-rick Kee-ee-ter," Lyon drawled the name slowly, for effect. "Just for the record, Kueter is spelled K-U-E-T-E-R, isn't it?"

"Yes."

Lyon smiled wickedly and turned toward the jury. "That's a German name, isn't it? In German, that 'ue' sound would be a 'u' with those two dots over it, right?"

"An umlaut, yes."

Blunt stood. "Objection! Of what possible relevance does the spelling of Professor Kueter's name have to do with the murder in question?"

"I'm coming to that, Your Honor," Lyon said.

"Then you may proceed, Mr. Lyon, but get to the point quickly, or I may reconsider," Judge Jamison replied.

Lyon bent forward in an oily bow of deference to the judge.

"Professor Heinrich Kueter, I understand you were asleep on the night of the prank?"

"I was asleep on the night of the abduction and murder, if that is what you mean."

Judge Jamison wagged a finger. "Just answer the question, Professor Kueter."

Kueter nodded. "I was asleep."

Lyon continued. "And a sound woke you?"

"I heard heavy footsteps and shuffling feet in the hall outside my door. Something didn't seem right."

"And what did you do next?"

"I quickly put on my slippers and went outside to see what was going on. I ran downstairs to the front door, and Mrs. Yaeger, behind me on the landing, asked me if thieves were in the house. Then I opened the door, and something hit me. I went out like a light."

"Out like a light."

Kueter nodded. "I had a big goose egg the next day to prove it."

"And that is the proof for your story, a big goose egg?"

"That and Mrs. Yaeger. She was there."

"Oh, I'll bet she was. Tell me, Heinrich, have you ever heard of Dutch Courage?"

Kueter set his teeth. "Yes."

"Had you had anything to drink that evening, Heinrich?"

"No, although I had had a beer or two at dinner."

"A beer or two at dinner?"

"Objection!" Blunt yelled. "What possible relevance does this line of questioning hold?"

"Every relevance!" Lyon yelled back. "This man is a German, a race known in these parts for its Sunday-go-to-drinking ways. I suggest to you, fine members of the jury, that Professor Heinie here had had a little too much to drink and sleepwalked until he fell down. Then, when he sobered up, he realized he needed a good story to tell."

"Order, order," Jamison bellowed, slamming the gavel on the bench and then pointing the handle at the lawyer like a long, bony finger. "I will not tolerate any more such grandstanding from you, sir! That might work in Kansas City, where they practice machine justice, but here in Franklinton, we believe in strict adherence to the law. You will argue this case on its merits, not on some cheap appeal to prejudice, or I will hold you in contempt."

Jamison glared at Lyon, who gulped and nodded. Blunt grinned. Heinrich boiled silently.

Heinrich trudged home from the courthouse, weary over his ordeal in court. An inch of puffy white powder lay on the ground from a snowfall the night before. Although brisk, the air wasn't too cold, just below the freezing point, with no breeze. While his testimony and cross-examination had drained him, at least the overall courtroom process, aside from Lyon's stunt, had appeared to be getting somewhere. And it was most important that justice be done. They owed that to Tommy Lee.

As he walked down fraternity row toward the Kappa Psi house, Heinrich began to feel as if he were swimming in a pool of gloom, accentuated by the quickly darkening sky. He noticed Old Ben Jones leaning against the burnt caisson of the Napoleon cannon. Wearing a worn gray overcoat and puffing on a cigar, Ben called out, "Hello, Professor!"

"Hello, Ben," Heinrich answered, trotting over to the remnants of the field gun. "You look like General Grant after taking the last Confederate redoubt at Vicksburg."

Ben laughed. "Reckon they'll make me president soon too? I could sure use the money."

"Couldn't we all," Heinrich nodded. "You been following the trial?"

Ben nodded and puffed his cigar. "Yeah, is that where you're heading back from?"

"Yes," Heinrich said, rolling his eyes. "It wasn't easy today."

Ben didn't say a word, just listened, drew on the cigar, and exhaled the smoke like an aging dragon.

"What's your opinion of the trial, Ben?"

Ben laughed. "You really want my opinion?"

"Sure, why not."

"Hell, sir, there wouldn't be no trial if Tommy Lee were a Negro. If it were just some sharecropper getting strung up, nobody would care but the colored folks."

Heinrich was taken aback. "You seriously think the law wouldn't do anything."

"Ten years ago, I saw my friend, Alex, get hung by a mob from the stone bridge over Stewart Creek. Ain't no white folks lifted a finger to help him. They just stood there watching him choke to death, swinging in the breeze."

Heinrich didn't know what to say. Ben took the last draw on his stogie, threw the stump on the paved stone front sidewalk and ground it in with his worn brown leather shoe.

"I would have helped if I'd been there," Heinrich said.

Ben put a wrinkled hand on Heinrich's shoulder. "I know, Professor, I know. There's still hope for you. Why do you think I mentioned it?"

Ben turned toward the fraternity house. "I gotta' get back to work," he said, but turned back to Heinrich and pointed a wrinkled finger at him. "Keep doing the Lord's work, now. The Lord needs good fighters on His side."

Heinrich nodded, a bit startled by the religious reference. It reminded him of something his father might have said.

Ben continued. "The trick is to make sure you're fighting for the Lord and not merely for yourself, because you like to fight. If you can honestly say that, you're on the right track."

The old man winked, said "Good Evening," and walked inside the Kappa Psi fraternity house.

After dinner, Manfred Dahlen dealt the cards for a game of rummy. Heinrich picked up his 11 cards and arranged them in his fingers. It was a middling hand, unspectacular to say the least, with a few potential groupings, but nothing set yet – a hand unsettled, like his mind.

"Tough day in court?" Manfred asked.

Heinrich nodded. "Yeah, I'd like to take a two-by-four to that fancy-pants K.C. attorney," he said. "You know, though, I just can't shake the feeling that there's something missing to the story. We know Tommy's neck wasn't broken; he was a fighter, yet he didn't fight; and then we have a cannon that exploded, but nobody knows who fired it."

"Heinrich, as an old artillery man, I can tell you from experience that sometimes cannons misfire or explode without warning. Sometimes, even for a weapon, the time to die comes. That ancient cannon's time had come."

Heinrich nodded slowly. "Maybe, but how could Tommy have been taken so easily? We know he could defend himself. We've seen him fight."

"Perhaps he was ill or a very deep sleeper," Manfred said. "Maybe he had too much to drink that night."

Heinrich shook his head. "Tommy didn't drink to excess."

Manfred laughed. "Are you kidding? He was a college boy. Even rational young men sometimes push the limits." Then he paused and said, "I hesitate to bring it up, but what about opium? The Chinese are famous for falling prey to it."

Heinrich pursed his lips. "No. Tommy was no opium fiend. That doesn't make sense."

Manfred looked Heinrich in the eye, a sober expression on his face. "Here's how I see it. Justice is being done. That Fairchild boy is an evil young man from an evil family, and he deserves the murder sentence that is coming. He doesn't have a Chinaman's chance in hell of escaping conviction, and once it happens, it will be time to let the matter go to God."

Heinrich nodded but remained unconvinced. He laid down a three of clubs to start the discard pile.

The next day, Prosecutor Blunt called Mrs. Yaeger to the witness stand. She marched forward solemnly in what looked to be her best black dress, the one she wore to funerals. Her brown hair neatly tied back in a bun, she placed her hand on the Bible and took the oath. The gray streaks were missing from her hair today, clearly colored away. If you didn't know her, she looked ten years younger. If you did know her, her hair just looked browner.

After she was sworn in, Blunt asked, "Was Professor Kueter's testimony about the night of the attack accurate?"

"Yes." She said it with conviction.

"Were there indeed men in your house that night, as Professor Kueter has stated?"

"Yes."

"About how many men, would you say?"

"I'm guessing about eight inside and that many more at least outside."

"Did you see Professor Kueter get hit?"

"Through the doorway. I saw someone hit him, a fist hit him, in the side of his head, and he fell down."

"Did you see who broke into your home?"

She shook her head. "No. They wore masks."

"Would you say the men were white or black?"

"Their voices sounded white. Most of them wore gloves, but the man who hit Heinrich had white hands. I remember the arm and the fist."

"Mrs. Yaeger, the defense attorney has suggested that it was not the Kappa Psis who invaded your house, but a roving band of renegade Negroes. Is that what you think?"

"No sir. They were white men; I'm near positive."

"One last question: Did Professor Kueter do any drinking at your house that evening?"

"Not that evening. Heinrich knows I have a rule against alcohol in my house."

"Does Professor Kueter follow your house rules overall?"

She smiled. "Yes, except sometimes he stays out too late and sneaks inside through the back door. He thinks I don't notice."

There were snickers in the courtroom. Several heads turned toward Heinrich, most grinning. Heinrich turned beet red.

"But did Professor Kueter stay out late that evening?"

"No, he came in early. He said he had some studying to do for his class the next day."

"Thank you, Mrs. Yaeger," Blunt said. "No further questions."

The trial dragged on for another week until early December, with much maneuvering back and forth. At the end, Mr. Lyon again pleaded with the jury to give the boys a chance. After all, it hadn't been first-degree, premeditated murder; at worst it was second-degree murder or more likely negligent manslaughter, he said.

"These boys lost control of a prank that was never meant to harm anyone," he said, his voice oozing with pathos. "Which one of you can cast a first stone," he asked, eyeballing each juror in a sweep of the box. "Can each of you men tell me honestly that you or someone you know has never been seduced by demon liquor? Because that's what happened to them. They fell prey to demon liquor and an impish sense of fun. The liquor clouded their judgment, and then their plans for a harmless prank went horribly, tragically wrong.

"The question is: Can you find the compassion in your hearts to forgive them?"

Lyon looked each juror in the eye individually, then wiped the sweat from his brow with a handkerchief and sat down.

Mr. Blunt stood up slowly to give his summation. He leaned over and looked at the jury. "Ladies and gentlemen, I would ask you a couple of questions. First, how many of you have a few drinks every once in a while?"

About half of them raised their hands. "O.K., now how many of you have ever gotten liquored up and put a noose around somebody's neck?"

"Objection!" thundered Lyon.

"Sustained," said Judge Jamison. "The prosecution will refrain from inflammatory statements."

Blunt nodded. "Of course, Your Honor. I merely wanted to point out the extraordinary nature of this act."

He turned to the jury. "It was an extraordinary event. This sort of behavior is not what young men – nay men of any age – under the influence commonly do."

One by one, he too looked each juror in the eye. "The question is not whether you can forgive their negligent behavior..."

"Objection!"

"Sustained," said the judge.

"I will rephrase my comment, Your Honor. The question is not whether you have the ability to forgive; it is whether you have the courage to do your duty. It is your duty to stand on behalf of your fellow citizens and provide justice for Tommy Lee. It is your duty to give these young men the sentence they deserve for murdering a young man in cold blood."

He looked at the members of the jury for a minute, then walked back to his seat. "The prosecution rests, Your Honor," he said.

Heinrich suspected the verdict would be guilty, and when it came a few hours later, his suspicion was confirmed.

Heinrich watched as John Fairchild stood stoically and faced the jury. When the jury foreman said, "Guilty," Fairchild's head dropped.

Heinrich nodded, a grim look on his face. Perhaps Fairchild really believed in his innocence, he thought. People could rationalize themselves into believing anything; criminals usually were innocent in their own minds.

"Will the defendant please rise?" Judge Jamison ordered. "John M. Fairchild, following the jury's recommendation, I hereby sentence you to life imprisonment in the state penitentiary at Jefferson City. While I might have chosen an even harsher sentence, the jury in its wisdom sees some promise in your potential rehabilitation. The bench hereby orders that you be held in the county jail until such time as you may be transferred into state custody. This court is now adjourned."

Jamison banged the gavel, rose and quickly left for his chambers, leaving behind great commotion in the audience.

As Heinrich turned to leave the courtroom, a white-knuckled hand grabbed his elbow. He swiveled and found himself face to face with young John Fairchild, who had slipped away momentarily from the bailiff.

"Professor, you've got to believe me; something was wrong with Tommy Lee that night," the animated Fairchild told Heinrich. "We never meant to kill him. It was an accident. Honest, we only put a noose around his neck to scare him, but we never figured we'd get that far. He was too tough."

The bailiff dragged Fairchild away. Dumbfounded and skeptical,

Heinrich stood watching the boy's pleading eyes as the door closed behind him. While it may have been an accident, the result was still darn near murder. Manslaughter by joke, perhaps? Nevertheless, the look of sincerity in young Fairchild's eyes startled Heinrich and made him think.

Heinrich methodically tried to sort out the whirl of thoughts circling in his head. Reason was his only hope, and his anger at the Fairchilds too easily got in the way of such ordered thought. He supposed it came down to this issue: Hypothetically, assuming young Fairchild was telling the truth, was there any objective meaning to it? In other words, if young Fairchild were telling the truth as he knew it, and if Fairchild's truth matched the objective truth, it would have to mean that someone else had murdered Tommy Lee. Someone else had to have fired the cannon to spook the horse, but such a possibility was outlandish, wasn't it? Who would have the motive and intent to do such a thing? It just didn't add up.

Clearly, the most obvious explanation made the most sense. Fairchild was simply mistaken; he had led a prank gone bad and would now have to pay the price for his perfidy or negligence, whatever label one wanted to paste on the stupid action. Still, a nagging sense that he had missed something tugged at the corner of Heinrich's mind. Rationally, he could see that young Fairchild must be guilty, but a stray, uneasy doubt would continue to pester Heinrich periodically for some time afterward. He continued to feel he was missing some element of the equation.

Happy to leave the drab outdoor world behind, Heinrich ducked into Murphy's for a quick hot lunch. Most of the leaves on the trees were long gone now, and a definite chill had arrived, the first clear harbinger of a cold winter to come. Along with winter came the Christmas spirit, marked by green wreaths on the streetlight poles along Main Street, courtesy of the local Chamber of Commerce.

While eating a hearty stew, the perfect meal for dreary weather, Heinrich read the *St. Louis Post-Dispatch*. Turning to the back page, his eyes settled on an article headlined: "Black Jack Heads Home."

Heinrich squirmed uncomfortably. He would forever associate his former commander, General John "Black Jack" Pershing, with the assault on Mount Bagsak. According to the article, Pershing had left the Philippines to become commandant of the Presidio in San Francisco, a plum post in a beautiful west coast city. Apparently, the Filipinos had hailed Pershing as a hero and honored the general by designating him a Sultan as he embarked on his ship with his wife and children. How nice for him, Heinrich thought with a smirk. He suspected the supposedly spontaneous honors were fictions generated for publicity purposes by the military, probably driven by Pershing himself.

Heinrich shuddered as he saw the image of Bud Bagsak's writhing pit of bodies in his mind. He took a large swig of beer. Black Jack was on the rise, as always. The ambitious Pershing, who years ago had been promoted in one leap from captain to brigadier by his friend Teddy Roosevelt, now had appointed himself Sultan. What would come next -- King Pershing? Why not just declare himself a god and be done with it?

Truth always suffers when propaganda is so much more satisfying, Heinrich thought. His abdomen tightened as he took another slurp of carbonation and remembered looking down the barrel of his carbine and firing again into the pit, sending to the grave a wounded Moro simply trying to crawl out of the bloody pile of body parts. In Heinrich's mind, Black Jack and Bloody Bagsak were forever linked.

Part of it was the general's dark nickname. Young Pershing had made his mark leading black troops into battle against the Apache, Sioux and Cree, and then against the decaying Spanish. Having finished off the Moros, Black Jack was moving on and moving up, a poor Missouri boy continuing to do his duty for the imperial United States.

Black Jack earned his moniker when, as a tactical officer at West Point, he frequently contrasted the prowess of his former black troops with the poor performance of his "weakling" white cadets. They began calling him "Nigger Jack" behind his back, and, over time, the nickname morphed into "Black Jack," which looked better in the newspapers.

Meanwhile, Pershing had been fortunate in the 1890s to befriend and then charge up San Juan Hill with his future commander in chief, Teddy Roosevelt. Like many officers at the time, Pershing had been stuck at captain for more than a decade. But mismanagement of the Spanish-American War proved that the high command held too many incompetent leaders who needed to be shown the door. Roosevelt cleaned house and then jumped Pershing to brigadier by presidential prerogative, much to the consternation of those officers whom Black Jack bypassed.

At first, Heinrich wondered whether Pershing ever felt guilt, but he doubted a man like Black Jack could afford owning up to a conscience. Heinrich, however, felt a need to reconcile his actions at the Bagsak crater. The image of himself, standing at the edge of the pit and continuing to fire into it until he was out of bullets, and then reloading and firing again and again. Yes, that had been him continuing to pull the trigger, mechanically firing into the mass of bodies, and he regretted it now.

What sort of Christian would do such a thing? A soldier under orders, that's who, a soldier who only wanted to do his time and go home, a soldier forced to face his own selfishness. A selfish man working for a selfish nation.

Heinrich took another swig of beer and tried to think about Sally.

Sally swished away a fly with her left hand and bit into the ham-and-cheese sandwich she held in her right hand. She realized she was chattering, as she did when she was nervous, in this case inanely singing the praises of freshly sliced, locally made, sugar-cured ham.

Sally was in love, which made her nervous. She knew it in her heart, but she didn't want anything to mess up the bliss the two shared. She worried, however, that her continuing to refuse Heinrich's marriage proposals might do just that. He might misconstrue her reluctance and become resentful. How sad that the demands of society to conform to its norms could become the chief impediment to a couple's happiness.

To pass the time and avoid too many negative thoughts, she talked for several minutes. Heinrich only heard or half-heard most of it, but he smiled at the thought that, as long as he could look into those deep blue eyes, he could listen to her all day.

It was unseasonably warm for early December, one of those strange Missouri sixty-five-degree winter days that come out of nowhere but don't last. The next day would probably be thirty or forty degrees and damp. Heinrich had heard a meteorologist say the weather's mood swings had to do with air patterns, which right now were apparently southerly.

She realized he really wasn't paying attention. "I've lost you, haven't I?" she said with a sigh.

So she changed the subject abruptly, as if pulling a new topic out of a hat in a desperate search for something that would pique his interest. "So, what do you think of the turmoil down in Mexico? Do you think your countrymen will get involved?" she asked. "The Kaiser certainly seems to be throwing his weight around these days."

Heinrich sighed. "If you mean my American countrymen, yes. We might become involved. I'm an American; they're the same countrymen as yours."

"Sorry," she said. "You have to admit you are a bit exotic for these parts. You have a definite air of Germany in you."

"Perhaps, but my Germany doesn't exist. My ancestors dreamed of a German democracy of free men, not this ridiculous empire with its Kaiser marching around in jackboots, playing with toy soldiers and ships."

"In other words, all the good Germans came to America and left the bad ones behind?" she asked.

"I guess so."

"Actually, I was a bit surprised that you would keep asking a woman like me out, and on a picnic, no less," she said. "I thought Germans don't like strong-willed women."

Heinrich laughed. "On the contrary, we like strong, virtuous women to run the domestic front, while we battle the forces of evil – thieves, politicians, and especially the French."

"If you have thoughts of me being your mistress of the home front, you'd better think again," she said with a hint of steel in her voice.

"As long as you learn to carry the beer at Oktoberfest and Maifest, I can live with that," he said, deadpan.

She gave him a mock sour look. "Good luck on that front, mister. And you won't ever see me out scrubbing the porch on my hands and knees either."

"Oh, that will never do. Remember, we Scrubby Dutch expect it. And we are very suspicious of women who want to compete in the man's realm."

"I not only compete, I win."

"Then you are rather exotic yourself, my darling suffragette."

They both laughed. For a minute, they silently watched the creek flow by from their perch on a secluded rock.

"Why did you ask me on this picnic?" she asked.

"You wanted a story about me, didn't you?"

"Sure, sometime. But from what I know about you now, I doubt you pulled me out here into the middle of the woods for lunch and an interview. Why?"

"Well, for starters, I was told not to associate with you, and I don't like orders like that."

He kissed her.

"Ah-hah. Because I am a fallen woman who thinks too much?"

Heinrich nodded. She grimaced.

"Perhaps I should explain the 'fallen' part. I've already told you about my former husband in Philadelphia. Shortly after I arrived here, I got very close to a man who told me he was going to marry me, but he wound up running off to California instead. So, in the eyes of some townspeople, I am a loose woman of questionable repute. It probably wouldn't shock them at all to know I've allowed myself to be carried out into the woods with an unmarried German. It can be rather liberating, actually, living up to such low expectations."

Heinrich laughed. "Please try to contain your wanton lust," he said, "and I'll try to contain mine."

She blushed. "I'll do my best to hold it in."

He laughed.

"But come now, that isn't all there is, is it?" she said. "You have something on your mind, I can tell. Some grave news, perhaps?"

Heinrich nodded. "It's just a nagging feeling, actually. I have no proof whatsoever, just gut instinct and rumor."

"About what?"

"I believe there was more to Tommy Lee's death than a tragic accident during a fraternity prank. I think it might not have been an accident."

"What do you mean?"

"Tommy was clearly a student of the martial arts, yet he hardly struggled when they grabbed him. It just seems odd."

She was silent for a minute, contemplating her pink lemonade.

Heinrich was silent too, half wishing he hadn't brought it up. It was too late now. He had done it again, saying the wrong thing at the wrong time. "I'm sorry," he said. "It's just been gnawing at me, ever since the trial. What do you think?"

"It's not entirely implausible," she said.

"How diplomatic. Does that mean it's plausible or not?"

She laughed, and he turned away.

"Oh, come now, Heinrich. You have to admit it's rather awkward. One minute we're eating a picnic, talking about the weather and flirting, and the next we're discussing a murder that has supposedly already been solved. Are you ever going to let it go?"

Heinrich nodded. "I know; I just can't get it out of my head. I think Tommy may have been drugged."

"There are certainly illicit substances available here; heck, he may have been abusing a drug, maybe opium," she suggested. "In many ways, this is still the Wild West. You've seen evidence of the violence that boils up every now and again and that results in a fight or lynching. Although Franklinton appears on the surface to be somewhat cleaned up and civilized, Fairchild's saloon is still a den of iniquity, and there are still plenty of other nearby towns that offer whatever vice you want. Have you spoken to the sheriff?"

Heinrich nodded. "He basically told me to mind my own business."

"Maybe you should take his advice," Sally laughed. "Listen, John Fairchild is an evil young man who got what he deserved."

Heinrich gritted his teeth, an angry look on his face. "Sorry," she said.

"No, it's all right. Manfred told me the same thing."

"Manfred is a wise man," she said. When Heinrich did not respond, she took a different tack. "Okay how do you believe it was done then? Do we have a murder weapon?"

"It looks like a straightforward accident. The horse bolts at the sound of gunfire, tightening the noose around his neck and hanging him. But the Doc said he may have actually died of a fever of unknown origin. I wonder…"

"Poison, perhaps? Arsenic, rat poison?"

"No, Doc Harris would have recognized common arsenic poisoning."

Sally moved closer to him and interjected a finger. "What if Doc was in on it?"

"I doubt it. I don't think he has the temperament for it."

"That's probably what they said about Jack the Ripper. Red Jack was probably some seemingly mild-mannered sort too."

Heinrich shuddered. He found it odd for a woman to talk this way, so blunt and gruesome. Ladies shouldn't do that, he thought. Then again, why shouldn't they?

"I must admit the idea is intriguing," she continued. "So, the killer may have been another student, but we don't really know. And we don't have a weapon yet. What about a motive?"

"Racism, perhaps?"

"Usually, lynchings are done in public to scare the colored folks into submission, but I've never seen it done to a Chinaman before. We really don't have that many around here, so it wouldn't seem necessary for that kind of public display."

Heinrich nodded. "There must be something deeper. Maybe if I can find out more about Tommy, I'll get a clue."

"And I'll ask around town. Sometimes people hear things."

"O.K., but be careful. I wouldn't want you to get hurt."

Sally giggled. She was close to him, closer than propriety allowed. She kissed him on the lips. Heinrich put his arms around her waist and passionately returned the favor.

After a moment, they came up for air. "Professor Heinrich Kueter," she said. "That was most pleasant."

Heinrich shrugged his shoulders sheepishly. "Thank you, my dear," he said. "You know, the marriage offer still stands."

"I'm still thinking it over," she said coyly. "Now, would you like to shoot for page one?"

A few days later, Sally's best stuff appeared not on page one but on 6A, the opinion page. She had written a scathing op-ed that railed against alleged discriminatory and crooked short-term loans by Truman Fairchild's brother, Arthur, who ran the family's Lucky Strike saloon.

For some time, Arthur Fairchild had floated short-term loans to his bar patrons, officially to cover the cost of a patron's bar tab. In fact, although some were short-term loans for legitimate purposes, the loans were most often connected to illegal gambling or prostitution in the saloon's back room. Drunken men were prone to make snap decisions to participate in nefarious activities if easy money were available. The illicit loans were lucrative for Arthur. Few were brave enough to cross him and his muscle, which could easily force reluctant borrowers to pay their debts quickly.

According to Sally's report, usually Arthur would charge 5 percent simple interest a day on a two-week loan of $100 or $200, and the patron could pay the debt off early and save any extra interest. The law didn't worry about such small amounts; the legal limit for larger, annual loans was simple interest calculated at 6 percent annual percentage rate, or 8 percent if it were written into a contract. On a $100 loan, therefore, the borrowing cost after two weeks would be $70.

Recently a few German and Irish customers had compared notes with other borrowers and found their rates to be significantly higher. They grumbled but did not press their case. However, now two families of Chinese railroad laborers sharing a dilapidated house next to the tracks had each borrowed $200 to fix their privy, which their landlord had refused to repair and which was leaking raw sewage into their backyard.

An enterprising businessman, Arthur Fairchild had gladly lent them the funds, but charged the Chinese daily compound interest for two weeks, making their combined costs more than $1,380. Fairchild had gambled that the families wouldn't contest it, but the Chinese spoke to Sheriff Thackeray. Upon hearing their story, Thackeray connected the families to an out-of-town lawyer who was more than willing to sue Fairchild for usury.

"Our community must understand that it cannot afford to give the cold shoulder to immigrants and expect to prosper," Sally's editorial stated. "It's bad enough when hooligans harass our immigrants who simply want to live in peace and pursue their own happiness. When we exploit them for illicit economic gain simply because of their ethnic heritage, the whole town loses out on economic prosperity."

Heinrich grimaced as he read the text in the classroom, while his students were taking a test on the Renaissance. At the end, she referred to Heinrich's incident with Truman Fairchild on his first day in town as an example of the town's dismal treatment of immigrants; Heinrich had literally gotten the cold shoulder, and he knew he might be in for trouble.

Sure enough, as he walked along the sidewalk in front of the administration building late in the afternoon, his footprints showing in the slush of the previous night's snow, President Tichenor's squeaky tenor voice came from behind, "Young Kueter, let's walk."

Heinrich stopped to let President "Ichabod's" bony apparition catch up. The president's undertaker eyes squinted, and he ground his teeth, making his demeanor particularly determined. A sudden, wishful vision of a headless horseman riding up to lop off the president's head flashed through Heinrich's mind, and he forcibly repressed a smile.

Instead, he opened with a syrupy gambit. "Mr. President, how nice to see you this fine afternoon."

"It is a nice, brisk afternoon at that, Professor Kueter. However, it would have been much better if I hadn't seen your name grace the pages of our local rag earlier today."

"Ah yes, Sally did hit it hard today."

"My concern is not with Miss Giddings; it's with your foray into the world of journalism."

"She referred to an incident that involved me; I hardly think that constitutes a foray."

Tichenor stopped and pointed his bony index finger at Heinrich. "Kueter, you will refrain from appearing in the press. Do I make myself clear?"

"Crystal, sir."

"Then good day to you." Tichenor marched back into the administration building.

"And to you too," Heinrich seethed as he walked on toward home.

Manfred later ribbed Heinrich about Sally's editorial and his role in it, but Heinrich no longer wanted to talk about it. Searching for a good way to change the subject, Heinrich stood and held his mug high. "I propose a toast," he said.

Manfred stood up shakily from his barstool and raised his glass, and Murphy poured a cold one from the tap and did likewise.

"To the Reverend Billy Sunday," Heinrich said, "the man who puts theology and the practice of religion back 400 years!"

"Here, here," responded his friends, as they clinked their mugs.

"However, I must offer a caveat," Murphy said. "May he keep driving business to my establishment!"

"And their horses to mine!" Dahlen added.

They all laughed. The news had only recently been announced that the Rev. Sunday's revival show would be stopping the following weekend on its way to St. Louis. Getting the revival so near to the Christmas Season would inject more dollars into the local economy than usual and make for a lucrative holiday. That was always a good thing. But enduring the atmosphere of over-charged, rabid Christian fervor could be difficult to stomach. Sally had asked him to attend the revival with her; she had to cover the event for her newspaper. Even though he wanted to find a reason not to go, it was an offer he felt he could not refuse.

Manfred put his arm on Heinrich's shoulder. "You'll have to represent us at the event, my friend," he said. "Please represent us well. We'll be here hiding out amongst the heathen, while you are busy finding true religion."

Heinrich had to laugh. Although he was in no way looking forward to the ordeal, at least he would be with Sally.

"Give me that old time religion, give me that old time religion, give me that old time religion, it's good enough for me," Heinrich sang loudly.

He didn't particularly like the song, mainly because of its undercurrent of unthinking adherence to dogma, but when in Rome — or in this case a wooden, Protestant tabernacle built especially for a visit from the Rev. Billy Sunday — one does as the Romans do. Although he hadn't wanted to attend Sunday's revival, Sunday certainly provided a great show and the big entertainment event of the week.

Sally had enticed him to come using various arguments, from the scientific – "Think of it as a sociological study of local culture" – to Billy Sunday's celebrity – "Whatever you think of the man, you have to admit he's a force that may help put our town on the map" – to the need for him to attend important town events – "You need to be seen, darling." Of course, the argument that actually swayed him was the personal – "I'll make it worth your while."

Billy Sunday's handlers led hymns to get the crowd worked up in preparation for the legendary evangelist's flashy entrance. A grand entrance is especially important when the show is more about entertainment than spirituality, Heinrich mused to himself.

"Turns out that Billy Sunday is a personal friend of Truman Fairchild," Sally told him. "That's how he got him to perform a one-night stop here on his way back home to Winona Lake, Indiana."

Heinrich nodded. He had been hearing the hammers pounding all week. At one time, Sally had told him, Sunday had preached in tents like other evangelists, but then his tent burned down. Ever since, Sunday demanded that towns wanting him to preach construct a wooden tabernacle according to his specifications. With a laugh to himself, Heinrich wondered if Sunday had given the dimensions in cubits.

The structure had been erected at great expense by Truman Fairchild as his gift to the town. The wooden tabernacle showed Fairchild to be a small-timer, thought Heinrich. A big-timer like Solomon would have used stone.

Of course, the funds more than likely came from the gambling and prostitution hidden from view in the back room of the Fairchild brothers' saloon, but Heinrich's father had often said that one of the mysteries of God was the Almighty's ability to turn petty evil to His own purposes.

The crowd began to chant, "Sunday, Sunday, Sunday…"

Shortly, the Rev. Billy Sunday made his entrance, with his choir singing, "What a Friend We Have in Jesus."

"Sunday, the best day of the week!" Sunday shouted with a laugh, to the glee of the crowd.

"Could I have an Amen?" he yelled, and a thunderous "Amen" erupted from his adoring audience.

"I want to thank you and your town's leaders for bringing me here this evening, and I especially want to thank my dear old friend, Truman Fairchild…Truman, stand up so we can clap for you." Truman stood up and bowed, a pious glow on his face. Apparently, he was truly feeling Jesus today.

"I also want to thank you all for these heaters," Sunday pointed to the four kerosene heaters in the corners. "They'll really help us on a cold night like this, and I like being reminded of my old days in tiny villages across this great country. Other than on a winter night, I can honestly say that Franklinton is no kerosene circuit town."

The crowd laughed. The kerosene circuit was the small-town trail for small-time evangelists that Sunday had left in the dust back in his youth. His show was now the biggest of its kind and had been for a long time.

"You know, it's really great to look out at all these shining faces," he continued. "They are the face of America, and the face of American religion. After all, it's people like you who form the American spirit, and that spirit is tied to the only true American religion, that of Jesus Christ."

And not, Heinrich thought, the spirit of the almighty dollar? A great cheer arose from the crowd, which stood and clapped resoundingly.

"I'm proud to be an American," Sunday continued. "It's amazing what that spirit of America can do to reform the foreign soul. It's simply amazing to see when an immigrant repents of his evil worldly ways and becomes Americanized. We're not just a melting pot; we're a smelting pot. Do I hear an 'Amen'?"

"Amen!" the mob shouted in adoration.

Sally looked at Heinrich with a sick smile. "Sorry," she said.

"You know, Sally," Heinrich answered. "I think I've been Americanized just enough." He stood up, turned on his heel into the central aisle, and walked out of the wooden tabernacle.

He needed a breath of fresh air. Away from the tent, he looked up at the stars. It was nice to gaze upon something actually made by God.

Heinrich shivered a little and turned up the lapels of his coat to better cover his neck. This revival was out of season. Usually, they were held in the blistering heat of summer.

Listening to snippets of Sunday's sermon inside, Heinrich was glad he had left the building: "Down in Nashville, Tennessee, I saw four wagons going down the street, and they were loaded with stills, and kettles, and pipes. 'What's this?' I said. 'United States revenue officers, and they have been in the moonshine district and confiscated the illicit stills, and they are taking them down to the government scrap heap.' You see, Jesus Christ was God's revenue officer. Now the Jews were forbidden to eat pork, but Jesus Christ came and found that crowd buying and selling and dealing pork, and confiscated the whole business!"

Heinrich felt the urge to vomit. Sunday had apparently decided to spout a variation on his "devil booze" theme. I could use a drink right now, he thought.

"I go to a family, and it is broken up, and I say, 'What caused this?' Drink! I step up to a young man on the scaffold and say, 'What brought you here?' Drink! Whence all the misery and sorrow and corruption? Invariably it is drink."

Heinrich would have gladly provided a rebuttal by suggesting that maybe there were more factors involved, like the exploitation of the working man by big business tycoons. The fact is the neighborhood tavern was the one place where a working man could go for fun. Frankly, a guy like Murphy would have made a better minister than Sunday. At least Murphy cared about his customers personally and was a good listener.

Heinrich quit listening and eyed a pile of scrap lumber left over from the tabernacle project. He hoped the city could recoup some of the costs by selling the used lumber from the building. Of course, Fairchild probably had already wangled a deal to sell it to contractors at a fair price and thereby line his own pockets.

Hearing the sound of feet marching across the gravel that covered the fairground, he turned to find Truman Fairchild coming toward him with a menacing look. And truly speaking of the devil, he thought.

"I'm glad you left the tent, you Heinie bastard," Fairchild said, "because you aren't welcome here." He tapped the silver-topped cane in his left hand.

"Mr. Fairchild," Heinrich answered. "Did I hear you correctly?"

Fairchild came nose-to-nose with Kueter, who could smell the liquor on the political boss's breath. Heinrich wondered whether the illustrious Reverend knew the true nature of his "good friend," but Heinrich didn't have time to consider the irony.

"You most certainly did," Fairchild sneered.

Heinrich blinked to mock his attacker. "Hmm. 'Bastard,' is probably accurate, but I don't cotton to being called a Heinie."

"Get used to it, you goddam Kraut. I shouldn't have just knocked you out of the way that first day. I should have finished you off for good. You sent my boy to prison, and I want satisfaction."

"Like father, like son. Isn't joining the murderous family business satisfaction enough?"

Furious, Fairchild swung the cane at Heinrich, who blocked it with his left forearm. It hit hard and hurt bad. The old hoodlum was serious; Heinrich knew there'd be a bruise. Circling, Fairchild swung again, but Heinrich ducked out of the way toward the woodpile, where he grabbed a three-foot length of pine two-by-two.

Fairchild attacked again, swinging his cane down from above with both hands, trying to hit Heinrich on the crown of his head. In response, Heinrich raised his makeshift club over his head, one hand on each end, and blocked the shot, then ducked and launched a powerful blow with his right hand into Fairchild's ribs. The older man fell, grasping his right ribs and lying on the ground in pain.

"You'd better bring some friends next time you go juramentado on me, old man, because I've got experience," Heinrich said through clenched teeth. He raised his wooden club. "You're lucky I don't have my Colt anymore."

As he was about to swing, he heard the cocking of a pistol behind him. "Drop the weapon, Kueter," Sheriff Thackeray said. "That's enough."

Heinrich dropped the lumber, after a moment thankful that the sheriff had stopped him from doing something stupid.

Fairchild got up, holding his rib cage.

"We aren't done, Kraut," he said. "But you're finished in Franklinton."

"So be it. We'll see if you've got the stones to make it happen."

"Truman, back off," Thackeray said. Fairchild complied, walking away toward the tabernacle, from which the strains of "Onward, Christian Soldiers" rang out fiercely. Sally came running out of the tabernacle, bewildered at the sight of her disheveled date.

"Sally, please take your man home," the Sheriff said. "He's had enough trouble for the night."

She nodded, grabbing Heinrich's arm. He winced at the touch.

Thackeray pointed a finger at Kueter. "I'll be seeing you if he presses charges."

Heinrich nodded, worried he had done it again.

CHAPTER 6

Heinrich had known this day would come, but through final exams and over the holidays he had tried to ignore its inevitable arrival. He immersed himself in his work, and then in holiday festivities, chess matches and hikes with Dahlen, poker games in the back room of Murphy's saloon and, above all, his growing romance with his beloved Sally, who still refused to marry him no matter how many times he asked.

This preliminary proceeding before the Faculty Disciplinary Board, held on a fittingly dreary mid-January Monday, would launch the drive to his potential termination. It had loomed large after his altercation with the elder Fairchild at the revival meeting. Under the guise of letting matters cool before soberly confronting them, the college faculty had decided to wait until the winter term to begin its formal disciplinary process regarding his case. The Christmas season was not made for scapegoating; far better to wait for Easter, Heinrich thought.

He had turned over the events of that fateful evening in his mind many times, but he still didn't know what else he might have done differently to avoid the situation, other than refusing Sally's invitation to the event or not raising the club to threaten Fairchild.

He wished he hadn't done that. He should have shown mercy and let Fairchild up, but his combat survival instincts, honed in the hand-to-hand warfare of the Philippines, had taken over at the time. Polite society in the States did not understand that a man must mentally adapt to the idea of killing without thinking. When at any moment a hidden Moro warrior might charge from behind the nearest tree or mango basket, there was no time to think, only to react. Likewise, a man must train to become a killer, and, once unleashed, the new "killer instinct" is difficult to control. He supposed he would have to promise to think before killing if he were to keep his job, but realistically, such a change in behavior might not be possible.

Heinrich surveyed his surroundings. He sat front-row and center where the audience would usually sit, in the college's main Smith lecture hall, named for an obscure alumnus who had dedicated his life to the relatively anonymous acquisition of wealth as an executive accountant under Andrew Carnegie. It made a fitting faculty courtroom. The three faculty members appointed to the tribunal sat solemnly in their formal academic robes in front of a gargantuan black slate chalkboard, the magic font of all academic wisdom, which covered the entire wall at the base of the amphitheater, and behind a sturdy maple table on which biology professors periodically dissected dead animals. Now the professors held Heinrich's carcass of an academic career in their hands.

Off to the right sat a dutifully expressionless President Tichenor, and Department Chairman Goforth, continually massaging his face with his hands, a pitiful picture that served as a portent of doom. Luckily, this hearing was just a start. A verdict would take some time. After all, the tribunal was, in effect, a faculty committee, and faculty committees are rarely given to speedy deliberation.

The tribunal chairman, a professor of Latin named Purcell who was seated in the middle, spoke first, "Mr. Heinrich Kueter," he said. "You are accused before the faculty of conduct unbecoming of your rank and status as an instructor and faculty member at Worcester College. Do you wish to make a statement?"

Heinrich nodded. "I would like to say that I regret the unfortunate incidents in which I have been involved through no fault of my own. However, my altercation with Mr. Truman Fairchild was unavoidable because he attacked me. I was simply defending myself."

"So noted," Dr. Purcell said. "This faculty tribunal will conduct an investigation and render a report and judgment in a month."

The tribunal stood and, like penguins in their black academic robes and tasseled waferboard hats, waddled out a side door. Heinrich stole a final glance at Tichenor, then stood up and climbed the slope to exit through the main doors of the lecture hall.

Heinrich needed to get out of his office. It had been two weeks since the preliminary hearing, a dark time spent buried in paper-grading under the cloud of his faculty impeachment proceeding. It was a sunny, frigid, late-January Friday, and the temperature hovered just above zero.

Donned in layers, with cotton underwear at the bottom and woolen long underwear beneath his suit, the extra clothing made Heinrich lumber along with a strange, stilted gait that made him wonder if he looked like one of H.G. Wells's Martian fighting machines.

Heinrich took the path along fraternity row toward town with his gloved hands in the pockets of his thick wool coat, his eyes on the barren trees, and his thoughts on the momentous events of the past few months. As they often did, his thoughts turned to the night of Tommy Lee's death, which had started the whole mess now threatening his career. If only he had not been half asleep, been a little more aware of his surroundings, or hadn't charged blindly out of the house, only to be knocked unconscious, maybe he could have defeated his unknown assailants and saved the boy. If, if, if…

If only he could forget about the incident, maybe he would be better off, he thought glumly. Between dreams about Tommy's death and Moro warriors on the attack, and his worries over potentially losing his job, he wasn't getting much sleep.

He decided to stop at his room to drop off his black academic robe, which was required attire for faculty in the classroom, before meeting Sally at Murphy's Tapped Keg for the evening.

When he arrived back at home, Mrs. Yaeger's face held a tired look, and her bottom lip quivered slightly. She was sweeping snow off the porch with a brand new straw broom.

"Hello, Mrs. Yaeger. Is that a new broom?"

"Yes, Professor Kueter. Good evening." She sniffled, then leaned on the gray painted front porch railing and began to cry.

Heinrich walked up onto the porch and put his right hand on her back. "Are you all right?"

"I'm very sorry, Heinrich. I need to clean out Thomas's room, and I miss him so much. He was such a special boy, so full of promise. I promised his family I would keep him safe, and I failed in that duty." Mrs. Yaeger, whose husband had died years ago, was a staunch member of the local Presbyterian Church. She had boarded Tommy Lee upon agreement with the missionaries in Korea who sponsored him.

"He was a fine lad and a great friend. I miss him terribly," Heinrich said. "I too wish I had done things differently that night, but you can't spend time blaming yourself for every misstep, or you will go mad."

Yes, he thought, pretend you aren't doing precisely the same thing.

She nodded. "You know, he told me you were one of his favorite teachers," she said.

"Really?" That did please him.

"Yes, because he said you stayed true to your beliefs."

"Why, thank you for the compliment." He supposed the statement was indeed true, although he might be better off if it weren't.

Mrs. Yaeger grabbed hold of his left forearm. "I never thanked you for your kind words at his funeral. It took great courage to say them."

"Perhaps courage, perhaps foolhardiness." He handed her his handkerchief, and she wiped her eyes.

She suddenly turned to look at him. Her blood-shot green eyes spat fire. "He was right, you know. You really stuck your neck out for him."

Heinrich nodded. "That's what friends do."

Mrs. Yaeger leaned over and kissed his cheek. "Would you mind looking over Tommy's things?" she asked. "If there is something you want, you may have it. He would have wanted it that way."

Heinrich doubted he would want anything, but he nodded. A nagging thought that he ought to look in Tommy's room had bothered him for a couple of weeks anyway. This way, no pretext was necessary. Maybe some new lead to the mystery would jump out at him, some clue that would explain why the young man had let the Kappa Psi hooligans nab him without a fight.

"I put his things in a box on top of the bureau in his room."

"Thank you." He headed inside and began to ascend the stairs.

"Any plans for this evening?" he heard her ask.

He mumbled something noncommittal as he walked across the landing halfway up the stairs about going out with friends. She didn't need to know he planned to go to Murphy's and meet Sally. He had heard her rail against the evils of the "saloons," and he knew better than to bring up the subject of a liaison with his *belle femme* in front of a disapproving matron such as Mrs. Yaeger.

He climbed the next half-dozen stairs to the second floor and entered Tommy's room, which was spartan and non-descript. There was a rickety twin bed, a dresser, and a washstand. In the corner was a teakwood kneeler with a weathered King James Bible beside it. Above the kneeler on the wall was a Chinese print on a small bamboo mat — a painting of a pagoda, a palm tree, and a tiger, distant and reserved, but pleasing to the eye.

Heinrich could imagine Tommy there, kneeling in prayer. Heinrich wondered how his friend might have prayed. Would he have prayed more like a Buddhist, pressing his palms together high above his head and then prostrating himself on his knees, palms and forehead, or had he simply kneeled like a western Christian? Did he clap to get God's attention as some Eastern worshippers were known to do? Heinrich suddenly regretted that he would never know this intimate fact about his friend.

Heinrich walked over to the dresser. In a box on its top lay a tarnished brass pocket watch, three handkerchiefs, and a wallet. He opened the pocket watch. On the inside of the cover was a painted, swirled, circular symbol that looked like black and white fish chasing each other's tails. Heinrich stared at it for a moment.

He remembered Tommy explaining it as the Yin and Yang symbol of Taoist philosophy. Yin and Yang, black and white, soft and hard, female and male. The white and black did not stand for good and evil, Tommy had explained. Instead, evil stemmed from an imbalance of the two forces. Clearly they were much out of whack lately.

The watch reminded him of his own talisman, the Teutonic Cross. He pulled it from his pocket and unwrapped the handkerchief that swathed it. Heinrich wondered whether its main cross, with smaller crosses on each arm might imply a similar message, with positive and negative forces embedded in the arms of the symbol. Of course, it all might depend on your point of view. No wonder the Prussians used it as their symbol. If you looked at it as all pluses, it might be hyper-masculine, an overdose of Yang. He laughed to himself. Those damn Prussians, that's their problem; they're completely unbalanced!

He opened the top drawer of the dresser. Nestled next to underwear and socks lay a small, blue-and-white, oriental teacup and a small canvas bag with a drawstring. Heinrich picked up the dirty teacup and studied it more closely; its blue illustration appeared to depict a Chinese male peasant. He put the cup aside and picked up the canvas bag, which was stamped in red ink with the words, "Chung's Chinese Market." The bag had a curious odor. Heinrich opened it, and the pungent smell quickly permeated the nearby air, then subsided a little as his nose got used to it. Inside was a ground plant material, perhaps a rough-cut spice or dried mushrooms. Heinrich put the teacup and bag in his pocket.

He opened the other drawers, but nothing stood out. He scanned the room; nothing else caught his eye. Disappointed that he would solve no mystery that day, he headed back downstairs to Mrs. Yaeger.

He showed Mrs. Yaeger the teacup. She studied the porcelain octagonal cup for a minute. "He would drink Chinese tea from time to time," she said. "He told me it was a special cup, given to him by a friend, I think."

He then showed her the bag with the drawstring. "Was this Tommy's? Do you know what it is?"

Mrs. Yaeger shrugged her shoulders. "I have no idea. They were probably an Oriental remedy. He often purchased traditional Chinese herbs, to help with his hay fever and such, from a Chinese store in Jefferson City."

"Would you mind if I borrow this bag?" he asked.

"Have you got hay fever?"

"No," he grinned sheepishly. "I'm just curious. I'd like to see what's in the mix."

"Sure, take them," she said. "Ain't no use to me anyway. I need to clean out the room for another lodger."

He thanked her, ran back up to his room to deposit Tommy's things, and then headed for the Tapped Keg.

The next morning, he walked to the college's science building hoping to speak with Dr. Miles McGovern, chair of the Worcester biology department, who also served as the county coroner. On Mondays McGovern often talked about his weekend experiments, so Heinrich knew there was a good chance the biology professor would be at his lab on a Saturday morning.

Indeed Heinrich found Professor McGovern in his laboratory peering intently into a microscope and looking very much the "mad scientist" in a white lab coat. McGovern was a balding man, with gray hair that ringed his head like a laurel wreath. His round, wire-rimmed spectacles rested on the crown of his head, as if they were eyes in a blank face staring at something on the ceiling. Heinrich stood patiently, silently waiting until the biologist came up for air.

McGovern looked up, startled. "Kueter, what a surprise! I had no idea you were standing there."

"Sorry to bother you, Miles." After the usual small talk about McGovern's family and health, Heinrich left the canvas bag and teacup with the biology professor, who seemed intrigued and promised to analyze them.

On Monday morning, McGovern dropped by Kueter's office to return the bag and teacup, and to relate his findings. Heinrich offered the biology professor a chair, but McGovern shook his head, patted his pocket watch in his vest and leaned against the doorframe instead. McGovern took off his glasses and nervously polished them with a handkerchief as he spoke. "The bag holds a species of amanita mushroom, *amanita phalloides*," he said. "It's known popularly as 'death cap' or 'death angel.' It's highly poisonous, lethal in most cases if ingested. Where did you get it?"

"I found it, actually."

"Well, don't eat it. Maybe somebody was using it for rat poison or something, but you sure wouldn't want it around where some child might get hold of it."

Heinrich thanked him, and McGovern walked away. There were no rats or mice in Mrs. Yaeger's house, at least as far as he knew. And Tommy was a smart boy. Heinrich couldn't believe the young man would have taken something so blatantly toxic on purpose; he wasn't suicidal. Where would he have gotten it? The best place to start, Heinrich decided, would be Chung's Chinese store in Jefferson City. He would need a good cover story for his trip to the state capital, and a piano concert he had heard about might serve perfectly.

Heinrich tethered his bay horse in the late afternoon the next Saturday outside Chung's Chinese Market, below a sign advertising "Oriental Herbs and Grocery" in Jefferson City. The ride had been cold, but the warmth of the horse beneath him helped ease the chill of the day, with a temperature somewhere in the mid-20-degree range, according to the morning newspaper. It would feel good to warm up near a stove, out of the northern wind.

He'd driven the mare hard, having left Franklinton on the 25-mile trek immediately after his 8 a.m. American History class. He really hated teaching on Saturdays, and he knew many students disliked it. Perhaps someday the college would get rid of Saturday classes, but he guessed the Calvinist puritanical reverence for work had entrenched the tradition for a long time to come. Regardless, the ragtime piano concert with Blind Boone provided a good alibi for making the trip. He planned to see the concert with Sally that evening. She would drive from Franklinton in her automobile to avert gossip. Then they would stay overnight in Jefferson City and head back the next day.

But first things first. Opening the rickety wooden door of the Chinese shop to the tinkle of bamboo wind chimes, Heinrich entered into a strange, aromatic world of incense, bamboo, and spices. Exotic roots hung in bunches from hooks in the ceiling and bins on the wooden floor. Best of all, it was warm inside.

The proprietor, a middle-aged Asian gentleman with silver hair, approached him. He wore a standard Western black suit, but with a white satin Chinese-style shirt with a Mandarin collar, as if he chose to remain firmly divided between East and West. "May I help you?" the man asked, with only a hint of an accent.

"Are you Mr. Chung?" asked Heinrich.

"Yes."

"Do you recognize these?" Heinrich handed him the small canvas bag and the teacup.

Mr. Chung looked at the figure on the teacup. "Niulang, the Cowherd."

Heinrich looked puzzled, trying to remember the story his friend Manfred Dahlen had told.

"It's from an ancient love story in Chinese mythology," Chung said.

"The Cowherd and the Weaver Girl?"

"Exactly," Chung said.

Mr. Chung then looked inside the bag. "I recognize the bag," he said. "I use them to sell various herbs and spices. Are you a policeman?"

"No," Heinrich laughed. "I'm a history professor from Franklinton."

"Ah, I have a customer from Franklinton, young Tommy Lee."

Heinrich winced and kept silent for a moment, unsure how to respond.

Chung's face looked puzzled. "Did I say something wrong?"

Heinrich shook his head and sighed. "Tommy is dead."

Chung's jaw dropped. He pointed to a couple of stools next to his counter. "Let us sit."

After they sat down, Chung said, "How did it happen?"

"Tommy was kidnapped during a fraternity prank and accidentally killed. He was my friend. When I looked through his things, I found this bag and was told you might have sold it to him."

"Let me see." Chung poured some out onto a piece of paper. "This is not the tea remedy I prescribed for him. My remedy was made from ground morel mushrooms mixed with some rare varieties of Chinese fungus. These look more like ground paddy straw mushrooms, which are often sliced and eaten in very good Chinese dishes…"

Chung stopped in mid-sentence. "I believe there is more to the story than you are telling me," he said.

Heinrich nodded. "Yes, Tommy did not act like himself during the incident on the night of his death. He was not the kind of man to be taken without a fight. To me, it doesn't add up."

Chung eyed Heinrich. "You believe he was drugged?"

"Yes."

"Then should I assume that you believe these mushrooms to be poisonous?" Chung asked.

"A biologist has studied them. The substance is *amanita phalloides*, also known as 'death angel,' and it is highly poisonous." Heinrich paused to gauge Chung's reaction.

"I can honestly say that I had nothing to do with this, whatever it is," Chung said.

"Let's call it murder," Heinrich said.

Chung blinked. "If so, I had nothing to do with it."

"Do you sell this substance?"

"Never. I sold him tea and sometimes Chinese mushrooms, but never anything toxic."

"Any idea how it might have gotten into his bag?"

The Chinaman shook his head. "None. Such a substance would be too dangerous to keep around here. I have children."

"Do you know where someone might get it?"

Chung rubbed his chin. "In the woods, perhaps? My guess is you would have to know where to find it growing wild. Either someone picked it and put it in my bag, or perhaps Tommy found and picked the mushrooms during one of his hikes, thinking he might save money. Maybe he ate them, not knowing they were poisonous."

Heinrich nodded. "I'd like to think it was a mistake, but I suspect it was no accident," he said. "Let me ask you this: were there any feuds within the Chinese community that might have led to a grudge against Tommy?"

Mr. Chung's face soured; the question appeared to offend him. "Sometimes, there are disagreements between rival gangs of criminals, or between royalists and democrats, but no more than might be expected, and certainly no more disagreements than Americans might have."

"Mr. Chung, I apologize; there was no ill intent meant by the question. I'm just trying to look at all possibilities."

"I understand," Chung said. "I know of no conflicts that would potentially have to do with Tommy."

Heinrich thanked Mr. Chung for his help and turned to leave. A concerned look on his face, Chung called out, "I hope you catch the killer," as Heinrich walked out the door.

Heinrich had arranged, using one of the college telephones, to keep his horse at a local tavern run by a German woman named Schmidt who mentioned she had known his father. So Heinrich had been forced to break the sad news of his father's death to her. Schmidt was a thin woman with a blonde bun, strategically placed to minimize the gray streaks in her hair. Her tavern was located on Jefferson Street, the main southbound thoroughfare, in the protestant German part of town known as Muenchberg, or Munichburg as the English-speaking neighbors called it.

Meanwhile Sally, looking very smart in an ankle-length black dress and a white fur coat, joined him for dinner at the tavern at 6 p.m. They dined with Mrs. Schmidt looking on disapprovingly, suspicious that they were up to no good under her roof.

Heinrich explained to the older woman that they were there to see Blind Boone play a piano concert at the Presbyterian Church, with funds going to help build the Second Baptist Church, a local black congregation.

"Ja, Mmm-hmm," she said, unconvinced, while filling their water glasses, preferring to believe that a clandestine tryst might be in the works.

"I will, of course, need my own room," Sally said. "Can you arrange for a porter to move my bags upstairs?"

Mrs. Schmidt's face brightened. Two rooms doubled the rent, and appearances would be properly kept. Even if the pair's intent was not totally innocent, at least a plausible excuse could be made to satisfy the outside world. "Of course. Bruno?"

A burly German youth with short blond hair and green eyes sauntered over. "Do you know how to open the trunk of a car?"

Bruno nodded. "If I have the key," he said.

Sally opened her black patent leather purse and handed Bruno her auto's keys. "Thank you so much," she said, and blinked her eyes in that girlish way that always melted Heinrich's heart.

Bruno headed outside. Heinrich and Sally continued their meal of delicious roast duck. One of two young men laughing loudly at a nearby table, obviously tipsy, stood and announced in a raucous voice, "Why would you want to listen to some blind nigger anyway? There's plenty of white piano players."

Mrs. Schmidt sat him down with a menacing look. "Mind your own business, Rufus McGill. And you'll not use such crass words in my house, do you hear?"

She turned to Heinrich and Sally. "Sorry about that. Don't mind him. He's the town idiot. He wouldn't know a pianoforte if it kicked him in the behind."

The Presbyterian church's nave was packed for the concert; Blind

Boone's reputation had preceded him. The crowd consisted of mostly young men and women, whites downstairs and blacks in the balcony. The blacks were ushered upstairs via their own separate, but hardly equal, entrance and hidden staircase on the back side of the building.

Heinrich and Sally found seats shortly before John William Boone made his entrance. After about five minutes, a rather undistinguished tall, thin black man with graying cropped hair appeared on stage. "My name is John Lange, John William Boone's manager," he said. "Since this concert is a benefit, Mr. Boone plans to have a more relaxed evening than his usual performance in a concert hall, so don't be surprised if he acts a little peculiarly.

"One last thing," Lange continued. "Up there in the balcony, could Mr. Boone borrow a child to lead him onstage?"

"Yes'm! My Jeremy'll do it!" yelled a woman's voice. The audience laughed.

"Wonderful. Could you bring him backstage, ma'am?" She nodded and stood up.

A few minutes later, a rotund black man lumbered onto the stage. Only five feet tall, he carried the small black child from the balcony on his shoulders. The little boy gleamed a huge, toothy smile. The boy whispered in Blind Boone's ear and pointed, even though Boone couldn't see his finger. Boone made his way to just short of the edge of the "stage," which was actually the church's raised altar area, and bowed only slightly, as the boy held on for dear life.

"Forgive me, dear audience, for not bowing fully, but we don't want any injuries here tonight," Boone said. The audience laughed and clapped.

Boone found the piano, his enormous "Big U"-shaped monstrosity, specially built for him by the Chickering Piano Co. He swung the boy down onto the mahogany piano bench and patted his shoulder. The boy began to get up, but Boone shook his head and grabbed his arm.

"Son, can you name me a bird?"

"A bird?"

"Yes, son, name me a type of bird."

"Uh, whipporwill," the boy said with a slight stutter.

Boone played a sound like a whippoorwill on the piano. The audience cheered. "I'll play a whole song about the whipporwill later," he said. "Any others?"

"How 'bout a woodpecker?" the boy asked.

"That's too easy," Boone said, and knocked on the wood of the piano with his fist. The boy laughed, and the audience roared. Boone thanked the boy and sent him scurrying backstage to his mother.

Boone began the main event with a rendition of Franz Liszt's Piano Concerto Number Two in A major, and then announced that he would play his own *Aurora Waltz*, a lilting melody, followed by his *Josephine Polka*, a soft dance, and his *Grand Valse de Concert*, a waltz. Heinrich was struck by the pianist's feather-like touch on the keys, the lilting, angelic tone of his harmonies, and his ability to blend elements of classical with ragtime music. While Scott Joplin was better known for his ragtime, Boone was a classical specialist first and a ragtimer second.

"We're in the presence of greatness," Sally whispered.

Boone then presented his soft, playful side with his *Whippoorwill* and *Hummingbird*. He pointed up to the balcony. "Now Jeremy, you listen for that whippoorwill, you hear? And see if you hear the quick hummingbird too."

After finishing his bird pieces, he played a rendition of the familiar hymn, *Nearer My God to Thee* and told the crowd they could sing along if they wanted to. Heinrich sang, in his rich baritone, and Sally followed, but not many audience members joined in, preferring to listen.

The chorus at first sounded a bit like an uncertain small church congregation, not quite confident in its singing ability and not quite in time with the booming piano, but their singing improved as the hymn went on. Boone finished with a dramatic ending that brought loud applause.

"I don't know," Boone kidded the audience after wiping perspiration from his brow with a white handkerchief. "I think First Baptist had a better handle on it!" The audience laughed appreciatively.

Before ending his printed performance with his loud signature piece, the *Marshfield Tornado*, Boone told the audience he had written it to represent the storm that had destroyed the town of Marshfield, Missouri, in 1880. The audience gave it a standing ovation, and, after the concert, Heinrich could hear audience members buzzing about how the piece was so realistic it gave them chills. Heinrich thought they must have had very active imaginations.

But Boone had more to give, and the audience would have been disappointed if he had stopped with the printed performance. John Lange came back out on stage, while "Blind" Boone drank a glass of water. The Tornado piece clearly took a great amount of energy – Heinrich had heard somewhere that Blind Boone had broken pianos playing it in the past, which is why he needed to use his special, heavy-duty instrument – and he was sweating heavily. Boone wiped his face with a handkerchief, while Lange gave his pitch.

"I have here in my hand a $1,000 bill," Lange said, stretching it gingerly between his hands and holding it above his head for the audience to see. "If Mr. Boone can't replay your song by ear, after you play it for him, you will earn this $1,000 bill."

Abuzz with excitement, the audience watched as, one by one, many of its members trooped up on the stage and plinked out tunes from *Mary Had a Little Lamb* to the "Alleluia Chorus" from Handel's *Messiah*. Boone played them all back from memory, even including the mistakes, and it earned him another standing ovation. Nobody won the bet that night.

The performance reminded Heinrich of the music parties his family would have on Sunday evenings back home. Boone rewarded the standing ovation with a double encore of his *Southern Rag Medley* and Stephen Foster's *Old Folks at Home*. After finishing, he rose from the bench and waved to the crowd.

"Good night, you've been a wonderful audience," he said. "Thank you all, but especially Jeremy, for helping me on stage!" He pointed into the balcony to Jeremy and then exited to thunderous applause.

On the way home to Franklinton the next day, Heinrich took a leisurely pace, not pushing his horse as hard as he had on the trip to Jefferson City. Sally had left in her motorcar early in the morning, after a bacon-and-egg breakfast with German potato pancakes under the icy glare of Frau Schmidt, who had clearly surmised that some hanky-panky had been going on between them during the night, a deduction that was entirely correct. Heinrich guessed it wasn't the illicit liaison that bothered Schmidt, just the fact that it had occurred within her domain and without her permission. Still, she said nothing about the matter, merely kept to her business. After all, they had paid for two rooms.

He thought about Blind Boone's performance and felt inspired by the picture it had given of a man so full of life and at peace with himself. Perhaps the hope for American reconciliation between the races might lie in music. After all, the man's music appealed to white and black alike, and Boone's motto, "Merit, not sympathy, wins," restated well the sentiment of the American Dream, Heinrich thought, combining the democratic American belief that people should succeed on their qualities alone with their always-present desire to venerate a winner. Perhaps there is hope for us someday, he thought, a future day when all Americans logically might allow blacks and other ethnic groups to rise on the strength of their own characters.

Of course, Tommy Lee's chance to rise had been stolen from him. Perhaps the turn of thought back to Tommy was inevitable; after all, it had been the true purpose for Heinrich's visit, for which the Blind Boone concert had provided good cover.

The temperature for the return trip back up the Franklinton Road was less bitingly cold, partly because his slower pace didn't generate as much wind in his face. Heinrich also sensed that today's air was more humid than the day before, and a light drizzle began to fall as his horse loped casually forward. Heinrich barely noticed, his thoughts having turned to his ever-present doubts that Tommy's real killer had been found.

The trial testimony gnawed at him. John Fairchild had insisted that there was something wrong with Tommy before the Kappa Psis had grabbed him, as if Tommy were drugged. Could there be something to that line of thinking? The amanita mushrooms were the obvious candidate. Assuming Tommy had ingested them, who provided them, and why? Heinrich knew he didn't have all the pieces to the jigsaw puzzle yet.

That was perhaps the biggest problem to solve, the motive. As far as he knew, except for a small number of students, everybody liked Tommy. And Tommy hadn't interacted all that much with the townspeople, as far as Heinrich could see. If someone unconnected with the college were the culprit, there had to be an emotional reason. Racism, perhaps? That was certainly rampant. Truman Fairchild would be a good bet. He had been known to rail against "slanty-eyed devils" in the past. Heinrich made a mental note to speak with the sheriff, Murphy, Dahlen, and Sally about the matter; perhaps they might know of townspeople who might have carried a grudge against Tommy.

As for the mushrooms, the Chinese grocer said he did not sell the poisonous amanita variety. Perhaps he was lying. Heinrich stewed on the thought, but it seemed unlikely. What motive would the shop owner have to kill a Chinese boy who was a customer? Could Tommy have angered him somehow, violating some sort of cultural honor code and then exacting retribution? The man had given Heinrich no hint of such a possibility, and Tommy probably would have mentioned such a clan conflict if it had existed. Tommy's personal problems lay with American college boys, not Chinese grocers, Heinrich figured.

After McGovern had pinpointed the substance in the cup and bag, Heinrich had looked up the subject in the library and had learned that the amatoxins given off by the amanita mushroom caused medical conditions such as fever, abdominal cramps, nausea, vomiting and diarrhea, followed by delirium, coma and death. Could Tommy have been in the early stages leading to a coma when John Fairchild and his cohorts grabbed him? It made sense.

If so, who gave Tommy the amanita mushrooms? That question brought the puzzle back to motive. Who, other than the Kappa Psis, wanted Tommy dead? What other motive might there be? The puzzle still lacked many pieces; Heinrich would need to find them somehow.

He touched the Teutonic cross in his breast pocket, unconsciously hoping for some luck to rub off, he thought to himself. The cross was a symbol, and symbols often drive men to do strange things. He thought of the elaborate prank set up by the Kappa Psis and their racist symbols. What might Tommy's death mean in symbolic terms to his killer? Oriental symbols, perhaps? He remembered Tommy's pocket watch, with its Taoist message of yin and yang. Yin and Yang, hard and soft, light and darkness, male and female? What did it all mean? That line of reasoning came to an end rather abruptly, leaving Heinrich stumped atop his horse. He needed to learn more. He touched his Teutonic cross again and prayed for guidance.

"Two," Sally said as she discarded two cards from her poker hand onto the table. Receiving her draw with her left hand, she placed the two cards into their proper places in her hand and moved one card from right to left.

She grinned. "Before I forget, I do want to thank the law firm of Murphy, Dahlen, and Kueter for inviting me to your Friday night poker game," she said.

Murphy laughed and replied, "No problem, Sally. If you suffragettes want to vote like men, you need to learn how to waste your money too."

"Yes, we are always ready, here at Murphy's, to fleece a new pigeon," Dahlen added.

Sally grinned again. "Perhaps the next hand," she said.

She lay down a full house, kings over threes; raked the penny-ante pot, worth up to about 50 cents, toward her; and began to stack the pennies.

Kueter groaned. "Never played poker before, eh?"

She batted her eyelashes. "Little old me? I just wanted to see what goes on in the back room of this saloon."

Murphy laughed and spread his arms wide to the display of

wooden crates and barrels of various spirits. "It's certainly shocking, I'm sure, but unfortunately my back room offers none of the evil pleasures available at the Lucky Strike."

"So I've heard," she said. "Prostitution, opium, and rigged roulette, I believe. Perhaps it's time you caught up with the competition, Murphy."

Murphy laughed. Heinrich looked uncomfortable, and Sally put her hand on his arm.

"Don't worry, dear, it's just a joke," she said.

"It's a cultural thing," he said. "We Germans believe in protecting our women from the dirty world of men."

"We women bear the effects of men's vices directly," she retorted. "We may as well confront those vices honestly."

Heinrich could certainly see the logic of the argument, but it still made him uncomfortable on an elemental level.

Murphy dealt another hand. As Sally adjusted her cards, she said, "Actually, I have secret, scandalous information that I'm dealing with right now. You'll see it in tomorrow's edition."

The men eyed her silently. "Okay, so tell us," Kueter said.

"I'm not sure how to say this in a ladylike fashion, so I'm just going to lay it out on the table," she said. "The Democratic Club held a wild Christmas party last month for supporters of the machine for their help in guaranteeing success in the recent elections. Apparently, the festivities included a dozen fallen women brought in from Kansas City."

Murphy whistled. "Sounds like a Fairchild operation," he said.

"Precisely," she said. "We live in a cruel world, gentlemen, and it exploits women who find themselves in desperate straits. It's just another reason we need the vote, and it's why women overwhelmingly support the Temperance Movement."

"And that is why the liquor industry will continue to fight against the women's vote," Kueter said. "They fear you."

"If the liquor industry were smarter, it would clean up its involvement with sordid behavior in the backrooms of its saloons and support moderate women who desire the vote," she replied. "Otherwise, when women eventually get our due rights, the militant crusaders may attain Prohibition soon after."

Murphy nodded silently, suddenly afraid for his business. Heinrich put down his discards and asked for three cards in return.

The scandal over Sally's story the next day raged for a couple of weeks. Most women were shocked at the actions of their menfolk. Male opinion split along social and political lines, with many angry that she had published the sordid affair, either because she had outed their backroom behavior or because of the strongly held Victorian belief that such matters should be kept secret. Sally's story included interviews with two of the prostitutes; that Sally made the effort to track them down and speak with them also caused much consternation, especially among the town's female population.

In subsequent stories, before he eventually stopped commenting on the issue, Truman Fairchild told the St. Louis Post-Dispatch that it was a "damned lie, concocted by political foes to ruin me and to fight my policies, which are vital to the interest of the community."

Privately, Fairchild vowed revenge.

After several delays, the faculty tribunal deciding Heinrich's fate met again on Wednesday, February 25. The penguins in their black robes and mortarboard hats regally marched into Smith Lecture Hall again and sat down in unison.

As before, Heinrich sat front and center in the audience section. The tribunal sat solemnly in their black academic robes at the maple lecture table in front of the slate chalkboard. In an earlier class, some English professor had written on the black chalkboard in white letters, "In all things it is better to hope than to despair. – Goethe."

Also as before, President Tichenor and Chairman Goforth were seated to Heinrich's right. Tichenor's face held a look of imperiousness, and Goforth simply looked ill, which Heinrich assumed did not portend well for his case.

The chairman, seated in the middle, rose to speak. "Professor Heinrich Kueter," said Latin Professor Purcell, the tribunal chairman. "You are accused of conduct unbecoming of your rank and status as an instructor on the faculty at Worcester College. You have testified in your defense that you were simply defending yourself against an attack from Truman Fairchild, one of our town's leading citizens, outside a tent revival meeting. Is that still your defense?"

Heinrich nodded.

Purcell continued. "After extensive review of your testimony, this tribunal has come to a decision. Do you wish to make a statement before we announce the verdict?"

Heinrich nodded. "As I stated previously, I regret my involvement in the unfortunate incidents under question in this proceeding. However, my motives have always been pure, either when simply defending myself or defending the memory of the recently deceased."

Heinrich looked at Goforth, who had covered his face by his

hands. Apparently, Heinrich had little to lose. With a sudden burst of inspiration, he decided to continue.

"As you gentleman know, our town's founding fathers named this community in honor of Benjamin Franklin, a man renowned for his innovative mind and an important voice for respect and tolerance in colonial America and the Revolution," Heinrich said. "Likewise, The Scottish Presbyterians who founded this college chose Worcester, at which the Scots battled the English in defense of their liberty. Our predecessors searched for a name that would stand for their continual fight for the democratic spirit of the Scottish Kirk and its Presbyterian church government, which would later form the basis for the Constitution of the United States. During the Revolution, Worcester became a symbol of our nation's similar conflict with England.

"But the desire for political freedom rages in the hearts of many peoples, not just the Britons. Friedrich Muench pointed out in his writings before the Civil War that the desire for freedom drives all the Germanic peoples, including the Britons and Americans, toward a better world civilization. A 'truly free Germany, England, and North America, united in close association, could force the rest of the world to strive for humane institutions and clear away the last vestiges of barbarism,' he said, and 'the more the German element…in North American life asserts itself, the more it assumes decisive influence over the future course of human history.'

"My ancestors left Germany to regain their rights in the light of American liberty, as many other peoples from around the globe continue to do so to this day. At the heart of that democratic ideal lies a respect for the importance and dignity of each individual, no matter his race or creed.

"Unfortunately, many in this town and college have forgotten that proud history and have chosen instead to follow a path of intolerance and injustice against those who look different or act differently than they. All of my actions, some of which I admit have been regrettably overzealous, have been taken against such intolerance. No matter what happens here today, I intend to continue to fight for justice and the rights of each individual, no matter his ethnicity or country of origin. You can depend on that."

Heinrich sat down. "A fine speech, Professor Kueter; however, many I am sure would disagree with your assessment of the motives of others," Dr. Purcell said. "This faculty tribunal will now deliver its verdict. Mr. Conrad, would you please read the verdict?"

The faculty member on Purcell's right stood. "We find professor Kueter guilty on all counts," he said, and sat down.

Purcell turned to his left. "Mr. DeSalle, please give the sentence."

DeSalle stood. "Mr. Kueter, you are to make immediate written apology to the college for your action. In addition, at the conclusion of this semester, your teaching duties will be terminated, and you will be expelled from the faculty, unless the president of the college commutes the sentence."

"All rise," Purcell said. After everyone in the room had complied, the penguins once again waddled out of the room, leaving Heinrich to be thankful that he at least had a job until spring.

Officially drummed out of the corps, Heinrich glanced at Tichenor's smirking face, gritted his teeth, and climbed the slope to exit the lecture hall.

CHAPTER 7

"...And therefore, Professor Jamison suggests that the Second Boer War could be the last of the colonialist wars this century," Heinrich said.

"Except for the Moro rebellion in the Philippines," responded Arnold Brady, a bright student in Heinrich's world history seminar. Brady was a tall, skinny kid with orange hair, a ruddy complexion, and freckles.

"Right, although we, of course, are merely bringing civilization to our brown brothers...at the point of a sword, naturally," Heinrich answered. "That's our story, and we're sticking to it!"

The class laughed. Heinrich pulled Tommy's brass pocket watch from his vest, opened it, and took a quick look. "All right, then. Please read chapter four, and I'll see you on Friday."

He waved as the young men scrambled from the class, eager to catch the end of a relatively warm, though windy, March afternoon. At lunch, Murphy and Dahlen had said they thought spring might be here for good, while Sally had stood against them saying it was a false spring. Heinrich wisely had demurred to her point of view.

Heinrich glanced at his watch again, then looked up to find Arnold Brady standing before him. There was something strangely familiar about the boy, but Heinrich couldn't put his finger on it.

"Professor Kueter," Brady said. "I've been trying to find the right time to tell you this."

"Yes?"

"There are quite a few of us, in fact many in my Gamma Sig fraternity, for instance, who are extremely angry about your being let go."

In Heinrich's eyes, the Gamma Sigma boys were an upstanding bunch, nothing like the Kappa Psis. The Gamma Sigs had fetched the doctor and helped him move Tommy Lee back to the boarding house on the night of the young man's death. The Gamma Sigma fraternity had started in Ohio, and he had heard its membership had more of a Northern-state, pro-Union base. Unlike the Kappa Psis, at least there hadn't been a rabid Nathan Bedford Forrest type among its founders, he thought.

Heinrich raised his palms at his sides. "Thank you for your concern, Mr. Brady, but don't worry too much about it. What's done is done. I have never felt entirely welcome in this town anyway."

Brady nodded. "I understand. That's a problem with this place. I'm half Irish, myself."

Heinrich laughed. "I thought so. The red hair gave you away." Then it dawned on him why he recognized the boy's voice. "I'll bet you're my library whisperer, aren't you?"

Brady bit his lower lip for a few seconds, not sure whether to answer. "Yes, that was me."

"Well your information was quite helpful. Thank you for your courage."

"Thank you, sir. May I say that your steadfast stand for justice provides an example for us all."

Heinrich shrugged. "No good deed goes unpunished, I guess."

"I have contacted my parents, who are good friends with two of the board members. They might be able to get you reinstated."

Heinrich put his right hand on the young man's shoulder. "Mr. Brady, I appreciate the gesture, but I am all right. After all, I am but a small player on this campus. What happens to me really doesn't matter that much in the grand scheme of things."

"Don't say that."

"It's the truth. Perhaps I belong in a larger city anyway."

"But it's wrong!" the young man burst out. "My fraternity brothers and I intend to do something about it."

Heinrich looked him in the eye. "Mr. Brady, once again, I am most touched by your concern, but please don't do anything that would get you into trouble."

The young man nodded. "Don't worry," he said, tipping his hat and leaving.

Of course, rash young men tend toward rash action. Two days later, while headed toward Academic Hall to teach an afternoon class,

Heinrich found himself in the midst of a student protest on his behalf, led by Brady and the Gamma Sigs.

Brady stood on the steps of the Greek Revival building goading about 50 young men through a cheerleader's bullhorn to shout in unison, "Bad Move, Ichabod!" and "Bring Heinie Back!" It wasn't the sort of militant demonstration brought on by a labor dispute; it had the flavor of a college cheering squadron at a football game. At least there would be no big-city mobs of working men armed to the teeth with axe handles and chains and brawling with Pinkerton detectives.

Embarrassed on many levels and unsure how to respond, Heinrich grinned self-consciously; he knew the boys' hearts were in the right place. He glanced up at the window of the president's office on the second floor. Tichenor stood at the window, hands clasped behind his back, stoically surveying the scene below, a sour look on his face. He turned slightly toward Heinrich and glared. Heinrich shrugged his shoulders, his palms facing upward, to signify that the protest was not his doing. Of course, he knew Tichenor would never believe that.

The mob soon spotted Heinrich, and somebody yelled, "Heinie's here." A great cheer rang out. Heinrich blushed. The boys grabbed his arms and pulled him up the steps toward Arnold Brady, who began a new chant, "Speech, speech, speech, speech..."

Heinrich raised his hands to try to calm them down. "Thank you, all of you, for expressing your support. While I appreciate your gesture today, I don't believe this sort of mob action will really help the cause. My current difficulties with the college leadership are not important in themselves. They are just a symptom of the greater problem in this community, in which racism and prejudice are allowed to run rampant. If you are going to demonstrate for a cause, march for tolerance and peace! That would do the world much more good. Thank you."

They cheered. He turned on his heel and headed up the steps into the building to teach his class as Arnold Brady yelled out, "Let's give them one last 'Bring Back Heinie,' before we go home today!"

The chant of "Bring Back Heinie" rang out for another two minutes, followed by somebody yelling "Hip, hip..." and a loud "Hooray!"

As he stepped into his classroom, his chuckling late-morning students gave him an ovation. "Thank you, thank you," the noticeably red-faced Heinrich said. "Now let's get to work."

Squinting down on the demonstration from his office's window on the second floor, President Tichenor's demeanor was downright grim. There would be no cheers from him. In the midst of a meeting with Truman Fairchild, "Ichabod's" face looked a sickly shade of green.

"Jim, as chairman of the Board of Trustees, I must warn you not to let this situation get out of hand," Fairchild said. "Those students must be taught respect for this institution."

Tichenor nodded. "Of course, John, but what can I do? They have a right to assemble and speak their minds."

"It's a problem amongst the boys," said Fairchild, with a thoughtful look on his pudgy face. "Perhaps we should let them handle it for themselves."

Tichenor raised an eyebrow, pondering the potential implications of Fairchild's remark. How would the students "handle it for themselves"? If the political boss intended to generate a melee on his campus, Tichenor would not stand for it.

"Mr. Fairchild, this is my campus. Please do nothing to interfere."

Fairchild said no more. Tichenor picked up the phone and called the college security chief, Daniel "Web" Webber. Looking out the window again, Tichenor could see that Webber had arrived on the scene and was yelling to the crowd, telling the students to disperse peacefully. He hung up the phone and turned back to Fairchild.

"There will be no brawling on my campus," he said. "The crisis is averted."

Fairchild nodded as if in agreement, then quickly moved close to the president and poked him in the chest. "Don't ever talk to me that way again," he snarled. "Don't you ever start believing you can tell me what, or what not, to do. I run this town, and I own you. Without my funds to prop it up, your college would be in serious financial trouble, and you know it."

Tichenor stepped back, his eyes wide with fear. Fairchild calmly turned and put on his hat. "You can't make an omelette without breaking a few eggs," he said on his way out the door.

Patrick Ringgold surveyed the back door of the Gamma Sigma house from behind a hedgerow that marked the property line. Through the eyeholes of his pillowcase hood, he could see only a couple of lights in rooms on the second and third floors.

Truman Fairchild had given him the idea for this bit of bald-knobbing when the gentleman had visited the house the day before. Ringgold, a junior and the house's unofficial leader since the jailing of John Fairchild, had secretly handpicked a group of six other adventuresome Kappa Psi fraternity brothers to take part in this raid on the Gamma Sigs.

An unofficial state of war had existed between the fraternities for several years, with escalating pranks that had turned quite mean recently. The two houses had been trading fire for some time via "human slingshot." To form the siege weapon, two boys would stand facing each other a couple of yards apart, holding rubber surgical tubing between them. A third student then would take up position between them, load a projectile and pull back, stretching the rubber tubing to its furthest extent and then letting go, launching it toward the enemy position. Last year, the projectiles had been innocent water-filled balloons, but over time, the students had graduated to paint-filled balloons, tomatoes, potatoes, firecrackers, dead rodents and even dissected animals, such as frogs, fetal pigs, or cats obtained from the garbage cans behind the science building. This week, the projectile of choice had become 6-or-8-inch rocks, which had broken a few windows in both houses' aging brick edifices before a truce was called between the house presidents.

The young men also would fire bottle rockets and roman candles at each other from time to time, as long as the chance of getting caught was minimal, but the college sternly frowned upon the use of fireworks. A few years back, the college had joined the National Fire Prevention Association's crusade against personal fireworks. A widely publicized 1910 statistic that 600 people died each year in firework-related accidents during the first decade of the new century had stirred popular anger at their irresponsible use. Of course, the students scoffed at such data; after all, they were young, male, and invincible.

As far as Ringgold was concerned, it was time for the Kappa Psis to up the ante on the Gamma Sig menace, and his heart raced with adrenalin on this new covert adventure. He pulled a brass pocketwatch from the right side pocket of his trousers. He had heard that soldiers were starting to use wristwatches, but he doubted it would ever become a fad among "real" men. No sissy wristlet for me, he thought to himself, although he had to admit that the pocketwatch was a bit bulky for an attack operation like this. He could feel it thumping against his thigh in his black wool pants as he sprinted toward the rear French doors of the Gamma Sig house in the moonlight. His assault team wore dark pants and shirts – his was black flannel – for this secret operation.

Pressing flat against the wall beside the door, he waited a minute before peering side to side through the glass. Seeing that the coast was clear, he motioned for his six brothers to join him. Each wore a pillowcase mask and carried a small baseball bat or ax handle as a weapon. Three of them also carried small wooden buckets of red paint with brushes inside.

Ringgold had chosen to carry a cast iron crowbar, mainly to "jimmy" the lock. In the pocket of his black wool jacket, he also carried his black tin Ever Ready flashlight. He had inserted fresh "D" cells earlier in the evening.

Testing the door handle, Ringgold found it securely locked. He wedged the teeth at the end of the crowbar into the space between the French doors just above the locked handles and pried open the door on the second attempt. The wood splintered around the lock, and the door opened with a slight groan of its hinges.

Ringgold hurriedly led the young men inside. They quickly moved up a hallway to the front foyer. There were no lights; the gas fixtures were off downstairs, although lantern light and laughter trickled down the stairway from an upstairs room. Ringgold shared a grin with his compatriots and pantomimed the act of drinking from a bottle. They smiled.

From the foyer, they turned right into the house's living room. It was pitch black. Ringgold switched on his flashlight and hooked the nickel-plated, glove-catch switch to keep the light on continuously. He shone its weak glow around the room, providing him and his accomplices with just enough illumination to catch their bearings.

Shining the light on the giant green and yellow Gamma Sigma crest above the fireplace mantel, Ringgold motioned to two boys and pointed there. They sprang into action, painting words above the crest in red, "N...I...G..." and so on, as he held the light. As they were close to finishing spelling out "Nigger Lovers" in foot-high letters, he moved his light to the opposite wall to check on the progress of other teams.

Two other youths were finishing "We Love Chinks" there, while a third pair worked on a cursive "Heinie Kraut Bastards" with artistic flair on the top of the grand piano in the corner. Enjoy the music, assholes, Ringgold thought to himself with a chuckle.

After they had finished their dirty work, Ringgold circled his index finger in the air. Grabbing their paint buckets, the boys headed for the front door. But as they reached the front foyer, a shout came from upstairs. "Hey! What are you doing? Fellows, wake up!"

Somebody charged into the foyer from the kitchen area, and one of Ringgold's boys quickly clobbered him in the gut with an ax handle. When the boy doubled over, another Kappa hit him in the head, and he went down for the count.

"Front door, go now!" Ringgold said in a loud whisper as he pointed. They ran from the foyer, exiting the front door with Gamma Sigs coming down the stairs close behind them. As a last gesture of humiliation, on their way by, they dumped their leftover red paint onto the stone lions that stood guard outside the front door and tossed the cans and brushes into an alley garbage pile as they ran away into the night.

Sitting across from President Tichenor's desk, Truman Fairchild's blood boiled. Such insolence, from a woman no less, would never have happened in Kansas City. Jim and Tom Pendergast would never let an affront like this stand. It was time to unleash his muscle.

"Just listen to her editorial, Jim," he said. "'The recent actions by racist fraternity members against the Gamma Sigma fraternity house on campus are appalling and simply should not be tolerated in a civilized society. Unfortunately, our town and our whole nation have tolerated such antics and worse for years.'

"'What else should we expect,'" he continued. "'Our young men have learned through the actions of older Know-Nothings and night marauders that such vigilante violence is a proper function of society. These are the fruits of past efforts, stemming from the stain of past lynchings of Negroes to more recent vandalism against Irish businessmen, harassment of Germans, and murders of Chinamen.' Can you believe that?"

Tichenor nodded, recognizing the uncomfortable nature of the situation. For a moment, he wished he had never come out here to Indian Territory. He didn't know what else to do. He couldn't afford to stand against Fairchild, but he knew the Kappa Psis had crossed a line with this recent escapade. He could lose control of the student population entirely if he completely ignored the incident. It had the clear mark of another prank gone too far, and he already had directed the dean of students to investigate it.

"This too shall pass, Truman. It's only words," Tichenor said.

Fairchild shook his head. "She's blown up a stupid prank, a simple case of youthful high spirits, beyond all proportion, and she's comparing that to the actions of your crazy Heinie history professor, who attacked one of your students and me in cold blood. What are you going to do about it?"

"I learned early on that you never take on somebody who buys ink by the barrel," Tichenor said.

"That's horse hockey, and you know it," Fairchild said, forcefully poking Tichenor's mahogany desk with his finger. "These foreigner-lovers are dragging me, my town, and our college through the mud. What's more, they're ripping at the fabric of our way of life. They're not going to get away with it, not if I have anything to say about it."

Fairchild stood up, turned on his heel and left the room. Tichenor quickly followed him to the door. "Truman, get hold of yourself. Don't do anything rash."

"Oh, it won't be rash, believe me," Fairchild said. "But it will be strong."

As Fairchild strode away, Tichenor hoped it wouldn't be deadly either.

Sally was proud of her first op-ed about racism and vigilantism thriving in Franklinton. It certainly had caused a stir, judging from newspaper sales and the buzz around town. Her follow-up would cause an even bigger one when the next edition was distributed in the late morning. As she read the copy one last time in the lamplight, she decided it was some of her best work. She enjoyed fighting the good fight; it got her blood flowing.

She looked up at her father's photo on the wall, staring down at her with that stern look that all Victorian photos seemed to show. Photographic plates were expensive, and it took time to get a good exposure, so photographers of that day often requested that subjects keep their lips closed. The grim visage did not suit her father, Thaddeus Giddings. He was full of life, always quick with a joke, and he was considered a man of great business acumen and a fearless newsman, even though he had always felt like something of an outsider in Franklinton because his father had taken a difficult stand as a staunch Union man in Little Dixie during the Civil War. Leading a company of Union militia, her grandfather had hunted bushwhackers before being killed during Sterling Price's 1864 raid through Missouri.

Sally's mother had died giving birth to a stillborn brother when Sally was three years old, so it had just been her and her father for most of her life. It was she and daddy against the world, that is, until her father caught typhoid fever during a business visit to New York in 1906. Inheriting the newspaper upon his death, she had promised herself that she would live up to his example of fearlessness.

The problem was she hadn't counted on falling in love; it certainly changed the equation. Even with his paternalistic side, perhaps Heinrich would be strong enough not to make her give up her calling in return for a marriage bed.

She glanced at the clock, and noted that it was nearing 1:15 in the morning. She really should be heading home. The printing press had been acting up lately, so she had stayed late making sure tomorrow's edition would be ready for distribution in the morning. She often did so, putting the paper to bed only shortly before she put herself there. Fred Carnahan, the pressman, would be in before dawn to print the paper.

There was a soft knock at the door. That was strange. Peering outside cautiously from behind a curtain, she saw nothing. She quickly snuffed out her dim lamp, unsure who might be calling at this time of night. Whoever it was, he certainly was up to no good. Something wasn't right.

She was about to ask, "Carnahan, is that you?" when a red brick crashed through the front window, just missing her. In the moonlight, she could see a man's hairy hand reach through and open the brass doorknob.

Truly frightened now, Sally ran into the back room, past the new Petersen Linograph machine, and hid behind the 13-foot-long Campbell Country Newspaper press, which filled the back of the room. She swore and prayed under her breath. Heinrich would not have approved of her language, she knew.

Crouching as low as she could get in her dress and black-buttoned shoes, she groped for a weapon in the dark. Her fingers found first an oily rag and then a foot-long wrench Carnahan used to install the printing plates.

She could hear several men milling around and snickering. Hopefully, this was just a retaliatory prank and not something more sinister.

"Did you hear something?" said a voice she didn't recognize.

"No, let's just do the job and be quick about it." That voice she recognized. It was Truman Fairchild.

Then a tin can crinkled, followed by the sound of splashes. She smelled the heady odor of kerosene. Her life was in danger now! She needed to escape.

She knew the back door in the hall alcove between the pressroom and newsroom would be her best hope. She crawled carefully toward the arched entranceway into the hall. Her skirt caught on a splinter in the plank floor. At least the dress protected her knees.

There were several loud crashes of metal hitting wood and scattering chunks of metal, like heavy dice being thrown on the wood floor. She knew what that sound meant. They were dumping and breaking up the typeset pages. Damn barbarians!

She peered out into the hall. The coast was clear, so she stood up and sprinted for the back door. If she could just turn the handle to pop it open, she'd be home…

Then something metallic hit her on the back of her head. She pitched forward, out cold, crumpled in a heap of skirts on the hardwood floor.

Before setting fire to the newspaper building, Fairchild and his half-dozen roughnecks had attached chains to a team of four mules. They dragged the press and linograph out onto the back loading dock and onto a waiting heavy buckboard, hitched to a team of four horses.

He felt no remorse about the woman. She got what she deserved, spreading her lies. He only regretted that his men hadn't found her first. When they had searched the newspaper office, they had found her warm lamp, but could not find her. At first, they figured she had run out through the loading dock, but they hadn't checked closely enough. Now she had to die. Perhaps it was better that way. It would end any threat from her for good.

Fairchild ordered the men to leave her in the hallway. It wouldn't be long before she succumbed to the smoke. Fairchild took her kerosene lamp, lit it, threw it into the press room just beyond the loading dock, and watched a sheet of yellow flame jump up in a stack of paper.

Yelling a loud, "Yah!" to get the horses moving, he and his men raced out of the alley and down the street, out of town. They wouldn't stop until they hit the river. That's where the silenced press would end up, dumped in the waters of the Big Muddy, next to an old steamboat wreck that served as a memorial to the industry that had built the town.

Headed back from Murphy's, Heinrich and Manfred were walking to the Austrian's home behind the stable to play a game of rummy, but they never reached it. They were discussing Hegel's philosophy when Heinrich spotted the newspaper building going up in flames.

"I'll go get the sheriff!" Dahlen said, and ran eastward through the street.

Heinrich sprinted up to the front door and peered inside. He could see what looked like a pile of clothing at the back of the center hallway near the rear door. Then he saw the pile move! The heap had a head. Sally!

The fire was too hot at the front, so he ran to the southeast corner of the building, then down the side alley to the back door. The loading

146

dock was open, but it was filled with flames too. He tried the back door and recoiled when it burnt his hand.

"Damn!" he explained, at his scorched fingers. At least the door was unlocked. He pulled down his sleeve to cover his palm and opened it.

He quickly pushed open the door, located Sally beyond the flames on the hallway floor and ran to her. He knelt and put his face close to hers. Only partially conscious, she mumbled something unintelligible. He scooped her up; she was as limp as a pile of laundry. He ran outside and took off as fast as he could down the alley toward the doctor's office, praying to God that she would be all right.

Doc put a hand on Heinrich's shoulder as he watched Sally's covered body sleep, limp on the bed in the physician's office. Her blonde hair lay across the gingham pillowcase in a dreamy scene of deceptive stillness. He and the doctor had removed her cream-colored dress, which was streaked with grease, blood and soot from the newspaper fire, before putting her beneath several blankets to ward off potential shock. The doctor wiped smudges of soot from her face with a damp towel.

"There's nothing more you can do, son."

"I told her to be careful," Heinrich said, angry at himself.

"She's a big girl, Heinrich. You know as well as I do that she rarely takes direction," Doc said.

Heinrich nodded. He loved her for it.

"Will she make it?"

"I don't know," Doc said. "She breathed in a whole lot of smoke, she's unconscious, and her neck is broken. I don't know if she'll walk again."

It took a moment for that news to sink in. "Who would do such a thing?" Heinrich asked out loud, although deep down he already knew. No matter what, he would avenge this attack. It was way past personal now.

For several days, Heinrich lived in a daze, going through the motions of his routines and doing his job. He answered expressions of sympathy from colleagues and students with a blank expression and a limp, "Thank you."

"It was a terrible thing." Well-meaning people had told him that so often that he wanted to hit the next person who said it. He screamed at

God too at least once a day, usually silently in his room, but he gave it full voice once while walking in the woods alone. He would curse God one moment, and then quickly apologize in prayer. He knew blasphemy and vulgarity would do Sally no good now, but it seemed to help him cope a little, just the same.

He visited Sally every afternoon before going to supper, held her hand and tried to talk to her. Doc was worried. The aging physician had thought she might come out of the coma, but now he wasn't so sure.

Heinrich drank too much every night for several days. Murphy and Dahlen dragged him home one night, and Mrs. Yaeger did not say a word. She just gave him a pitiful look as his friends slung him onto his bed and took off his shoes. If she felt remorse over her disapproval of Heinrich's relationship with Sally, the proud landlady keep such feelings to herself.

A week after the fire, he woke up hung over and angry as usual – angry at God, the world, and especially the people who would even dream of hurting Sally.

On his lunch hour, he walked downtown to Watkins General Store. Over the past few months, he had been eyeing the pistol in the display case, lying one shelf below the jars of tubestick candy and lemon drops, over the past few months. The "black lady" was familiar. It was a Colt .45 service revolver, just like the one that had brought him through the Philippines campaign. The urge to feel the familiar heavy steel in his hand and its powerful recoil again had become too powerful to ignore.

It was time; psychologically, he needed to arm himself. He asked George Watkins, the store owner, to let him look at the pistol. The leather grip fit his hand like a glove. He sighted the weapon on the far wall, pretending to aim at an imaginary Moro warrior, just like the one he had dropped in the Jolo marketplace — only this time, Truman Fairchild, with his cold, beady eyes, was wearing the turban.

Yes, he wanted this metal lady; he needed her. He had no plan yet, but he would soon. He purchased the gun, along with an Army surplus holster and a couple of boxes of ammunition.

He thanked the proprietor and turned toward the door. Beside the door, Sheriff Thackeray leaned against an open barrel of brown leather work gloves, trying on a pair.

"Going to do some target shooting, Heinrich?"

Heinrich nodded. He said nothing.

The sheriff lowered his voice and looked him straight in the eye. "Don't do anything stupid. You let the law handle this, you hear?"

Heinrich nodded. He'd leave matters to the law for now, but he felt better holding the firearm. Now he was ready, ready for anything that would come his way.

Later that same afternoon, Heinrich stood in class, his back turned to the students. As he erased his notes from the chalkboard, a commotion blew up behind him. He whirled around to find two students circling, Arnold Brady of the Gamma Sigs and Patrick Ringgold of the Kappa Psis. A crowd of the other young men, unsure what to do but fascinated by the fight, had formed around the combatants as they swung punches.

"Take it back, swine," Ringgold said through gritted teeth.

"Afraid of the truth, are you? You racist thug," Brady responded.

Ringgold lunged and connected with a right cross on Brady's chin. Brady staggered back, then came again at Ringgold, who bobbed and weaved, keeping away from the other youth's punches.

Heinrich rushed forward and put himself between them. "What in blazes are you doing? This is a classroom, for Christ's sake."

Ringgold growled. "I don't have to take any guff from you, you goddam Kraut!"

He then swung a right round-house punch, this time at Heinrich. Heinrich stepped back, allowing the punch to miss by inches. He then stepped forward, grabbed Ringgold's arm and pulled it downward. At virtually the same time, untwisting his upper body like an uncoiling spring, Heinrich hit Ringgold in the back of his head with his elbow. Ringgold dropped to the floor.

"In my class, you'll take whatever I give you," Heinrich said.

Another Kappa Psi, Bart Connelly, shooting Heinrich a dirty look, bent down to help his friend stand up.

As Connelly helped him to his feet and pulled him out the classroom door, Ringgold spat at Heinrich, "We're not done with you, Heinie! Not by a long shot!"

Heinrich, watching the door warily, figured as much.

Web Webber ran his hands through what was left of his gray hair as Tichenor eyed him icily. College security wasn't supposed to be this difficult. Usually, the worst part of the job involved emptying bottles of smuggled liquor onto the ground.

"You're telling me that you cannot control the rabble?" Tichenor asked, but it wasn't really a question. "Then, tell me again: What do I pay you for?"

Webber grew irritable. "Mr. President, I'm giving you an honest assessment of the situation on your campus. Sir, this battle between the Kappa Psis and Gamma Sigs has grown to the point that other students and even whole fraternities are taking sides. There are fights breaking out all over campus, with rival bands ambushing other students. Events are quickly spiraling out of control into a full-blown student civil war, and I do not have the resources to control it."

"Then what do you suggest, Mr. Webber?"

"Get the sheriff in here immediately, and seriously consider a request to the governor to get help from the state militia," Webber said.

Tichenor blinked. "You can't be serious. I have many donors whose sons have apparently taken leading roles in this unfortunate affair. I cannot afford to alienate them, not when we are so close to meeting our fundraising goals. Why, I just had Truman Fairchild in here warning me that if I do anything, he'll pull his gift for the library wing."

Webber was furious now. "Dammit, sir, if we're not careful, pretty soon there may not be a library! We're damn near close to anarchy here, and you're sitting here fiddling while the campus burns!"

Tichenor rose to his feet. "How dare you swear at me, you washed-up reject from the police department! You are dismissed, you hear! Permanently!"

Webber smashed his right fist into Tichenor's chin, and President Ichabod crumpled to the floor. He leaned over Tichenor. "That's all right, Mr. President, sir, because I quit. I'd rather work in a goddam factory."

Webber marched out of Tichenor's office, thinking a factory was probably where he would wind up now. But it had been worth every tooth scrape on his knuckles. Let the campus burn on Ichabod's watch. It would serve him right.

Taking his firearm along for company, Heinrich had left campus after the classroom confrontation to clear his head. He intended to find an isolated spot to get some target practice. Lost in thought and high on the adrenaline from the fight, he walked a long distance that cold afternoon. It had been a tough day.

He started walking along the creek but then began to randomly take this dirt path and that, muttering to himself and alternating between despair and fits of rage at his situation. The love of his life lay in a coma, possibly dying, and he had been forced to trade fisticuffs with racist hooligans.

Heinrich walked for at least an hour and a half. He really didn't know where he was going. It was as if he were being led somewhere he had never seen for some purpose he could not comprehend.

He was on somebody's farm now, well outside of town. As he crested the next hill, he could see a large lake, probably man-made, but much larger than the average farm pond, probably about an acre in size. The far bank appeared to be far away across the water.

Someone had built a small sand beach at the southern end of the lake. Heinrich felt drawn to it. He walked down the hill toward the sand.

Then he saw the sign: Franklinton Reservoir. Okay. It was the town's water supply. That made sense.

He thought of turning, but something compelled him toward the beach. He walked onto the sand and sat down on a wrought-iron bench. Suddenly feeling exhausted, he leaned back, the revolver beside him, and watched the sun play on the water. It was tranquil. He watched a duck paddle across the water. Then his eyelids drooped, and he fell asleep.

He was no longer on the shore of Franklinton Lake. He was on the shore of Lake Michigan. Looking east and west, he recognized the confines of Evanston's Greenwood Beach, his father's favorite childhood hangout. His father had wiled away many a summer there, long before he ever became Papa Kueter. But the scene had a strange amber glow, as if from a constant sunset. The scene was not of this world. Heinrich's skin tingled with goosebumps as he let the golden, liquid air of the magical place wash over him like a waterfall.

Time stood still as a young man emerged from the water, dripping and grinning in the sun. "Isn't it great, my boy?"

Heinrich squinted. "Dad?"

It was indeed his father, but a much younger version wearing old-fashioned swimming clothes with long shorts and a striped shirt.

His father stood before him, speaking directly into his mind without using his bronze-tinted lips. Heinrich stammered something unintelligible.

"Son, I just wanted you to know that I am where I want to be. It's great fun. No time to discuss. I have a message for you. Everything is going to be all right. Remember your Teutonic Cross. Let it lead you. Follow the cross no matter where it takes you. Remember, everything is going to be all right..."

His father's voice faded, and the image melted away. Heinrich awoke with a start. He was on the shore of Lake Franklinton again, with a cow mooing nearby.

Heinrich shook his head to clear it. He knew it was just a dream, but it was a special dream, a transforming dream. It felt much more real than the usual night-time hallucination. He wondered if he would ever be the same. He felt a rush of adrenaline surge through his body.

As he retraced his steps, he ran it through in his mind. Apparently, he had been led to that spot at that moment to receive that message: everything is going to be all right. The implications were difficult to fathom. Perhaps it meant there was a reason for all of this, for him, for his predicament.

Above all, he had no more time for anger at the Lord. Heinrich would simply have to let God's time play itself out. Perhaps he really was in the capable hands of an all-knowing God.

He laughed to himself when a rather silly thought flashed through is mind: If this was how predestination worked, maybe he'd have to join the Calvinist Presbyterians after all.

As with most altercations between groups of young men, what came to be known as the Battle of the Greeks began as a rather innocent tangling of antlers. According to later reports, Arnold Brady of the Gamma Sigs made the mistake of walking past the Kappa Psi house, although others would later say that Brady did it intentionally, starting the altercation on purpose.

Sitting on the front porch, Ringgold yelled something hostile about staying away from Kappa territory, adding some fine Anglo-Saxon epithets regarding Brady's ancestry and sexual proclivities. Brady responded in kind with similarly heated words and a raised middle finger. The situation then quickly escalated when Ringgold charged across the lawn to confront Brady up close. They exchanged more words and grappled.

Riggold shoved Brady, who slipped on gravel in the street and fell to his knees. Angered by Ringgold's assault, Brady grabbed a white pebble and flung it at his assailant.

Unfortunately, Brady's aim was off. The rock zinged past Ringgold's ear and shattered one of the front windows in the Kappa Psi house. The clatter of broken glass brought a dozen more Kappas running out to survey the damage and to back up Ringgold.

Meanwhile, two houses down the street, a whistle blew, and about 20 young Gammas came running out of their house to the defense of their president. Half of them carried baseball bats or axe handles, and a couple carried chains. Others picked up bricks or sticks along the way. The weapons were of the type commonly preferred by striking workmen, but in this case, the young men weren't demonstrating for workers' rights. This fight was about masculine pride, about pure tribal dominance, fueled by the hearty anger and fiery testosterone of youth.

Seeing the advancing force, the Kappas yelled for reinforcements, and the Gammas did the same. Within 15 minutes, about 80 young men in wool jackets and shirtsleeves filled the front lawn of the Kappa Psi house, engaged in hand-to-hand combat with their hated rivals. Wounded students fell to the ground as arms and legs grappled in the grass, fists, knees, and elbows flying. Some fell with more serious wounds in the full-blown melee as bats, axe handles, shovels, chains and knives hit their mark.

Heinrich, returning from his walk, came upon the scene in time to see a Kappa slash a Gamma's chest with a hunting knife. Bewildered by the fracas, Heinrich dropped to one knee to help the injured boy. When the boy with the knife threatened to attack him too, Heinrich pulled his Colt from his pocket and aimed it at the boy, who ran to the Kappa porch, his face white with fear. Heinrich knew full well his gun wasn't loaded, but the ploy worked. He quickly pulled out six bullets and loaded the revolver, then dropped down to help the bleeding boy, one eye warily on the kid with the knife.

Then Heinrich saw Sheriff Thackeray, arriving with two deputies and Web Webber, shotguns at the ready. The Sheriff gave Heinrich a nod, and Heinrich stepped in to join them. Soon Murphy and Dahlen, armed with hunting rifles, also arrived to help.

The sheriff fired off two loud shotgun blasts that echoed through the street. Some students quit their fighting, raised their hands, and backed off at the sight of the determined lawman. Thackeray then reloaded and fired two more rounds. The two sides backed away from each other for good this time with bloodied noses and angry looks at their opponents.

"Disperse, now!" he yelled in a growling bellow, "or the next shots find real targets."

Heinrich knew the sheriff was probably bluffing as well, but it worked.

The Kappa Psis warily backed away toward their house, carrying their wounded with them, snarling epithets under their breath. At the same time, the attacking Gammas shouldered their wounded and filed back to their house too.

Thackeray pointed the barrel of his shotgun at first Riggold and then at Brady. "You two, come with me. You are under arrest."

A deputy grabbed each youth by the arm and pulled them toward the sheriff's office.

Stumpy turned to Heinrich, Murphy, and Dahlen. "Thank you, men, but your services are no longer needed at this time."

He walked away, following a good six feet behind his deputies.

Heinrich turned to Webber. "Should we call the doctor?"

Webber nodded, surveying the trampled lawn.

"I don't envy you," Heinrich said. "This is a mess."

Webber's face brightened. "It's no longer my problem," he said.

Heinrich raised an eyebrow.

"I quit earlier today," Webber said. "Our fearless President Tichenor can handle it himself."

Webber laughed and walked away.

.

CHAPTER 8

Nearly two weeks of relative calm followed the Battle of the Greeks, as the college and community took stock of the situation, trying to understand the outburst of anger that led to the incident. Behind closed doors, President Tichenor gave stern lectures about the melee to the leadership of all the fraternities on campus. He then expelled Ringgold and Brady and closed the Kappa Psi and Gamma Sig houses, suspending them from campus for the rest of the semester. Local landlords enjoyed the resulting rush of students seeking alternative lodging, but Mrs. Yaeger kindly did not raise Heinrich's rent.

On Thursday, March 26, an overcast, rainy day, Heinrich sat at a table at Murphy's eating a dreary supper of corned beef and cabbage. He had thought the dish to be Irish, but Murphy had laughed and said it was really an Irish-American creation. He enjoyed the dish on occasion as a change from the norm, but today the meat's corduroy texture and strange salt-and-vinegar taste, combined with the limp, bland vegetable matter just made him depressed. The events of the past few months weighed heavily on his heart. He missed Sally. He missed Tommy. He hated Franklinton and wanted to leave town, but he couldn't. Nothing could drag him away. He wouldn't leave the woman he loved behind.

Murphy shot Heinrich a concerned look, hoping the meal was to his liking. Heinrich manufactured a quick smile and mechanically shoveled in another bite. Reassured, Murphy walked away to wipe off another table.

Heinrich pulled the Teutonic cross from his pocket and placed it beside him on the table in his booth, remembering the dream about his father that he had experienced at the lake. His faith in a just and righteous God could sure use a boost right now, he thought. It was slipping.

Someone cleared his throat to announce himself. Heinrich looked up. It was Old Ben, standing in front of Heinrich's table and shifting his weight awkwardly from one foot to the other. Heinrich experienced a momentary surprise, as blacks were not seen in Murphy's. Murphy did not enforce segregation in his tavern; local convention simply told blacks they weren't welcome in white establishments.

Ben read his mind. "Murphy let me in; I told him I needed to talk to you most urgently, sir," he said. "Do you mind if I join you for a moment, Professor Kueter, sir?"

"Of course not, Ben. I could use the company. Please sit down." Heinrich put the cross back in his pocket.

Ben sat, periodically shooting wary looks around the room.

"Don't quite know how to say this…" Ben mumbled.

"Then just say it."

"Some of the Kappa Psi boys was involved in that newspaper fire; I'm plum sure of it."

"What do you mean?" Heinrich responded

"I'm positive young Mr. Ringgold was in on it, and maybe some more. He and a couple others came in late that night; I saw them when I was up following nature's call. I heard them talking about a hot fire, and keeping Miss Sally quiet. It was pretty clear they helped. Sounds like old Mr. Fairchild led it, though."

Heinrich nodded slowly, not completely surprised.

"You're a brave man to tell me, Ben."

"Sometimes you just gotta do the right thing even if it ain't the safest."

Heinrich nodded in agreement.

Ben continued. "People got to stand up to evil sometimes. Look at Jack Johnson; he done stood up to Jim Jeffries and won!"

Heinrich had followed the black boxer's ongoing saga in the newspaper since the "fight of the century" three years earlier.

"Yeah, but he's been hounded ever since," Heinrich said, "and he's been on the run in France for nine months. You don't have enough money to sail to Paris, do you?"

Ben laughed. "No way, no how. Can't see myself as a Frenchie, anyway."

"Seriously now, Ben," Heinrich said, feeling a sudden sense of foreboding. "You stay safe. There's some bad people in this town."

Ben nodded and got up to leave. "Ain't that the truth? Tommy and Sally deserved better."

Heinrich gritted his teeth. "I'll say."

"You deserve better too, Professor Heinrich," Ben said, then lowered his voice. "There's something else brewing, something bad, but I don't know nothing yet. I'll tell you once I find out more."

Heinrich nodded.

"Fine, Ben, but don't do anything that'll make you a target. You probably don't want to be seen around me. At the first sign of trouble, you get ahold of the sheriff or secretly get word to me through Manfred or Mike, Okay?"

"I'll be careful," Ben said with a nod. "But you be careful too. They got Miss Giddings. My guess is you're next."

Heinrich sighed as Ben walked away. The old man was probably right; he'd better keep his revolver loaded and close at hand.

Ben nodded to Murphy and closed the door behind him. As he walked away, he didn't notice a young man leaning on a pole across the street, who watched him depart and then walked away in the opposite direction.

A few days later, Old Ben trudged home on the dirt path from the brick plant where he had taken a temporary job sweeping until the Kappa Psi house could be reinstated. As the path disappeared into a grove of trees and headed downhill toward a creek, Ben Jones stopped to look at a red cardinal perched on a tree limb.

At that moment, eight hooded young men jumped him. One man on each side grabbed his arms, while one in front punched him in the gut. As he crumpled over, the wind knocked out of him, a fourth gagged him and grabbed him in a bear hug from behind.

Ben struggled, but he was no match for the surprise attack. They picked him up, carried him several yards to a waiting wagon and threw him in the back. After a 15-minute ride, the hooded kidnappers dragged the aged man, frightened out of his wits, into an old barn behind an abandoned farmhouse, where they tied him to a chair.

"We understand you been looking at white women," one of the masked men said.

"No, sir. That ain't true."

"Maybe not, but you done worse, ain't you? You been talking to that Kraut professor, ain't you?"

"I never told him nothing."

His main interrogator grabbed Ben by the shirt and roughly pulled him up out of his chair, brandishing a billy club in his face. "That's bull, Ben, and you know it. You spilled the beans to that Heinie, and you're going to pay."

Ben realized his time was short, but he refused to talk. The leader clubbed him on each foot. As Ben screamed in pain, the hooded leader laughed and stuffed a dirty rag in the old man's mouth. Though gagged, Ben continued to cry out, so his sneering tormentor clocked his prisoner with a right hook to the cheek. Ben began to cry quietly with resignation.

The leader then handed the club to another assailant, and the kidnappers took turns beating him with it, handing out slow, hard blows and alternating left and right to keep the damage even. Ben gave them nothing but muffled screams in response. At the end, Ben accepted the pain, silently begged God for deliverance, and prayed that the Lord would keep his family safe.

The next morning, a passing student found Ben swinging from a rope in the rafters of the wooden, covered bridge that carried the main highway over Stanford Creek on the way to Kansas City. A stunned Sheriff Thackeray cut down the body, beaten and bloody, and gave it solemnly to Ben's wife for burial.

The next day, Heinrich found the sheriff seated and whittling at his usual spot on the boardwalk in front of his office.

"Hello, Kueter," the sheriff said. "I'll bet you are here about the investigation of Old Ben's death now?"

Heinrich nodded. "Any leads?"

"None I'd tell you about. But I hear he talked to you yesterday. I swear, son, death seems to follow you wherever you go."

Heinrich set his teeth. "Just find out who did this, sheriff. If I can help, you let me know."

"What did he talk to you about?" Thackeray asked.

"He said he overheard a conversation between Ringgold and a couple other Kappa Psis. He told me they were involved in the attack on Sally, and he said that Truman Fairchild was behind the attack."

The sheriff nodded. "Makes sense. I figured as much. You got any proof to back up those accusations?"

Heinrich shook his head. "No, just his word. He said something else was afoot, and he was going to try to find out what they had planned."

A look of concern flashed across Thackeray's face. "Damn, will this foolishness ever stop? Who knew there was so much hatred in this quiet little town?"

Heinrich stood stoic and silent. "I wish I had a good answer for you, Sheriff; some quote about Cain and Abel might suffice, I suppose."

"Thanks, Preacher," said Thackeray, rolling his eyes. The sheriff massaged the bridge of his nose with his right thumb and forefinger as if he had a headache coming on. "I'll have to be on the lookout then."

"You and me both," Heinrich said.

Thackeray shook his head. "You let me handle this, Kueter. You've done too damn much already. The gravediggers have been working overtime since you came to town."

Heinrich burned with anger over Ben's murder and shame at his race's treatment of the black man as he listened to a quartet from the African Methodist Episcopal church sing "Amazing Grace." He was one of only a handful of whites at Ben's funeral, a fact that made him ashamed of his own skin.

Old Ben hadn't had a chance, and it was partly Heinrich's fault for talking to him in a public place. He paid his respects to Ben's graying wife, Mary. "He was a good man, and very brave," was all he could come up with.

She nodded, "Yes, he was."

Heinrich stared at his toes; she touched his arm. "Don't you worry, Professor Kueter," she said. "Ben's in a far better place, a place where justice reigns."

"I hope to do Ben justice here too," he answered.

She looked him in the eye. "You be careful. There's a pack of wild wolves running loose around here that's just plain mean. They'll be gunning for you too."

Heinrich nodded. Good thing he had his revolver, he thought. At least he would be ready to shoot back.

President Tichenor and Department Chair Goforth called Heinrich in to a meeting in the president's office the next day. He stiffly shook each of their hands and sat down in a single chair across from Tichenor's mahogany desk.

Heinrich could tell he was in trouble again. Surely it was no accident that the Spartan wooden chair reserved for him had been placed alone in front of the president's large desk, as if he were facing the Inquisition. Goforth sat just to the right of the president's desk in a comfortable seat, clearly the designated witness of the day to what the president planned to do. In addition to an academic degree, Tichenor had earned a law degree earlier in his career; presumably, Heinrich would now see the president's blood-sucking-attorney side spring into action.

"Professor Kueter, it has come to my attention that, after repeated attempts to get you to cease and desist, you still insist on doing detective work," President Tichenor said. "Is that true?"

"Anything I have done is on my own time, sir," Heinrich bristled. "I have done nothing illegal or unethical, I assure you."

Goforth nodded. "What worries the faculty is that you are not paying enough attention to your regular duties as a faculty member at this college. This sleuthing is taking too much of your time."

"You have already made it clear that I am to be expelled from the faculty at the end of this semester; what else do you want from me? And, as I have said, I believe it is my own time to give."

Tichenor chimed in. "Professor Kueter, I tell you with all candor that a faculty member's job is not just your average nine-to-five, 40-hour-a-week endeavor. I have had to give similar advice to many a young professor. As a faculty member at a small institution of higher education, you must spend time being seen at college events – its lectures, musical and theatre entertainments, and its sporting events. I notice, for instance, that I did not see you at the basketball game last week."

Heinrich shook his head in disbelief. "Let me make sure I understand you. Two students and an employee are dead. The editor of the local newspaper has been beaten into a coma. We have seen rioting and fights all over campus. My employment is to be terminated when the semester ends in six weeks. But you want me to attend basketball games?"

Tichenor wouldn't give. "I am asking you to take part in the life of the college that you still work for; it is part of your job, Professor Kueter."

Goforth piped in, "The Quiz Bowl is next week, for instance. If you don't care for athletics, perhaps you should consider making an appearance at that event."

Heinrich began to get hot. "Gentlemen, I repeat, how I spend my free time is my concern."

"Not if I say it isn't," Tichenor shot back. "Kueter, we have a local constable. Let him handle the police work."

"Mr. President, does it not bother you that some of your students have proven to be racist murderers? These crimes are tearing at the fabric of the college's moral foundation, yet you do nothing."

Tichenor's face grew red. "That is my concern, not yours. You don't seem to understand that I hold the cards here, not you. I hold your career in my hands, and I will finish you if need be, here or at any other institution at which you wish to teach. Let the authorities handle the detective work without interference, or you will be summarily fired from this position, not just let go at the end of the semester. If you do not cease and desist, I promise you I will make it so that you do not work in academia ever again. Do I make myself clear?"

Heinrich nodded. "Am I excused?"

Tichenor waved him away. As he reached the anteroom outside the president's office, Goforth came out and grabbed his elbow.

"Please consider what is at stake, Heinrich," Goforth said. "You are a fine teacher. You have a brilliant career ahead of you. Don't throw it all away."

"Dr. Goforth, the love of my life is lying in a hospital bed in a coma, hanging by a thread. My life is in danger from roving packs of thugs. My career is the least of my worries right now. Clearly, the principles upon which I have staked my life are under attack, and if I do not stand up for them, I sell myself, my friends, and my ancestors short."

"Dammit, this isn't about your principles and ancestors, and you know it," Goforth said. "It's about doing your job and letting others do theirs. Put aside this nonsense, and be the teacher you were meant to be."

Heinrich did a double take. He'd never heard Goforth swear before. In fact, he'd never seen the mousy man this passionate about anything.

He paused before replying. "Erwin, if I don't show my students that my most cherished beliefs are worth fighting for, then I would lose their respect, and it would be impossible to teach them anything."

Goforth shook his head. "Son, you are headed down the wrong path, and if you continue, I can no longer protect you."

"Protect me? I'm already been forced off the faculty."

"Heinrich, that is nothing. That will simply be a small pothole on the road to your future. If you continue along this path, you are in for much worse. What is going to happen won't happen tomorrow, but you can expect it soon."

Heinrich nodded. "Then I'll have to live with it," Heinrich said. "Thanks for nothing."

Heinrich shook Goforth's hand and headed out the front door.

Later that evening, sitting on his usual hickory stump on the porch outside his office and whittling in the twilight, Sheriff Thackeray whistled "Down by the Old Mill Stream" and "Let Me Call You Sweetheart." His prisoners — Ringgold, Baker, and young Fairchild and his cohorts — had been fed and, he hoped, soon would be asleep for the night.

Yesterday, when he had received the news that his prisoners would soon be moved to the state penitentiary in Jefferson City, probably next week, he breathed a sigh of relief. He'd been housing them way too long as it was in a small, somewhat vulnerable facility that was never meant for long-term housing of inmates.

He heard a scratching noise, like a foot dragging gravel, on the east side of his building. The sound stopped too quickly, as if someone were trying to hide, out of his sight.

"That you, Keith?" he asked, thinking it might be one of his deputies, who was a little slow this evening getting back from supper. Unsnapping the holster strap over his ivory-handled Colt .45 peacemaker, he slowly got up from his stump.

There was no answer. Something was up; he smelled danger. Thackeray drew his pistol with his right hand and quietly eased over to the front door of his office, trying to not give away that he was moving inside. He turned the knob slowly behind him with his left hand. It whined quietly; damn, he'd needed to oil that thing for a while.

He quickly stepped inside and shut the door. Grabbing his Winchester Model 1910 repeating rifle from the rack on the wall, he opened a desk drawer and pulled out four loaded .401 magazines. They held four 250 gram bullets each, and he had prepared them for just such an emergency. He inserted a magazine into its slot on the underside of the stock and waited.

"Stu-u-u-m-py!" a voice called from outside.

"Yeah, who is it?" he yelled back.

"We want you, Stumpy!" came the answer, along with a wicked laugh. "We're coming to get you!"

"Come on then, what are you waiting for?" Stumpy Thackeray said, whispering under his breath a few extra words, "...you little shits." He quickly checked the chambers of his pistol to make sure they were loaded and felt around his waist to make sure that he had plenty of extra pistol bullets in his gunbelt.

Thackeray crouched behind his desk, preparing for the coming assault. "You waiting for an engraved invitation or something?" he said.

"Don't shoot, then. We're coming in; we just want to talk."

Thackeray knew better.

Suddenly, two men wearing pillowcase hoods smashed through his front windows simultaneously, carrying pistols. At nearly the same instant, a third hooded man kicked in the door and stood like a live scarecrow in the moonlight holding a double-barreled shotgun.

"We've come for the prisoners," said the man in the doorway, an inviting target.

Thackeray nodded and took aim with the rifle. The man moved hesitantly toward the jail cells, as two more armed men walked through the doorway.

"Take 'em, over my dead body," Thackeray said, firing his Winchester at the leader, who crumpled with a hit to the shoulder. The man crawled behind a table and tipped it over with his feet, scattering pencils on the stone floor. Thackeray dropped down to one knee and fired again, hitting the thigh of one of the gunmen in the front window, who fell and crawled back out the front door, where he continued to fire at Thackeray through the doorway. The third assailant found cover behind a filing cabinet, trading shots with Thackeray, pinned down behind the desk.

Thackeray continued to shoot the Winchester, keeping the men from reaching the jail cells through his steady firing, until he emptied three of magazines. Then he switched to his peacemaker, firing six bullets at a time and reloading quickly from his belt. His adversaries would need the keys to open the cells, and the keys were in the desk. He desperately fired and reloaded his Colt, trading shots with the attacking men and hoping they would retreat soon. If not, he might have to surrender.

When he ran out of the bullets in his belt, he pushed his last magazine in the Winchester until it clicked. Kneeling, he fired over the top of the desk out the front door at the man on the porch, then whipped open the second desk drawer to find more ammunition. As he did so, he saw peripherally to his left a figure in the east-side window, the one spot from which he knew he might be vulnerable. He swung around, Winchester at the ready, but not in time. A shotgun blast came through the window and hit him in the chest. He fell to his knees, and a second shot went through his left temple, killing him.

The lead gunman with the wounded shoulder hurriedly kicked Thackeray's body out of the way and ransacked the desk. He found the keys in the top drawer and promptly used them to open the cells, releasing Ringgold, Fairchild and his lieutenants.

With nowhere to hide, Baker, the Gamma Sigma president, dived under the steel bunk in his cell. Ringgold grabbed the sheriff's warm rifle and took the keys from the lead gunman, one of Truman Fairchild's thugs. Ringgold opened the door to Baker's cell, pulled the bunk out of the way and fired its three remaining rounds into the defenseless Baker, who died with his back against the brick wall, begging for his life, a fish trapped in a barrel.

Eyeing his nemesis's body in a bloody heap, Ringgold put the rifle down. "Sometimes you win; sometimes you lose," he said.

Fairchild shook his head. "We haven't won yet."

Their work done, the group ran out the door and disappeared into the moonlight, leaving the bodies behind them.

The violent jailbreak shocked the town of Franklinton, whose townsfolk believed in law and order and hadn't seen anything like it since the James Gang had roamed the state during the Reconstruction era. Who would do such a thing in this modern day?

The answer seemed pretty obvious to Heinrich, but he couldn't prove it yet. He began to carry his loaded revolver with him everywhere, concealed in a holster under his suit jacket. His compatriots, Murphy and Dahlen, kept their arms handy as well. Heinrich knew the gun wouldn't save him from an ambush all by itself, but at least he had the comfort of knowing it gave him a chance to defend himself if the situation should call for it.

The mayor appointed Deputy Keith Anderson temporary sheriff until the next election in August. He and his fellow deputy, Toby Richards, were both about six feet tall and known to most as "Stumpy's Smith and Jones." Until now, the lean and relatively nondescript figures had operated in the background. Both were veterans, Anderson from the Army and Richards from the Marines; each possessed that certain swagger honed through years of military discipline. While rarely ill-tempered, neither was known for having a particularly engaging personality, but Stumpy hadn't hired them for their bantering abilities. He hired only men with steel eyes and salt in their veins.

The day after the jailbreak, Heinrich stopped by to speak to Anderson, but the deputy wasn't in the mood to engage in much conversation. Heinrich could see he was overwhelmed and distracted by the new responsibility placed upon him. Heinrich simply expressed his support and said he hoped the lawmen might track the vicious killers, but Anderson only grunted noncommittally about how he planned to do it.

"Can't see forming a posse right now," Anderson said. "Don't know where to go or who to chase."

Heinrich got the distinct impression Anderson didn't like him very much. Perhaps the deputy didn't much like anybody or really didn't like Germans. He even may have blamed Heinrich for Stumpy's death. Hell, Heinrich thought, he ought to blame himself for tarrying too long over dinner. Heinrich thanked and saluted Anderson as a sign of respect, but he left the jail feeling unsatisfied and uneasy, guessing the two would gossip about him the minute the door closed behind him.

Meanwhile, Heinrich had other worries. Every day after classes were over, Heinrich visited Sally at the hospital. He would watch her, hoping for movement, but she remained motionless. He would often read to her from a book or talk to her, but there was no response. Discouraged, he watched as she lay lifeless, her mind somewhere else.

But she was breathing. He could feel her breath on his face when he leaned over to kiss her cheek or lips. Unfortunately, he was no Prince Charming; his Sleeping Beauty stayed asleep.

Exhausted, ten days after the jailbreak, he lay back in the wooden rocker beside her hospital bed, dozed off and began to dream...

His young father appeared, once again in swim clothes, water drops glistening on his skin, a golden sunset behind him.

"Keep swimming for the truth. Swim the river of the sky that divides the night. Read the tea leaves. Look to your cross, and find the truth," his father's ghost said in a hollow voice.

"I will, father, but what do you mean?" Heinrich answered.

His father turned and walked into the water and vanished in the breakers of Lake Michigan without another word. Strangely, the back of his father's swim shorts held a painted yin and yang symbol, with its black and white swirls, like the one on Tommy Lee's pocket watch...

Heinrich woke from his nap with a start, wondering what the dream meant. He pulled out the Teutonic cross from his pocket again, studied it and sighed. He didn't know whether he had chosen the quest or it had chosen him. But he had made the decision months ago to follow the trail, and he would see it through.

He figured he had little choice now but to continue to search for the truth about Tommy's murder, and he would continue the fight for justice, no matter what. It was a moral imperative. Duty called, and his ancestors demanded that he act.

Heinrich grinned. Often Stumpy had jokingly called him "Preacher," and now he was preaching to himself. Maybe there was more of his father in him than he liked to think. As for the fight Heinrich had taken on, it didn't really matter whether others believed in it; he just knew the fight against these murderers was important, for reasons he could not express in words, and he intended to see it through to its conclusion.

Heinrich sat at Murphy's bar conversing with Murphy and drowning his sorrows in a beer when a large, authoritative man walked in and sat down beside him.

"You Heinrich Kueter?" he asked gruffly. The man's black business suit, vest, and black hat carried the thin gray film of road dust.

Heinrich nodded. "That Austrian fellow up the street said you might be in here. Name's Jeremy Hunt, U.S. Marshal from St. Louis."

"And you are here to find out about the recent jailbreak and killings?"

Hunt nodded. "You kill a lawman, the feds take notice."

"We definitely need your help," Heinrich said. "The situation around here has devolved into the Wild West."

Hunt put a paw on Heinrich's shoulder. "This is Missouri, son, the nursery school for the Wild West. You think it was an accident that Jesse James was a Missourian? Outlaws like him learned their trade here in the guerrilla warfare on the Kansas Border before the Civil War, and they perfected the craft afterward. Apparently, we now have some modern-day rebel hoodlums following the same tradition. They may be a bit more educated these days, but it's the same old story."

"Cain hates Abel because he is favored in God's sight."

"You got it, son. It's damn near as old as forever," Hunt said. "People say the love of money is the root of all evil. Hell, that ain't so; it goes deeper. Selfishness is the root of all evil. Man wants something the law tells him he can't have. He goes and gets it anyway using all means at his disposal, no matter how low-down. It won't surprise me at all if they start up robbing banks and trains again. Who knows, one of these days maybe motorcars and aeroplanes'll be next."

Heinrich nodded.

"Now," Hunt said. "Tell me what you know about this case, from the beginning."

So Heinrich talked, while Hunt listened, nodded and asked short questions for clarification. When he had finished interviewing Heinrich, Hunt got up from his barstool and said, "Son, don't leave town. I may need your help catching these weasels."

On a cool, damp Saturday night in April, Heinrich walked toward home, letting the internal, warm buzz from a little too much alcohol slowly dissipate. He had left Murphy's an hour earlier and dropped off a tipsy Dahlen at his stable. Getting a little drunk had seemed a good way to crown one of those tantalizing Missouri April days when spring gave a quick taste of its coming charms, and then the weather returned to its usual blustery winter dreariness. Now he could see wisps of foggy breath in the humid air.

Heinrich didn't feel too drunk to function, just drunk enough to get into trouble. Suddenly driven by a maudlin desire to see Sally's house, he ambled his way across town, thinking sad thoughts mainly of Sally, with a little of Stumpy, Ben, and Tommy mixed in.

Had his thinking been a little more lucid, he wouldn't have turned onto Water Street. He could see a commotion in front of the Lucky Strike Saloon from a block away. Suddenly, a man flew backward through the front shutter doors and landed on his back in the street; then two men, bouncers, marched out close behind and promptly began to beat and kick him. Heinrich began to turn around and walk away, but stopped when he heard the man on the ground wail in a plaintive voice that he recognized. It was a student, a Gamma Sig named Ed... Ed Blaine.

"Please, she stole my money," Blaine cried. "I just want it back, that's all."

"Shut up and get the hell home boy," shouted the thug kicking him.

Getting involved was not really a conscious decision; Heinrich simply reacted. The lad was in trouble; Heinrich moved quickly. He ran down the brick street and surprised the nearest bouncer, a mid-sized stocky man, with a football-style block that knocked the man to the ground, where he landed hard on his hindquarters.

Heinrich then turned to the taller man, a little over six feet in height, and grappled with him. When the man widened his arm to throw a punch, Heinrich shot his hands up around the man's neck. He interlaced his fingers, and pulled the bouncer's face down to meet his upcoming knee as he lunged it upward. Two strong strikes with the knee and a right hook to the thug's temple put the bouncer down in the street on his hands and knees. Heinrich kicked the man in the chest, and he stayed down.

When the stocky man then grabbed him from behind, Heinrich swung his upper body from side to side and wriggled out of the fat bouncer's grip by leaning downward and hitting the thug in the ribs with backward elbow thrusts. Heinrich then turned to face his attacker and twisted his upper body, coiling it like a spring and firing his elbow forward like a projectile into the attacker's jaw. The second bouncer crumpled to the bricks too.

Heinrich knew there wasn't much time before they'd recover and come after him, probably with reinforcements, so he quickly grabbed the prone Ed Blaine by the shoulder and belt and pulled him to his feet. "Run!" Heinrich yelled. Blaine let out a frightened wail and staggered westward down Water Street.

Meanwhile, a dozen angry and liquored men poured out of the saloon and quickly circled Heinrich before he could follow Blaine. They took turns shoving him and throwing punches like picadors taunting a prize bull, prepping it for the arrival of the matador. Surrounded, he really wished he had Tommy Lee in the ring with him.

In the bright yellow light of the saloon doorway, Heinrich could see Truman Fairchild, laughing like a devil on the porch, the great fiery maw of Hell behind him.

"You made a mistake coming here, Dutchie! A big mistake!" Fairchild announced with a twisted laugh.

Someone kicked Heinrich in the gut hard. He dropped to his knees and suddenly felt fear. A taut fist connected with his left ear. He fell onto his side, and his vision clouded over. Then he heard a distant gunshot and passed out.

Heinrich awoke in his room in bed, his head throbbing, with Marshal Hunt's beady black eyes looking at him.

"Well that was real smart, professor," Hunt said. "You're damn lucky to be alive, son. Next time, consider taking along some backup, Mr. Prize Fighter. Those apes mighta' killed you."

Heinrich winced at the throbbing pain on his face and felt the lumps and bruises distributed relatively evenly around his head. Of course, he realized Hunt was right. It was a stupid thing to do. He should have been more careful. "Did you bring me back here?"

Hunt shook his head. "The deputies responding to the commotion did. Good thing that Blaine kid made some noise. I happened to be nearby, so I helped by closing down the saloon. Now look, you rest up, and don't do anything else foolish, you hear?"

Heinrich nodded. Hunt got up to leave.

"Thanks, Marshal," Heinrich said, putting his head back on the pillow as Hunt closed the door behind him.

He awakened later to the sound of pounding on the door.

"Heinrich, you awake?" asked Mrs. Yaeger's voice.

Heinrich looked at the clock on the bedside table. It was almost 6:30 a.m. He must have slept for several hours.

He touched his swollen face, sore head and tender abdomen. He could tell he had some deep bruises.

"Yes, Mrs. Yaeger. I fell asleep. Just a second."

He put on his shoes and walked to the door.

When he opened it, Mrs. Yaeger gasped. "Professor, your face…"

"Yeah, I know. I fell down some stairs."

"More likely you fell into a brawl down at Murphy's tavern. Haven't I told you about that place and its dangers?"

Heinrich grinned. Apparently, the marshal had not told her what had happened. A regular old bar fight would take less explanation. He didn't want to get into it right now. "What is it, Mrs. Yaeger?"

"President Tichenor's office sent word that you are to see him immediately."

Heinrich was silent.

"As in right now," she said.

"Okay. Thank you, Mrs. Yaeger."

She waited for a moment to get an explanation, but he didn't want to give one just yet. He put on some socks and a fresh shirt; it was time to face the music.

A half an hour later, Heinrich told himself to hold his chin high as he trudged into President Tichenor's outer office — although the sun was up, the front office was in shadows, the secretary's desk was quiet and unmanned — prepared to take whatever the despot dished out. After all, he'd killed men far better than Tichenor. The thought of putting a bullet in the man's head produced a momentary grin on Heinrich's face, but he quickly swallowed it in the wake of a wave of Christian guilt. Just the same, Heinrich had reached the end of the line and was in no mood to play nice. Fed up with the constant harassment and intrusion into his personal life, Heinrich would let the dictator have it with both barrels if necessary. No job was worth this abuse. It was time; he had little to lose.

As Heinrich crossed the threshold into Tichenor's inner office, Chairman Goforth was already present as the president's witness to the execution, seated grimly in a walnut chair placed to the right of the president's prominent walnut desk. Also present were Dean of the Faculty Stephen Meyer, another of Tichenor's toadies, standing by another chair to Tichenor's left; and interim Chief of Campus Security Hamilton Curry, who had been Webber's deputy and who stood on the wall opposite the president, behind the "hot seat" in which Heinrich soon found himself. A brawny, tough customer with wavy, black hair,

Curry had been placed strategically in the room to provide muscle in case Heinrich were to stoop to physical action. Heinrich gave Curry a nod, which the security man returned. Fellow ex-Army men knew the score.

"Please have a seat, Professor Kueter," Tichenor said cheerily while indicating the "hot seat" with a wave of his hand, as if the lynching of Heinrich's career were a matter of great personal pleasure.

As Heinrich sat, so did Tichenor and Meyer. Curry remained standing in the back of the room, ready to react.

Elbows on his desk, Tichenor formed a pyramid with his fingers and looked over the tips, preparing to yank the lanyard and fire the first volley. "Professor Kueter, after spending the entire evening dealing with a brawl you allegedly began at the Lucky Strike Saloon, I have called you here tonight to let you know that I am initiating dismissal procedures that will result in the immediate termination of your employment with Worcester College. In numerous conversations with you, I have tried to impart feedback regarding your job performance, but you have not listened to my counsel."

Heinrich sat stoically silent, crossed his arms and cocked an eyebrow.

"Instead, although warned several times against continuing such combative behavior, you have persisted in activities not in accord with your position on the faculty, matters which are the legitimate domain of law enforcement, not teaching or research. In addition, earlier this evening, you went out of your way to assault the employees of an important alumnus and donor to the college, thereby jeopardizing funding for an important college building project. Truman Fairchild has today withdrawn his financial support of our new library addition because of your brutal attack on his establishment this afternoon. Do you have anything to say in your defense?"

"Sure, as if it matters. I simply responded to save a student from a vicious attack by his goons, who were beating young Mr. Blaine within an inch of his life. I fought them, but ultimately lost, and it is his brutal handiwork that you see before you in evidence tonight," Heinrich said, pointing to his bruised and cut face.

"Don't lie to me, Sir. You attacked his bouncers, who were lawfully executing security within their place of business," Tichenor said.

"Hmm, I suppose you could say, being street thugs, that they were in their element, since that's where the fight happened, in the middle of Water Street," Heinrich replied.

"Drop the smart-aleck tone, Mr. Kueter; you are standing on the thinnest possible ice."

Heinrich composed his thoughts for a moment. "Mr. President, you are free to make me a scapegoat as you wish. My father taught me that some things are more important than keeping a job or funding a library."

Tichenor shot back, "You, sir, are out of control."

Heinrich nodded, resignedly. "Perhaps, but at least my motivation is pure. You choose to clothe yourself in piety, hiding your naked selfishness and greed under a cloak of righteousness. Your day of reckoning is coming, sir."

Tichenor pressed his fingertips together in front of his face, fuming inside. Heinrich continued, "My father told me once that sometimes a good man must give up his comfort to fight for love and tolerance. Sometimes he must stand against those who promote a cruel agenda of hate under the guise of Christian decency, such as Fairchild and you. You are an evil, petty man, sir, and that is why we find ourselves in conflict."

Tichenor turned beet red. "You dare to accuse me of unchristian ways, young sir? I am an elder in the First Presbyterian Church, and I attend every Sunday."

Heinrich nodded. "Exodus 34:12: Take heed to thyself, lest thou make a covenant with the inhabitants of the land whither thou goest, lest it be for a snare in the midst of thee," Heinrich said. "Your willingness to accommodate the rampant racism in this town in order to build the college endowment blinds you to the evil cesspool in which you swim."

Tichenor turned to Curry. "Get him out of here. Watch him as he cleans out his office."

He turned back to Heinrich. "How dare you disrespect this college! You are a disgrace, Kueter, and I intend to see to it that you don't get another teaching position ever again if it is the last thing I do."

"That's fine, Mr. President, because I resign. You are no longer worthy of my respect; you are rotten to the core."

Curry grabbed Heinrich by the elbow and led him out of the president's office, leaving Tichenor to seethe and pace in circles.

Once outside in the cold again, Curry let him loose, almost apologetically. "I hope you understand, Mr. Kueter. Nothing personal; just doing my job."

Kueter softly tapped Curry's shoulder with his fist. "Called to duty; boots on the ground," he said. "We all have our roles to play."

Although Heinrich felt shame and remorse at losing his job, he also felt relief at finally being rid of the evil Ichabod's regime and its reign of terror over him. Heinrich moved in and out of the euphoria of new freedom and the knowledge of failure. Learning the extent of one's personal limitations is never easy; he had failed to sail his boat successfully through the difficult political shoals at Worcester College, and he would have to live with that failure.

On his march back to his apartment the day of his dismissal, carrying a wooden crate of his belongings from his now vacated office, Heinrich promised himself not to allow the Fairchilds and Tichenors to run him out of town. He could not leave yet, not with Sally still alive, and the murders of Ben, Stumpy, and Tommy unsolved and unavenged. For most locals, the recent violent events had driven Tommy's death far into the past, as if it were a forgotten memory, but the boy would not be forgotten as long as Heinrich had anything to do with it.

For several days, Heinrich checked out and read a few books from the town library, played chess and gin rummy with Manfred Dahlen, and drank a bit too much in the evenings at Murphy's. Seeing occasional concerned looks from Mrs. Yaeger, worried about the source of her next rent payment, and from Mike Murphy, concerned about Heinrich's hefty bar tab, led the young ex-professor to realize he would need a new source of income soon.

One evening a week later, as Murphy poured him another beer, the bartender broached the subject. "You know, Heinrich, if you're planning to stick around, you ought to start looking for another job."

Heinrich nodded and was about to respond when Marshal Hunt walked in the door and dropped onto the adjacent barstool in a neighborly way. "Sometimes, if you're lucky, the job comes to you," Hunt said.

Heinrich turned to him. "Yeah?" he asked.

"Kueter, I have a proposition. I would like to appoint you deputy marshal of the central Missouri district, to be based here in Franklinton. How about it? The pay's not as good as a professor's, but it'll get you by. And you even get to wear a star."

Hunt placed a deputy marshal badge on the bar. Heinrich stared at it for a moment; did he want it? Yes, for now.

Heinrich picked up the badge. "How could a mad professor pass up an offer like that?" he asked, and pinned the deputy marshal's badge to his vest.

"It looks good on you," Murphy said with a smile.

Hunt thumped Murphy's chest with the back of his hand. "You're just thrilled he's good for his tab now," Hunt said. "You owe me one, my friend. Heck, maybe I should just pay Kueter in beer; he spends so damn much time here."

They laughed. "Now, Kueter, remember. Wearing the badge doesn't give you the right to take on Fairchild," Hunt said. "A cool head and some restraint are what I need from you in this town right now. That and some evidence. I have to head to St. Louis for a few days. I need to check out some fingerprints I found at the sheriff's office and newspaper."

"Fingerprints?" Heinrich asked, with a puzzled squint.

"It's a new process. You ink the little ridges on your fingers, and it identifies you. The SLPD started using it ten years ago. Some snooty Scotland Yard detective showed off the technology at the St. Louis World's Fair in 1904."

"And this ink is supposed to help us how? How do you get criminals to ink their hands?" Heinrich asked.

Hunt rolled his eyes. "For a professor, you ain't too smart sometimes. People have oils on their skin that leave marks on things they touch. You dust some promising surfaces at the crime scene with white chalk or charcoal dust, depending on whether it's a light or dark surface — you know, door handles, windows, potential murder weapons, that sort of thing. Then you compare it to an inked print from your suspect."

When Heinrich's face showed that he remained unconvinced, Hunt put his hand on his new deputy's shoulder. "Just trust me, Okay? It might nail the people who attacked Sally. It's worth a shot."

Hunt paused and waved his index finger under Heinrich's nose. "The main thing is I don't want you to do anything rash while I'm gone. Clear?"

Heinrich nodded. "Crystal clear, Marshal."

Hunt looked him in the eye. "One last thing, Kueter," he said, and handed Heinrich a box of 12 Schofield revolver cartridges. "I understand you have a Colt .45 and know how to use it. I'd like you to get in some target practice."

Heinrich nodded. "The Colt's an old friend."

Hunt raised his left eyebrow. "Your relationship with your firearm doesn't concern me; ditch the gunfighter talk," he said. "You're no good to me dead."

Heinrich nodded again.

Hunt got up from his barstool. "All right then, Deputy. I expect to see you in my office on Thursday, bright and early. I'm serious now, don't get into any trouble. I want to give you some training before you run off and get yourself killed."

"Yes, sir."

"Good to have you on the team," the marshal said. He patted Heinrich on the shoulder and left the tavern.

Heinrich decided to make a return visit to Ed Blaine and thought it best to do so after dark, when there was less chance of being seen by his enemies. He had visited the young man at the Gamma Sigma house the previous week, after the fight outside the Lucky Strike. Blaine had been groggy but thankful for Heinrich's effort to save him that night. Having no illusions about Tichenor's eagerness to have him arrested for trespassing, he approached stealthily by way of the alley and entered through the back door of the Gamma Sigma house. He knew from previous experience that the boys regularly kept the back door open.

He entered a back hallway by the kitchen and walked toward the front of the building, where a large great room opened off to the right and stairs went upward on the left to the second floor. A young man with short red hair and a ruddy complexion who was lying on a couch looked up from a biology textbook.

"Hello, professor Heinie," he said with a grin.

Heinrich nodded. He had found it wise to tolerate the nickname. The students meant no harm by it.

"Is Ed Blaine still in the same room?" he asked.

The boy nodded. "Up the stairs and to the left."

"Thanks." Heinrich turned and walked upstairs. As he turned left into the upstairs corridor at the top of the stairs, he could see a white baseball flying back and forth across the hall between two open doorways.

Heinrich cautiously waved his hand in front of the door on the left and then peeked inside. The ball whizzed past his head, barely missing him.

"Sorry, professor!" It was Blaine's voice. "Frank and I were just playing a game of catch."

Heinrich gave a small wave and grinned at Frank in the opposite room, then walked inside Blaine's room. "You're looking better," he said to Blaine.

"I feel much better, sir, thanks to you."

Heinrich looked down at his shoes. "Only trying to help a soul in need."

"Yeah, well, thanks just the same."

Blaine paused, then continued. "I sure wish we could get those crooked bastards back. After I was drunk, they hooked me up with that cheap harlot, Diane, in the back room, and she picked my pocket. I lost thirty dollars."

Heinrich nodded sympathetically. "Take it as a lesson learned. Next time be more careful in your choice of entertainments."

Ed smiled. "You know, what I'd really like to do is go back, sneak into the back room, and get my money out of the safe."

"No," Heinrich said. "Don't even think about it. They'd get you on a burglary charge. Besides, that saloon never sleeps."

"You're right there. Still, I'd love to pull a prank on them just to show them who's boss."

"Don't do it; it's not worth the risk," Heinrich said. Still, even as the words came out of his mouth, a similar plan of his own began to form in his mind. Hunt wouldn't like it, but too bad. Hunt wasn't here.

Heinrich stopped to see Old Ben's widow, Mary. For his plan to work, he would need her help.

He found her, looking lonely, on the front porch of her tiny gray bungalow in "browntown," the term the white population used for the section of Franklinton where she lived. She perked up when she saw him.

"Well, I do declare, professor," she said. "What brings you down here?"

He sat beside her on the porch and explained his plan, in which she would play a small, but integral, part. She grinned and agreed to help.

"I'm doing this for Ben, you understand, because you and he were friends," she said.

Heinrich nodded. "Ben deserves revenge, doesn't he? Plus, you'll have a story to tell at your next shine party."

"Oh no, professor. This one needs to be our secret."

Three nights later, Heinrich launched his operation to break into the Franklinton Democratic Club. Mary Jones obtained the key for the offices from her friend, who cleaned Truman Fairchild's house once a week. The friend let Mary borrow it for a few hours, and Heinrich nonchalantly had a duplicate made at Watkins hardware store. He then returned the key to her quickly.

Two days later, Heinrich looked at his pocket watch, which read

10:10 p.m. Perched behind a woodpile a few doors down from the Lucky Strike saloon, he watched the Democratic Club building across the street closely for signs of life. Truman Fairchild had left the office, come down the stairs, and headed down the street to his brother's saloon fifteen minutes earlier. Two Fairchild goons stood guard outside as usual.

Heinrich turned his head to peek toward the saloon through a hole in the woodpile. As he had hoped, a group of eight ladies, Mrs. Yaeger included, from the local chapter of the Woman's Christian Temperance Union had stationed themselves outside, picketing with signs bearing slogans such as "Save Our Girls," "Wine is a Mockery" and "Rum Means Ruin." Although he could not make out her face, he could tell the group included Minnie Tichenor; he recognized her by her pompous bearing and stiff gait. Although he couldn't see her face, it was sure to hold its usual sour expression, he thought.

Mrs. Yaeger, apparently the group's song leader, occasionally led the women in temperance tunes, with melodies borrowed mainly from old, well-known favorites, such as "America the Beautiful," "Hail to the Chief," and "Old Dan Tucker" — fierce choral odes soaked in preachy platitudes about the evils of booze.

At present, Mrs. Yaeger had them singing something to the tune of "Yankee Doodle" that was apparently popular among the hatchet-waving hordes:

"Cold water is the drink for me,
Of all the drinks the best, sir;
Your grog, of whatever name it be,
I dare not for to taste, sir.
Give me Dame Nature's only drink,
And I can make it do, sir;
Then what care I what others think,
The best that ever grew, sir.

"We've had enough of license laws,
Enough of liquor's taxes.
We've fumed the grindstone long enough,
It's time to swing our axes.
This deadly upas tree must fall —
Let stroke be strong and steady,
Pull out the stumps! Grab out the roots!
Oh, Brothers! Are you ready!"

Heinrich had to admit, the tune was catchy. The women then

switched to a song based on "Auld Lang Syne," a rather maudlin ditty about the "Days of Drinking Wine," which was much less so. He grimaced at a line at the end of the first verse, "A temperance hour is worth a power of days of drinking wine."

Waiting for the annoying ditty to end, he checked his watch again. He expected Ed Blaine to arrive at any moment to cause the distraction he sought, although the temperance women were causing enough commotion that Blaine's ruse might not even be necessary. Then again, their protest might give him enough cover to make a speedy getaway later.

A few deliberately off-key drunks had shuffled onto the porch and joined the chorus, parodying the ladies' efforts. Someone hurled an insult from inside the saloon, and one of the ladies yelled something back.

Then Heinrich heard the sound of a galloping horse, the sound he was waiting for. When he saw Blaine atop the black mare borrowed from Dahlen's stable, he had to laugh at the young man's disguise, an old gingham dress whose long sleeves and skirt covered his arms and legs, although his leather riding boots were decidedly masculine. A pillowcase hood covered Blaine's head and face, but this was no ordinary, bald-knobbing hood. It had a female face with bulbous red lips and black eyeliner painted on it, and it sported golden pigtails made from yarn and tied with red calico bows — a nice touch, Heinrich had to admit.

On both flanks of the horse, "Temperance is Coming!" was written in white painted letters directly in the horsehair. A good rider, Blaine galloped up the street at a controlled clip while swinging an axe. He reared the horse up for a few seconds in front of the saloon and then plunged forward, still on the horse, into the doorway of the Lucky Strike.

"Support our sister!" screamed Mrs. Yaeger, and the WCTU women rushed into the saloon, from which loud screams and sounds of crashing glass could be heard. Heinrich saw the two guards at the Democratic Club look at each other, drop their cigars, and run down the street to the saloon. The diversion gave Heinrich the chance to sneak in unawares.

Heinrich quickly ran across the street, carrying a flashlight and laundry bag in the pockets of his overcoat, and up the back stairs to the second floor office as quietly as he could. He inserted the brass key into its matching faceplate and turned it to unlock the latch. As he turned the beaux-arts decorative brass knob to enter, he heard a particularly loud crash from the saloon behind him, a sound which he would later learn came from Ed Blaine hurling his axe to shatter the mirror above the bar. He hoped Ed would exit quickly before Fairchild's henchmen came around to using their guns, although he guessed gunplay would be a last resort around the group of women.

He knew he didn't have much time. Blaine could not stay in the bar long enough to get caught, just enough to pull off the prank and keep the guards' attention. How the ladies would react was a complete unknown; they hadn't been part of the original battle plan, but were a good addition.

He stopped inside and quietly locked the door behind him. He walked past the secretary's station, now dark, and headed for Fairchild's office, not knowing exactly what he was looking for, but hoping he'd find proof of wrongdoing.

Fairchild's office door was open, and he entered, shutting the door behind him. He looked around quickly. The Confederate battle flag and photo of Pendergast with those beady, malicious eyes stared down at him from one wall, and the painting of the attractive Asian princess in an alluring gold lame dress smirked at him with bedroom eyes from the other.

Heinrich opened the drawer of a walnut file cabinet and quickly rifled through four drawers of files. He found nothing particularly interesting, except for a hidden fifth of Old Granddad in the top drawer. On a shelf next to the filing cabinet sat a toy cannon and boxing glove. Something about the cannon, boxing glove, and Asian woman bothered him, pulling at his subconscious, but he couldn't put his finger on exactly what they might mean.

He then turned to Fairchild's rolltop desk and sat in the padded executive chair, which was black, or perhaps navy blue, depending on the accuracy of the soft glowing light from the flashlight. Damn, the desk doors were locked; he hadn't thought of that. He looked under the desk, but found nothing.

Then it came to him. He checked the top drawer of the filing cabinet again. Next to the bottle of whiskey was a small key he had seen earlier, attached to the front of the drawer with white surgical tape. He tried it on the top desk drawer. The key turned and worked the lock. He opened the drawer.

As he dug through the drawer, the first item of interest was a manila envelope filled with photos of men and women in various stages of undress. The common pose, over and over again, was of a man holding a highball glass or beer mug in one hand and a topless or totally nude woman in the other. He whistled softly, then remembered where he was and silenced himself.

These photos must be from the orgies held for Fairchild's supporters, which Sally had chronicled in the paper. Fairchild probably kept them for blackmail purposes. He could make out the mayor, county commissioners and even President Tichenor all making a little too merry in the photos. Heinrich almost felt sorry for Tichenor's wife — almost. He set the envelope aside.

Then he saw ledger books. That was the sort of thing he was looking for. The entries included hundreds of thousands in donations from the Lucky Strike saloon and large gifts to the Democratic Club from other donors. Heinrich guessed that some of those donations had probably been coerced with assistance from the illicit photos of men cavorting with women who were not their wives. It was no wonder Fairchild never found himself short of cash.

In addition, the two books showed outgoing monies being deposited directly from the saloon's take into the college's bank accounts, a fact that raised Heinrich's eyebrows for a moment. He continued to rifle quickly through the rest of the desk, then relocked the drawers, and placed the key back in the filing cabinet.

Then, taking one last look under the rolltop, he saw a long, slender piece of heavy, dark gray steel, about the size of a very thick ruler, in one of the cubbyholes. He pulled it from its slot and shined his flashlight on it to look at the surface. Then he realized what he was looking at — it said "Franklinton Democrat," in negative with an eagle and bunting. It was the "flag" of Sally's newspaper, what many people think of as the masthead.

"That rat bastard," whispered Heinrich.

A sound came from outside. Heinrich switched off his flashlight and ducked down behind the desk, quickly sliding the newspaper flag, the envelope with photos and the ledger books into his laundry bag and tightening the drawstring.

Somebody was checking the lock; probably the guards had returned. He could hear them tromping back down the stairs to the street.

It was time to go. He needed an alternative escape route. Once out in the hallway, past the secretary's station, he turned left and headed down the hall to a window. Looking outside, he could see the branches of a strong oak tree that came down behind a small fence that enclosed garbage cans and an outhouse.

He tied the sack around his neck — probably not the best way to carry it, but it would have to do for now. He then exited the window, climbed onto the nearest tree limb, and methodically worked his way down the bough and trunk, trying to make as little noise as possible.

He could still hear commotion around the Lucky Strike, but he couldn't see it. Reaching the ground, he crouched behind the privy shed for a moment, listening intently. All he could hear were excited voices coming from the saloon's direction.

He imagined the sheriff's deputies would be taking accounts from all the witnesses, but he thought it most prudent to leave that fact for others to confirm. He entered the main street and walked nonchalantly away from the action as quickly as he could along the sidewalk, swinging his laundry bag. He would surely hear more about the saloon riot later.

Heinrich awoke with a start. Someone was knocking loudly on his door. Moonlight from the window shone on the brass bedframe. He got up, rubbed his eyes, turned on the bedside lamp and looked at his pocket watch. It was just past a quarter after 2 a.m.

"Yeah, what is it?" he called to the door.

"Heinrich, Marshal Hunt is calling for you," said Mrs. Yaeger from the other side of the door, with a voice tainted by distress. "He needs you. It's urgent."

Heinrich winced. He hoped the Marshal hadn't learned somehow about his nocturnal activities; he wanted to tell Hunt about that himself.

"In the middle of the night? I thought he was still in St. Louis?" Heinrich answered.

"He came back to town early," she said. Something wasn't right about her tone; there was an edge in her voice.

"Are you okay, Mrs. Yaeger?" he asked as he eyed his loaded Colt holstered in the gunbelt hung on the bedpost.

"Yes, just tired and startled is all." She sounded as if she'd been crying. Heinrich got up from the bed.

"Just a minute," he said.

He put his shirt and trousers from the day before on over his union suit and pulled on his boots. Seeing his laundry bag beside the bed with the items from Fairchild's office still inside it, he made a quick decision. Just as a precaution, he quickly wrapped the newspaper flag in a dirty shirt, placed the envelope of photos inside the cover of one of the two ledgers, wrapped them in a pair of trousers, and put it all back in the laundry bag. "Heinrich?" Mrs. Yaeger asked again.

"Just a minute," he replied.

He opened the small flap to the laundry chute underneath the desk, and dropped the bag in. He heard a muffled "flop" sound from below in the basement, where Mrs. Yaeger kept her big laundry bin. He quietly closed the cabinet door to the laundry chute and placed the nearby rectangular wicker wastebasket in front of it. Holding the pistol in his right hand, he stood sideways to the door and turned the brass doorknob with his left hand.

The door creaked open slowly at first. He could see Mrs. Yaeger in the dark, a grim look on her face. Suddenly the door burst open wide, and six men in pillowcase hoods pushed into his room. One of them held Mrs. Yaeger from behind with a strong arm. He dragged her across the wood floor and held a knife to her throat.

Heinrich aimed his peacemaker at the man's head and thought about chancing a shot.

"Put the gun down, Kueter, or the lady dies," the man with the knife said. Heinrich turned to aim at one assailant, then another. He ended up back again at the man with the knife.

"Drop the gun, Kueter," the man said, gripping Mrs. Yaeger. "I'm not going to tell you again."

Heinrich recognized the voice. It was John Fairchild.

"Don't be stupid, Kueter. Put it down."

It was a lost cause. He was a good shot, but he couldn't count on it with his unpracticed aim. And he couldn't afford for her to be hurt on his account. Too many had died already. He said a silent prayer, put the gun on the bed and raised his hands.

"That's a good Kraut," Fairchild said. "I believe you know my night riders. You're coming with us."

One of the scarecrow-faced men tied Heinrich's hands behind his back and stuffed a rag in his mouth. Fairchild picked up the Colt and released Mrs. Yaeger, but immediately clubbed her in the head with the pistol. She crumpled to the floor in a heap of skirts.

"Let's move," Fairchild said. Two young men grabbed Heinrich by the arms and hustled him down the stairs toward a waiting buckboard. They threw him into the back. A sharp pain shot through his left shoulder and elbow when he landed on his side in the wooden buckboard. A splinter lodged in his left cheek.

The driver yelled out, "Giddap!" and the buckboard lurched forward. The men held him down on the floorboards with their boots, but he could tell the buckboard was following a winding path out into the woods, maybe to a secluded hunting spot. Peering between his feet, he could barely see that they had passed over an old bridge over Smiley Creek that he knew was a popular gathering place for secret keg parties that the college administration was not supposed to know about.

The wagon stopped. The men pulled him roughly out and pushed him through the front door of a hunting cabin. Inside it was pitch black, and it stank of sweat and damp mud. Fairchild shoved him onto a wooden chair, and his partners in crime tied Heinrich tightly to it.

"We'll come for you later, Nigger lover," Fairchild said with a smirk before locking the door shut. Heinrich could see it had a modern steel lock, not the old-fashioned string-through-a-hole setup. "Just think: You can learn how the Chink felt on his big day."

CHAPTER 9

In the ink-black darkness of the cabin, Heinrich struggled with the ropes binding his wrists, ankles, and chest to the chair. He could feel the rough-hewn oak timber against his skin. Flexing his neck to the rear, he rested his head against wood and could tell the chair had a high back that extended above his head.

He wondered why his captors hadn't just killed him; he had no money to speak of and wouldn't bring a good ransom. The answer had to be that they hadn't yet found the photos and ledger he'd stolen from Truman Fairchild's office. If he stayed put, they would most likely torture him for the information.

He hoped Fairchild's thugs wouldn't hurt Mrs. Yaeger; they might if she didn't give them what they wanted. Certainly, they would ransack his room, but it would be difficult to search the entire boarding house without raising the suspicions of the other boarders. He wondered how long it would take them to figure out his laundry chute maneuver. Of course, none of it would matter if he couldn't get loose. He needed to escape; better to die on his feet fighting.

Turning his head sideways, Heinrich felt a protruding knot in the wood against his left ear. Maneuvering his tongue, he pushed the rag in his mouth outward while simultaneously craning his neck to the left, but he couldn't quite make the rag reach the knothole. He then tried pressing with the back of his neck and rubbing the rag knot against the rough chair. After a few minutes, he had loosened the rag enough to snag a corner of it on the wood knot, which provided the leverage to slowly work the gag out of his mouth. He gasped for air as he managed to spit the gag out. Cool, fresh air flowed in quickly. He took several deep breaths in through his nostrils and exhaled through his mouth, partly just to calm down. He knew he couldn't make too much noise and attract attention. If he were lucky, he might have one chance to free himself. He needed to make it count.

Testing the restraints on his legs, he could tell that the rope on his right ankle seemed a little looser than the one on his left. He leaned back in the chair, tipping it as far as he dared, and moved his ankle up and down until he worked the rope off the bottom end of the chair leg. With his right ankle free, he focused on freeing his other ankle, pushing downward with his opposite foot until it too came loose.

During his hour or so of captivity, his eyes had become accustomed to the darkness, and he noticed a small length of bailers' twine hanging on a rusty nail in the far wall. Pushing with his feet, he scooted his chair across the dirt floor to check it out. The nail stuck out about four feet from the floor; he figured some hunter had hung gear on it.

Heinrich slithered his chair into place so that the back of the chair rested against the log wall and the nail. He pushed with his feet to work himself and the chair up and down, as if he were using the wall to scratch his back, over and over. The rope on his chest alternately tightened painfully and slackened with each thrust of his legs. After 15 grueling minutes, the rope began to weaken. He had to rest for a moment; the sweat of exertion drenched his body and caused him to shudder in the chilly, drafty cabin. After catching his breath, he began the leg thrusts again, counting them in sets of ten and then stopping to rest. After another quarter hour's workout, he had loosened the chest ropes enough so that he thought he might wriggle loose if only he could free his arms.

Heinrich noticed that the chair's left arm had a slight wiggle. He couldn't see why in the dark; the supports where it attached to the seat were weak, perhaps from rot, a wood split or old glue gone bad. Heinrich decided to chance hitting the chair arm against the wall as hard as he could. He pushed with his feet and slammed his left side against the cabin wall, gritting his teeth at the pain shooting through his forearm, then stopped to listen carefully to make sure nobody could hear what he was doing. He heard nothing but the sound of distant laughter and an Indian drum. Emboldened, he crashed the chair arm into the wall again and again. Of course, while hitting the wood against the wall, he could not avoid whacking his own arm in the process. It hurt like hell, and the bruises on his arm mounted, but he had no choice. He had to get loose. After what seemed like an eternity, he heard the crack of splintering wood.

Success! He slammed against the wall one final time and broke the arm of the chair out of its socket in the seat. With the chair arm still tied to his bruised left forearm, he reached across with his left hand and worked at the ropes on his right arm, then wriggled out of the chest ropes. In ten minutes, he was completely free and holding the F-shaped chair arm as a makeshift weapon.

Peering out through a knothole in the door, he could see the glow of a campfire in the distance with a dozen men milling about and sharing bottles of whiskey. He assumed the leader was John Fairchild, holding court with his renegade Kappa Psis. Their clothes looked tattered; many wore ragged shirts with dirty dungarees or dusty riding chaps. Each also wore a hood made from a pillowcase or feed bag.

Heinrich studied the scene but could not detect Truman Fairchild or his henchmen. Probably still at the boarding house, he thought. Heinrich saw John Fairchild stand and point to a noose, probably meant for him, hung from a limb on a nearby tree. Apparently, they were to make an example of him for their entertainment. We'll see how that works out, he thought, grinning warily. He would enjoy avenging himself on them, but first things first. He needed to get away.

He looked closely at the door and tried the knob, which was locked. He studied the hinges, which appeared to be made of iron. Inspiration! He felt in his pocket and pulled out the Teutonic cross. He was surprised his captors hadn't taken it; maybe religious superstition had stopped them. Using the top extender of the cross like a screwdriver and the broken chair arm like a hammer, he tapped upward on the cross to knock out the two hinge pins. It worked! In no time, he had disconnected the hinges and then pulled the hinge side of the door inward carefully, not wanting it to fall and make a sound. Opening the door about eight inches, he slid between the door and frame and then quickly fit the door back into its hinges, although they wouldn't hold the door if anyone pushed on it. He then dropped to his belly and slithered low through dirt, leaves, and wood chips as silently as possible into the moonlit night.

Staying as low as he could on his hands and knees, Heinrich crawled to a woodpile about 20 yards to the right of the cabin. From the pile of logs, he pulled out a stout broken limb about two feet long that might be useful as a crude club. Hearing someone coming, he hid behind the stacked logs.

Crouched low, he saw one of his captors headed for the cabin with a handgun and a bowl of soup or beans, presumably for his final supper. Realizing the guard would soon sound the alarm, Heinrich made a split-second decision and crept closer to the cabin door. The guard put the pistol in his waistband, pulled a key from his pants pocket, and unlocked the door.

"Shit, what the hell...?" Heinrich heard the young man exclaim as he pushed on the door, which collapsed into the cabin, and peered inside.

As the man turned to run out of the cabin, Heinrich hit him with his log club, first in the stomach and then the head, before his enemy could make another sound. The young man toppled to the ground unconscious.

Heinrich recognized the young man as one of the Kappa Psis, but he couldn't remember the youth's name. Heinrich took the lad's revolver and put it in his waistband. He dragged the young man inside the cabin, reinserted the pins in the hinges, and locked the door with the key he found in the youth's pocket. Then Heinrich ran back to the woodpile and crouched behind it. He pulled the revolver from his waistband and checked its cylinder for bullets. It was empty. He needed another weapon. Looking around, he saw a hatchet lodged in a nearby log, but it wouldn't help him much unless he could get in close to his enemy – and he didn't want to be any closer than he had to be.

Peeking out from his hiding place behind the logs, Heinrich counted nine Kappa Psis around the campfire, including the jail escapees and others. Heinrich had no intention of sticking around to witness their barbarity firsthand, so he headed toward a nearby tree, intending to work his way out of the area using whatever cover was available.

Then he heard a rifle bolt click shut. "Hold it right there, Kueter," said a voice Heinrich recognized. John Fairchild stood behind Heinrich, alone, with a rifle trained on him.

Heinrich's first instinct was to swing around and fire the pistol, but he knew he had no bullets. And he didn't want gunfire to bring the other renegades to their leader's rescue. He turned slowly, the pistol still in his right hand.

"You may as well drop it and give up," Fairchild said. "That was Andy's gun you stole. He didn't have any ammo for it. That is, unless you're planning to throw it at me."

Heinrich complied, swearing under his breath. He couldn't afford for Fairchild to fire the rifle and alert his friends. He desperately sought a way out, but all he had available were rocks, wood, and a rusty hatchet. "What are you going to do to me?"

"Oh, that's easy. Once we find the things you stole, you're tonight's main attraction. Your Mick-loving, Chink-loving, Nigger-loving life ends this evening."

"So you're just going to throw away your life too? I thought you didn't kill Tommy Lee," Heinrich said. "That's what you told me at the trial."

"I didn't, but I have killed too many others. I've gone too far to stop now."

Heinrich shook his head. "There's still a chance to reverse the decision, you know. I've come to believe you; I know you didn't kill Tommy. I just can't prove it yet."

"Quit grasping at straws, Kraut. You and your Chink friend ruined my life, and now you're going to pay for it."

Fairchild raised the rifle and took aim. Heinrich had only one chance. He quickly looked past Fairchild's shoulder toward the front of the cabin as if someone were behind the young man with the rifle, quickly nodded and said, "Now."

As Fairchild whirled around instinctively to fend off an attack from a nonexistent assailant, Heinrich dived over the woodpile, grabbed the hatchet, and hurled it, targeting Fairchild's chest as the younger man turned back around in a fury.

"You goddamn..." Fairchild gurgled, sinking to his knees. Heinrich realized with a flash of regret that the young man wouldn't speak again. The hatchet had flown a little high and lodged just above Fairchild's breastbone, in his lower neck, below his Adam's apple. However, as the youth fell to the ground, his rifle fired – too late to save his life, but not too late to warn the other outlaws.

Heinrich moved to Fairchild, who had rolled onto his back, gasping his final breaths from the mortal wound. Fairchild grabbed the sleeve of Heinrich's shirt with his right hand and pointed with his left index finger.

"I didn't kill Tommy..." he said, his eyes filled with fear. "I didn't..." Heinrich felt the life leave Fairchild's body and pulled his arm back to wrest it loose from the grip of the dead man.

Heinrich could hear the other young men heading toward him with shouts and crackling leaves underfoot. Time for combat. Heinrich grabbed Fairchild's rifle and took off running as fast as he could through the woods, jumping boulders and dodging tree limbs in the dark, doing his best to stay ahead of his pursuers. He scraped his knee on a low tree limb and turned his ankle in a six-inch hole, but he had to keep going. Luckily, visibility was just as poor for the young men chasing him as it was for Heinrich. If he could find a landmark to catch his bearings, or some good cover, he might have a chance.

Suddenly, he entered a clearing between two stands of trees.

Instinctively, he knew such terrain meant trouble; he needed the cover of trees. Just the same, he had to keep running and decided to chance the open field. He sprinted across it and headed for the next stand of trees.

He could see a thick group of trees about 20 feet in front of him when the ground quickly dropped into a ditch. Running so fast that he couldn't stop, he stepped into the trench before he knew it was there and fell forward onto a gravel road, dropping the rifle and scraping his cheek and hands in the stones. Rising to his knees, he felt the sting on his palms and face, but he would live — for now, anyway.

Hearing the approach of a galloping horse, he dropped to his belly and aimed the rifle in its direction.

A dark horse appeared on the dimly moonlit road and slowed its gait to a hesitant walk.

"Kueter?" the rider asked.

It was Marshal Hunt. Heinrich stood up. "Boy am I glad to see you."

Hunt shined a flashlight on him. Seeing the dirt, blood, and torn clothing, the marshal whistled. "What in tarnation happened to you?"

"There's no time to explain," Heinrich said. "The renegades. They're after me."

Hunt grunted and nodded. He tossed Heinrich a badge, a Colt revolver and some cartridges.

"You find cover and stay here," Hunt said. "Smith and Jones are back down the road. I'll get them, and we'll circle around and bag 'em from behind."

Apparently now serving as the bait for the trap, Heinrich scrambled to the ditch on the other side of the road to face his pursuers. He loaded his weapons and waited; you never wanted to be the prey, but at least this fox had teeth now. Heinrich was no stranger to killing; he'd make these boys pay.

He didn't have long to wait. The renegades soon appeared, working their way through the brush on his trail.

"He must have come into the clearing about here," he heard Ringgold say. He could see Ringgold clearly in the moonlight. He sighted the rifle – a Springfield M1903, which he knew well from his Army days – and waited. He knew that firing would give away his position, so he wanted his shots to count.

Just a little closer, Mr. Ringgold, he thought. Just a little farther this way. At 50 yards, Heinrich decided the time had come. He fired a shot into Ringgold's left thigh. The youth screamed and fell, holding his leg. The other eight young men fell on their bellies.

"You Heinie bastard!" Ringgold yelled.

"You're damn lucky I didn't kill you," Heinrich shot back. He realized it was a stupid thing to do, providing another clue to his position for little gain.

One of them fired a shot in his direction, but it sailed well over his head.

A minute later, Hunt's voice bellowed from behind the renegades, "Boys, it's over! Drop your weapons and hold your hands high, or by god, I'll shoot every last one of you where you lie!"

For a moment, nobody moved. Then, one by one, the outlaws stood with their hands in the air. Marshal Hunt rode forward with the two deputies, who dismounted and shackled the prisoners.

"Take 'em to the county jail and hold 'em," Hunt told Smith, who nodded.

"Marshal, we need to make sure Mrs. Yaeger is all right," Heinrich said.

Hunt nodded, pulled Heinrich up behind him on his black horse, and began the ride toward town. "You can fill me in on the way," he said.

Heinrich and Hunt stopped quickly at Manfred Dahlen's stable to drop off the exhausted horse, which had worked up a sweat hauling both of them back to town. They found Dahlen and Murphy there playing checkers. The two quickly volunteered to help, and the marshal deputized them. Dahlen strapped on an aged and holstered European revolver and handed Murphy a Winchester 97 repeating shotgun.

Noticing Heinrich's interest in the revolver, Dahlen said, "It's Austrian, Rast and Gasser; I used it in the Boxer Rebellion."

Hunt nodded. "Always handy to have an old friend in a fight. Is it clean?"

Dahlen crossed his arms. "As an artillery man, I take care of my weapons. While she may look a little rusty on the outside for character, I assure you her insides are *wunderbar*."

Hunt laughed. "Just making sure. Didn't mean any offense."

As the first hints of impending dawn peeked over the eastern horizon, they walked down the street toward the boarding house at a quick trot and then carefully circled around behind the college chapel across the street to reconnoiter. The Marshal quietly moved forward to scout the immediate situation at the boarding house and quickly returned.

"Okay, here's how it looks," he told the others. "There's one guard each at the front and back doors. My guess is Fairchild's still inside looking for the stuff you stole; he needs to find it quickly before the other guests start waking and getting suspicious."

Heinrich nodded. On the way to town, he had told the marshal about his foray into Fairchild's office and the events surrounding his capture. None too happy that his deputy had launched a solo operation without backup, Hunt had responded that if Heinrich could develop some brains to match his guts, he might make a good lawman someday. Heinrich laughed at the comment, but Hunt hadn't been in the mood to joke.

"I'm not kidding, Kueter. You're damn lucky to be alive."

Heinrich said nothing. The marshal was right.

"Mrs. Yaeger will need to begin preparing breakfast for the boarders soon; he'll probably have a guard posted on her," Heinrich said. "And he's probably got somebody in my room, ransacking it."

Hunt nodded. "Right, but the good news is he probably can't have many goons inside; he can't afford to make too much fuss, for fear of making her other boarders suspicious," he said. "That should help us: We're probably about even, and I hope to have surprise on our side."

Hunt quickly outlined the plan of attack. Murphy and Dahlen would distract the guard at the front door. Simultaneously, the marshal would neutralize the guard at the back door, and once inside, would head toward the front door to help the others. Meanwhile, Heinrich would enter through a first-floor window and make his way to the basement to retrieve the information from Fairchild's office that he had dropped down the laundry chute. Hunt reminded them to work fast and quietly to keep surprise on their side. If the boarders were to come forth, all hell might break loose.

"If we aren't careful, we'll have a disaster on our hands," he said. "Any questions?" There were none. "Then let's get going."

Dawn was emerging, but the shadows were still murky and provided good cover. From across the street to the west, Heinrich watched Murphy hide his shotgun behind a wide-trunked box elder tree in the southwest side yard. Then he and Dahlen walked nonchalantly toward the house on the front sidewalk. Heinrich sprinted across the street, shimmied through a gap between two honeysuckle bushes that were starting to leaf out for the spring and headed for the side of the house, looking for the back-corner kitchen window that he knew Mrs. Yaeger often left open to help vent cooking smoke from the stove. He knew that, even when she closed the window, she rarely locked it; she needed to be able to open it quickly in case of a stovetop accident.

As Heinrich began to push the window upward with his palms, a voice to his left said, "Hold it right there."

Heinrich turned to face the voice. Apparently, the guard from the back door had seen him cross the yard. He raised his arms in surrender and pretended not to see Marshal Hunt sneaking up behind the man.

Hunt put a pistol in the man's ear and whispered, "Not another word, if you want to live. Drop your weapon."

The guard dropped his pistol and raised his hands. Hunt frisked and cuffed him, stuffed a bandana in his mouth and hit him over the head with the butt of his revolver.

Giving Heinrich a nod, Hunt pointed to his own chest and then to the back door. Heinrich nodded his understanding, and Hunt left to enter the back door as planned.

Heinrich turned back to the window and pushed up on the bottom frame with his palms. A little stiff, the window made a slight creak as it went up, which worried him. With his back to the wall, he quickly moved toward the front of the house and saw that Murphy and Dahlen had started their performance on the sidewalk just outside the white picket fence that skirted the perimeter of the immediate front yard.

Although he couldn't see the guard, he could hear the man chuckle as Murphy called Dahlen a "dumb Kraut" and pushed him into an evergreen bush. A furious Dahlen retorted that Murphy was a "drunken, stupid Mick" and tackled him, pushing him over the fence into the front yard. They play-acted their parts well, keeping the guard entertained and allowing Heinrich to finish pushing open the window. He quietly climbed over the threshold into the kitchen. Looking around in the gray light of early dawn, he saw it was neat as always, with not a pot or dish out of place. Apparently Fairchild had not searched in here yet, nor had Mrs. Yaeger started to cook breakfast. He hoped she was all right.

He guessed that the cunning gangster would begin by searching his room and then would try to figure out other alternatives. Whether Fairchild had figured out about the laundry chute was anybody's guess, but sooner or later, he surely would consider the possibility. Heinrich headed toward the basement stairs. Even though it would be a bad place to get ambushed, safeguarding Mrs. Yaeger and obtaining the evidence had to be his highest priorities.

Heinrich moved cautiously into the hallway. The loaded Colt revolver felt heavy in his right hand as he moved stealthily toward the basement door. He paused and leaned against it. His heart was pounding. At that point, Hunt entered the hallway from the back door and nodded toward the front door as he sidled past Heinrich. The sign meant Hunt planned to help Dahlen and Murphy secure the rest of the house first, while Heinrich stood guard over the basement door.

Heinrich took his post and watched Hunt head for the front door.

In the entryway, Hunt looked out through one of the tall windows that flanked the front door. From the front, the house looked as if it had two vertical slit eyes framing a large nose.

Hunt eased open the front door carefully. The guard did not notice the slight creak from the hinges, engrossed as he was in Murphy and Dahlen's vaudeville act.

"Don't move, and don't make a sound," Hunt whispered, putting a gun to the man's head. The gun against the man's temple clearly implied the result of doing otherwise. The guard raised his hands, and Hunt hit him over the head with the butt of his revolver. The man crumpled to the floor, and Murphy and Dahlen soon entered through the front door, weapons ready. Hunt pointed them upstairs, and they quietly climbed to the second floor.

Hunt then turned to Heinrich and pointed to his eyes with his left index finger and forefinger, indicating either that Heinrich should stay and keep watch or watch out; Heinrich wasn't really sure which. Hunt then headed upstairs behind Dahlen and Murphy.

Heinrich stayed put for a moment, but then heard a crashing sound and a woman's whimper coming from the basement. He opened the basement door slightly so that he could listen. He could hear Fairchild and Mrs. Yaeger downstairs.

"Mildred, I've had enough lies. Where are the items the Kraut stole from me?" Fairchild shouted.

"I don't know," she replied. Heinrich could tell Mrs. Yaeger was crying.

"That's a lie," Fairchild said, followed by another crash, which worried Heinrich. He quickly glanced upstairs, but there was no sign of Hunt or the others. He had to make his move downstairs for Mrs. Yaeger's sake and hope that Hunt would follow him soon.

Quietly, with deliberate steps, Heinrich made his way down the wooden stairs into a large basement room, the stone walls of which were lighted by a single, dim bulb installed only recently. Mrs. Yaeger stood with her back against a tall oak cabinet that held mops, brooms and cleaning supplies. Fairchild faced her, his hands pinning her arms to the cabinet.

"Tell me where you've hidden them, you Mick whore," Fairchild hissed, then slapped her face hard with his right hand. She fell against the cabinet, creating the crashing sound Heinrich had heard from upstairs.

Heinrich aimed his revolver. "One more move, and I'll blow your head off," he said.

Fairchild whirled and dived behind a steamer trunk that sat on a pallet on the dirt floor. Mrs. Yaeger ran in the opposite direction, jumping for cover behind her prized new Thor electric clothes washer. The wringer atop the device was known to be dangerous, which is why she did not allow children in her basement. Many careless women who got too close to the wringer while it was running were rumored to have been injured by the Thor machine in the few years since its invention.

"Stay down, Mildred," Heinrich called, finding cover for himself behind a pair of stacked wooden crates. Fairchild fired a shot at him with a pistol, and Heinrich fired back with his Colt.

"You goddam thief!" Fairchild yelled. "I should've killed you long before now."

"Yeah, too bad you're too incompetent to handle the job," Heinrich answered. He moved to a box nearer to Mrs. Yaeger, trying to maneuver himself between Fairchild and her so that she might escape up the stairs.

"What say we let Mildred go?" Heinrich asked.

"No, she stays," Fairchild said, firing a round at him simultaneously.

Heinrich peered in the direction of the voice. Fairchild appeared to have moved from his previous position. Heinrich continued to move in Fairchild's direction, threading his way between boxes of bottles, sacks of potatoes and crates of onions. He came to a green, wooden workbench, probably built by Mrs. Yaeger's late husband. Crouching low next to it, he found the spot where Fairchild had been, but of course, the gangster was no longer there. Whatever happened, he couldn't let Fairchild get away; he might even have to head back upstairs and wait the thug out. Either way, the conflict must end today — right here, right now.

As Heinrich turned back toward the stairs, suddenly Fairchild stood and fired his pistol. The bullet sailed over Heinrich's head and shattered the basement lightbulb, plunging the room into darkness. Heinrich dropped behind an old baby crib, looking furtively in all directions, hoping his eyes would adjust soon to the limited light. His eyes did adjust, but only in time to see Fairchild lunging at him in the darkness.

They grappled. Suddenly Heinrich's chest burned with pain as Fairchild slashed him with a knife. Heinrich instinctively clenched and hunched over, his arms holding his bleeding torso. Then Fairchild kicked him in the gut. Heinrich fell with a thud on the dirt floor and dropped his gun. In the darkness, he could feel the legs of the Thor washing machine next to him on his right. Heinrich rose to his knees as Fairchild towered over him, his left hand leaning on the machine's wringer, and the pistol in his right hand.

"It's over for you, Kraut," he said, panting, and aimed his pistol to fire point blank at Heinrich.

His right hand clawing desperately for some weapon in the darkness, Heinrich suddenly found the lever for the wringer on the side of the machine and pulled it downward to turn it on. The wringer roared quickly to life and grabbed hold of the cuff of Fairchild's shirtsleeve. The gangster screamed and clawed at it with his other hand in the darkness as it pulled his hand into its unforgiving jaws. The pistol fired high, and Fairchild's knees buckled as he reached desperately for the electrical cord to unplug the machine.

Suddenly Mrs. Yaeger arrived at Heinrich's side and thrust a heavy, metallic, strangely textured, and thick piece of steel into Heinrich's hand. "Hit him!" she yelled, and he complied, clubbing Fairchild in the head over and over in the dark, all the while yelling like a savage caveman hitting a rival over the head with a rock, until Fairchild's body went limp. Heinrich took Fairchild's pistol from the gangster and trained it on Fairchild, who was at least unconscious, perhaps dying. Meanwhile, Mildred Yaeger found Heinrich's Colt on the floor and traded weapons with him. He stood over Fairchild for a few more moments, looking for a sign of life, but none came.

"Mildred, go get a flashlight," Heinrich said.

She ran up the stairs, and he could hear her rummaging through a kitchen drawer. She returned, with Hunt, Murphy, and Dahlen behind her.

"You okay?" the marshal asked.

"I'm not dead," Heinrich said, his breath short and his chest on fire from the knife wound.

Mrs. Yaeger shone the flashlight on Fairchild, whose face was a bloody mess. Heinrich felt for a pulse in the man's neck. There was none.

"He's dead," Heinrich said, marking the obvious. Still holding the thick piece of metal that he had used as a weapon, he trained the flashlight beam down on it to see what it was. It was the iron typeset flag from Sally's newspaper. He would later appreciate the irony of using it as a club, but for now, he needed a doctor to bind his chest wound, which would take 20 stitches to close.

"Where did you hide it?" he asked Mrs. Yaeger, waving the newspaper flag.

"I found it and the other things you dropped down the chute in the laundry pile and hid them in the washing machine with a load of laundry," she said. "I figured no man would look there."

"Apparently, you were correct. I suppose it was as good a hiding place as any," he said. "Good thing nobody turned on the water."

The others laughed nervously. It had been a rough night.

Heinrich began to feel faint from loss of blood and staggered forward. Murphy and Dahlen caught him, put his arms across their shoulders and carried him upstairs between them.

"You fellows all right?" Heinrich heard himself ask.

"Great," Murphy said. They were both still a bit high on adrenaline from the excitement.

"Exhilarated," Dahlen said. "I had forgotten the rush of feeling one gets from combat; I haven't felt so alive since I battled those damn Boxers…"

But Heinrich didn't hear all that, having begun to lose consciousness.

CHAPTER 10

Of the renegade Kappa Psis brought before him, Judge Jamison let only two off with probation or short jail terms of six or fewer months. He declared them minor players, "too ignorant or immature to understand the seriousness of their actions." The majority were convicted and sentenced to long prison terms as accessories to kidnapping; the murders of "Old Ben" Jackson, Sheriff Thackeray, Martin Mason, and Tommy Lee; the assault on Sally Ann Giddings; and the kidnapping and attempted murder of Heinrich Kueter. Likewise, all but one of Truman Fairchild's hired thugs received long sentences for their role in his schemes.

The judge posthumously convicted both John Fairchild, for the murder of Sheriff Thackeray and the kidnapping of Heinrich. Likewise, he convicted Truman Fairchild of numerous crimes. Most satisfying to Heinrich was the elder Fairchild's conviction for the attack on Sally and the arson at her newspaper. In addition to the metal flag of the *Franklinton Democrat* being found in Truman Fairchild's possession, the fingerprints that Hunt had found after the newspaper fire placed Truman Fairchild at the scene of the crime.

As Heinrich's chest wound healed over the next couple of weeks, tremors from the scandal reverberated throughout the community. Marshal Hunt brought in more federal help to investigate the Fairchilds' activities and their connection to Worcester College. Sifting through Fairchild's ledgers and other records with a fine-tooth comb, Hunt found that President Tichenor had helped Truman Fairchild funnel proceeds from the Lucky Strike saloon's gambling, prostitution, and thievery operations through the college's accounts.

When combined with rumors that he had helped cover up the

murders of two Worcester College students and the turmoil on campus, the illegal financial dealings were the final straw for Tichenor's presidency. First the faculty passed a nearly unanimous no-confidence resolution. Then the Board of Trustees voted to force his resignation, replacing him on an interim basis with the academic dean. Finally, the interim president named Erwin Goforth as acting dean, a move Heinrich saw as a positive step forward.

On a Friday afternoon in late May, Hunt found Heinrich playing chess with Dahlen at the stable on a rough oak table, with two whiskey crates for chairs. Although the aroma of horse manure smelled a bit pungent that day, Heinrich didn't mind. The game was just one of many they had shared over the school year, but something about today's game unsettled Heinrich. The unsolved murder of Tommy Lee still bothered him, and something about the symbolism of the game nagged at his mind, something he couldn't quite put his finger on.

No matter, he thought. First he had to rescue his queen, which was in grave danger of being forked by a knight. We can't have knights forking queens, he thought to himself, with an amused grin, but didn't share the ribald joke. Heinrich moved his queen one space to the right to get her out of her predicament.

When Hunt knocked on the door and entered, Heinrich looked up. That was Hunt's way; he would often knock for courtesy's sake but rarely waited for permission. His official role allowed him to break social convention when he wished.

"It's time," Hunt said to Heinrich.

Heinrich nodded. "Okay, then let's go."

Heinrich had known the visit to Tichenor's house would come soon. The visit was sure to be most unpleasant, and Heinrich held mixed feelings about it. Arresting the former president seemed like overkill; Heinrich doubted the man would risk fleeing to freedom. At the same time, he strangely felt drawn to the event; he couldn't miss the final scene of the drama even if he'd wanted to.

Kueter and Hunt marched the four blocks to the president's federal revival style home, with its round white columns out front. Rumor had it that the Tichenors had received notice to vacate the premises by July, and they were preparing to move out soon. Heinrich followed Hunt up the stairs to the front porch, and Hunt rapped his furry knuckles on the white door.

Mrs. Tichenor answered the door with a scowl. "What do you two vultures want?"

Hunt tipped his hat. "We need to see your husband, ma'am."

A sudden look of despair crossed her face; Heinrich almost felt sorry for her. "To arrest him?" she asked, and began to cry.

"Yes, ma'am; sorry, but it has to be," Hunt said.

"Why did we ever come to this godforsaken place?" she asked with a sob.

Heinrich remained silent. After all, what could he say to an Easterner out of her element? That disillusion is inevitable here? This is Missouri; get used to it. Here, you are always a short-timer, passing through on your way to someplace else. We're either just a stagecoach stop on your way to a fortune in gold, furs, land or conquest — or we're where you retreat when your expedition into the western land of milk and honey has failed. Heinrich now really wished he hadn't come.

She turned to him. "And you – I wish we had never met you, you spawn of Satan."

Heinrich nodded, suddenly feeling a tinge of remorse. "Now, I am become death," he said. "The destroyer of worlds."

She said nothing, but her eyes blazed with hate. Then she spat at him, a move he hadn't expected. He turned away and wiped the spittle off the lapel of his dark gray suit with a handkerchief. Hunt took her by the shoulders and led her to an overstuffed chair, where she collapsed in a heap.

"Kueter," Hunt said. "Your bedside manner needs work."

Heinrich smiled weakly. "Sorry.

Dr. Tichenor entered the room with a regal gait reminiscent of King Charles at the gallows and comforted his wife. After a moment, he stood up, his defiant gray eyes blazing with fury.

"So, have you merely come to torture my wife, or are you here on business?" he said.

Hunt sighed and shook his head. "Strictly business, sir. We are here to arrest you for laundering illicit funds through the college accounts. Do I need to cuff you, or will you come along peacefully?"

"No handcuffs are necessary," Tichenor said. "I won't run."

A few weeks earlier, after all the derision he had received from Tichenor, Heinrich would have enjoyed kicking the tyrant when he was down and had even had periodic daydreams in which he stepped on Tichenor's fingers as President "Ichabod" hung by them from a cliff. But today, he felt pity for his adversary and touched the cross in his pocket.

"Sir, I'm sorry things turned out the way they did," Heinrich said. "God placed me in a situation over which I had little control."

"It appears I owe you an apology too, Professor Kueter, for your injuries and any undue anguish I may have caused. Apparently, when choosing my friends, I chose unwisely."

Heinrich nodded. "If there's one thing I learned from Black Jack Pershing in the Philippines, it's that a leader is often best served by those who tell him what he least wants to hear, not by the fawning sycophants who paint rosy pictures for the boss."

"I'll keep that in mind, Professor Kueter." Tichenor held out his hand, and Heinrich curiously found himself shaking it. "I lost my way, sold my integrity cheap, and now must pay for my mistakes. Young man, remember to keep your integrity intact; other than one's innocence, integrity, once lost, is the most difficult of all virtues to regain."

Tichenor paused for a moment, then reached with his right hand into the left inside breast pocket of his black suit and pulled out a small pistol.

"No!" Mrs. Tichenor screamed.

Tichenor placed the revolver perfunctorily in his mouth and pulled the trigger. Blood and brains sprayed out like a fountain from the back of his head onto the fleur-de-lit wallpaper behind him, and his lifeless body dropped to the floor.

"Good Lord!" Hunt said in disbelief, as he shot forward to do something, anything, as Mrs. Tichenor knelt over the body and sobbed hysterically. Heinrich could do little but stand, dumbfounded, in shock.

A week later, Dean Goforth sent word to Heinrich that he wished to speak with him. When Heinrich arrived, he found Goforth on the telephone, but the dean waved the younger man to a seat. Gorforth ended the call quickly, hung up the phone, and silently looked Heinrich in the eye.

"I'm not sure where to begin, Heinrich," he said. "I want you to know how sorry I am personally about the distress this college administration put you through."

"Thank you, Erwin; I appreciate that."

Goforth looked down at a sheet of paper on his desk. "What I would like to do is offer you your old job back, with a substantial raise in pay. Yesterday, the faculty voted unanimously to reinstate you. You could start again next fall, if you like."

Heinrich looked out the window at the barren trees and shook his head. "You know, Erwin, a couple of weeks ago, I might have taken you up on the offer. But the answer is 'no.' There are still some loose ends to clear up as deputy marshal, and I'm beginning to believe the Man Upstairs has something else in mind for me after that."

Goforth stood up, and Heinrich followed suit. "That's too bad,

Heinrich. You're a fine teacher and a man of principle. If you wish to reconsider, let me know."

Heinrich nodded. "Thank you," he said, and shook Goforth's hand.

As he walked toward the door, Heinrich turned back. "Could you do me a favor, Erwin?"

Goforth nodded. "Of course."

"Teach your students that, if our nation is to maintain its place among the great peoples of history, we must all be men of principle, willing to take a stand."

Goforth nodded, and Heinrich left Worcester College for good.

The next day Heinrich went to see Marshal Hunt.

"So how is my Dutchie Deputy doing today?" ribbed Hunt with a twinkle in his eye.

Heinrich gave a mock grimace, but he didn't mind the Marshal's occasional barb. After all, Hunt had saved his life. Heinrich needed to make an odd request, and he wasn't sure how to broach the subject. He rubbed his chin with his thumb and forefinger.

"Got something on your mind?" Hunt asked, although it was more an observation than a question. "Usually best to just spit it out." Hunt was a straight shooter all the way, and Heinrich had grown to appreciate that quality in the man.

"John, we need to exhume Tommy Lee's body. I don't know how to go about doing that, but there it is."

Hunt frowned. "It will take a court order. I'll have to talk to the judge. I think I can make it happen. But why? Why am I going to all this trouble to dig up a dead body in a case that's closed?"

"I think I know who really killed Tommy Lee."

Hunt sat back in his chair. "I thought the court already established that Fairchild and his fraternity brothers were responsible for that crime," he said, listening for an explanation.

"John Fairchild swore to me at the trial that he was not responsible for Tommy's death; he even denied it as he died," Heinrich said.

"Son, criminals have deathbed confessions all the time..."

"Yes, but I believe him this time. I know Tommy, and he would have put up more of a fight that night. I believe the only reason he didn't is because he was poisoned."

"Oh, come on, Heinrich. Who on earth would have a motive other than the college students, and all of them are either dead or in jail already."

"But what about the mushrooms?"

"The mushrooms from the Chinese grocer down in Jeff City?" Hunt said. "Do you really expect me to go tell a judge that I'm digging up a body on the word of a crazy Chinaman?"

"No. I expect you to act as a lawman in a murder investigation and ferret out the truth about what really happened," Heinrich said. "Jeremy, we need to know that justice was indeed served. I need to know."

Hunt nodded and thought for a minute. "Okay, Heinrich, you win. I'll see if I can make it happen. But if you're wrong, you owe me a steak dinner."

Heinrich smiled. "It's a deal." They shook hands on it.

Heinrich and Hunt stood back as biology Professor Miles McGovern, in his role as county coroner, examined Tommy Lee's body, laid out on a steel table in a storeroom behind the biology lab at Worcester College.

For Heinrich, it was as if all of the year's events were wrapped in the shrouded figure of his friend. As McGovern unwrapped the stark, white cotton fabric from Tommy's body, Heinrich envisioned in his mind a cocoon opening to release a butterfly. Something old had ended, but something new was taking flight.

Getting the body exhumed hadn't been as difficult as Heinrich had thought it might be. Hunt said the judge had been intrigued by the idea, and there was no family to oppose the exhumation.

McGovern studied the body meticulously, carefully looking at each extremity and wound, and taking detailed notes. The process seemed to take forever. When the professor had finished, he put down his clipboard, tore off his rubber gloves, threw them into a metal wastebasket and washed his hands in a nearby utility sink. He then leaned against a wall, pushed his wire-frame glasses higher on his nose, and rubbed his right hand through   hair.

"I guess no matter how many autopsies I do, I never feel completely comfortable with them," he said. "There's still something strange about working with a dead body."

Heinrich nodded. "What did you find, professor?"

"To my mind, the primary cause of death is still the hanging. I can't rule it out yet, and it is the most obvious reason. Although the subject's neck is not broken, there is heavy bruising, which means great strain and trauma to the body and potentially a blood clot headed to the brain that might have caused a stroke. Also, the constriction around his neck would have made it very difficult for the young man to breathe."

Heinrich was disappointed. "It was my hunch; I owe you a steak," Heinrich said.

Hunt grinned. "Look, sometimes hunches don't pan out," the marshal replied. "Don't let it bother you; it was worth checking."

McGovern raised a finger. "But my conclusion is not definite yet. There are a few more tests I still need to do. For instance, I want to examine the contents of his stomach. If he was truly poisoned, that information might be significant."

Hunt nodded. "Take as much time as you need to get it right. We don't want to go off half-cocked."

The next day, McGovern met with Kueter and Hunt late in the afternoon in his office, which was lined with shelves filled with scientific books and laboratory specimens suspended in jars filled with formaldehyde. On the wall behind his desk, a large starfish, about five feet in diameter, stood guard eerily over the proceedings; one would hate to run into such an unearthly monster in the dark, Heinrich thought to himself.

McGovern explained that he had performed tests on Tommy Lee's bodily tissues for arsenic, strychnine, thallium, plant alkaloid, digitalin and morphine, and all the tests had come up negative.

"Fine," Heinrich said. "But what about the amanita?"

"Ahhh, that's the interesting part. When I analyzed the stomach contents, I found amatoxins and phallotoxins, more than enough to kill him, indicating poisoning by *amanita phalloides*. In addition, the amatoxins had infected his liver, kidneys, lungs and heart. I believe he either ingested the mushrooms by eating them whole or drinking them in a liquid about a week before his death."

"So he might have ingested them by drinking tea?" Heinrich asked.

"Yes, any liquid — tea, coffee, water."

Hunt raised his hand. "Let me get this straight. Would drinking tea laced with this poisonous mushroom incapacitate somebody?"

"Among the final symptoms of amanita mushroom poisoning are delirium and coma."

"So Tommy Lee was possibly delirious or comatose the night he was abducted," Heinrich said.

McGovern nodded. "That would be my guess."

"Is there any connection to the teacup? Did you find the toxins there?" Hunt asked.

"Yes. In my opinion, this teacup was probably the main vehicle through which he was poisoned, and the poisoning probably occurred over a few days," McGovern said. He handed the teacup to Heinrich.

Heinrich thanked the chemist and shook his hand.

"Hope it helped," McGovern said.

"Immeasurably," Heinrich answered.

Outside, Hunt gave Heinrich a blank look. "So what does it all mean, Sherlock?"

"I don't know yet. I need to think about it."

Hunt nodded. "Okay, let me know when you've got something. You can find me down at Murphy's."

Heinrich held the Chinese teacup up and studied it in the sunlight. Might there be some hidden message baked into the porcelain? Alas, no. He slowly turned it in his hand, hoping that some secret information might reveal itself. Drawn in blue, the peasant man leading a cow behind him stared back at Heinrich, his tiny face holding an inscrutable expression. Apparently, no revelations would spring forth today.

Holding the teacup, he walked back to Mrs. Yaeger's place. Sitting on a bench under an elm tree in the chapel yard across the street from the boarding house, Heinrich watched Mrs. Yaeger beat a Persian rug she had hung from a clothesline with an aged badminton racket. The dust came out in billows that made her sneeze several times.

He knew Mrs. Yaeger loved the imported, woven rug. Her husband had purchased it, she had told Heinrich, at a bazaar in North Africa while serving in the Navy. The fanciful image of an Arab woman working on a loom in a Saharan tent flashed in his mind, but he had no idea whether such an image accurately represented Arab reality or was just a romantic figment of his fertile imagination.

He looked down at the teacup in his hands, with its blank-faced peasant, and then thought again of the Arab weaver. Something clicked. A flood of images poured into his mind. The yin and yang symbol from Tommy's watch and the knick-knacks in Fairchild's office all came together like pieces of a jigsaw puzzle. The painting of the Oriental beauty, the toy cannon, and boxing glove – they all made sense.

Suddenly he knew the answer and stood up with a start. With a quick wave to Mrs. Yaeger, who looked concerned at his strange behavior, he ran down the street to find Marshal Hunt.

He found Hunt leaning on the post on the boardwalk outside

Murphy's. "Jeremy, we need to go visit Manfred Dahlen's stable."
Heinrich looked pleased with himself. Hunt shrugged. "Why?"
"I'll explain on the way."

A short while later at Dahlen's house, the Austrian made tea while
Marshal Hunt sat at the table. Heinrich surveyed the antiquated
wooden bucket from a butter churn next to the fireplace that was filled
with tools. "I never really paid attention to it before, Manfred, but I'll
bet that rod with the sheepskin wrapped around it is an old-fashioned
cannon rammer and sponge." He looked at Hunt, who raised an
eyebrow.

"Ya, from my days as an artilleryman," Dahlen said. "About ten
years ago, I collected the essential tools: an old powder ladle, a wad-
screw, a priming iron, and a botefeux."

At Heinrich's puzzled look, Dahlen explained that the botefeux
held the slow match that fired a cannon.

Heinrich's Austrian friend put the teapot on the table and sat
down. Heinrich joined them at the table.

Dahlen and Hunt sipped their tea. "I presume we would also find
gunpowder and slowmatch in your shed?" Heinrich asked.

The Austrian shot Heinrich a wary look. "I may have some lying
around. Why?"

"Because you are an artillery man who could fire a cannon,"
Heinrich said.

Dahlen looked stunned. "What is this all about?"

Heinrich took a sip from his teacup and looked Dahlen in the eye.
"The tea is wonderful, as usual," Heinrich said.

"Thank you. It is imported from China."

"As is your tea set, I believe." Heinrich walked to the mantle
above the fireplace and placed the second blue-and-white teacup, taken
from Tommy Lee's room, beside the teacup of the young Chinese girl.
They were the same size and the same octagonal shape. They were
male and female. That's the symbol, Heinrich thought, the symbol on
Tommy's watch. Yin and yang, hard and soft, male and female.

"The Cowherd and the Weaver Girl," Heinrich said. Hunt looked
puzzled.

"It's a story from Chinese mythology," Heinrich continued. "Star-
crossed lovers separated forever by forces they cannot control."

A sick look flashed across Manfred's face as it dawned on the
Austrian that he was caught.

"It was you, wasn't it, Manfred?" Hunt asked. "You fired the cannon that night."

Manfred didn't answer.

"Your wife was the Weaver Girl, and you were the Cowherd," Heinrich said.

Manfred nodded. "We were. How did you know?"

"Mr. Chung saw the Cowherd when I showed him the teacup," Heinrich said. "I just didn't make the connection myself until today. Did Tommy ever drink your tea?"

Dahlen's eyes narrowed. "Maybe once or twice. It reminded him of home."

"Isn't it true that you bought tea for him often?" Heinrich asked.

"I don't think so... not too often... I don't really know..."

Marshal Hunt joined the conversation. "That's not what Mr. Chung said."

Dahlen began to grow angry. Heinrich lifted his right hand. "We talked to him, Manfred. He said you often purchased green tea and Asian vegetables for Tommy."

"So what if I did?" the Austrian asked. "I felt sorry for him, so far away from home."

Hunt nodded. "You had dinner with Tommy Lee about a week before his death?"

"He and I had dinner every week or two, yes."

"And you gave him some special herbal tea then, didn't you?"

"I don't remember, but even if I did, giving a person tea is no crime."

"You're right. It's not a crime..." Heinrich paused, "...That is, until you lace it with poison."

The Austrian turned white. "You have no proof."

The Marshal pulled a small jar with a metal lid from his pocket. "Do you recognize this, Manfred?"

The Austrian shook his head. "Well, you should. We found it hidden behind a sack of oats in your barn," the Marshal continued.

"It's Amanita mushroom; isn't it, Manfred?" Heinrich asked. "You put it in the boy's tea."

Manfred shook his head, dazed.

"You may as well tell the truth," Hunt said. "A chemist who analyzed Tommy Lee's teacup detected amanitin and other toxins consistent with the Amanita, or 'Death's Head,' mushroom."

"Murphy told me, and I bet there are many in the town who would agree, that you're one of the town's foremost experts on mushrooms, Manfred," Heinrich said. "What I don't completely understand is why you did it. Am I right to suspect that it's about the Boxers?"

Manfred put his head in his hands, his elbows resting on his oak tabletop. He began to cry. "Those Chinese bastards," he mumbled between sobs. "They killed her, and I swore revenge."

Heinrich nodded in understanding. He patted Manfred's arm sympathetically.

Marshal Hunt cocked an eyebrow and looked puzzled. Heinrich explained, "The Boxer Rebellion. The Chinese killed his wife."

"My Liesl, *mein Liebchen*. She was everything to me. She was my life," Manfred sobbed. "I thought I was through with the slanty-eyed devils, but then Tommy showed up. Every time I saw him, I saw them attacking her, violating her, beating her. I should have been there to save her, but my unit got called away. By the time I could return, it was too late."

"Her death is not your fault," Heinrich said. "But Tommy's is."

Manfred pulled his arm away from Heinrich's grasp and shot him an angry look. "I thought you were my friend," he said.

"And Tommy Lee thought you were his," Heinrich answered. "Our friendship cannot trump murder. You covered your tracks well, thinking people would believe he died from an accidental hanging. But you poisoned Tommy, and then you fired the Napoleon outside the Kappa Psi house to spook your Lippizan horse and finish him off. You killed an unsuspecting boy who trusted you; he was your friend."

The Marshal pulled Manfred to his feet and put handcuffs on his wrists behind his back. "Sometimes friendship isn't enough," Hunt said.

Manfred continued to sob. "What have I done?" he wailed.

Heinrich had no answer. He had thought solving the mystery would be a triumph, and in a way it was. He should feel exhilarated, but he felt empty instead. He had lost another close friend, and he didn't have too many of those left.

Hunt tipped his hat silently to Heinrich as he led Dahlen away. Heinrich nodded, then turned to look out the window at the white Lippizan stallion in the pen outside — a beautiful animal, with its sinewy muscles moving fluidly under its white coat. The steed snorted, and its red eyes looked uneasy, even angry, Heinrich thought.

"What about me?" the horse seemed to ask Heinrich. "What will happen to me without my beloved owner?"

Heinrich had few answers to offer the horse, and even fewer answers for his own questions. He could feel this phase of his life ending, yet he had no idea what new challenges might lay on the horizon. He looked at the Lippizan again; it snorted and patted the ground with an impatient hoof. You and I have much in common, he thought. Even though we two have survived intact, we are both still casualties of war.

As he had done for much of the spring, Heinrich visited Sally nearly every day in the hospital for the next month. He would sit beside her bed and pray desperately for her to come out of her coma. Sometimes he would hold her hand or read out loud, hoping to elicit some response, but to no avail. She lay on the bed, passively breathing but showing no outward sign of awareness.

Early on, when Doc Harris had checked her skin reflexes and corneas, Heinrich asked the doctor what could be done for her.

The aging physician shrugged. "Pray, I guess."

When Heinrich began to snarl a retort at the answer, Doc held up his hands. "I don't mean to be flippant. Medical science just doesn't know enough about this condition. We know that it can be caused by cerebral hemorrhage, in this case bleeding caused by trauma in the brain. There's a new theory that it has something to do with increased intracranial pressure, the pressure inside the skull, but we just don't know all the ins-and-outs yet.

"So, as her doctor, I have to fall back on my Hippocratic oath to do no harm, while hoping for the best. I'm monitoring her blood pressure, and it is okay for now. If it gets too low, we can elevate it through artificial respiration or send more blood to her heart by raising her legs or compressing her abdomen. We can also give her a salt solution or drugs such as ephedrine, atropine, or strychnine."

"Rat poison?" Heinrich asked.

"Only in desperation," Harris said. "Unfortunately, this sleeping beauty won't come to with just a kiss. Her body needs to heal first."

Doc told Heinrich to continue speaking, reading, and singing to Sally in the hope that she might recover. "Look, there is very little at this point that I can do for her as her physician," he said. "It's up to God now. So pray for her."

At the beginning of June, Hunt returned to St. Louis, leaving Heinrich behind on a small hourly wage as his deputy. Heinrich had grown to enjoy the Marshal's company; Hunt had even suggested that Heinrich relocate to St. Louis when his ordeal with Sally came to an end.

Heinrich gave a noncommittal answer. While he hadn't said "no" yet, Heinrich had for some time felt a growing urge to head west to get a new start.

On June 21, he left Sally's bedside for a quick meal at Murphy's. In the middle of a hearty shepherd's pie, he felt a hand on his shoulder. It was Mike Murphy.

"Heinrich, you'd better go quick," Murphy said. "The Doc says Sally needs you."

Heinrich threw his napkin on the table and rushed down the street to the hospital.

He found Sally awake but blurry. Doc grabbed him by the shoulder as he ran in the door of her room. "Don't get her too worked up," the doctor said, his index finger wagging under Heinrich's nose. "She may only have a few minutes before she slips back into a coma again."

Heinrich nodded, and Doc left the room. Sally opened her arms to Heinrich, and they hugged for several minutes.

"I'm so sorry. Thank you for spending so much time with me. How long was I out?" she asked.

"About two months."

She sighed. "I could hear you sometimes, and knew you were here, but I couldn't respond."

"Don't worry about that. You just get better," he said. He pressed his lips against hers. She did not feel warm, as he remembered, but cool and clammy, which disconcerted him.

"I love you, Heinrich," she said softly.

"I love you too. Now, you just need to recover. I want you to marry me, and I refuse to take no for an answer. I have big plans for us."

"Wow, a shotgun wedding, with the groom holding the gun," she grinned and giggled weakly. "What more could a girl ask for?"

Heinrich laughed.

Suddenly, she winced and held her arm to her abdomen. "It's a wonderful dream," she said, "But I fear it may not come true."

Something was wrong. Heinrich grasped her hand.

"Heinrich, my dearest, I'm afraid you may have to let me go."

"No, Sally Ann, you hold together. Do you hear me?"

She laughed softly, as if she were only half there. He could feel her slipping away.

"My love..." she said, her voice trailing off.

"No!" He turned toward the door. "Doc, Doc! Come quick!"

She gripped his arm. "It's all right, Heinrich. It's going to be all right."

The words brought back his dream by the lake, with the ghostly image of his father mouthing the same words.

"Please, Sally, don't..."

Suddenly her eyes became glassy and clear. She gripped his arm tighter and pulled him to her.

"Keep up the good fight, Heinrich, no matter what happens," she whispered in his ear, a determined look in her eyes. "Carry your cross; it will be your guide."

She gasped and exhaled a long breath, as if her soul had poured from her body in a rush. He kissed her again for a moment, but stopped after she fell completely limp.

"Sally? Sally?" She was no longer there. He no longer felt her breath on his cheek.

Doc, who was standing just inside the doorway, pushed Heinrich out of the way and tried to resuscitate her, giving her mouth-to-mouth on her pillow for about five minutes, but it soon became clear that it wasn't doing any good. He quit and stood up.

"Heinrich, I'm sorry…"

Heinrich pushed him aside. "Let me try." He had watched Doc's maneuvers over the past few minutes; the physician had alternated breaths with pushes on Sally's chest. Clumsily, frantically, Heinrich tried to do the same.

After a couple of minutes, Doc put his hand on Kueter's shoulder. "It's no good. Son, when it's over, it's over."

Heinrich quit pushing and fell on top of Sally's body, sobbing. "No, no…"

Doc gave him a few moments. Heinrich grasped Sally's body and cried. A few minutes later, he sat up and looked at his love's dormant face.

"Oh God, I cried, give me new birth, and put me back upon the earth," he said.

The doctor said nothing. "Edna St. Vincent Millay," Heinrich explained. "Her favorite poet."

Doc nodded and said gently, "Heinrich, help me with the sheet."

Doc handed Heinrich one corner, and they covered her face. Then Doc led Heinrich out into the hallway.

The next few days of preparation, and then Sally's funeral, passed in a blur for Heinrich. Numb, he went through the motions of public grief as her neighbors and family met to honor the life of his beloved and put her in the ground.

Later, he would remember shaking many hands and hugging numerous relatives of Sally's whom he didn't know. He would remember singing "Amazing Grace" at her memorial service, throwing flowers on her casket as it was lowered into the ground and crying buckets of tears. It was all so unfair, a waste of a good life.

Heinrich felt most dreary when her family held an auction of her effects. One by one, the fast-talking auctioneer held up pieces of jewelry and antiques, most of which sold relatively quickly for pennies on the dollar. While Heinrich wanted something to remember her by, he had very little money saved.

When her Model T came up for sale, the auctioneer asked, "What'll you folks give me for this fine convertible touring car?"

Heinrich immediately put up his hand. "Fifty dollars."

After a farmer in green canvas overalls bid $55 and the florist bid $60, Heinrich laid all that he had on the line. "Seventy-five dollars," he yelled, pointing to the sky.

The farmer shook his head, but the florist upped the bid to $80. Heinrich was out of money.

That's when Murphy stepped forward. "One hundred dollars," he said.

The florist stepped in to up the bid once more, but Murphy glowered at him. Clearly, the Irishman was going to outbid him. Seeing the writing on the wall, the florist bowed out of the bidding, shaking his hands with his palms out in front of him. He didn't want the car badly enough to cross swords with Murphy.

Murphy marched over to Heinrich and tapped him on the shoulder. "The car is a gift to you," he said, "but I want your $75 to pay off your bar tab."

Heinrich grinned and handed him the money. It was a steal anyway. A brand new car would easily cost at least $650. He was lucky that nobody wanted to outbid Murphy.

He gave the barkeep his horse to make up for the other $25.

Although his friend's good deed led to a temporary moment of good cheer, overall Heinrich felt angry and betrayed by his Lord during the mournful period of grief at Sally's passing. He had trouble sleeping, his nights often filled with tossing and turning, as strange dreams filled his mind. One night, as he slept, Heinrich put God on the witness stand and grilled the Almighty for taking her life early.

"How could you allow it to happen?" he asked the Lord, who sat enthroned in regal repose, eyeing Heinrich with a cocked brow and an inscrutable, but silent, look. It was the same question Heinrich had been asking in the darkness, which always seemed to follow him, night or day, inside the palms of his hands as he pushed on his eyelids. No particular answer ever came, only silence, and none came in the dream either. Heinrich awoke, sweating and filled with guilt. He rolled over and tried to think about something peaceful. He supposed that, at least, his dreams of combat in the Philippines came less often now.

On Sunday, June 28, he sat in his usual pew at the Lutheran Church only half listening to the pastor's sermon. He would leave town tomorrow, so it would be the last service he would attend in this wretched little town whose people he had come to love and hate at the same time. The time had come to leave Franklinton.

He pulled the Teutonic cross from his pocket, studied it intently, and asked himself how a God of love and peace could allow so much hate to thrive, so much discord, destruction, and death in the world of His creation? Heinrich smiled wryly to himself, knowing he was not the first to ask the question. Certainly, his father had asked it in more than one sermon before his congregation.

The cross simply stared back at him, stoically silent.

Later that night, he dreamed about the courtroom again, but something appeared different this time. While awake, Heinrich had always pictured God as a wizened old man with a long white beard.

In this dream the Almighty appeared on the witness stand in full-dress Army uniform, looking strangely like Black Jack Pershing, with his trademark Sam Brown belt strapped diagonally across his chest. Before Heinrich could ask a question, the terse, regal military man stood in the witness stand, and slapped the railing with his swagger stick.

"Have you figured it out yet, Crusader?"

Heinrich looked down in silence at his feet. He certainly had no answers and could think of nothing positive to say.

The General marched over and inspected him from top to bottom. Pershing looked him straight in the eye with an unwavering stare. "I understand you're some kind of fighter," he said. "But I don't see it in your eyes."

Heinrich gritted his teeth, unable to speak.

"I'll bet you would like to take a swing at me right now, wouldn't you?"

Heinrich gritted his teeth and nodded.

"Well, go ahead, if you think you're man enough." The General took off his hat, tossed it aside and said to those assembled in the courtroom, "Rank is no issue here."

He stood in front of Heinrich, hands on his hips, an easy target. "Come on, take your best shot."

Heinrich looked from side to side. Suddenly, the anger welled inside, and he launched a left jab and a smashing right cross combination. The General simultaneously sidestepped the left jab, ducked the right cross, and cold-cocked Heinrich in the nose with a hard vertical, bare-knuckle boxing punch that laid Heinrich flat on the floor.

The general stepped back, retrieved his hat, and put it firmly on his head once again. "Son, you're not the first trooper into whom I've had to knock some sense. A commander never needs to explain his reasons, but the fact is that her enlistment was up. She was ready; you aren't. You still have work to do here, and I expect you to get up and get cracking. It's time to function, Private Kueter."

The general paused, tipped his head and winked. "Remember, son, there are many ways to fight the good fight, and they don't all involve a fist or a gun."

The general nodded once to Heinrich, as if to punctuate his point, and marched out of the courtroom, his brown, leather cowboy boots rapping a cadence on the stone floor.

Heinrich awoke with a start. He rolled over but could not go back to sleep. He rolled back the covers, got up and turned on the light switch to look at his pocket watch, which said 4:14. He sat down for a minute to think, then turned out the light and went back to bed. He needed the sleep for his drive tomorrow.

He slept later than he had planned, waking up a little before 10 a.m. Mrs. Yaeger insisted that he could not travel on an empty stomach and cooked him a brunch of scrambled eggs, bacon, and toast. She sat with him and talked about his future plans, avoiding the events that had embroiled them all during the past year.

He finished packing up his possessions, loaded up the Ford, and said goodbye as Mrs. Yaeger fretted about the wisdom of travelling in something as unreliable as an automobile. In an uncharacteristic show of affection, she hugged him and said she would miss him. He said he'd miss her too.

Since the Model T had been sitting for a few days without being driven, its engine would be cold. He checked inside to make sure the ignition was off and that the handbrake was on, which put the transmission in neutral. Otherwise, the car might run over him when he cranked the engine from the front. As Mrs. Yaeger watched from the front porch with concern in her eyes, he moved to face the front of the vehicle and pulled the front choke lever out to prime the engine. With a smile toward her, he grabbed the metal engine crank in his left hand, and simultaneously stepping toward his right while grabbing the right front fender for leverage, cranked the engine a half-turn. The engine roared to life.

He then gave a theatrical bow to his audience on the porch and waved to Mrs. Yaeger one last time before getting in the driver's side door. He made sure the choke knob on the dash was in to lighten the fuel mixture, adjusted the throttle lever on the right of the steering column, and the spark advance to the left to tune the engine to its best-sounding RPM. With a final wave out the window, he drove to Dahlen's stable and, leaving the engine running, paid the stable boy now in charge of the place for another two weeks of lodging for his horse. New owners were negotiating the purchase of the business while Dahlen's trial commenced.

He took one last look at the white Lippizan, wondering what would happen to it, and, as promised, headed to Murphy's for a final meal on his way out of town at just before 5 p.m. He planned to stay the night with a friend in Boonville, about two hours or so depending on road conditions. As long as he hit the main road before it got too dark, he'd be okay.

When Heinrich entered the door, Marshal Hunt, just arrived from St. Louis, was seated at the bar. Heinrich shook his hand warmly and sat on the padded barstool next to him.

Murphy gave Heinrich a steak, and Hunt handed him a copy of the morning's St. Louis Post-Dispatch. "This means trouble," Hunt said, and pointed to the dominant front-page story above the fold.

Heinrich whistled. "Black Hand terrorists assassinated Austrian Archduke Franz Ferdinand and his wife yesterday in Sarajevo," he read. Some young, enterprising killer named Gavrilo Princip could now stake his claim to historic infamy, an international John Wilkes Booth whose action might spark conflict in the Balkans, the newspaper report said.

"Just you wait. The Austrians will blame Serbia, so it might mean war with Russia," Hunt said.

"Surely, cooler heads will prevail," Heinrich said.

Hunt nodded, "Let's hope so."

"So where you headed?" Murphy asked, changing the subject.

"I'm going west, young man. I'll start with Kansas City, maybe hit Denver. Not sure really where I'll stop."

Murphy nodded. "What do you plan to do?"

"I don't know yet. Maybe Dodge City needs a new marshal."

Hunt grinned. "If so, you'd best call me."

Murphy laughed. "Listen to your mother, Heinrich. You'd make a better minister."

"You may be right." Impulsively, Heinrich made a decision. He placed his Colt revolver on the bar. "Marshall, I want you to have this."

Hunt raised an eyebrow. "I guess that means Dodge City is out, and you are out of the law enforcement business, after all?"

Heinrich nodded. "It's time to put away the gun."

"Good thing. The world's changing quickly," Hunt said. He stood up, picked up the revolver in his left hand, and shook Heinrich's hand with his right. "Buena suerte, amigo. You take care of yourself."

With a tip of his black hat, and a final wave, Hunt walked out the door into the street.

"We'll certainly miss you," Murphy said, almost tearing up. "We kinda need a good Kraut around here."

Heinrich laughed. "A good Mick like you should cover the foreigner element nicely."

As he finished his steak, the player piano in the corner played the song, "After the Ball," a Tin Pan Alley hit from twenty-some years earlier. He got up, wiped his mouth on a napkin, and reached for his wallet. Murphy put his right hand on the top of Heinrich's before he could turn it over to hand the Irishman the cash.

"This one's on the house," he said. "You're family."

Heinrich smiled and thanked the Irishman. He put some of his cash back, but reconsidered and plunked half of it on the bar for a big tip. "Make that the start of the Tommy Lee Anti-Intolerance Fund."

"You got a deal," Murphy said. Heinrich shook the Irishman's hand one last time, and he said, "Mike, you're the one man it might be worth staying in town for."

"Go on, get out of here, Dutchman," Murphy said, walking around the bar and hugging Heinrich. "You wait much longer, there won't be any daylight."

Murphy followed Heinrich out to the Model T. As he was opening the driver's side door to get in, Heinrich said, "I almost forgot. Murphy, remember to feed my horse. She's over at Dahl... at the stable, paid up for two weeks. Feed her something special every so often, kay? She's been a good friend."

Murphy nodded. Because the engine hadn't been off too long, there was no need to crank start the Model T. Heinrich got in the Ford's cab, started it from the inside, released the brake, and drove away. At the end of the block, he rolled down the window and gave Murphy one last wave goodbye before heading off to find Route 2, known as the St. Joseph Road, into the rolling farmland west of town. The sun was sinking lower in the west, leaving him about two hours or so of daylight to get to his destination.

With his right hand, he checked his breast pocket one final time to make sure he had his Teutonic Cross. As always, it was with him.

Author's Notes

Introduction

This novel began with a tombstone.

One day while working as the public relations director for Westminster College in Fulton, Mo., the president came into my office and told me he had found an old headstone while tramping through a historic cemetery that had the name of an Asian student from the early 20th century. He wondered if I had ever heard anything about him. I hadn't, but I got to thinking, "What if that student had been murdered?" That question led to me write this novel.

As I said in the preface to my first book, a non-fiction study of five Missouri generals, I am not a historian, but a writer who is also a history buff. As with most people I know, I am especially interested in the stories of history.

So that's what I created in *The Teutonic Cross* – my own story of history – and I hope you enjoyed the novel. In addition to trying to create a good story with interesting characters, I also did my best to infuse historic fact into the narrative. While I'm sure that some enterprising historian, steeped in deeper knowledge of the time period than I possess, may try to pick the story apart error by error, I did my best to keep it factual and believe that I have kept the story true to the spirit of the time.

The early 20th century, prior to World War I is downright fascinating. It holds the beginnings of modernity, from the creation of the income tax and direct election of senators to automobiles and airplanes. And it's the beginning of the American Empire.

As backstory, the Philippine Wars of the early 20th century loom large. If any armed conflict could be called a truly "forgotten war," the Moro Wars in the Philippines would certainly qualify, at least for history students in the United States. Judging from survey classes, which jump straight from the Spanish-American War of 1898 to the start of World War I in 1914, you might get the impression that nothing of particular importance happened in the interim.

Nothing could be further from the truth, as shown in their formative properties for Heinrich Kueter, the protagonist of this novel. After the United States took the Philippines from the Spanish with the help of an already potent insurgency that had fought its Iberian overlords throughout the 1890s, the U.S. then fought those previously allied Filipino insurgents for three years in an early version of "meet the new boss; same as the old boss," to borrow words from a song by "The Who."

Although the Philippine-American War officially ended in 1902, the conflict continued unofficially as remnants of irreconcilable rebels joined in the Moro Wars that began in 1904 and continued ostensibly until 1913 with the Battle of Bud Bagsak. Other than the Barbary Pirates in the early 1800s, the Moros were America's first Islamic adversary, and one could make the case that the situation is still unresolved since there is still an ongoing Muslim insurgency in the Philippines even today led by the Moro National Liberation Front, which was formed in 1969.

Regardless, as our first conquest of natives beyond the North American continent, the Moro Wars of the early 20th century can be instructive today as we fight Islamic extremists around the globe. And the conflict tells us much about the empire-building process. The Moro Wars can be seen as a continuation of our conquest of the native peoples of North America. Just as Spain needed an outlet for its conquistadors after driving the Moors from Iberia and therefore founded an overseas empire in the New World, the United States likewise needed an outlet for its conquering heroes and therefore stole the remnants of Spain's empire to begin its own.

As the conflict helped create the character of Heinrich Kueter, it would forge and solidify the careers of many other military officers who would achieve fame later, such as George C. Marshall and John J. Pershing, whose 1905 promotion by President Theodore Roosevelt from captain to brigadier general rocked the military establishment. Black Jack Pershing plays a preeminent role in the novel, just as he did during this time period and subsequently, as the demigod-like mentor to the U.S. crop of generals who would later win World War II.

Likewise, since readers may be interested in the historical information presented in the book, I have decided to provide notes, chapter by chapter.

Chapter 1

The growler pail incident is based in stories that my grandmother wrote about and told me of life in Carondolet, a German enclave immediately south of St. Louis. On a hot summer day, the neighborhood would send one of its youngsters to the local tavern with a tin growler pail full of cold beer. The neighbors would congregate amongst each others' porches and down the cold brew to beat the heat. As it often does today, the beer fueled many a fine block party, providing the neighborhood's adults with an excuse to converse while the children created their own amusements such as large games of tag and other general mayhem.

For those of you who are familiar with the *black-only Model T*, it turns out it did not come about until after 1914. A knowledgeable early draft reader made me aware of the fact. The tire-changing procedure is accurate, as far as I can discern. The early tires were much like bicycle tires today.

Although they have now been pretty much completely assimilated into the U.S. racial category of Caucasian, *Irish and German immigrants* had much in common, both being outside the sphere of those of English descent. Missouri's German immigrants made an especially strong effort to hold onto their customs and language from the old country until America's entrance into World War I made many of the practices seem unpatriotic and forced them to assimilate. In Missouri, the Germans were often the target of resentment because of their outsider image and their integral role in keeping the state in the Union during the Civil War.

While Kueter's flashback image of the Battle of Bud Bagsak is somewhat stylized for effect, it is a relatively accurate depiction of what happened in that battle and the earlier battles of Bud Dajo, during which the Moros fortified the tops of dormant volcanos and wound up being massacred. Since I have never seen the terrain personally, I do not claim total accuracy here, but the general pattern of the engagement is correct. The Moro warriors who chose to stay and fight were surrounded and were not given quarter by Black Jack Pershing.

When Kueter speaks inane niceties with Tichenor at the college mixer, the subject of *the fighting fraternities* comes up. My great-great-great grandfather, Friedrich Muench, at the University of Giessen was a member of the Black Brothers, one of the *Burschenschaften*. The Black Brothers fought duels with other students in the name of democracy and the ideals of the Enlightenment.

Sometimes their politics got them into deeper trouble than battling fellow students. Friedrich's brother-in-law and best friend, Paul Follenius, was the young brother of a German revolutionary, Karl Follen, also a member of the Black Brothers, who wound up having to flee Germany after falling under suspicion for being a co-conspirator in the assassination of August von Kotzebue, a conservative diplomat, by Follen's friend, Karl Ludwig Sand. Soon after his arrival in the U.S., Follen was named the first professor of German at Harvard University.

Although I have dabbled in my ancestral tongue and have tried to myself to speak it, my ancestors are probably angry with me because I learned French instead. Likewise, as a member of a college fraternity myself, I unfortunately missed out on the potentially fun swordplay over philosophies of government. Instead, like most fraternity men, I drank copious amounts of beer and participated in and/or witnessed similar antics to some of the fraternity practices mentioned in this novel. But that is the extent of my revelations on that score. I'll take the fifth...of whatever people are drinking at the time. (Just kidding.)

Tommy's fight at the end of chapter one is based in my experience as a student of the martial art of Tae Kwon Do. Although I have not practiced the discipline for several years now, it came in handy when choreographing a good fight. While I claim no resemblance to a true talent such as Bruce Lee, I did earn a second-degree black belt in the American Taekwondo Association and lost many sparring matches against people who had abilities similar to Tommy's.

Chapter 2

Juramentado attacks were the norm in the Moro Wars of the Philippines. At least the warriors did not strap on explosives as they do today.

The story of the Germans keeping Missouri in the Union is true, and the anti-German feeling was still alive for many years afterward. Part of the reason for Blue Laws on Sundays, for instance, was to harass the Germans. Even as late as the early 1990s, I can remember receiving anti-German hate mail after I objected to a local newspaper editorial touting all the great things Southern culture had brought Columbia. "Yes, but what about slavery?" I had responded, and some local yokel took offense, suggesting most vehemently that I should take my German keister and leave town.

If people mistakenly believe that history does not live on in our culture and language long after active events with dates, they misunderstand its very nature. We are the result of our history; it truly lives in us and through us.

For the discussion of Morris "Railroad Bill" Slater, I am indebted to the *Greenwood Encyclopedia of African American Folklore* (Greenwood Press, 2005) and its author, Anand Prahlad, who allowed me to read his copy. The three-volume work was an eye-opening experience for me to African-American experience and history, much of which I had not encountered before.

As for the Grand Duchy of Dixie, Callaway Countians in Missouri will recognize this echo of their story of the notorious rebel Jefferson Jones, who negotiated with the Union Army and thereby created the "Kingdom of Callaway" legend.

I also am indebted to Kenny Greene, jeweler and Tai Chi Chuan master in Columbia, Mo., who has taught me much about the Chinese martial art. It's easier on the joints, and I hope to practice it more when I have time in retirement.

In regard to the story of the Cowherd and the Weaver Girl, I do not remember when I first heard the tale, but I think it was in elementary school.

The conversation between Dahlen and Kueter over German unification finds echoes in my family's story. I have often wondered whether German and world history would have been different if so many democratic-leaning Germans such as my ancestors had not left the Fatherland to come to America. Might they have turned German political structures toward a more enlightened model if they had stayed behind, rather than following their utopian dream of recreating a better Germany in the United States? Certainly, the unification of Germany under the militaristic Prussian state did not turn out well, but like so many other "what ifs" of history, we will never know.

The menu at the Titanic dinner party is taken from an actual menu served at a sorority banquet in mid-Missouri at the time. Many thanks to my wife's grandmother, who saved it and passed it on to her. I have no idea whether anyone would think of having such a tacky party theme a year after the tragedy, but if someone were to do it, it would have been Madame Tichenor. The idea came to me after visiting the Titanic museum in Branson, Mo., and the ubiquitous 100th anniversary specials playing on multiple cable channels ad nauseam in 2012.

It sometimes amazes me that people still find the disaster so fascinating. After all, there are plenty of other big ships that have sunk with wealthy people aboard, but this particular story has so many elements that make it a stirring morality tale: the arrogance of proclaimed "unsinkability," the daring of Mother Nature and her icebergs, the lack of safety precautions, the class struggle of upper and lower decks, and the wrath of God all make for a powerful myth.

For the "Shine" aspect of the story, I once again am indebted to the *Greenwood Encyclopedia of African American Folklore,* in which I first learned of it. The story adds a whole other dimension to the class struggle aboard the ship.

The ragtime music seemed appropriate to the period especially since Scott Joplin lived in St. Louis. Missourians have mostly forgotten their ragtime roots, but it's here if you look. I had visited the Scott Joplin State Historic Site shortly after it opened while working for the State of Missouri, and I recently brought my family to see it. It's a hidden gem. Likewise, I hope that Columbia, Mo., will finish its restoration of Blind Boone's home and the reclamation of his ragtime legacy.

For the quote from Friedrich Muench in Heinrich Kueter's lecture,

I am indebted to Anita M. Mallinckrodt , the intrepid historian of Augusta, Mo., and her pamphlet, "What they Thought II: Missouri's German Immigrants Assess Their World –1860s," (Anita Mallinckrodt, 1995), in which she translated a few 1862 articles by my great-great-great grandfather from the *St. Charles*, Mo., *Demokrat* that provided a contemporary analyses of slavery by one of the leading Missouri German thinkers of his day.

Tomahawks and throwing axes have been used throughout history. The native Americans used the tomahawk, derived from a Powhatan word, as cutting and killing tools, but did not have metal tomahawk heads until they obtained them in trade from Europeans. According to various Internet sites, the French employed a tomahawk design that may have been derived from early weapons used by the medieval Franks and other Germanic peoples including the Anglo-Saxons.

Chapter 3

While my college fraternity never conducted such a sinister operation as the one depicted in this chapter, we did participate in many nocturnal hijinks of various types, mainly intra-fraternity pranks conducted by pledges on actives or inter-fraternity pranks and "black op" vandalistic raids on other houses. I suspect that similar activities have occurred between groups of young men since time immemorial. A certain tribal instinct lives in the hearts of young men, an inner hunter-gatherer that in our culture becomes somewhat tamed with age and the civilizing influence of women. It is interesting, for instance, that crime rates have been dropping over time as the median age of the culture has risen as the baby boomers have gotten older.

The September 1864 Battle of Pilot Knob in southeast Missouri culminated at Fort Davidson as the Confederacy was on the ropes. Confederate Gen. Robert E. Lee's army was under siege at Petersburg, Va., and Atlanta had recently fallen to Union Gen. William T. Sherman. Confederates under Gen. Sterling Price conducted a last-ditch raid through Missouri aimed at diverting Union troops from the front lines east of the Mississippi, destroying Union war materiel, damaging the Union war effort behind the lines, and bringing more recruits to the rebel cause.

While en route to St. Louis, Price's 12,000 men, half of whom were recent Confederate draftees and a fourth of whom were unarmed, attacked a force of 1,450 men commanded by Union Gen. Thomas Ewing, a relative and confidant of Gen. Sherman. Price hoped to overwhelm the fort, take its stores and prevent Ewing from reinforcing St. Louis or the state capital of Jefferson City. Ewing held out for a day of onslaught but, out of ammunition, abandoned the fort under cover of darkness early in the morning of Sept. 18, 1864, blowing up the remaining supplies.

Because of the mauling Price took at the Fort, losing 1,000 men in casualties, his raid was unable to threaten St. Louis. Ewing, whose force suffered only 200 casualties, then replaced the garrison at Rolla, Mo., which moved to protect Jefferson City from attack by Price's forces. Price then headed westward, his forces fanning out and fighting engagements in several central and western Missouri towns. Finding Jefferson City too heavily defended to attack, Price's forces continued toward Kansas City, where his army was soundly defeated in the Battle of Westport by Gen. Samuel R. Curtis in what is now the Country Club Plaza area of Kansas City. Price's raid wound up failing miserably and, in effect, clearing the state of its most effective rebel guerrillas.

"Baldknobbing" is a slang term from the Missouri Ozarks for such hooded vigilante activities engaged in by such groups as the Ku Klux Klan, although the modern Klan would not officially form until 1915 and reached its heyday in the 1920s. The term came into common use with the successful 1907 novel, *The Shepherd of the Hills*, by Harold Bell Wright.

As a child, I always believed the carved teakwood "shishi dogs" my parents brought back from Okinawa were cool looking. Apparently, the "kara-shishi" are usually lions and lion-dogs that guard Buddhist or Shinto temples, which sounds even cooler. To me, I've always been partial to dragons, which would be the coolest-looking yet, but nobody has asked my opinion.

Chapter 4

My college fraternity, Sigma Alpha Epsilon, held a three-day Paddy Murphy party every spring. In our ritual, he was an Irishman who died of inebriation, and we gave him a wake and funeral, of course. At that age, any excuse to party is welcome. Apparently, many other ΣAE chapters across the nation have similar traditions, only with far more elaborate stories concocted that sometimes involve Prohibition, Al Capone, and the Untouchables. In the 19th and 20th centuries, Paddy Murphy became a sort of Everyman Irishman used as the butt of jokes, and there are multiple folk songs written about him.

The Know-Nothings were an antebellum nativist political group. Please allow me some literary license here. Yes, they were of an earlier era, but nativist sentiments have been always present throughout our history, and they are often revived by traditionalists who look back on bygone mistakes with nostalgia (as evidence, see the creation of the modern KKK in 1915 or the recent "states rights" and "nullification" rhetoric from the right wing – you'd think we'd have resolved that line of argument with the Civil War). For instance, we see many similar nativist arguments today against immigration reform. As a culture, perhaps we need to be continually reminded that history is not a static thing with locked in dates, but it keeps being lived and revived by later generations.

*President Millard Fillmo*re, a one-time Whig, refused to join the new Republican Party and ran for a second, non-consecutive term as president in 1856 on the American Party ticket. The American Party was the political expression of the Know-Nothing movement. The party took third in the election, winning 21.6 percent of the popular vote.

Before they became famous outlaws carrying on a personal guerrilla war after the Civil War ended, Jesse and Frank James fought under Missouri guerrilla leaders William Quantrill and Bloody Bill Anderson. Quantrill, the more moderate leader, was eventually supplanted by Anderson, who believed in more violent tactics. For instance, Anderson appalled Sterling Price during the 1864 Missouri raid by encouraging his men to collect Union scalps.

Will Doniphan was a Missouri lawyer, politician and self-taught military general who led the First Missouri Volunteers into New Mexico during the Mexican-American War and took it for the United States. In his spare time while preparing to head farther south into Mexico proper, Doniphan wrote the new law code for the New Mexico Territory. Sterling Price followed Doniphan later with the Second Missouri Volunteers, who helped cement the new territory into the United States.

Although the Confederate Army of the West under Gen. Earl Van Dorn met with initial success at the March 1862 Battle of Pea Ridge in Northwest Arkansas, the Union Army of the Southwest forces under Gen. Samuel R. Curtis carried the battle on its second day when the Confederates ran out of ammunition. The rebel defeat effectively kept Missouri in the Union. According to the U.S. National Park Service, nearly half of the enlisted troops and many of their officers in the battle spoke German as their primary language.

For the facts related here about the Pendergasts and prostitution in Kansas City, I relied on primarily *Pendergast!* by Lawrence H. Larsen and Nancy J. Hulston, University of Missouri Press, 1997; and *Annie Chambers: Painted Ladies, Parlor Houses and Prostitution in Kansas City, Mo., 1869-1923*, by Courtney Ann Culp, Emporia State

University Press, 2009.

"Star Halma" is what we call "Chinese Checkers" today. Halma was originally invented in the 1880s by George Howard Monks, an American thoracic surgeon at Harvard Medical School, who was inspired by a British game called "Hoppity." The game board was a square grid with 16 by 16 spaces. A German variant of the game, "Star Halma," was developed in the 1890s, and U.S. marketers gave it the Chinese name later, perhaps because of its resemblance to the star on the Chinese flag from before the Communist Revolution of 1949.

The Colorado strike in 1913 against a coal mine in Ludlow, Colo., owned by John D. Rockefeller would turn deadly a year later. In what is now known as the "Ludlow Massacre," the Colorado National Guard attacked a tent city of striking workers and killed men women and children, many of whom were merely hiding in their tents. In retaliation, armed mine workers attacked national guard troops at mines throughout the state for 10 days afterward.

Mary Harris "Mother" Jones, a former schoolteacher and dressmaker, became a famous organizer for the Knights of Labor and the United Mine Workers unions and co-founded the Industrial Workers of the World. She was arrested during the Colorado coal mine strikes that led to the Ludlow Massacre. Christened "the most dangerous woman in America" by Teddy Roosevelt and "the grandmother of all agitators" on the floor of the U.S. Senate, a left-leaning news magazine is named after her, and Carl Sandburg suggested that she was the woman in the song, "She'll Be Coming Round the Mountain When She Comes" as she organized mine workers.

I bumped into the story of the $50 monthly payment by Black Jack Pershing to a lawyer in Manila on behalf of a woman of a child he fathered during the research for my book on Missouri generals. It reportedly comes from Gen. Leonard Wood's diary.

Chapter 5

Apparently, John J. Pershing was a big hit as a ROTC trainer at the University of Nebraska. However, when he later became a tactical officer at West Point, his cadets were less enthusiastic. As it says in the text, the cadets, tired of hearing how poorly they compared to his Black troops who had excelled in battle, began calling him "Nigger Jack," which later morphed into "Black Jack," which was more acceptable to the newspapers.

Pershing was indeed named first a "datu" and then a "sultan" for his work in the Philippines, although it was probably mainly a public relations gimmick.

Pershing is also noted for inventing "jumping jacks." The West Point commandant called him in to his office with the news that the laundry was complaining because it couldn't get the cadets' white pants clean because Black Jack was making the cadets repeatedly "drop and give him twenty" pushups. The commandant asked him to devise a new punishment exercise, so Pershing lined the men up in rows. The first row would do what we know today as the arm movement of the exercise, the second row would do the leg movement, and the rows would alternate. Decades later, Jack LaLanne combined the arm and leg motions and popularized the exercise.

When Old Ben and Heinrich talk about lynchings, it is important to understand that they happened in Missouri, not just the deep south. For instance, in 1923 James T. Scott of Columbia, Mo., was accused of raping a white woman, and a mob broke into the jail and hung him from a bridge. No members of the lynch mob were ever convicted. Similarly, Lloyd Lionel Gaines sued for admission to the University of Missouri Law School and won in 1938 but disappeared in 1939 before he could arrive on campus.

The account of the Billy Sunday revival is accurate according to accounts I found on the Internet of his services, and his quotes come from one of his famous sermons.

Chapter 6

The balance of yin and yang finds expression throughout the eastern martial arts. For each attacking move, there is a defensive one to counteract it. For each action, there is an equal reaction. Likewise, balance is the norm. When you move one arm or leg, the other is moving too in a way that maintains your balance.

Yin and yang are not the same as good and evil. Evil happens when an imbalance occurs between the hard and soft forces. Philosophically, I would suggest that, in essence, Hegel's dialectic (although it gets his name, other philosophers may have developed and popularized it) is a western attempt at achieving such balance. A thesis and antithesis are proposed, and a synthesis results. And that's how democracy is supposed to work too. Two opposing sides forge compromise, a synthesis. Of course, that would mean considering that the other side is not evil, but just disagrees – and may have a good point. Maybe Congress could learn from yin and yang!

The amanita phalloides mushroom is indeed poisonous. People sometimes mistake it for edible varieties.

"Pianoforte" was the original name of the instrument we now just

call the "piano." It was called so because greater dynamics could be employed by hitting the strings with little hammers rather than plucking them like a harpsichord did.

John William "Blind" Boone was a ragtime giant, literally as well as figuratively, whose influence on the musical style was as great as the more famous Scott Joplin. He was a large, blind man who could repeat and play any melody by ear. He lived in Columbia, Mo., and the city is now debating whether to complete repairs to his home. The concert that Heinrich and Sally attend is based upon accounts of his performances.

The more I have learned about the development of the Prohibition movement in the United States, the more it has become clear to me that women's suffrage and prohibition tended to go hand in hand. The main reason men did not want to give women the right to vote is that they suspected that the first thing women would do with that political power would be to take their booze away.

But what was much worse to women than the booze itself was the saloon culture that had developed among their men, partly because of the Victorian idea that sex was an impure thing that had to be hidden. Every neighborhood had at least one saloon, and much of what was going on in the back rooms of those saloons was bad for women and their children. At the end of a long work week, men would socialize with other men in the saloons and get drunk. Once drunk, thieves, gamblers and prostitutes would take their money in the back room. In addition to the venereal diseases to which she would be exposed, the wife and her children, who were reliant on the husband's paycheck, could become destitute quickly upon its disappearance.

Although first exposed to this phenomenon in a college history class when I read the book, *Deliver Us from Evil: An Interpretation of American Prohibition,* by Norman H. Clark (Norton, 1976), I didn't really understand the implications of the problem at that time until I became a husband and father myself. In addition, reading about the underworld of prostitution and white slavery system of the time, and seeing that it still exists today even in my relatively small city, further opened my eyes.

The Battle of Worcester in 1651 was the final battle of the English Civil War. Oliver Cromwell and the parliamentarians defeated the royalist forces supporting Charles II, who had allied himself with Scottish Presbyterians who were fighting for the right to govern their own churches as they pleased rather than be dominated by bishops imposed by the Church of England. While the battle could be seen as a victory for representative government by the people, it was seen by the

Scottish Presbyterians as a defeat for representative government in their individual churches, the "kirks." Incidentally, many of the rebels were sent into exile in the Americas, where they would be afforded the opportunity to fight the British again and win.

Chapter 7

The Boer Wars were fought in 1880-81 and 1899-1902 between the British and two republics set up by the Boers, who were Dutch farmers, in South Africa. The later conflict was particularly brutal and drawn-out and foreshadowed wars to come in the 20th Century. Although the British eventually won, with the Boer republics of Transvaal and Orange Free State affirmed as self-governing entities within the British Union of South Africa, they did so by putting the Dutch population in concentration camps.

The Pinkerton National Detective Agency became synonymous with strike-breaking in the late 19th and early 20th Centuries as its agents were employed in such deadly labor-management conflicts as the Homestead Strike, the Pullman Strike and the Ludlow Massacre.

Although my fraternity antics never took a particularly violent turn, we did sometimes pursue nocturnal activities similar to this raid on a rival fraternity house. Our activities in the 1980s were rarely racially motivated, however, and were more a matter of young bucks proving their mettle in the eyes of their peers, something that the young men of any era find new ways to do. When society finds ways to channel this "yang" energy toward positive goals, mountains can be moved.

The idea for the attack on Sally's newspaper came from the story of Elijah Lovejoy, a Presbyterian minister, abolitionist and newspaper publisher whose press was destroyed three times in St. Louis before moving to Alton, Ill. Then an abolitionist mob murdered him, pushed his press out a window onto the Mississippi riverbank, broke it into pieces and threw it in the river. Yes, it was an antebellum attack, but mobs are mobs in whatever era. In Sally's case, it was an orchestrated and premeditated attack by a particularly evil man.

Chapter 8

Jack Johnson, the "Galveston Giant," was the first African-American world heavyweight boxing champion. In the 1910 "Fight of the Century," he pummeled former champion James J. Jeffries. He would eventually lose the heavyweight title to Jess Willard in the 26th round of a 45-round match, although he is rumored to have thrown the fight because of his personal difficulties. He had married three times, all white women. He was convicted on a Mann Act violation after taking his future second wife, Lucille Cameron, across state lines "for illicit purposes." She had been an alleged prostitute, but the prevailing reason appears to be because he was a black man attracted to white women. Skipping bail, he fled to Montreal and then France with Cameron. He later returned to the U.S. and continued fighting, mostly underground, until 1945. He died in a car accident in 1946.

As discussed earlier, lynchings occurred with some regularity in Missouri. There were 81 lynchings in the state between 1889 and 1916, according to NAACP data cited in an April 14, 2006, article by Jenny Filmer, "1906 Lynchings Grew from Tensions, Racism," in the *Springfield, Mo., News-Leader.* Interestingly, before 1897, most victims were white, but after that date, they were predominantly black.

Interestingly, the story about fingerprinting being introduced to the United States by Scotland Yard at the St. Louis World's Fair in 1904 is true.

The WCTU protest scene is based on actual signs in photos of similar protests of the time and includes songs that can be found on the Internet from the time period. Of course, the transvestite horseman riding into the saloon is my addition.

Chapter 9

The Thor electric clothes washer was the first such device in the United States, designed in 1907 and patented in 1910 by the Hurley Electric Laundry Equipment Co. in Chicago. Invention of the first electric clothes washer is disputed, according to Internet sources. Before electricity was added to power the machine, clothes washing machines used some form of hand power to crank or turn them.

Chapter 10

Regarding Kueter telling Tichenor that Pershing taught him to not rely on sycophants, there is a story from World War I that is telling about Pershing's character. While Pershing was inspecting Lt. George C. Marshall's unit at the front, Black Jack dressed down Marshall's commanding officer in front of the staff, pointing out numerous deficiencies and placing the blame on his commander. Marshall grabbed Pershing's arm and told him emphatically that the criticism was unfair and pointed out the reasons why. Pershing was taken aback, and Marshall's peers told him he would probably be sent home on the next ship. Instead, Pershing called Marshall the next day and asked him to join his headquarters staff.

Pershing served as an indispensible mentor, and Marshall would become known as "the Wizard" for his management ability. When the Wizard became Army Chief of Staff the day after Hitler invaded Poland to begin World War II, Black Jack's acumen for character came to fruition. President Roosevelt grew to count on Marshall's management abilities so much that he couldn't spare him the opportunity to command the D-Day invasion, which fell to Dwight D. Eisenhower. And Marshall would later win the Nobel Peace Prize for the economic rescue of Western Europe.

Pershing fought hard with Washington to keep the Sam Brown belt, which goes diagonally across the chest. Its main purpose is to provide more support for a saber, which few soldiers by this time employed on more than a ceremonial basis.

Conclusion

Harry Truman said: "There is nothing new in the world except the history you do not know."

I hope you enjoyed the story I created and the imbedded history within. Perhaps you learned something new. I know that I did while writing the novel. We are all swimming in a sea of history, and understanding it helps us not to swim in circles.

"I think if I couldn't tell stories, I'd die," said President Abraham Lincoln to an impatient political ally who didn't want to listen to one of his anecdotes.

To me, it's the stories of history that make history live, and the interesting people who populate the stories, that make it fun. Stories and the people who live them make history worth the effort of learning it.

ABOUT THE AUTHOR

James F. Muench is an author, free-lance journalist, public relations consultant and writing instructor.

His first novel, *The Teutonic Cross*, was published in May 2013 by Silver Tongue Press of Milwaukee, Wisc. His first book, the non-fiction *Five Stars: Missouri's Most Famous Generals*, was published in 2006 by the University of Missouri Press.

After working for more than a dozen years as a strategic communicator with the State of Missouri, Westminster College and the University of Missouri, Muench launched his second career as a free-lance writer and consultant in 2001. Muench's byline has appeared in such periodicals as the *St. Louis Post-Dispatch*, the *Columbia Daily Tribune*, the *Columbia Business Times*, *Inside Columbia*, *Columbia Home and Lifestyle*, *Jefferson City Magazine* and *Sports Illustrated for Kids*.

Before going solo, he served as director of communications for the Missouri Department of Economic Development, director of public information for the Missouri Division of Energy, director of publications and media relations for Westminster College and science writer for the MU News Bureau.

Muench holds a bachelor's degree, cum laude, in English-Creative Writing from Westminster College and a master's degree in print journalism from the University of Missouri School of Journalism. In the past, he taught English composition at MU and Westminster College and public relations at Stephens College. At present, he teaches basic news writing at Mizzou and developmental English at Columbia College.

Muench and his wife, Fran, will celebrate their 26th wedding anniversary in July 2013 and live in Columbia, Mo. They have two children: Nolan, 20, and April, 16.

Made in the USA
Charleston, SC
08 September 2013